The FALL OF THE KING

LIGHTNESS SAGA

BOOK 3

STACEY MARIE BROWN

Copyright © 2017 Stacey Marie Brown
All rights reserved.
Cover by Dane at Ebook Launch (https://ebooklaunch.com/ebook-cover-design/)
Developmental Editor Jordan Rosenfeld (http://jordanrosenfeld.net)
Edited by Hollie (www.hollietheeditor.com)

ALSO BY STACEY MARIE BROWN

Darkness of Light
(Darkness Series #1)

Fire in the Darkness
(Darkness Series #2)

Beast in the Darkness
(An Elighan Dragen Novelette)

Dwellers of Darkness
(Darkness Series #3)

Blood Beyond Darkness
(Darkness Series #4)

West
(A Darkness Series Novel)

City in Embers
(Collector Series #1)

The Barrier Between
(Collector Series #2)

Across the Divide
(Collector Series #3)

From Burning Ashes
(Collector Series #4)

The Crown of Light
(Lightness Saga #1)

Lightness Falling
(Lightness Saga #2)

Dedicated To:

David Gandy
(my Lars)

You made this story so easy…

but really embarrassing to write in public.

The Fall of the King

Chapter One

Lars

The lock clicked, released from its hold, and the sound reverberated off the stone walls deep underneath the house above. The heavily spelled door swung open, and my shoes clipped loudly on the stone floor as I stepped into the small room. Magic slammed into me, gripping my lungs. No matter how much I guarded this room with enchantments, they would never be fully contained.

The blood ignited in my veins as the power laced with my own, rushing up my spine like a geyser. My hands trembled.

One other knew of this room beside myself, but I trusted Goran with my life, a privilege only a handful of others had ever achieved in my entire existence. After I saved him from a life of being a slave for a sexually sadistic overlord, who beat and humiliated him until he was unconscious, he dedicated a life of faithfulness to me until his last breath.

A dominant force drew me to the first compartment on the wall, while the other two farther down the row were quiet. The fourth box sat empty, waiting to be filled.

Soon it will be. Soon the entire collection would be mine.

I was no fool; I understood the consequences of obtaining these objects and the power they held. However, my not having them would be an even bigger catastrophe.

The four Treasures of Tuatha Dé Danann were almost as ancient as fae themselves. The treasures were designed by Druids as gifts to honor the ancient fae kings and queens when Druids had yet to be taken into our gods' and goddesses' embrace, and still worked as teachers, seers, practitioners, and war consultants for the royal fae. Even then fae were aware of the Druids' special abilities and their magic fae did not possess.

Like anything good, the offerings proved to be too tempting to the fae, who used them for their own gain. Only two of the treasures, the Sword of Nuada and the Spear of Lug, were neutral by nature, merely taking on the intent of the holder, be it good or bad.

The other two, the Stone of Fáil and the Cauldron of Dagda, developed their own desires. The stone grew gruesome with greed and power, wanting it all for itself, but the cauldron has enough power to counterbalance the stone.

Individually these treasures were more powerful than any fae. They were not meant to be together. The

Druid who realized the ramifications of these objects' power took them back and hid them from the world. They became legend, little more than folklore over the centuries, but they were no bedtime story. I had found all but one: the cauldron. And soon that would be remedied.

A tapping sound drummed against the metal of the cabinet. The stone wanted out. It longed for me to grasp it in my hand and let it free of its isolation.

My fingers slipped over the lid of the box, stroking it like a lover. My lids squeezed together, the call almost unbearable. Even alone, it was unpleasant to reveal the weakness I felt in its presence, to admit I might not be as strong as I believed. Demons craved power and control. I was no different, but my will was stronger than any others. My understanding of what these objects could really bring about kept me from indulging my desires.

One touch. The power I could give you. What we could do together. A voice entered my head, low and ancient. *Do not fight me, like the human, for in the end it is pointless. You both will succumb.*

"I will not. I am no ordinary fae you can manipulate," I said back in my head. "I am your proprietor. You will do as *I* wish. As for the girl, she already defeated you. She was strong enough to fight you."

She tricked me, the stone replied. *But I left my mark...she will hear my call when the time comes. She will not be able to help herself. And neither will you.*

A smile curled my mouth. "You greatly underestimate the girl. And me."

I had met the human-turned-fae girl prior to the war, and she had significantly surprised me. Zoey Daniels was stronger than most fae I'd ever met. What I had learned about her life, what she had gone through, showed me she was remarkable. She grew up fast and tough in the foster care system, jumping from house to house. Abused by one of the men she lived with, she became a street fighter to never be the victim again. It also enabled her to get extra cash to help take care of a disabled foster sister, Lexie. Somehow Zoey still tried to finish school, and landed a job with the government to hunt fae, only to find out *she* was the government experiment. I respected her. Liked her. I could say that about few people in my lifetime, fae or human.

She had survived through a transfer of fae powers from a Wanderer. Where most humans would have died the instant the magic touched their soul, she took it in and flourished. Then she outwitted and withstood the power of the Stone of Fáil. High kings and queens had fallen to its power, yet she had not. I understood, similar to others before, how hard it was to fight the draw of the stone. It showed you everything you desired, promising you power and your deepest wishes to come to life.

Yet it was finicky in its attachment. It did not speak to everyone who touched it. The stone had fixated on the street fighter, perhaps even falling in love with her, if a stone could do such a thing. It wanted her, even more than it wanted me. The stone was not the only one who could feel desire in the air. I could sense its true longing for her. Whether for revenge or something else, it craved Ms. Daniels.

The world will be in chaos because of you. You will need me to fight it. Deep down you know it is the truth, the stone whispered, wrapping around my mind, squeezing out doubts.

My throat tightened, my teeth clenching. Every hair along my neck pricked with energy, my muscles contracting with deep-seated desire.

The stone was not wrong; I knew what was going to happen. My fate showed its hand in small but profound ways lately. It woke me up at night, and left me pacing around my desk in the day. A battle was coming, one I feared I couldn't stop from happening unless I took preemptive steps to control it. This was why I had worked so hard to collect all the Treasures of Tuatha Dé Danann. What was heading our way would take more than what I had alone.

One touch, King. Your power will be impervious to any threat. Inside and out. You will rule without worry for the rest of time. I can give you this and more. The stone lured me closer to the box where it was contained. *I also know your other desire...I can bring her back.*

Images of a woman flickered through my head. Long red hair framed the most beautiful face I had ever known. Light violet eyes rimmed in a darker shade of indigo sparkled from under her dark lashes. She was tall, her toned legs peeking out from the slit in her dress, a smile, so blindingly beautiful, growing on her face.

Aisling. My heart called her name.

You three can be a family. You know she is yours. You can have it all.

Another girl joined Aisling in the vision. She was a

mix of the woman I loved and myself. Or my twin brother, Devlin.

Ember's face and mannerisms were so similar to her mother it sometimes wrenched my heart to look at her. She had one yellow-green eye from her demon ancestry, the other eye a violet match to her mother's. Ember's jet-black hair hung to her waist, the color the same as her father's, with streaks of red through it, representing her mother. Daes—half fae, half demon—took after both their parents in appearance. It was easy to spot them with the different colored eyes and hair.

The secret of Ember's parentage died with her mother's murder. Aisling had told me Ember was Devlin's, but that had been in a middle of a fight, when she had wanted to hurt me. Looking back, I could see why she had. Besides being so angry and hurt when I broke her heart, Devlin would have been a stable, loving father. A child to me then would have been an inconvenience. A hindrance to my goals. I had been foolish and stupid, picking power over her love.

Even when she left me for my brother, Aisling and I could not stay away from each other, our passion too strong to fight.

I had always sensed Ember was my child, but I had no way of proving it. Demon twins were identical down to the last DNA strand. Respecting Aisling's choice of father, I told Ember I was her uncle. In truth, I hated it. Ember was mine. *My* daughter.

Don't you want that? Your lover back in your arms and in your bed every night? Your daughter undeniably yours? Everyone thinks you only crave power, but I know the truth. You want a family. Love.

My fingers rolled up into a fist. The stone pulled out my most secret desire, which sounded sad and weak. I was a king! I had all I could ever want, in my bed and out, but none of it filled the hole Aisling left when she died. Nothing filled the emptiness when I mistook a need for power over her love. If I had seen what was in front of me, she would be alive, and Ember would have grown up under this roof, instead of with her adoptive mother, Lily. She would have crawled around my office, learned to walk in the family room, trained in her powers early with Alki, and been spoiled silly by me. Actually, by this whole house. Marguerite would have doted on her and plumped her with food. The love of my life and my daughter would both have been happy and healthy in my arms.

One decision changed my life in so many ways. One I utterly regretted.

With a shaking hand, I reached for the box, hooking the lid of the container. The other strongboxes were pregnant with power but did not taunt me like the stone.

Yes, demon. Aisling could be yours again. Your heart aches for her. One touch and I can take all that pain and regret away.

The top of the container opened, causing my lungs to draw in large gulps of air. *Stop. You are stronger than this.* A voice in my brain berated me, but my hand continued to inch down.

Almost. Just a little bit more. The stone vibrated, shoving off waves of energy, pulling my hand down even closer to its surface. My body quaked with its power, cutting a craving so deep, I felt as though I was going through withdrawals. *I need it. Just a little taste.*

"Sir?" A voice behind jerked me around with a start. I wrenched my hand back from the case. Goran stood in the doorway, his eyes pinched at the corners. "Sir? What were you doing?"

"None of your business." My neck stiffened, my chin rising. "What do you want?"

"The Queen is here to see you. Again." Goran shifted on his feet, his attention flicking to my hands briefly. I slipped my hands in my trouser pockets. "She demands to see her sister."

I tried to fight back the groan on my tongue. Kennedy Johnson had been here twice already this week. I wasn't the one keeping her from her newfound sibling. It was the extremely powerful, pain-in-the-ass Druid I had locked up in my cell. Fionna, the eldest daughter of Keela and Raghnall and descendant of the great Cathbad, one of the most formidable Druids to ever live, refused to see her sister.

I hated to admit Fionna was wise. I had forced Ms. Johnson to promise to find the cauldron, the one Fionna knew the whereabouts of. She understood, though, if she and her sister were in the same room, there was a chance Kennedy would get the location from her.

Fionna would do everything in her power not to let me acquire the cauldron. She had almost kept me from getting the spear. She would not let this slip through her fingers so easily. She was strong and probably one of the toughest people, or fae for that matter, for me to break, but I would find her weakness.

"Sir?" Goran hauled me away from my thoughts.

"Yes, I will be right up." I nodded to him.

14

His stern face pinched again, his large muscled body slightly turning away, as though he struggled with leaving me here by myself.

"Go, Goran. Let her know I will be there shortly."

He nodded, knowing he could not refuse my order. He gave me one last look before ascending the stone steps.

Air released in a heave from my lungs, and my gaze drifted down. Even tucked in my pockets, I could feel the tremors rattling my fingers. I drew them out, bringing them up. My gut tightened as they shook violently. The magic of the treasures was so thick, it wasn't wise to stay more than a few minutes. But I was the High Demon Unseelie King. I could handle more than most, and I refused to be intimidated by this level of magic.

I shoved away the unease, straightened my back, walked confidently to the door, then shut and locked it. I greatly respected Kennedy, but if she went against her promise, I would do anything to keep my reign secure and my people safe.

Chapter Two

Fionha

"The Queen was here again." A deep voice rubbed up against my ear from the doorway, like a purring lion. Sultry, confident, and deadlier than being thrown into a pit of hungry sharks. It was part of his alluring character, which made fools think he was too charming to hurt them. If you were that much of a daft wanker, you deserved to die.

I was not and did not. Staying silent, I folded my arms over my chest, curling my legs on the squeaky cot, my view pointed at the stone wall of the windowless room somewhere below the King's compound.

"Ms. Johnson is quite upset. She wants to see you." The King walked deeper into the tiny chamber, his shoes, which likely cost a thousand euros, clipping against the stone and chipping away at my nerves. The energy bounding off him was enough to set my teeth on edge, but his smug confidence ground my sanity into dust.

"All I need is a location. That is it, and you would be free of this room. Of me." Lars came into my peripheral vision, his deep red tie taunting me like a matador's blanket.

I snorted, turning my body farther toward the wall.

Free of him? Sounded like heaven, but I knew it was a lie. He wouldn't let me go easily. I've learned things while living in hiding most of my life—number one, never trust a fae. Especially a demon.

Still, I was surprised he hadn't forced me to face Kennedy. Most captors would not care what you wanted, but when I said I didn't want to see her, he respected my decision. This only made me distrust him more; he was up to something. He also had yet to torture or starve me; I was doing the latter one on my own.

What kind of ruthless king was he, anyway?

"You disagree?" The fabric of his slacks swished as he slid his hand into his pocket. I could see why any woman or man would keel over with lust at the sight of him. No model or actor I'd ever seen in a magazine or a movie came close to his perfection. His thick, slightly wavy jet-black hair was brushed back off his face and displayed bright yellow-green eyes and olive skin. Stubble lightly lined his chin and mouth, only drawing more attention to his full lips and strong jawline. He stood tall, broad, and dominant. Without a word, sexuality, assurance, ego, power, and danger rolled off him, drowning anyone close. I had never seen a man similar to him in person, but instead of falling under his charm as most women or men probably did, I wanted to punch him in the face or toss him across the room with a few words and rip the almighty leader off his self-proclaimed pedestal.

Lars, the Demon Unseelie King, made me nauseous with abhorrence because of what he allowed to happen to my people and what he'd done and still wanted to do.

He unwisely thought trapping my sister into helping him gain information from me would lead him to the cauldron. Little did he know.

"You think starving yourself is showing strength and courage?" Lars huffed, kicking at the tray of untouched food at the foot of my bed. "All you are doing is weakening yourself."

I twisted to look at him and snarled. "You did that the moment you put me in this room." He was closer than I thought, and I automatically jerked back into the wall. I tried to cover up my reaction, but comprehension curved his mouth.

"You thought I would let you use your magic on me?" Lars lifted an eyebrow.

I turned back, finding a crack that trailed up to the ceiling. The prison surrounding me somehow blocked my magic. When he first put me down here without my mouth covered, I attempted to do a spell, but no magic found its way into the room. Impenetrable. It frightened me because no fae had ever been able to block us. Druid magic was different from fae magic. We could not only challenge them, but in some ways overpower them, which was why fae feared and killed Druids throughout the centuries.

But I still needed the energy from the earth, needed life to enter my words for them to be effective. Here, all energy was blocked. And the only way he could do that was if he blocked himself in this room as well.

My lips twitched at the edge, ready to push back and see if my theory was true. How I wanted to wipe the arrogance from his face. The King needed to be taken down a few notches, understand he couldn't control everything. Especially a Druid such as me.

I was not beneath him. I was an heir of Cathbad, one of the most powerful Druids ever known. I would not cower to a fae, King or not.

My legs swept to the floor, and I bolted up. Lars took a step back, not expecting my sudden movement, his jaw tightening.

"I didn't think you'd *let* me..." I countered his step, coming within a breath of him. My neck cranked back to look up at him. "But I don't really ask for permission. I do what I want."

A nerve strained along Lars's jaw as he stared down at me, his eyes burning into me. "So. Do. I."

"Then go for it. Torture me...get the information you want," I whispered. He was so close I could smell the mix of fae—sweet and woodsy—with only a breath of cologne, manly and warm, like a glass of a top-shelf whiskey. Just enough to make you want to step closer to get a better sniff. "What are you waiting for, King? Take what you want from my mind. Force me to speak."

Challenging the Unseelie King might not be wise, but the moment he let me out of this cell as I hoped, I would match his power with my own.

Another nerve twitched at his temple before a slight smile curved his mouth. "Have this all figured out, don't you?" He leaned in, his breath curling down my cheek. "Get me riled up so I will foolishly try that exact thing? I've been King since you were young. It will take more than a Druid who thinks way more of herself than she should to rattle me."

I looked at him through narrowed eyes, annoyed by the intensity of his nearness. Lars chuckled, low and dark, the noise vibrating against my skin.

"Do not challenge me." Lars tipped even closer, barely an inch from my mouth. My chest locked up, but I didn't move. I would not show fear. "You will find, *Druid*, you are quite unprepared for the likes of me."

"Or maybe it's the other way around." I peered up, holding his gaze. "Is that why you won't take me from this room? I'm not the only one who can't do shite in here. Aren't I right, *King*? Without your magic, you're all talk. A balloon full of hot air."

"You sure you want to keep this up?" A ghost of conceit twinkled his eyes. "I was trying to cordially work with you, however, you are forcing my hand."

"Cordial? Keeping me prisoner and binding my sister is what you consider cordial?"

"Very." He slanted his head, his expression momentarily open, as if he were being the kindest, most gracious person. "But I see being nice is not something you respond to. You answer to a little rougher game. We all have a weakness, it's just a matter of finding yours."

Sensing the first string of doubt leaking through me, my mouth pinned closed.

There was no way he would find out.

"That is what I thought." He smirked and stood to his full height. "You have one more day to come to your senses before I stop playing this game with you. For the Queen's sake, I was hoping we could come to a mutual solution. However, I see your sister is not your vulnerability."

"Was your brother yours?" I shot back at him. Lars's lids narrowed. "You did what was best for the masses, not for your blood. Kennedy, above anyone, would understand. Keeping you from another piece of the treasure is something I will fight for." I stepped closer to him, now only a hair apart, our bodies touching ever so slightly. "Until my last breath."

Lars's intense eyes stared down into mine. "If that is the way it has to be." He lifted one eyebrow. "I always get what I want in the end, Ms. Cathbad. Always." Lars turned, exiting the door with a speed and quietness that screamed supremacy.

The door clicked, continuing to secure me in my magic-empty prison.

Chapter Three

Lars

The moment the prison door shut, Travil found his step behind me, causing me to growl under my breath. Strong women were nothing new to me and found little admiration in weakness, but this woman was making me crazier than most.

And that was saying a lot.

Ember's stubbornness and power could be a challenge. Yet as frustrated as I could get with her outright disobedience sometimes, I was never riled this easily. It took a lot to really make me angry. As a demon, I learned to keep my temper under control at all times, else I might destroy cities. Whether it was because this woman had sent strighoul to my compound, almost killing Marguerite, or because she was keeping me from what I wanted most, I was slipping into anger faster than usual.

At first the similarities in looks to her younger sister with her long silky brown hair, deep brown eyes, and petite physique had me treating her with a little more care than I normally would with a prisoner. But I no longer saw the kindness and quiet strength of the Queen. Fionna Cathbad had grown up quite differently. Hiding from fae for decades in Ireland had turned her tough and ruthless. She was not shy, sweet, nor did she have the luxury of being empathetic and kind. And I would never admit it, but I was impressed she'd taught herself black magic and Druid spells.

She was a force to be reckoned with. One strong enough to challenge fae.

It was true I had done nothing to stop the killing of Druids. After Aisling died, I was dealing with my brother, his insanity, and his murdering thousands. Druids were of little consequence to me.

Losing Aisling destroyed me, but Devlin kept me from completely going under by misplacing his sanity enough for both of us. I had to marshal the strength when he lost his. But when he entirely lost his mind, I had no choice but to end his reign. End him.

The door to my office hit the wall as I strode in, my shoulders still tight around my ears. "Get..." What was my new secretary's name? For the life of me I could not remember. "Whatever her name is... I want to hear from Garrett and Cadoc in the next hour. I need something on Ms. Cathbad. Now," I yelled at Travil, my palms smacking my desk harder than I meant to.

"Yes, sir." He bowed his head, stepping out of my office and closing the door.

I let out a breath, staring absently down at my desk.

What was wrong with me? My temper was skimming the surface too easily, and I didn't like it. I prided myself on control, fairness, and making the best decisions for the survival of the world. If I showed any sign of weakness or recklessness, the European Eastern bloc wouldn't be the only countries wanting to exit my rule.

"Majesty?" A slight, Latin American brunette entered the room, her five-inch heels still only bringing her up to my chest. She was a pretty little thing with caramel skin, straight brown shoulder-length hair, soft brown eyes. But something about her still irritated me. Actually, every secretary had...since Rez.

I pinched the bridge of my nose. Her name was still a sore subject with me. Theoretically I was happy for her, that she'd found her mate, but it had come at my cost. She was mine. I had brought her into my home, given her a job and a life. After all I did, she left me for a lesser fae.

Still, I was no fool. The dark dweller, West, and Rez were perfect for each other. You'd have to be a fool not to see it, which made it impossible to be around them, reminding me of what I had lost so long ago.

I had cared deeply for Rez but was never *in love* with her. Aisling had taken all my heart, leaving nothing but a carcass. I wasn't capable of loving someone else. Not anymore. And Rez deserved better, which was the only reason I allowed them both to live. Any other Demon King would not have been so lenient, but my respect for Rez and the dark dweller softened my retaliation. Still, I had punished them. The law of my rule demanded it.

Perhaps the worst part of it was no secretary could live up to Rez in skills. Rez and I worked extremely well together. The majority of the time she knew what I wanted even before I did. She was a hard worker, excellent lover, and took care of the business of the compound like she was made to do it. I missed her. Every day. No one had even remotely come close to filling her shoes, and my patience for these new ones had me firing them almost as soon as they were hired.

My assistant had to do a lot more than just help run my house and businesses. I had also tried several men to fill the role. They had only lasted a few hours. I found women much more efficient, able to multitask and handle all I threw at them. This new one was competent, but I knew she wouldn't be here much longer. She already was exasperating me by asking endless questions.

"Get me Garrett on the phone now." I sat back in my chair. "Also get me all the files you can on Olwyn O'Sullivan. I want to know everything you can find on her."

"Yes, sir." She tried to curtsy, but her pencil skirt almost made her stumble over. Her cheeks flushed red, and she bowed her head, trying again.

"Just. Go. Now," I growled, clenching the arms on my chair. She wasted my time trying to perfect her curtsy with those ridiculous heels and skirt. She teetered out of the room, closing the door.

"Marguerite?" My finger pressed the button to the kitchen.

"Yes, Mr. Lars?" Marguerite's accented voice came through the box, calming me. She had been with me since she was a little girl. Though I was far older than her by centuries, she had taken on a maternal role in this home, and her cooking could challenge the most famous chefs. Besides Ember, she was the only one I allowed to hug me. I loved that woman. If anything happened to Marguerite, I wasn't sure I would be able to stay sane.

"Can you get me a list of new potential assistants?" Marguerite had to approve them as much as I did.

"*Si,* Mr. Lars." I could almost hear the smile in her response. She had yet to okay any of the replacements either. "Made devil food cake. Will bring."

I smirked. What began as a joke, to bake me devil's food cake whenever I was irritated or upset, had now become our tradition. She had made me a lot of cake lately.

"Thanks, Marguerite." I couldn't help but smile. My mouth watered already at the thought of her cake.

"Nic! *Mi hermoso chico, para de comer.* For Mr. Lars!" I heard Marguerite yell through the speakers before it went silent. I chuckled softy, my head shaking.

I had discovered Nic, like Rez, in a sex den. It was a flea-infested slum and the drug of choice was magic-infused crack. They had him so strung out between the ceaseless sex, a natural high for an incubus, and actual drugs, he was close to brain damaged. Magic healers and speech therapists helped with his recovery, but the ghosts of his past haunted him a great deal. He had lost his eye in the war. As an incubus, he was afraid this would hurt his "hunting." It did not, as the women and men seemed to only be *more* intrigued and lust-filled with the pirate-looking Spanish god.

Now the stone's statement flooded into my head, stirring me in my seat. *Everyone thinks you only crave power, but I know the truth. You want a family. Love.* I had never thought about why I filled this house with broken people who needed a home. Each one came here from a horrendous situation. Was I trying to fill a gap? Create a family? A house full of noise and love?

I shoved the thought away. I was a demon. A king. I had more things to worry about than love or feeling lonely. They were weak qualities that caused lesser beings to seek approval and acceptance.

The two things I could never permit.

~~

"Majesty, I have Garrett on speaker, and here is everything I could find on Olwyn O'Sullivan." My assistant stood before me, handing me a walkie-talkie device and a file. Her hair was now twisted up in a knotted bun. I really should learn her name, but my concentration was on the file in front of me. It was thicker than I thought it would be. I glanced up at her. She appeared somewhere in her late twenties and was a raccoon shifter, which were known to be good thieves. Maybe I should get her stealing instead of being my assistant. "I also had Garrett send me all the files they found so you could go through their research." She smiled, a breath of pride curling off it.

One eyebrow curved up in surprise. Maybe I would keep her around a bit longer.

"Thank you, uhh…"

"Sofia." She tried to curtsy again and failed miserably.

My lips pinched together holding back my sigh. I dipped my head, letting her know she was free to go. The moment she exited the room, I swiveled in my chair to the device sitting on my desk.

"Go ahead, Garrett."

"Sir." He spoke in his thick Irish accent through the newest version of a cell phone, one not even on the market yet. "This Druid was exceptional at covering her tracks and staying hidden. No credit card, no phone records, no internet trace of her. I thought we'd never find anything on her. Even the people in town said she and the old lady were hermits. Barely ever seen. They had nothing useful."

"Get to it," I growled, my impatience for all things related to Fionna Cathbad was already fraying my nerves. I never failed in getting what I wanted. Never. But if I didn't find her weakness, the thing which would make her buckle, I didn't know what I would do. This anxiety was a new experience, and I didn't like it. Torture would be pointless; she would not succumb. She would rather die for her cause. She also knew perfectly well I couldn't touch her sister, not really. I bound Kennedy to find the cauldron, and by doing that, I hoped Fionna would step up. She did not.

"Well, sir, until we found a document in a file at the county hospital on Olwyn giving birth to a girl. It was misfiled in a completely different department. But with my skills I was able to uncover it."

I flicked the folder open, flipping through the pages until I landed on a stapled set stamped by the University Hospital Galway.

"The second and third page caught my attention. At the fourth one, I knew I found what you wanted." Garrett cleared his throat. I sat back in my seat, turning to the second page, my eyes scrolling over the page quickly.

"If you look at the next document," Garrett suggested. I turned the next one, my eyes widening the moment I understood what I was looking at.

"You see, sir, Olwyn's daughter died at the age of twelve. About sixty years prior." He paused, his energy bursting through the walkie-talkie at his own discovery. "But this says she had a baby about five years ago, giving it up for adoption. I think we all know that would be physically impossible. Five years ago she was still way over a hundred."

Satisfaction twisted up my mouth, elation filling my chest.

"Good work, Garrett." Approval coated my words. "I am extremely impressed with what you attained."

We found it. The information I needed.

"You know what I am going to ask you next." I bolted from my seat, energy buzzing up my calves. Walking to the French doors, I overlooked my property. Spring was on the horizon, but you wouldn't know it from the angry Pacific Northwest rain spitting down in an endless stream, saturating the fields and plumping the creek running near the house.

"Already done, sir. We didn't want to contact you till we followed the trail and retrieved what you wanted. Cadoc is doing it now."

"Excellent." I had been unsure of Garrett and his group when I first took them from the lowlife demon,

Vadik. However, those who survived the war had turned into faithful soldiers, Garrett especially. His intelligence and hacking skills would be legend one day. "Head home the moment you do."

"Ta, sir." The device clicked, going quiet.

I returned to my desk, going through the rest of the documents Sofia had added to her research. What I learned was horrific and shocking, stirring anger deep inside.

I had tried to find something on Fionna originally to bend her to my will. Now I realized my actions were for the best.

"You are mine, Fionna Cathbad." I smirked, my hand rubbing my mouth. "I have you."

Chapter Four

Fionna

I could feel his presence even before the door opened, which considering the absence of magic in this room, was a statement of his power. Lars was his own energy field, pulling you to him like gravity.

Kicking my dinner tray away, I tucked into myself on the bed, facing the wall. I had no sense of time, only my meals giving me a base of measure. When I got eggs or oatmeal, I figured the day was beginning for most above. Sandwich or soup equaled midday. Stew, burritos, and chicken told me the sun had probably already set on my prison.

Going off this, two days had passed since the King's last visit.

Once I gave in and started eating after Lars left the last time, I realized what a fool I was for letting all those other meals go to waste. I'd give Lars one thing, the prison food here was amazing. Rather than gruel, I was getting chef-style meals, better than anything I'd ever had in my life.

What was up with that? Why treat me so well? It didn't make sense. Was it because of Kennedy? Or was he doing some strange reverse psychology bullshite on me? Was my chicken enchilada a device to break me? Get me sucked in by the delicious sauce so I'd let my guard down? If he took it away from me now and gave me gruel, I might break.

Goosebumps flushed over my skin the instant he walked in. I rolled away and folded in tighter against the feel of his presence.

"Ms. Cathbad?" His deep voice slid over my shoulder, entering my ear.

I was a prisoner, and he still called me by my family's given name. Names held respect. It was another thing that annoyed me—the possibility his formal pleasantries would make me mad.

I turned to address him, air halting in my lungs. *Bloody hell.* Today he wore a deep navy suit with a yellow-and-gray striped tie, his hair brushed back. It never looked gelled or greasy. Most likely his hair was too scared to disobey his order to wave back in perfection.

My mouth pinched together, my gaze snapping back to the wall.

"I will take that as an answer to my final chance I have so generously given you."

I snorted.

"Get up." His voice went icy cold, drawing my attention back to him. The King stared at me; his heavy gaze held power and irritation. "Now."

"Done playing nice?" A smile twisted my mouth; sweeping my legs to the floor, I stood up. "It's about fucking time. Now we can finally start getting to the point."

"Yes, we can." He replied so unemotionally a chill scampered down my spine.

He tilted his head down at me. Fear coiled in my gut. Something had changed. His confidence burst out of him similar to an overstuffed turkey.

"Travil?" he called, keeping his attention on me.

The guard who caught me in Ireland stepped into the room. He had long dark hair pulled back with a band. He stood an inch or two shorter than Lars, built wide and muscular. Not someone you wanted to run into in an alley. I could never imagine him cracking a smile. His beefed-up bow and arrow hung from his back and a beautiful carved knife draped against his hip.

Fabric hung from his fingers, draping like chains.

With nowhere to go, my legs still took me backward toward my bed. He held Druid's kryptonite. A gag. How sad was that? A piece of cloth could bring Druids to their knees.

Travil was in front of me before I could blink. I hated how fast fae could move. It was unnerving.

"Open up." Travil ordered me, his eyes glinting with glee. He was enjoying this immensely. His dislike for me was palpable every time he dropped off my meals, clouding the room in a dense fog.

33

Glowering, I pinched my lips together.

"Even better," he said so only I could hear, his hands clamping down on the sides of my face, the cloth pushing at my lips, trying to divide them.

I tried to turn my face, but his fingers dug sharper into my skin. With a grunt, he parted my teeth. The gag skated back, ramming into the corners of my mouth. I shoved against Travil, my head waggling, trying to break free. But it was too late; a knot dug into the back of my head as he tied it.

"You should always be this way." He knotted it again. "Muzzled."

"Travil." Lars said his name like a warning. Travil backed up, but his glare still fixed on me. "Ms. Cathbad, you wanted to see the level I will go? Let us go find out." He turned for the door.

Tying my hands behind my back, Travil yanked the rope as if it were a leash, forcing me to follow the demon. Anger boiled inside, ready to spout out, though physically I could not do anything. I was only five-three and a wee thing next to these brutes. Only my magic made me a giant among fae.

I never believed Lars would play fair. He was a cruel, selfish, demented man, caught up in his superiority, thinking himself untouchable. But the moment I could, the King would find he'd met his match.

"Come, Ms. Cathbad, you have guests." Lars's smug gaze drilled into mine.

Guests? More than one? I figured my time was up and he was going to force me to face my sister, but he was too smug, too haughty for it to just be Kennedy.

Sour acid pitted deep in my gut. *No. He couldn't have found out. There's no way.* The King had the means to find out things others couldn't, but what I hid was untraceable back to me. I had made sure.

My throat struggled to swallow. Travil pushed me to trail after the formidable King, his bloody expensive shoes snapping the floor like yipping dogs in front of us.

Travil's fingers dug into my arm, shoving me rougher than he needed to down the hall. Clearly he was one of those still bigoted against Druids. He disliked me purely because of what I was.

Well, okay, he might also hate me because he almost died in a bombing when I planned to kill a group of vile noble fae. To be fair, I did not know the King and Queen were there. Killing the King and his men would have been a lucky happenstance. And yes, I sent strighoul to attack the compound, but only after my first warning went unheeded, and the King dispatched a dark dweller and a siren to come for the spear. I learned my lesson. My warning had not been enough; I was too soft. So, yes, I ordered the strighoul to take one of his people and threaten him with them.

Lars would have done no less to me.

Protecting the Treasures of Tuatha Dé Danann was my first priority. History had shown us they should not be obtained by fae, especially all the objects together. Devastation and destruction would follow. The power was too much for anyone to handle. Every fae before thought they would be the one to have the strength to control them. They never did. And kingdoms had fallen.

Lars already had two I was aware of, but it was possible he had three. There had been whispers in Ireland, years before the war, that the Stone of Fáil had been turned up by a Wanderer and a human girl. As fast as the buzz came around, it went silent. There was a great probability he had found a way to secure it from them, the same way he obtained the Spear of Lug from me.

I hoped I was wrong. If he had it, we were in so much trouble. The only thing that could challenge the stone was the cauldron, but that didn't make me any more inclined to hand it over to him. For now all I could do was guard the Cauldron of Dagda with all I had and keep a final piece from him.

Lars stopped at a door at the end of the hallway, turning to look at me over his shoulder. "Last chance, Ms. Cathbad, before you force me into extreme measures."

I glared at him, hoping my eyes screamed *fuck you*.

His lip curled into a slight smirk. He opened the door and stepped in, and I followed along with his crony. I was ready to see a torture apparatus or at least my sister. I found neither of those. My neck turned my head to survey the room.

It was stone like my cell, rectangular and empty. A large, dark window took up most of the wall on one side. My eyes couldn't penetrate the darkly tinted glass, but I knew we were still far below the ground surface. This would not be a window looking outside.

Travil moved me to face it. I gulped, acid burning my esophagus. Anxiety alighted all over me like sudden cold snow. I trusted my intuition, and it told me to be scared. Whatever he had planned for me, I might be wishing for torture.

"I would love to untie and ungag you." Lars came up beside me, sliding one hand into his pants pocket. He was at ease, which only twined my nerves into clusters. "However, I have little faith you will not try to attack me."

I shifted my chin higher. He was right. No point in denying it.

"I have tried from day one to work with you, Ms. Cathbad." He flicked his chartreuse eyes toward me. "But you have forced my hand. You want me to play dirty?" The color in his eyes deepened in vibrancy. "I am a king. A demon. I can go to depths you never even dreamed of to get *what I want*."

The intensity of his gaze and the authority in his voice stirred a burning heat through my body. I snapped my head away from him, feeling abhorrence and anger explode against the heat similar to a buffer. My hands clenched, letting the hate rise inside me and pushing back against whatever disgusting response this demon could make me feel.

"Go ahead, Travil." The demon nodded to his man. The dark-haired brute walked over to the wall and flicked on a switch. It was exactly what I thought—a two-way mirror.

Light from the other side brought the room to life, showing what he had in store for me.

A gasp clogged my throat. "No!" I tried to scream through the gag, but it came out muffled. My feet moved me to the glass, my arms trying to wiggle out of the binds behind my back.

Olwyn!

My heart dived down to my toes at the sight of the old woman who raised me. She sat in a rocker, a blanket over her, her lids closed as she tipped the chair back and forth, sound asleep. She had hit a hundred and twelve last year. She only continued to live because I had extended her life. Even though she had lost most of her mind and her health a long time ago, she was all I had, and I didn't want to be alone.

I should have known Olwyn wouldn't be safe from him. But did he really think she was my Achilles heel, which would crumble me to a pile of rubbish and spill all my secrets? I didn't bend for my sister; did he think a woman of almost one hundred and thirteen would have me selling out humanity?

I turned to stare at the King, straightening, my gaze level on him.

Another disturbing smile ghosted his mouth as he moved closer to me. "I figured."

My forehead crinkled in confusion. If he knew she wouldn't break me, then why act as though he had a winning hand? Another dose of fear flooded my gut, swiping at the lining in my stomach.

"Goran?" Lars hit a speaker button next to me on the wall. "Bring her in." He shifted his head, his face close to mine, his voice a low whisper. "I warned you there is no depth I would not go to get what I want, to discover your most hidden secrets."

In my peripheral I saw movement in the small chamber next to Olwyn's. Time began to move slowly as I rotated around to see the bodies walk in. One large. One small.

Oh. Gods. No.

The earth buckled beneath me. My knees crashed to the ground and a guttural scream lashed against the fabric in my mouth. Like clamps cranked down on my airwaves, oxygen stuck in my lungs and locked in my chest.

He did it. He found the one thing I thought I had hidden so deep no one could ever find. Not just my Achilles heel, but my soul.

Fire ripped through my chest as I blinked back hot tears threatening to come. She was supposed to be safe, far away from me, from this life.

I stared at the little girl holding Goran's hand, a stuffed animal wrapped tightly in her other, and her long brown hair shielding part of her face. Goran leaned down, whispering something. She looked up and a gasp hitched in my throat.

Deep blue eyes like her father's glistened in the light, but everything else was me. My family genes, down to the freckles sprinkled over her nose.

She was beautiful. Perfect.

My daughter.

Chapter Five

Fionha

Pain and love pounded in equal tempo, more tears cascading down my face. I could not stop staring at her, my hands aching to reach out.

"Mother" was a word I had never claimed for myself. I had given birth to her, but I was no mother. I never even let myself hold her before they took her away.

It was for the best, I'd told myself. She would never have been safe, surely used against me by an enemy, and would spend her life in a world of death and darkness. I thought I had done the right thing, protecting her from my world.

Lars came up beside me, his figure towering over me, arms behind his back. He watched the little girl as Goran sat her down with some toys. She didn't move to them, rolling her arms into a knot at her chest, while longing flooded from in her eyes. Goran, the huge asshole, was on his hands and knees, trying to gently encourage her.

"You hid her well. But my men are considered the best for a reason." Lars broke my attention from her. "I did not want to use a child. You gave me no choice." My head shot up so sharply a vein popped in my neck, heating it with blood. He slowly turned his chin down to me, his green eyes set on mine. "I am going to untie you now, Ms. Cathbad, because you understand perfectly what is at risk if you do anything to me. You grasp what will happen if you do not say yes to my request?"

My nose flared, fury boiling in my stomach. He had me completely under his command and he knew it. An inferno of hate seared through the tears trailing down my face. I had no choice.

Nodding, my lids squeezing together, the last tear soaked into the cloth wrapped around my mouth. With a nod from the King, fingers dug into my wrists, undoing the rope binding my hands. Once freed, my palms flew to the glass, pressing against it. Travil ripped out strands of my hair removing the gag, but I hardly felt it, all my attention on her.

"Ms. Cathbad, I bind you from using magic on me, anyone in this home, attached to me or this property. No loopholes or tricks. Do you understand?"

"Yes," I whispered, feeling as if he were stripping me of my soul.

"Do you agree to this contract?"

I sucked in air, letting it flow over my lips in a long exhale. Staring at my little girl, I only had one response.

"Yes." The moment I agreed, energy descended on me as palpable as when Lars's ogre had decided to use me as a chair. My shoulders sagged under the weight, my teeth gritting through the pressure. Then it was gone. But I felt the bind wrap around me like a noose.

Goran sat down with the girl and nodded toward the toys. She sat but still didn't move to touch the toys; her long silky hair blocked most of her sweet face. I couldn't take my eyes off her for more than a moment.

"What kind of a man are you, using an innocent little girl?" I hissed.

"If you saw the family who had adopted her, you'd be thanking me for taking her." Lars slid his hands in his pockets, nodding toward the girl. "She's an extremely special girl. It is incredibly lucky we found her. Got her away from there...from *those* people," he snarled.

"Where was she?" I croaked out, peering up at him. "What were they doing to her?"

"She was near Dublin. The family from whom I took her have filed reports several times with the police and adoption agency. They complained of her being possessed by the devil, that her tongue was controlled by demons." Lars tugged at the cuffs of his sleeves, his forehead pinched.

My neck swung back to the tiny child. *Bloody shite.* She was too young to be getting predictions. She was only five. I had hoped her fully human father would water down the Druid magic, but it seemed only the opposite had happened.

I'd thought about her every day after that warm June morning when I had to give her up, wondered what she was doing, what her life was like. If she was happy. Had friends.

"They hoped beating her would expel the demons," he growled. "When that didn't work, they tried to get her exorcised."

My hand went to my mouth, doing little to hold back my anguished cry. Guilt pummeled me and bent me over. I was unable to swallow over the agony I felt, air fighting to get down into my lungs.

What had I done to her? What horrors did I let happen to her because I thought I was doing the right thing?

Gasps ricocheted out of me. Air wouldn't make its way over the barricade in my throat. My nerves trilled with fear and anxiety.

Fingers came up under my chin, forcing it up with a jerk. Bright greenish eyes caught mine. "Calm down," the voice ordered me. "Take a deep breath."

Without hesitation my body followed the command. My shoulders dipped lower as I halted the short breaths, taking a long controlled one.

"Again."

I sucked in through my nose, feeling the blockage dissolving on my tongue after a few more inhales. Slowly my panic ebbed, allowing me to notice the King squatted down next to me, his fingers wrapped around my jaw.

"Thank you," I mumbled out so low most ears wouldn't have heard, but Lars was not like most.

He nodded at my appreciation, his expression holding no emotion. "One more time."

"I'm fine." I tried to pull away from his hold.

"Humor me." He leaned his head to the side, keeping his grip firm.

Normally at the first hint of anyone, especially him, telling me what to do, I would have swung out a right hook. Instead I took another deep breath, closed my eyes, and centered myself.

"She will never be harmed again. That I can *promise* you," he said quietly, his voice like butter, coating me in warmth. A promise to a fae was binding. They did not toss them around casually, Lars least of all. He meant it.

Fionna, wake up! Don't get caught in his glamour. This is all a trick!

I yanked away from him, scooting backward, my defenses slamming up.

"What is your game then? If you aren't going to use her against me?"

He watched me for a few beats before rising.

"I never said I wouldn't use her against you."

Fuck. Shite. I knew it.

I flew to my feet, my shoulders rolling back. An overwhelming need to protect my daughter caused me to snarl the same as a wild animal. Magic clawed up my throat, ready to strike.

"Don't." Lars glared. "I warn you, even if you physically attack me, I will retaliate. You have something to live for, Ms. Cathbad, so don't take away this little girl's mother again."

His words were a knife in the chest. I stumbled a step back, remorse slowing me down.

"She is safe now and will remain so under my care."

Dread trickled down my throat like an IV. I understood what he meant. "I need to do what you say or I will never see her again." The instant I set eyes on her, I knew I could never walk away again. It killed me the first time when my need to protect her had been my reason to give her up. Now none of those reasons existed anymore. DLR was dismantled, and most of my people were dead from our battle with Luc, a noble fae trying to end the monarchy. I was no longer the commander. I had been swept off the board and was no longer a threat to the fae.

Lars was anticipating a mother's instinct for her child. That *I* would do *anything* for her. Anything…even betraying my own beliefs and principles against everything I fought for.

Sorrow punched at my heart. I glanced at my daughter, still too scared to play with the toys, probably fearing she would get punished if she made a wrong move. I dropped my head in shame. *Do what you need to do. She is worth everything.*

"I have one condition." I sucked in, lifting my head, locking eyes with him.

Lars raised one lip in the hint of a smile. "You have gumption, Ms. Cathbad. I will give you that." He slid his hands into his pockets.

"I want you to unbind Kennedy. She has nothing to do with this. She knows nothing. This is between you and me only."

The smirk expanded over his whole mouth, and I realized it was exactly what he always wanted. Checkmate. He hadn't cared about Kennedy's involvement. He wanted me to be the sole member in this game. As he promised, he had won this round.

Lars took off promptly after I agreed to his terms. He didn't tell me where he was going, but I hoped it was to Kennedy. To break the bind on her.

When he got back, we were to have a "meeting," which meant I was going to have to tell him where the cauldron was.

However, I still had cards up my sleeves he would not be expecting. Ones that might get me killed.

Do what you need to do, Fionna, I repeated in my head. *She is worth any sacrifice.*

Chapter Six

Lars

By the way the Druid held herself, you could easily forget she was only a handful of inches over five feet. Her power wasn't close to any other Druid's I had ever felt. Her strength, stubbornness, and ferociousness, even when used against me, were ironically the precise things that kept me from killing her.

She intrigued me.

The woman who attacked my compound, using strighoul against me, kidnapped Marguerite, and threatened my life should be dead. I should have ended her the moment she used her magic against me in Ireland. But I didn't for two reasons: my respect for the Seelie Queen and the need for the cauldron. Fascination only went so far.

"I also want to see my daughter." Fionna clicked her chin a level higher, her lips pursing together.

"You mean the one you gave up five years ago?" I rubbed my chin. "To religious fanatics who abused her?"

She flinched, her teeth clenching each other. "I-I didn't know. I thought I was doing the best for her." Fionna glanced over her shoulder at the child.

The little girl was watching as Goran played with a toy, trying unsuccessfully to engage her. Something critical and assessing showed in the young girl's gaze as it moved over Goran. She seemed unsure of his sincerity. Probably because she was used to being hit with the same hand that embraced her.

When she was first brought here, she walked straight up to me. Not fearful, but mildly curious. She didn't say a word, but her eyes bored into me until I felt as though she was peeling back my soul.

"What is your name?" I had peered down at the tiny thing. She looked so similar to her mother and aunt, even the same brush of freckles over her nose and cheeks. She continued to stare at me, her eyes much wiser than any child I had ever encountered. "Do you have a name?"

Nothing.

Children in general did not scare me, but for some reason the intensity of this little girl was unnerving. I looked away from her penetrating gaze.

"Goran, take her to Marguerite. She needs to be fed." I waved to my second-in-command, shifting on my feet. "And a bath."

He walked up to the girl, nudging her. She tilted her head, her blue eyes still watchful of me, as if I were a puzzle she was trying to decipher. She reached up, took Goran's hand, then turned and walked out with him.

I had faced the scariest and deadliest of enemies, dealt with life-threatening situations, but nothing made me feel as exposed as this five-year-old had.

Her mother was almost as talented. However, Fionna inspired anger in me, a need to marshal control.

"Please, let me see her." Fionna set her brown eyes on me.

"There." I held up my hand toward the girl on the other side of the glass. "Don't say I did not give you what you asked for."

"You know what I mean." Fionna stepped forward, her hands in knots at her side. Magic bubbled under her skin. "Let me talk to my daughter, wanker."

In a blink, Fionna flew back against the wall, her hands reaching to wrench away the invisible hand gripping her throat. Just enough to let a little air in but bottle up any words in her throat.

"You. Forget. Yourself," I ground out, making my way to where her body was pinned to the wall. "You are my captive." I leaned into her, my warning licking her ear. "You threatened and tried to kill the King. You should not be alive. My rights say I can kill you. Torture you. I have been *quite* generous." I added a little more pressure to her throat. "However, my patience is thinning, and my respect for your sister will only go so far. You do not make demands. I do not need you as much as you'd like to think." I stepped even closer, the scent of the shampoo I provided her wafting up my nose. "I can do whatever I want to you. I own you."

The whiff of soap and her natural smell, something close to a crisp rain and baking apples, gripped my chest. A low growl vibrated up my throat. My muscles tightened, my body jerking back in reflex. *Fuck. Where had that come from?* My hold on her dropped, and she fell to the ground, hacking and gasping for a breath. Fury circled up my windpipe, spilling over into the room, thickening the air.

"You will see her when I say you can." I tugged at my cuffs. "The sooner you show me where the cauldron is, the faster you can be with her."

Fionna's head slowly peeled up from her knees, her lids narrowed with rage. "You are a monster."

"Something I have never denied." I moved a hand to straighten my collar as I faced the mirror. "And what makes you even more disgusted is you would do the same. You are no fool. This is how it works, Ms. Cathbad. You understand that perfectly."

Her nose flared, her head jerking away to stare at her daughter. Both of us were quiet for a few moments.

"What is her name?" The question came out like wisps of wind.

"Her name on the adoption papers is Mary, but when Marguerite asked, she told her it was Piper."

Fionna gasped, covering her mouth with her hand, her eyes filling with tears. "What?"

I turned toward the rising figure, watching her hands press against the glass.

"Th-that…" Fionna blinked, but a single tear escaped, trailing down her cheek. "It was the name I was going to give her."

My gaze shot back to the little girl, who was now helping Goran put a puzzle together, her eyes never swaying from him. How was it possible? How would she know the name she was never given? Did she have the power to see the future and past?

"She's too young to be this powerful," Fionna whispered to herself.

"She is." I nodded. "That means she needs you more than ever to help guide her. Power without understanding can only lead to destruction. Of herself. Of others."

Fionna wiped away a single tear, her expression losing all emotion, before she faced me.

"Fine. Let's get started."

A smile curved over my mouth. "Exactly what I was hoping you'd say."

Chapter Seven

Fionna

"You get twenty minutes with her." Travil yanked my arm roughly to the closed door. Lars's kindness only extended to this brief time with Olwyn. He would keep Piper from me until I did what he wanted. It hurt being this close and not being able to touch her or hear her voice. However, the pain was mine alone. She did not even know I existed, much less I was here. At night she would call out for the people she considered Mummy and Daddy. Not me.

I would have to live with this. My choice had been both right and wrong. There could be no resolution to this, and I would have to come to terms with it.

Travil opened the door to a large room that stole my breath away. It looked as though a princess should inhabit this space with its intricate chandeliers, four-poster bed, lush rugs, and designer furniture. A huge fireplace burned bright, and in front of it an overstuffed rocking chair held the woman I knew better than anyone.

I grew up in a tiny, drafty shack on the coast of Ireland, where fog and rain seeped so deep into your bones you forgot what warmth was. I slept wrapped in a moth-eaten comforter on a thin mattress in a loft, a bucket next to me to catch the rain coming through the hole in the roof.

Not once did I look at it as an encumbrance. It made me tougher, inside and out, and I relished nothing could break me...cold, poverty, hunger...and especially fae. Anything that made me stronger to fight them, I welcomed.

This room only held warmth, softness, and beauty, not qualities I understood. I was cold, hard, detached. A leader for the Druids. A killer. The fae had made me into this. To play their game I had to become everything they were. I prided myself on it and empowered other Druids to be the same.

Yet in less than an hour Lars had been able to strip back layers of me with the two people I'd let myself care about. The woman who raised me, shared love with, even if her hand was firm, and my baby girl who I thought I'd never see again. She should have had a better life than mine and been loved and held with warmth and softness.

I didn't think I was capable of that.

"Olwyn?" I pulled free of Travil's grip and rushed to the woman sitting by the fireplace. Her lids were closed, a soft snore rattling from her chest. She would have died naturally years before, but selfishly I kept her alive with my magic.

I was afraid to be alone, without her.

I went down on my knees, taking her hands in mine. Thousands of life lines ran deep over her face until it was hard to remember the woman she'd been when I was a little girl.

"Twenty minutes, starting now," Travil snapped, leaning against the doorjamb. My glare did nothing but make him grin viciously at me.

"Bastard," I mumbled.

"Heard that."

"I know. I wanted you to." I whipped back, turning my attention to Olwyn. I bit my lip, rubbing my hand over Olwyn's.

Her eyes finally fluttered open. "Onie?" Joy and love rushed over her pet name for me. "Ya returned ta me."

"Yes, Owl. I am so sorry I was gone so long." She got confused so easy and didn't understand time the same anymore.

She gripped my hand, her breath coming out in gulps. "Ya know how proud I am of you?"

My jaw locked down, keeping the emotion from her words back. She was not one to say she loved you or was proud of you often. When she did, it felt similar to being swallowed by an ocean.

"Hear me, girl? I am so proud..." Heaving in air. "Of who you have become."

"Shhh, Owl." My fingers caressed the side of her face. "Just rest."

"No…" Gasping. "I need ya to hear me."

"Why are you talking like this?"

Her lids drifted closed for a moment before lifting to mine. "It's time, Onie…it's time to let me go."

Panic.

Fear.

"No!" My head waggled back and forth. "No. Not now." *Not ever.*

"Yes, girl. It's time." She took both my hands. For someone so old and with little strength left, she seized them with a bone-crunching grip. "Your journey is just startin'. You have your wings, girl. Use 'em. Fly."

Dammit. My throat thickened with emotion.

"I had no magic. Not like you, but I still feel it."

"What?"

Olwyn licked her lips, scanning around the room. "Ye're home."

My brows furrowed, not understanding.

"It's why I can leave ya." She stumbled over her sentence, as though exhausted. "Now, let me go. Promise me."

"Owl…"

"Promise me," she gritted, determination set behind her eyes. "I want ta. Don't be greedy, girl. Not meant for this world anymore."

A cry clogged my chest. I knew I was being selfish. She was ready; she had been for a long time. I had held on for dear life. I leaned over and dropped my head into her lap like a child. She ran her fingers gently through my hair. I had vague memories of my real mother, but

Olwyn had raised me, cared for me, taught me, pushed me to be more. To fight.

Tears slipped out and I sighed. The unbinding enchantment came out so quietly it hummed in the air like a lullaby. Olwyn began to rock in her chair, magic encircling her. Then it broke the spell keeping her alive. She sighed happily, as though the world was no longer weighing on her shoulders.

"I luv ya, Fionna. Never told you enough," she muttered, then her hand went limp in my hair, sliding out to her lap. The last bits of her life flew from her body, finally free of their cage.

Silently I sobbed, my heart breaking into splinters. This had been coming for a long time and I had known that, but it didn't take away the loss in the moment. She really was gone forever now. I understood I wasn't alone. I had my sister, my daughter. But without Owl, I was truly an orphan.

My skin prickled at the sound of Travil on his walkie-talkie. I hated his intrusion in such a personal moment, so I blocked his clear position of my heartbreak. But I wasn't fae; I didn't count or matter in their eyes.

"Get up!" Travil was standing over me, his face tight. Pissed.

"Fuck you." I glowered up at him.

"Not if you begged." His fingers wrapped around my arm and yanked me off the floor. "Now move!"

Brutally, he tore me away from Olwyn's body. Rage bloomed in my chest like spring flowers. Every insult I could think of gushed from my mouth, still reaching for Olwyn, her hand sliding from my fingers.

"Shut the fuck up!" He dragged me out of the room and down the hall.

"No. I won't, you arsehole!" I tugged and wriggled the same way as a snake, trying to liberate myself from his grip. How I wished I could spell his ass with magic. The Dark shite. I wanted to fling him out of the house and crush his brain.

"Stop," he yelled, slamming my back into the wall, knocking the air from my lungs. "This compound is being attacked right now." He growled, getting into my face. "By strighoul...and if we find you had anything to do with it..." A vicious grin displayed his white teeth. He didn't startle me, but his statement did. Attacked? By strighoul? "Let's say, the King will have fun shredding you into bits. And I will be there watching."

Fuck.

Chapter Eight

Lars

"We will be there in three minutes," Goran yelled back at me from the front of the car as he jerked the wheel and tore down the private road to my compound.

Fae were supposed to be these great magical beasts, but I couldn't feel more human in this moment. Every second I sat in the car, my home and the people in it were under threat.

The magical doors weren't reliable enough to use since the wall fell. Only Ember seemed to be able to find her way through them without ending up across the world. I wasn't willing to risk it. Not tonight. But taking the car seemed archaic. I wanted to be there *now*.

The moment Rimmon contacted me, letting me know we had "guests" waiting at our barriers, I struggled to stay in my skin.

I had given her every luxury. I had never given the liberties and privileges to any other prisoner I had granted Fionna. Not only did she show no gratitude, now she sent her mangy pets to try and break her out? The only pleasure I took in this was she had not predicted I would find her daughter. With this attack, she was putting her little girl's life in jeopardy. I was told they had yet to strike, but just stood there clanking their weapons and howling warrior cries.

"That fucking little bitch." Fury rattled the monster inside me, the one I worked hard to keep contained but lately had been frequently slipping. I wasn't sure if I could keep myself from killing her this time.

Kennedy was firm in her thinking Fionna had nothing to do with the confrontation and demanded she come along, but I forbade it. I didn't want her to bear witness or try to stop me from dismembering her sister. The Queen could believe what she wanted, but the Druid had attacked my home before with strighoul, so why wouldn't they come for their patron?

"Hold on, sir." Goran whipped the car off the paved road, the car bouncing as it hit rocks and trenches, and crashed through the creek that ran through my property.

My knuckles turned white as I gripped the door handle. We couldn't come in through the front door. The strighoul formed a crescent around the front part of my property, making it necessary to slip around from the back.

The tires slipped over the wet ground as he spun the wheel, tearing us past the spell-protected barrier, driving the magic and bulletproof automobile up on the lawn to the deck. Goran had not even stopped the car before I hopped out, running for the house.

"Marguerite?" I called the moment I entered through the back door to the kitchen.

"We're in here, Lars," Nic's deep voice called out.

"Do you have…?" I came around the corner to the kitchen, seeing Nic on a stool next to Piper, eating ice cream. Marguerite stood by the stove.

"Mr. Lars." Marguerite rushed up to me. The sight of her released the tension in my shoulders. If they had gotten her again, I would have shredded each of them, taking extra time with their benefactor. I would deal with her soon.

Nic stood protectively next to the little girl. He turned to face me, his body relaxed, but his unpatched eye was serious.

"Go downstairs in the special room until we have this taken care of." My hands went to Marguerite's shoulders, while my eyes fixed on Nic. Piper, wearing flannel pajamas, her hair freshly washed, set down her spoon and stared at me. She tilted her head, seeming to find me interesting.

"But I have cupcakes in the oven." Marguerite swished her hand, twisting around me for the stove. "Vanilla with sprinkles. *Para la niña.*" She smiled warmly at the little girl, whose small face bloomed with happiness. I had yet to meet anyone who could fight the love that burst out from Marguerite.

"Marg—"

"No, Mr. Lars. *We* will go after she's finished." Her eyebrows tapered down, her jaw set. "Then it is movie night, right, *niña*?"

Piper's grin widened and she nodded eagerly.

"Fuck," I mumbled to myself. I could get men of all species to cower before me, but not this human. She was a mule, but also one of the only people in the world to do whatever she pleased, whenever she wanted. That was how much I loved and respected her. She was smart and understood life here. This was not the first time we had been threatened, and she knew when the time was to go into hiding. Some of my tension eased when I realized she was taking charge of Piper.

"I will be here to make sure they stay safe." Nic turned to Piper, tickling her. "Uncle Nic's got this. Right, little one?"

Piper let out a piercing giggle, wiggling on her stool. Nic and Marguerite would shower this little girl with love. No one could fight their charm, especially together. Piper was safe.

"My liege." Travil walked into the kitchen from the other end of the house.

Her mother, on the other hand, was not safe. Not from me.

"Where is she?"

"Tied up in your office." His eyes glinted like he had enjoyed being the one to do it.

"You get all the fun." Goran came up to my side.

"Report," I demanded.

"So far they are just dancing around and making a lot of racket. Rimmon counted about a hundred or so. Not the numbers or the same level of magic as last time," Travil responded.

I rubbed the spot between my brows. This "attack" did not make sense. They lost the benefit of a surprise assault. They weren't beating at my protection wards with magic. And I was no longer sure if my absence just happened to be a coincidence.

"Rimmon has the men ready to act?"

"Yes." Travil nodded. "At your word."

"All right, let me talk to our houseguest. See if she can enlighten me." The demon inside perked up, rumbling my voice. "Be ready for my go-ahead."

"Yes, sir." Both men bowed their heads, heading outside to join their fellow warriors.

While Marguerite took the rainbow-colored dessert from the oven, a special treat for the little girl, I stormed down the hallway, planning to give the mother a whole different kind of reward for her behavior.

Torture *was* dessert to my demon.

Chapter Nine

Fionna

The King had his own force field. Like a tornado, I felt him heading for me, rumbling and ripping away everything in his path. The energy coming off him prickled my skin. He was pissed.

No, furious.

The magically bound rope cut into my wrists and dug deeper as I wiggled my back to the wall where Travil had tied me.

I would never be one to cower, no matter how much force came at me. That was not how Olwyn raised me, and not the foundation my real mother and father ingrained in me before I left them. I took things head-on.

The door swung open with such force the door handle crashed through the wall and snapped the hinges. The thick plank of wood creaked, smashing to the floor behind the King.

His face was bleached white, his eyes black. Not even a hint of white bordered his pupils. *Shite.*

At the sight of his demon, fear gathered in my limbs, and I curled my legs farther up to my chest, as though they could block me from his wrath.

He sped toward me with silence and grace I found disturbing. Things like stomping, yelling, threatening with weapons came with anger. Scary as it could be, your brain understood that, even expected it. What Lars could do went past fear, his movement struck my most primal need to run. Cry. Pee myself.

I fought every instinct, but my chin trembled. I forced it to rise higher.

His black pits stared down at me.

"I, I..." I swallowed over the quake in my voice. "I didn't..."

The rope fell away from my arms, and a hand clutched my throat, my body rising so fast up the wall I didn't have a chance to gulp for air.

"Stupid, Druid," he snarled, getting close to my face. "Think your pets can save you? That they could seize my walls?" His hand crushed my windpipe, not letting me speak.

I shook my head back and forth, trying to tell him it wasn't me. I would not be this foolish. My legs knocked against the wall as I kicked into him. My lungs burned with the need for air, my hands scratching at his fingers. He wasn't using his powers to strangle me; he was doing it himself.

"Though I'll bet you weren't counting on your daughter being here." He slammed me again against the wall, blackness fringing my vision. "I should walk her out there, let them get a whiff of the magic already coming off her."

Something snapped inside me.

Feral. Protective.

I went wild; one of my kicks hit him right where I hoped. Fae or human, King or beast, you could always count on the same weakness: their dicks. With a grunt, he released his hold on me, and my body landed on the wood floor with a *thunk*, pain jolting through my tailbone. Oxygen wheezed down my throat, so raw it felt as if I were swallowing nails, but my lungs hungrily consumed as much as they could.

A deep growl vibrated through the room, and I knew I only had seconds to convince him I didn't send for the strighoul.

"This. Wasn't. Me," I croaked, shoving back onto my feet, one hand still rubbing at my raw throat. "I had nothing to do with the strighoul tonight."

Still bent forward, his empty eyes stared at me from under his eyebrows, his lips twisted into a snarl.

"I'm not stupid. Lars, you *know* that. I would never make a mistake like this." I stood to my full height. "I'm actually a little insulted you would think this was my doing."

"Why shouldn't I, Druid?" He slowly straightened. His skin had a little more color in it, but his eyes stayed black pools of anger. "You attacked me before using those foul things. You almost had me, my men…your sister blown up."

"Yes, I did." It was all I could respond. He would either believe me or not. "But this time it's not me."

In a blink, his face was in mine, leering down. The muscles along his jaw twitched. "If I find out…"

"You won't," I replied.

A crackled voice came from Lars desk. "Sir, some are in the field. They have torches and looked to be building something. Waiting on your word, sir." Without looking away from me, he reached back, grabbing the walkie-talkie on his desk.

"Attack," he said to his men, then set the device back down, his attention on me again. "I think it's time you tell me where the cauldron is, and let me warn you, Druid, I am not in the best of moods tonight."

He didn't say it, but the threat gurgled under every word. My daughter was up on the table. *Shite. Shite. Fuck. Shite.*

One of the cards I had, if played, might—no, would—end everything right here. I swallowed, letting the lie roll off my tongue with confidence.

"Prague."

"Where in Prague?"

I pinched my mouth together.

"Ah." He grinned, which looked more like a sneer. "You think if you tell me, I will kill you. That I'll have no need for you anymore."

"Exactly."

"You think me a fool?" He tilted his head. "The treasure would be layered under spells and protections. Ones, I have a feeling, only a Druid could undo. You are coming with me."

66

"Coming with you?" My eyes went wide. I was hoping I had more time. Time to get my daughter and run.

"You will be attached to my hip, Druid, until the moment you put it in my hands." Terror filled me. *Hide it, Fi. He will be able to feel it coming off you.*

"Sir!" Goran's voice broke again over the device.

Lars took a beat, then finally turned his head, breaking his intense gaze from me.

"Did you take care of them?"

"Yes. Most are dead, some got away, but I have men running them down."

"Thank you, Goran."

"Uh, sir, I think you need to come out here."

"Why?"

"They left a message for you, sir. That's what they were building out here."

Lars made a strange noise, set down the walkie-talkie, and grabbed my arm, pulling me with him.

"Let go of me." I stumbled and tripped trying to keep up with his long legs.

"I told you, Ms. Cathbad. You will be glued to me from now on."

With his speed, he practically dragged me out to the field, only releasing my arm when we reached his group of men. I could hear the crackle of the fire, and what appeared to be several bonfires were flaming behind the soldiers.

Goran stepped aside, letting Lars walk past him. Curiosity drove me and I found myself alongside him, staring at the display before our feet. Lars's body went rigid.

"Definitely not me," I muttered.

When Lars looked at me again his eyes were back to the bright yellow-green, fire reflecting off them. Then he stepped forward, crouching down close to the flames, and touched an oily leaf not yet ignited.

The foliage used as kindling was not brush you normally found around the Pacific Northwest.

"Is that…?"

"Olive tree." Lars rubbed it between his fingers, his expression distant, almost lost in thought.

"Olive?"

"Yes, just like the ones from my home country. Similar to the ones on my parents' property." He stood, whirling away, striding back to the house.

I gazed back down at the ground, the heat of the flames crackling my skin. Written out in fragments of olive branches…

Coming for what is mine.

Chapter Ten

Lars

"If you need anything else, sir, just let me know." Melanie handed me my glass of Scotch from a bottle over a hundred and fifty years old. My extremely long lifespan gave me the luxury of waiting for Scotch to age well and feeling as if it had only been months in the scheme of things.

"No, thank you," I snapped, wanting her to go away.

A flirty smile spread across her face as she winked. "I'm here to serve, my liege." Her hips swished as she walked over to Goran and Travil in the front of the plane.

Travil was sound asleep, but Goran sat straight, alert. He was always on, even in the absence of a threat. Goran's bulky body sat on the bench seats against the window so he could keep an eye on me. However, it seemed he was really keeping an eye on Ms. Cathbad.

Glaring actually.

Goran and Travil did not like the Druid, especially after they learned she had bombed the hotel room in Zurich, almost killing all of us.

Melanie served Goran his spritzer and strolled past me again, her fingers grazing my sleeve, her cue she was ready at any moment for me to call on her. The moment Rez no longer occupied my bed, Melanie made it clear she wanted to be in it. Both Melanie and Jessica were rare air fairies called sylphs. Not many remained, as air pollution killed most of them. Air to a sylph was like placing a water fairy in a river. They overly generated energy, which then needed an outlet.

I had made a rule a long time ago to not mix employees with pleasure, and I had kept to that rule. Rez had been the exception. My first and last.

It saddened me, but I missed how easy it had been with Rez. She was fierce in bed and exceptionally smart at running my business. I'd had the best of both worlds, except I never loved her. She had deserved it, but it had been a while since I'd been able to love like that.

As I swirled my glass, the smoky aroma drifted up my nose, taking the edge off my coiled muscles. Unfortunately, alcohol was not going to relieve what I felt at the present. Only one thing would help me. Fucking.

My teeth ground as I stared out the plane window, trying to calm the demon. I had yet to sleep, my mind preoccupied with the events of last night and organizing our trip to Prague. Not that I needed much sleep, but this morning I was more agitated and short-tempered than normal.

My instincts over the centuries were honed and always spot on. However, I still did not want to acknowledge the fluttering voice telling me the incident on my compound with the strighoul was far from some insignificant fae trying to undermine me and challenge my throne.

The olive branches were significant, as was the specific specie of tree cultivated in Greece, my birthplace. I'd been raised there with my twin brother, Devlin. Greece was my home of origin, Ireland and Scotland were where I became a man, and the Pacific Northwest was where I became a ruler.

Devlin is dead. Stop being paranoid.

The glass in my hand groaned under the pressure of my grip.

"A bit tense today, eh?" Fionna's Irish accented voice trilled like music in my ear, reminding me of another woman I kept so close to my heart sometimes I couldn't breathe. Aisling. Her memory haunted me, an ache that did not diminish with the passing years. The Irish lilt took me back to a time in my life when I'd felt joy, love, and abandon as only the young and naïve could have.

Regrets were a pointless waste of thoughts and energy. But I could not deny I sometimes wondered what would have happened if I had done things differently. Chosen her.

My gaze swung to Fionna in the seats across from me. She sat with her back to the window facing me, her knees up to her chest, headphones on, and a laptop on her lap. Though it pained me to admit it, she was stunningly beautiful even without makeup. Her huge brown eyes seemed to see through you, with awareness and knowledge, and her rare smile could bring any man to his knees. But it was her strength, her unabashed willingness to survive without apologies I found most attractive.

A rare glimmer of a smile tipped at her mouth and glistened deep in her dark eyes, like she had been watching me for a while, ready to provoke me. The smile grew full of mocking and stirred a need in my body.

A rumble came up my throat, and I turned away from her. I needed to fuck. The demon didn't want her per se; it just felt restless and agitated.

I tipped the expensive Scotch into my mouth, not even tasting it as I drank it down.

Being King was always stressful, but lately it seemed relentless. Last night's event only layered another burden onto my shoulders similar to bricks. The tension came from something I did not want to admit to myself. A shift somewhere deep inside my brain, realizing I was losing self-control of my demon and weakening the hold on my kingdom.

Your brother is dead. You killed him. Stop being ridiculous.

"I don't even want to know how much that Scotch you just guzzled cost."

"No." I looked over at her. "You don't."

"Just think if you spent the money on the homeless," she challenged. "Or protecting those who have been discriminated against."

Anger brushed up my shoulders. "I contribute more money to causes than you could possibly dream up. I am the leader in finding cures for diseases and birth defects. A trailblazer in creating new technology and businesses. I just helped open an orphanage in Seattle. I have reopened colleges and schools. Setting laws to equalize human and fae..."

Her eyebrows curved up. "I don't think it's the engine keeping this plane afloat. Your ego would keep us up here indefinitely."

I slammed my glass down, shattering it into a thousand pieces and making tiny incisions all over my palm. Travil jerked up from his slumber, and Goran looked as if he were ready for my order to lock up Ms. Cathbad again. I was losing control. This seldom happened, but when it did, it was never good. It seemed to be occurring a lot more frequently.

Melanie and Jessica were instantly at my side, cleaning up the glass before I could even blink. It bothered me, them rushing to my side like I was a baby, cooing and pacifying me.

I curled my hands into fists. The spot between my shoulder blades quaked with the need to act. To release. The need was so violent I felt I might snap.

Shit. I was about to break one of my rules.

"In my office now," I ordered the blonde fairy.

Melanie jumped to her feet, rushing toward the back before I changed my mind, a huge grin on her face. My gaze slid only briefly over to Ms. Cathbad, whose lips were parted, mouth open in complete disbelief and disgust. Her judgment only fueled my anger. Who was she to condemn me?

Honestly, I would have taken both stewardesses in the moment just to shove her revulsion back in her face. But Jessica and Travil had a liaison, even though they both tried to pretend otherwise, and were unaware I was knowledgeable of it. That was a no-go for me.

Rez was the only one I had been with for decades, even when our bed went cold. Since she left, I needed constant release. It was never more than a onetime association, and always took place in a hotel or my car. Never at my home, my sanctuary, but more like a transaction. And I wanted it that way.

My private jet was an extension of my home. Melanie had been with me since the beginning. I was being rash. Damn, I was never a fool. Slamming the door to my office, I was ready to tell her to get out, that it was a mistake. Except Melanie was already down to her underwear, leaning against my desk, a coy smile curling her mouth. She was beautiful, and I couldn't deny my body wanted hers, but my head was telling me the opposite.

The one thing with fae…we never had to worry about sexual transmitted diseases, and I had taken precautions right after I became King so I could not impregnate anyone. Otherwise they would come out of the woodwork, declaring they had the King's love child. I was far too responsible and smarter than that.

"I've wanted this for so long," she purred. "But you were with Rez, and I could tell a man who would never cheat on his mistress." She strolled over and grabbed my tie, slowly undoing the knot. "Do you know how much sexier it made you?"

Her free hand moved to my pants, rubbing me. *Fuck.*

The demon clawed my muscles, and I reached for her.

"I can give you all you've been missing." She tipped her face to mine as she unbuckled my pants. "Let me pleasure you, my liege. Wherever and whenever you desire."

Her voice grated on my nerves. "You will not become my mistress," I growled as her hand slipped down my slacks. Weakness. I hated I was not above it, needing my ego stroked. But after Rez left me for another man, the dark dweller, their prowess notorious throughout the fae world, I couldn't fight the need for validation.

"Of course, my liege." She smiled as though she did not believe my declaration for a moment. Fairies had huge egos about sex.

Melanie was desperate to impress me, working me with more vigor than I'd expected. I groaned. She was talented, I'd give her that, but this was just sex. Nothing more.

"I can do so much more if you let me."

"No talking." I shoved her back onto my desk. Lust billowed off her at my dominance, her chest rising and falling with need. Her arms stretched to go around my neck, to pull my face to hers. "And no kissing." I grabbed her wrist and flipped her around, bending her over my desk. Kissing was much too personal. It created an intimacy I neither desired nor wanted. Trust was something I did not give freely. I fully trusted only a handful of people, and she was not one of them.

She made happy whimpers, gripping the ledge of my desk. I didn't bother undressing her more, just slipped the fabric of her panties to the side.

"Yes! Now, my liege!"

I snarled in irritation, wanting her to shut up.

I heard a noise outside my office, and my gaze drifted to the door. It was as though the Druid's magic was seeping through, and I could feel her here with me. Energy blistered my chest, swelling it with rage. The feel of her magic bleeding into me from a room away snapped my demon free.

With no hesitation or consideration, I slammed inside the fairy with all I had. She moaned so loud it rattled the furniture. "God, yes! You feel better than I imagined."

My hips moved with relentless speed, all my anger and frustration pounding into her. My vision shifted and I knew my demon was showing, making me very glad Melanie could not see me. My demon was frightening. People saw the version I let them see, the one scary enough to make the toughest bastard pee himself. I never let anyone see my true form, especially during sex. Not even Rez or Aisling.

"Fuck me! Oh gods...my liege!" She started going crazy, bucking and moaning like she was possessed. And my demon could sense she was not faking one bit of it, rendering me even harder. But I was a fucking demon and a king. Those two might not equate to being exceptional at sex, but I had made a lot of women pass out from orgasms.

My hand wanted to cover her mouth, to keep the deafening moans from leaving this room, but more of the Druid's magic flooded into the room, pulsing with fury, knocking into my skin.

The Druid was turned on and pissed about it.

A smirk spread my mouth, and the tips of my daggered teeth dug into Melanie's fragile skin. *You feel that, Ms. Cathbad? How about this?*

My bones strained at my skin, hollowing my cheeks. The demon filled the room, taking up every inch of space and air, though it cared nothing for the woman below me. It shot its energy at the closed door as though it was trying to break it down.

A voice deep in my mind told me to stop, but the demon was out too far. Every thump of the Druid's magic against me made it want to lash out.

I clutched the air fairy's hips, pushing deeper and harder. Objects splintered and shattered around me. Melanie made cries of ultimate pleasure. Sweat poured down my chest and back, sticking my dress shirt to my skin, my release just starting to build up my spine. I could feel her tightening, ready to go over.

"Noooo." I growled, not ready for her to be done, which only egged me to reach mine faster. I hauled her off the desk, bending her all the way over, her hands still using the desk to keep herself up.

"Fuuuuuck!" she wailed, hitting her climax.

I did not stop; I was not close.

Then I felt energy from outside the room. It almost seemed like a hand sliding down my chest, wrapping around my hips and slowly caressing down to the base of me, gripping me firmly. Fire sparked up my back, singeing all my muscles. A noise deep in my throat broke out of my mouth, and my body convulsed violently with release. I roared, my head falling backward. My vision blurred, and I lost track of all time and space. My legs gave way and I stumbled back into the wall, and to the floor. I sucked in clipped pulls of air, trying to calm my pounding heart.

What the hell was that?

My eyes cleared enough to see the girl was out cold, a lump on the ground. Similar to an incubus, a demon took, gorging on the energy of the act. Wolfing down the strength of the companion, but in doing so, it flooded them with endorphins, giving them the highest pleasure they could ever receive. Humans could actually die from it, overloading their system. Some lower fae could become brain dead.

Shit.

I peered down at myself, my tie loose and crooked, and my shirt soaking and crumpled. My pants were around my ankles, my dick exposed and glistening with sex and sweat. My demon was sedated enough, but I was livid. Mortified.

Not only was I a mess, but I had utterly lost control.

The Unseelie King did not lose self-control.

"Sir?" Goran's voice came through the door.

"Yes. I'm fine," I snapped, getting to my feet, yanking up my pants. My legs shook under my weight.

Goran snorted. "I don't doubt it, sir. No one in the vicinity would doubt. I think you forced lightning to hit the plane."

I growled. I hated everyone knew my business. No, I hadn't thought of Travil, Goran, Jessica, or the pilot. It had all been meant for Ms. Cathbad. My throat vibrated with anger.

"Just wanted to let you know we will be landing in thirty minutes."

"Thank you, Goran." I went over to the stewardess, picking up her limp body. I carried her to the sofa, placed her on it, and covered her with a blanket. Melanie hummed happily, a grin spreading on her face. She would need to sleep for the rest of the day to replenish.

Irritation at myself only grew the more I thought about my rashness. I walked into the shower attached to the bedroom next to my office. The warm water glided over my skin, washing away the evidence, and I scrubbed as if I wished to cleanse away the act and the aftermath I knew would result.

Melanie would not settle for just the one time. Arrogant? Maybe, but it was the truth. I had learned this the hard way. The reason I never allowed myself to let the demon out was because most become addicted. Not settling for just a onetime experience.

No matter how abrasively I scoured my skin, it did not rinse away the notion that not only had I lost restraint, but the element tipping me over the edge was an infuriating woman. And not the one I'd fucked.

A tiny woman. A tenacious young Druid who had tried to kill me and almost succeeded, and who challenged and bucked me at every turn.

She was my enemy and possessed strong skills in black magic. Kennedy's sister or not, I understood she was too dangerous to keep alive.

After she got the cauldron, I would end her. I *had* to.

Chapter Eleven

Fionna

Fucking fae. Seriously. They were all arseholes, especially the one next to me. He acted reserved with me since we got off the plane. Fine with me. The less we said to each other, the better.

I kept my gaze out the window, watching the beautiful city pass by.

The car swung around the corner, and the Prague castle exploded into view across the passenger side window, like a piece of art. My breath caught. The spires of the cathedral propelling up into the air past the gates of the castle stilled me in my seat. Believe me, we had an abundance of castles and manors in Ireland, but ours were a little more understated. The awe-inspiring design of the Gothic St. Vitus Cathedral clearly intended to amaze and perhaps intimidate its visitors. The spires reached for the sky as the enormous creamy yellow limestone building loomed over the people below.

Goran swerved the town car down a cobble lane and pulled the black sedan up to our location. I stared at the luxurious hotel and could already sense the snobbery and elitism wafting off it. The intricate vaulted entrance of stone and iron welcomed its guests...but only the ones with money. The white stone grandeur was only steps away from the Prague Castle and came with a reputation for its famous restaurant. What a waste of money. I rolled my eyes, shaking my head.

"I was not looking for your approval, Ms. Cathbad." Lars voice sounded clipped, his mood cantankerous. He set the files he was reading between us and touched the bridge between his eyes.

I was the one who had to listen to *him* have sex, the one who *didn't* get off. I should be the grumpy one, not him.

On the plane I had been so close to going to the bathroom to relieve myself of the throbbing between my legs, but no way would I admit him having sex could affect me that way. Instead I turned my music up louder, although it hadn't stopped the feel of his magic pumping into the room, crawling across my body, as if his fingers were caressing my skin.

My chest tightened, and I jerked my head out my window, pictures sweeping through my mind. It was natural to get turned on hearing someone have sex. Perfectly normal. No matter if the person disgusted you or not...right?

The car door opened on Lars's side, Travil holding it for his King. He and the other stewardess had also disappeared to the bathroom on the plane, which only added to the sexually charged atmosphere.

Lars slid out gracefully, tugging at his cuffs and the bottom of his jacket when he stood, appearing every bit the smooth, composed, deadly, sexy King. Emphasis on deadly.

He was back in control.

I knew his type. Narcissistically clean, starchy, and anal. Probably had a sick and twisted sex fetish, too, because he was so uptight in his everyday life. Men like him annoyed the hell out of me. Give me a beer, a guy with a beard, hands that could build stuff, and crazy wild sex.

Wrenching the door open, I got out as staff ran from the hotel, bustling around the car similar to planets revolving around their sun, Lars.

This was going to be a long, painful few days...if he let me live. I was no fool. He would kill me sooner or later. Either way, I knew he'd try. *Try*. He would not succeed if I had anything to say about it.

"Ms. Cathbad?" He motioned for me to join him. I grumbled to myself, his hand lightly touching my back to escort me into the hotel. I jerked away from the contact, and he dropped his hand.

"Sir, Travil and I will check the premises." Goran dipped his head toward Lars the moment we were safely inside, then he and Travil stepped back outside.

Lars headed toward the hotel lobby desk. A woman greeted him before we even reached it.

"My liege, we have your room ready. Everything is prepared exactly how you like it." She spoke with a thick Czech accent, her blonde hair rolled into a firm bun, her curves fitting nicely into her hotel uniform.

"Thank you, Lucia." He took the card from her hand, and the bellmen whisked away our suitcases.

"Anything you need, Majesty. Mikolas, the chef, is at your command. Day or night."

"*Diva.*" I coughed into my hand, causing Lucia to blink at me with confusion. She probably wondered if she heard me correctly, maybe awed I dare speak to the King in such a way.

"Tell him I look forward to whatever he prepares me." Lars grabbed my arm roughly, tugging me toward the elevator.

"Lars?" A husky voice, thickly accented, drifted from behind us. Lars and I swiveled around.

The woman was tall and runway thin, with shiny black hair so dark it had a hint of plum to it and cut in a long sleek bob that brushed her shoulders. Her dark eyes focused solely on the King, with undeniable interest. She was stunning, gorgeous, her features symmetrical in the way magazines adored. Her heels, tailored to fit, and her leather polka-dotted pencil skirt, cream blouse, and jacket screamed wealth and style. She held herself with elegance and superiority only someone born with money had. Romanian? Between her looks and accent, I was pretty sure she was from somewhere around there.

"Margo," Lars said. I could not gather how he felt about her because no emotion softened his features or his voice.

"It is so amusing finding you here. Our paths keep crossing." She leaned into him, air-kissing both his cheeks, getting as close to his lips as she could. She pulled back, peering at him through her lashes, then a smile broke her perfect red mouth. "What a wonderful coincidence. Are you stalking me, or is fate trying to tell us something?"

"I do not think you would consider it stalking." Lars eyebrow twitched, his statement direct.

She let out a deep laugh, her eyes twinkling with mischief. "I think I'm owed at least a dinner, after you left me in the bar so abruptly in Zurich."

"Important business came up."

"Yes. For a man in your position, business always comes first. Something *I* understand." She looked straight at him, giving no doubt what she wanted. It seemed exceptionally clear if they hadn't once been lovers, she *really* wanted them to be. Lars as usual was an enigma, showing no cards.

"Tonight, then?" She was confident as though he would never turn her down. To look at her, likely no one had ever said no to her. She was perfect for him, another uptight, snobby elitist with too much money and a diva complex. I had learned early to hold my head high no matter what my status was to others. I knew who I was. But I couldn't help feeling like the help next to this woman. Her class and confidence sucked up the air and left me dangling like wet laundry.

"My room?" She touched his arm. Expensive gems circling her fingers and wrist, but the jewels only highlighted the way her nails drifted and circled over his sleeve, full of promise. "I *happen* to have a bottle of Glenfiddich in my room."

Annoyance crackled along my shoulders. After the situation on the plane, I didn't want to see or hear another woman cry out Lars's name. She was probably kinky in bed. A screamer. My nose wrinkled, disgusted at the thought.

"Tonight I am busy." Lars leaned back, placing his hand on my back, pushing me forward. "Maybe some other time."

Margo's gaze darted to me, as though she finally noticed I was there.

"Oh, *my apologies*." She sounded anything but apologetic. "I did not know you were here with someone." Displeasure pressed her mouth shut. She looked me up and down, disgust at what she saw thinning her lids.

"We're not." I stepped away from his touch.

"She's upset with me," Lars whispered as he moved back to me, his palm driving me with force toward the elevator. "Have a good night, Margo." He nodded at her.

She stared after us, her face stone, but tiny blasts of black, deep red, and muddy green leaked out of her aura. Her dark penetrating eyes shot hateful daggers at us until the elevator doors shut.

"What went wrong? You two seemed so perfect together." Sarcasm laced my tone. The elevator started to the top floor.

"You do not know me, Ms. Cathbad." He stood stiffly beside me, tugging at his cuffs. "Do not presume to understand my needs or wants."

A shiver galloped over my shoulders and down my

arms. Even his hinting at sex or his desires in bed had me stirring uncomfortably.

"Trust is earned. And I have to be exceptionally careful with whom I give it to."

"So...magnificent Margo didn't pass your trust test?"

"Very few do." He shot me a quick look.

I snorted. "Margo seems like she would be quite high maintenance."

"No. She would be low maintenance." His eyes met mine. "It would be merely sex. She is wealthy, independent, and not looking for anything to hold her down either. The ones who want more become difficult in my line of work."

Heat crawled up my neck. "Then why did you turn her down?"

"Because." He leaned over me, his mouth only an inch from mine. Heat lapped at my lips like a dog's tongue. "I am *stuck* with a pain-in-the-ass Druid and have a job to do tonight. Business first, Ms. Cathbad. Always."

Ding. The elevators opened and Lars strutted out leaving me rolling in fury.

Fuck him.

Wait, let me rephrase that.

Fae suck.

Wait...

"Coming, Ms. Cathbad?" He didn't even glance over his shoulder. He was taunting me. Batting me around like a toy.

If he thought I was similar every other woman or person he could play with because he could, he had another thing coming.

~~

"Wow," I whispered to myself as I stepped into the giant suite after him, trying not to let my mouth drop. It was probably one of the prettiest rooms I had ever been in. Okay, my idea of a hotel was above a pub, where you could hear rats scurrying in the walls. Doubt there were any rats here.

Heavy with floral print, the main room was divided into a living space with fireplace, office, and an entertainment area. The ceiling curved, only adding to the baroque style of the room. An open door on the far wall led to a single bedroom. The four-poster bed was centered in the room, draped in rich textures and fabric. A bathroom with a spa bath and shower was connected.

"Where are you sleeping? The sofa?" I came back out to the living room, where Lars stood at the office desk, reading over some papers.

"Amusing, Ms. Cathbad."

"I am, aren't I?" My hand brushed along one of the chairs, the soft velvet gliding under the tips of my fingers. "Or do you, Goran, and Travil cuddle? I'll bet you're the middle spoon."

His gaze flashed up from under his lashes. "Sorry to disappoint. They have connecting rooms on either side of me." He went back to his documents.

Of course they did. They would keep the King surrounded and protected from other patrons and threats.

"You're hilarious. Anyone ever tell you that?" I shook my head, roaming to the bar, where I found a basket of ground coffee, chocolate, whiskey, and sea salt and vinegar crisps. This was what he asked for? Not terribly demanding, I had to admit. For a king.

"All the time," he replied dryly.

I opened a bag of chips, shoving one in my mouth. The tang of the vinegar seeped onto my tongue, and I groaned happily. It reminded me of home, making me nostalgic for the rolling green hills of Ireland.

Lars closed his file and looked up at me, his demeanor shifting. "I've been patient with you, Ms. Cathbad." He wrapped his fingers around the top of the curved back chair at the desk. "It is time you told me where the cauldron is."

My teeth scraped against each other as I tossed the rest of the bag of crisps to the side. "I'm starving." I strolled to the window, peering out at the gorgeous view of the city, rubbing my rumbling stomach. Crisps were good, but I needed food. "I have to say your staff on the plane were *less* than stellar. I didn't even get a bag of peanuts."

Lars watched me, the atmosphere thickening with his annoyance.

"Though you sure got yours." I lifted an eyebrow, ready to play back. "Or really, she got hers."

A cloud of fury billowed off him, and his attention grew more intense when I smiled with self-satisfaction.

"Do you think yourself so untouchable?" His words came out composed, but the green in his eyes flickered with darkness.

"Yes." I held his stare, pressing my shoulders back. "You need something from me. You're so bloody desperate for it you can't even think straight. So, yes, right now. I am untouchable."

Lars was in my face in an instant; the air didn't even have time to react. The force from his body slammed against mine, shuffling me back. Forcing my feet to hold their ground, I inhaled deeply and stared up at him in defiance.

"For this moment only. However, tonight you will take me to it. Do not forget I still hold a card you do not want me to play, Ms. Cathbad." He leaned in, his voice low and husky, limiting even more of my oxygen. "A little girl waits back at home for you."

The thump of my heart echoed in my ears.

"I think we can drop the pretense." I matched his tone and body language and pushed against his body, trying to ignore the way my muscles twitched. It felt like being close to an electrical fence. He didn't move a millimeter, his breath curling down my neck. Smugness glazed his eyes; he understood me perfectly. We both knew he was going to dispose of me the moment I was no longer useful. I was too much of a threat to him. Weirdly, I found great pride in that. I was up at his level then.

"Take. Me. To. The. Cauldron. Druid."

"Food. First. Demon." I didn't back down an inch, my jaw cracking with force.

Time halted, waiting for the first one of us to act. Black rushed through his chartreuse eyes like a wave coming to shore then receding. His head tilted to the side as he observed me. The line between the King and demon was thin, and he gave no sign of which way he was going. Mercy or reprimand? It was what caused him to be so frightening.

Slowly a grin tugged up his mouth, a chuckle rumbled from his chest, and he tipped his head back. I went on defense, stepping back, my body curling forward ready for an attack.

Lars only laughed louder, causing my heart to patter like raindrops on a roof. His laughing or smiling generated unease in me. He was a ruthless leader. Not a...man. Humor, heart, or even a personality? No. It didn't mesh with the monster before me. In that same laugh, he could literally cause my head to blow up without even touching me.

"Fine. Dinner first." He chuckled, turning back for the desk.

"What?" My mouth dipped open, peering around for something else to jump out and attack me.

Lars reached for the internal phone on the desk. "Yes, Lucia. Can you make reservations at the restaurant?" He paused. "Yes, thank you." He hung up.

I still hadn't moved. The swift change in his mood threw me off center.

"You certainly can't go to dinner in that, Ms. Cathbad." He set down the receiver and raked his gaze over me through his dark long lashes.

"Excuse me?" I peered down at myself. I was in jeans, riding boots, and a black jumper. Nothing special, but certainly nothing to be snotty over. I had grown up a poor outcast. Kids had thrown rocks at me, pushed, tripped, beat me up, and called me every name in the book. Nothing cut me more than when I went to primary school and kids teased me because I was wearing something Olwyn had gotten secondhand, something these kids had given away.

I was proud of who I'd become, of Olwyn. But it didn't mean those old wounds ever went away. I could feel the burn of old humiliations crawling up my neck.

"I'm not a doll. I don't dress up for anyone. This is me. How I dress," I snapped. "Nor do I want to go to some snobby restaurant where you get one carrot and a bit of some decorated ram balls and call it gourmet."

Lars's eyebrows drew up, a ghost of a smile haunting his mouth again. "Please don't tell me you came all the way to Prague and want to eat at McDonald's."

"Could your frickin' nose be any higher?" I scoffed, curling my arms at my chest. "What's wrong with McDonald's? Just because you were born with a silver spoon doesn't mean the rest of us were. It was a special treat for me when I was a kid. We couldn't afford it, but on exceedingly rare occasions Olwyn and I would go into the city to get new herbs, and she would splurge."

My lids blinked back the emotion those memories brought up. Her loss still so fresh, I almost forgot she was really gone. I turned, looking out the window at the castle in the distance.

Lars strolled around the desk, a couple meters away from me. "Okay. You pick the place then."

My neck jerked back to him in shock. "Really?"

"Yes. Any place you want."

My forehead crinkled, watching him. He was hard to look at for a long time; his beauty and sex appeal were like incense, covering up the stench of rational thoughts.

I wrinkled my nose at his tailor-made, pricey suit. "Well, you *certainly* can't go to dinner in *that*."

~~

"I cannot believe you are going to make me eat this." Lars picked up his Quarter Pounder, twisting it between his fingers as if he were trying to find an entrance.

"You have to try McDonald's once in your life. The fact it's taken you this long..." I slurped at my milkshake, shaking my head. I twisted on the stool seats we sat on, bringing me quickly back to my youth. "Pitiful. You should be ashamed of yourself."

"*That* is what I should be ashamed of?" He scoffed, his chest filling out his fitted T-shirt even more. Not that I was staring, but when someone who wears suits every day switches to jeans, combat boots, and a black T-shirt, it's a dramatic shift. I could tell he was built under his fine garbs, but now? *Holy shite.* The shirt wasn't skintight, but he appeared so muscular through the chest, arms, and shoulders, it conformed to him, like it wanted to hug his body too.

Too? I didn't want to hug his body. Absolutely not. Phhhhffftttt.

"Come on." I nudged him with my elbow. "I promise it won't kill you." I took another pull of shake, mumbling, "Yet."

He sniggered, inhaling his breath as if he were about to plunge off a bridge, and opened his mouth, taking a huge bit of the hamburger. Sauce and chunks of tomato squeezed out the other side, dripping on the wax paper.

He leaned over, his jaw working the enormous mouthful.

"Damn. You didn't have to take such a big of bite." I snorted, covering my mouth with my hand as I continued to laugh at him. Both corners of his mouth were covered with sauce. Lips together, he grinned, making him look like a little boy. Happy. Carefree. Despite myself, I smiled too.

He chewed the burger then swallowed. Wiping his mouth, he placed the rest down, which wasn't much.

"So?" I leaned forward.

"Nothing in that being even remotely healthy or really could be considered food."

"Besides that." I swished my hand.

"Then not so bad."

"Ha!" I punched my arms up into the air in victory.

He waggled his head, a grin growing over his features, lighting his eyes.

"Okay, now fries dipped in milkshake." I pinched the fried food between my fingers and plunged them into my vanilla milkshake, tossing them into my mouth, the salty sweet exploding over my taste buds. I tipped my head back with a happy grunt.

I felt Lars's eyes on me, searing my skin like meat on a grill. My gaze danced to his two minions a table over. Goran and Travil both looked disgusted and angry they were being forced to eat here. Goran kept sniffing his burger as though he couldn't figure out what it was. Travil ate, but his glower danced between the food and me.

They didn't say a word, but on the entire walk over, I sensed their opposition to my dinner plans. They also hated that Lars agreed to walk to the restaurant. However, my legs ached to stretch after being stuck in a cell for weeks and then a plane, and my skin desired the fresh air.

As the leader of DLR, I had always been extremely aware of my surroundings, of possible threats and attacks. My intuition was strong and magic was always ready on my tongue. The entire stroll over, I felt nothing but the energy of tourists and locals going on with their day. But Lars had suddenly stopped, his head snapping to a cluster of people gathering around the castle.

"What?" I stopped. My attention danced between him and the group. He didn't respond, his body tense and rigid, like a setter dog primed on a pheasant. A snake coiled in my stomach seeing the splash of alarm in Lars's eyes. Nothing seemed to ever rattle the King. But for an instant, that was exactly how he appeared.

"Sir?" Goran came up to his side, finally breaking Lars from his trance.

He shook his head. "I thought I saw something... But it's impossible." He rubbed at his temples, rolling back his shoulders, returning to his kingly demeanor.

"You have not been sleeping, my liege," Goran said.

"I'm sure that's all it is," Lars replied and started to walk again, his firm stride pushing away whatever had concerned him with every step.

The sound of the top of Lars's drink popping off turned my attention back to him. He poked a fry in his chocolate drink, eating it with a shrug. "Interesting."

"You should have ordered the vanilla, as I recommended," I scolded him.

"But I enjoy chocolate more."

"So do I...but not with fries. Always vanilla with fries. That's rule one." I scooped another fry into the vanilla cream and held it out to him. "Trust me."

"I didn't know McDonald's came with a rulebook."

"Oh, fledgling, I have so much to teach you."

Lars chuckled, taking the fry from me and dropping it on his tongue. He nodded. "You're right. Vanilla is better with fries."

"I know I'm right. About time you figured it out." I swung forward in my seat with a wink. Lars, let out a full, deep laugh. It was as though a tsunami crashed down on me.

What was I doing laughing with this man? Lars was my enemy. The dictator I was trying to bring down. This man was going to kill me and would keep my child from me. He was also damn sure going to destroy the world with his need to be the most powerful. The King who killed and looked the other way at a Druid genocide was hard to see in the man next to me laughing, joking, and eating frickin' McDonald's.

You're playing him, Fi. Just as he's doing to you. This a game. Do not forget it. My appetite was gone; my stomach rolled into itself. I wiped my hands on the cheap paper napkins, tossing them down on my tray. I could sense he felt the swing in my mood.

Lars cleared his throat, his spine straightening. His relaxed nature dissolved back into the tough skin of a king. "The sun has set." He reached for his thigh-length, classic wool jacket on the empty stool next to him, putting it on as he stood. "It's time."

Staring at my tray, I nodded, lost in thought, shoving back the mounting terror in my gut.

"Now."

I grabbed my jacket and beanie, the early spring in Prague still quite chilly, especially after sunset.

Unfortunately, things were going to get a whole lot colder, really fast.

Chapter Twelve

Lars

The last rays of the sun clung desperately to the top of the green dome of St. Nicholas Church as if they were clamoring to stay while being tugged away by the encroaching night. The narrow cobble street I stepped onto was already heavy in shadows.

I flipped up the collar of my navy coat as the temperature slid away with the last bit of sun. The incident earlier, when I thought I saw something impossible, still danced along my neck. For a moment, I was able to push it away, actually enjoy dinner, which I hadn't in a very long time. The deaths of Koke and Maya, the loss of Rez and Ember in the house, had made my own home feel the same as an oubliette— cold, empty, holding past echoes of laughter that had once occupied the house, just to torture me.

My obsession with obtaining the treasures kept me from acknowledging a truth I did not want to face. One I had no use for on my rise to the throne, because when you're young and determined, you don't worry about loneliness, which is merely a weakness. I might have still thought the same if Ember had never walked into my life. The moment Rimmon brought the unconscious girl through my door, I knew in my soul she was my daughter.

Pain jabbed my heart and forced me to take a deep breath. I had been such a fool. I had everything and I gave it away because I thirsted for more power. If I had only known hunger was contrived. I gave up everything I ever needed and turned the woman I loved to my brother and missed out on so much of my own child's life.

I made choices and had to live with them, but lately those choices had come back to haunt me. Almost as though Devlin had come back to torment me.

Buttoning up my coat, I shoved the thoughts back, twisting to face the girl who stood stubbornly between what I wanted and me.

"You said Prague. Now, *where* in Prague?" I stretched my shoulders, letting my size loom over her. Intimidation, conscious or subconscious, was a strong weapon. "And if you lie to me or waste my time trying to stall…" I leaned down into her face. Her features tightened, her nose flaring with defiance. My gaze dropped to a speck of salt resting on her bottom lip.

My arm rose with an overwhelming need to brush it off with my thumb. *Stop,* my brain ordered. I rolled my fist into a ball, forcing it back down to my side. Her eyes followed my hand, then went back to my face, her brow furrowing.

Gradually a smirk hitched her lips. "You think hitting me is going to get you what you want?" *Hitting? She thought I was going to hit her?* "You don't think I've been hit before?" Anger from her statement caught me off guard, filling me with the need to track down those who had struck her, even kill them. "I might be little and may resemble a great candidate for a bully to take out their anger on..." She moved in closer, her words more brusque. "They couldn't break me...and *you* certainly won't either."

"Someone hit you?" The question came out before I realized I was talking.

Her dark eyebrows crinkled again. "What do you care?"

I jolted back, reaching my full height.

"You've strangled me with your magic, chained me up, held me prisoner, and used my innocent five-year-old as leverage against me. Now, please, tell me why you give a rat's arse if I've been slapped around before?"

I stared at her. I had no idea. Why did I care? "I don't," I sneered. "But do not act as though you are so innocent, Ms. Cathbad. You sent a missile into a hotel room, slaughtered people, and almost killed the rest of us, including your sister. You have murdered and tortured hundreds of fae. Sent strighoul to strike my compound and kidnapped an innocent human, one of my own. A woman so kind she still would not let me feed you gruel as I wanted." I clenched my teeth. "And you've attacked me. On several occasions."

"I am sorry for Marguerite." She nipped her bottom lip. "She's one I do regret."

"And the others?"

Fionna's huge brown eyes met mine. "The others...not at all."

A rumble came from my chest.

"Don't give me that," she scoffed. "Like you would have done any different or felt remorse for your actions in any way. I was only doing what you fae do best...protecting my own." She whirled to walk away, but I reached out and grabbed her arm, flinging her back to face me.

"I never attacked or killed your people."

Fury boiled in her eyes like molten liquid. "You never stopped it either," she spat. "What is worse? The ones who blatantly cause genocide or the ones who stay quiet and look the other way, *letting* it happen?" She yanked her arm from my hold. "At least I knew where Aneira stood. You? Where do you stand, Lars? Besides by *yourself.*"

Fionna whipped around, marching down the lane, her boots heavy on the stone. Folks on the street parted and moved out of the way of the force bowling through them.

"She will not speak to you that way." Goran plowed forward, looking as though he was going to grab her and drag her back by her hair.

"Leave it." My words stopped him in his tracks. He whipped his head between the fleeing outline of the Druid and me.

"But, sir."

"I *said* leave it."

His mouth dipped open in either shock or rebuttal, but he snapped it shut with a firm nod and started to follow her trail.

I could understand his disbelief. Besides Ember, no one spoke to me in such a way. *No one.* They would not live long if they did, but I not only let her do it, I felt the repercussions of her query. I had looked the other way during that time. It hadn't affected me, and with all my brother's madness, I ignored the thousands of lives Aneira sentenced to death. Their lives had not meant enough for me to challenge the previous Seelie Queen.

My lids squeezed shut, the notion like an avalanche.

"Sir? Are you all right?" Travil's words startled my eyes open.

"Yes." I cleared my throat, letting the heaviness float away.

What was done could not be undone. But a heaviness still weighted my chest as I took steps to pursue Fionna. I used to be so sure in my decisions, whatever the outcome. I never had second thoughts concerning my choices. Lately, it seemed all the ghosts from those options were coming back for me.

Fionna led us to the castle, now closed to tourists for the day, as the security guards tried to hustle out the stragglers. I reached her side when I felt the icy fingers of someone watching me. Warning bells flicked on as they had earlier. My boots came to an abrupt halt, my head swiveling around, desperate to find the source of this unease.

"What?" Fionna sighed as though she really didn't want to talk to me, but curiosity forced her to.

I shook my head, not fully able to put my weariness into words.

"Sir?" Goran went on defense, scouring the area for what sign he missed. "Fae?"

"Yes." I nodded. At least I could feel that. Magic was extremely dense in Europe, and Prague all the more so, making it hard to decipher magic coming from a particular person.

"We don't have long to get into the castle." Fionna tugged on my sleeve. "They won't put the alarms back on until everyone is out. We need to go now."

My head bobbed, but I still couldn't stop scanning every dark corner. What I thought I saw earlier had unnerved me. It was impossible. I knew it logically. Lack of sleep and enormity of the stress I had been under were affecting me and messing with my mind.

Groups heading to dinner or home moved around us in clumps. The darkness enveloped the city, beckoning in fog that made it hard to distinguish faces.

My gaze circled the square and stopped. Oxygen pulled sharply in my lungs. A figure stood in an alley across the plaza, drenched in shadows. His face was hidden by the darkness, but his yellow-green eyes burned through the mist, right into my own.

He stepped forward, and a streetlamp flicked over half his face. I froze. Could hardly breathe.

It couldn't be. There was no way...

A sneer curled up on the man's face, then he slipped back into the shadows and disappeared from view.

"No. Wait," I muttered, my legs already moving without thought, desperate to reach him, to touch a solid person, to know I wasn't going crazy. I bolted through the people, pushing and shoving anyone blocking my way. I could hear Fionna as well as my men call for me. But nothing stopped my pursuit. I reached the spot where the man had been and followed his only path out. The alley dumped out on another tourist-populated square.

So easy to dissolve into a crowd.

I stopped, spinning in a circle, searching to see anyone exiting the square with purpose and hoping to slip away. My gaze darted to groups, to singles, to couples. No one watched me or looked out of place. I couldn't stop searching, making myself dizzy as I spun. He couldn't disappear.

Not if he were solid flesh.

A queasy feeling rolled in my stomach, distress sinking in deep. My shoulders curled over, and I forced in gulps of air.

"Lars?" A hand touched me gently, and heat sparked down my spine. "What's going on? Are you all right?" Fionna leaned over trying to see my face. I bolted up, turning away from her.

"Sir, I think we need to get you back to the hotel. You need to rest."

I glowered at Goran.

"You haven't slept in days...maybe weeks, my liege. You need to relax."

"You are not my fucking mother, Goran," I bit out.

"No, but I am here to protect you. Even if it's from yourself."

I moved, stepping up to him like a bull. "Do not forget yourself. I brought you in, saved your life. Do not get our roles mixed up."

Goran's teeth gritted. "I haven't forgot, sir. Nor will I ever. I swore to protect you with my life, and I plan on keeping my promise till the day I die. *Nothing* will stop me from doing that."

Even me. He didn't have to say it. Even if his King turned mad and could no longer understand reason.

Like most of the men in my family had.

I gazed over his shoulder and searched for the mirror image I had seen twice now.

Was I going crazy? Seeing the dead image of my insane brother would kind of be ironic. Was my conscience using him as a symbol of my own descent into insanity?

I stepped back from Goran, massaging the spot between my eyes. "Leave me for a moment," I ordered. Travil and Goran nodded, stepping far enough away I felt relieved from their constant presence.

"You too," I sniped at Fionna.

"No."

"No?"

"No," she replied even firmer.

"You know I am a king," I exclaimed. "Not just any king...but *the* King."

"That's nice for you."

I groaned, leaning my head back. What the hell was wrong that I could not get this maddening woman to do anything I asked?

"Are you okay?"

"I'm fine." I peered back down at her, her inquisitive eyes sparkling under the lights strung overhead.

"No, you're not," she huffed, folding her arms. "This is the second time today you've gotten spooked by something." She shuffled closer, tipping her chin to look up at me. "Who did you see? Someone who scares you." The way she said it came out blunt and direct. Just like her. I bristled at her awareness, feeling exposed.

"No one." I tried to move around her, but she sidestepped, blocking me. "And *no one* scares me."

"Tell me."

"Don't worry yourself about it," I growled, shoving past her and heading back for the alley leading to the castle. "We have more important matters."

Saying it out loud would confirm I was slipping. A king losing his grasp was a vulnerable king. I would be challenged at every turn. And the girl feigning concern was one of my top enemies. She was probably searching, waiting, and working me to find my liability. Of all the beings, I would not be brought down by a Druid.

She caught up with me. Goran and Travil flanked us, one slightly ahead, one slightly behind.

"The cauldron is hidden in the old royal palace?" I didn't bother looking at her, my sight straight on the closed gate to the royal palace.

"The Treasury of St. Vitus Cathedral to be precise."

I halted. "You mean to tell me one of the most powerful objects in the world is displayed for thousands of tourists to see every day? It is sitting in a glass box for anyone to steal? Please tell me you are joking, Ms. Cathbad."

At Fionna's silence I finally turned my head. Her cheeks were rosy from the cold. She knew I was staring at her but didn't acknowledge me.

"Ms. Cathbad?"

"It is well guarded."

"You are not answering my question."

"Sometimes the best hiding spots are out in the open."

She was far from stupid. In fact, she was extremely clever and shrewd, so much so she kept me on edge always trying to find her true motivation.

Piper was the only button I had to press, but I was still unsure Fionna wasn't playing me in some way. I despised that feeling. My demon was already walking a thin line, which grew ever finer with each step we made toward the palace.

The building we needed stood behind the castle walls, was gated on three sides, and heavily alarmed.

We scaled the wall off a small garden on one side and slipped in to the least guarded gate inside.

"Guards patrol every ten minutes through this area."

All of us tilted our heads, taken aback by her knowledge of their movement.

"What do you think I was doing on the plane?" She lifted her eyebrow at me. "I spent it breaking into the castle's database. And what were you doing? Oh right." She snapped her fingers.

My teeth ground together. What a fool I'd been to let myself lose control.

"Well, if you recall, Ms. Cathbad, I was unaware of where we were going until about ten minutes ago. I could have disabled the alarms had I known."

She rolled her eyes back in exasperation. She motioned her hands over the gate and began to chant. The words rolled out low but strong, the Latin rumbling through me with its power. With a *clunk* the lock rolled over, the entrance squeaking softly as it opened for us.

"Not needed. But thanks for the offer." She winked with snarky smugness, pushing through the opening and slinking into the darkness.

Aggravation torqued my muscles into knots. "That girl," I grumbled.

"She's the kind you either fuck or kill," Travil said impassively. Both Goran and I twisted to look at him. He was not a man of many words and most of them were about fighting.

"Remember your place," Goran snarled. "And she's a *Druid*."

"Druid or not, I think she's starting to grow on me." Travil shrugged, reaching over his shoulder for his bow.

Amusement found me out of the blue, and a slight grin inched along my face.

"To even insinuate a *fae King* would—"

"No, Goran, he might be right." I switched back, watching her sneak fluidly across the quad as if she were one with the shadows. The instant Travil put it out there, the demon woke up. Clawing. Wanting.

The problem was I didn't know which one it wanted to do more.

Chapter Thirteen

Fionna

Nerves cavorted in my stomach similar to a hyper bunch of frogs.

What was I doing? Ignorance of your own foolishness was one thing, but when you were doing it outright and labeling it self-preservation, it was plain stupidity. What kept me going was my daughter and a small chance I could pull this off, though it could backfire with deadly results.

My jacket scraped against the white building. Not surprisingly the long, rounded tip of the structure was shaped like a penis. What was it with men that even their architecture needed to be erect?

Speaking of... The sensation of a body silently sliding up next to mine warmed half of me. I had to admit my experience with Lars thus far showed he didn't shove his insincerity in my face or overly display his manhood. He didn't need to, and I doubted he ever did, which was what made the incident on the plane seem odd. I didn't really know him, but the blatantly loud sex, as though he wanted me to hear, seemed out of character for him. Even his men had acted bewildered by his actions.

"I'm going to pause the door alarm and the feed into the cameras. It will take a lot of energy from me, so get in as soon as I nod my head. All right?" I whispered to the men. This was not something easy to do, even for a Druid. In my line of work, it came in handy, but only worked on limited technology. Thankfully Prague's system had not been updated since the fae war. In my "research" I learned guards watched sensory alarms and video cameras in a booth somewhere. If anyone dismantled them, it would be noticed right away. But if I "paused" them with magic, we had a chance of slipping in unnoticed.

"You're giving us orders now?" Travil snarled, gripping his weapon.

"Yes. And you will follow them," I replied flatly. I had no time for this shite.

Lars's brow curved up, but he said nothing in response, only nodded at his men.

My shoulders hitched up as I drew in a deep breath. This was it. The spell forming on my lips coiled toward the door inside while my mind's eye pushed it through the security system, wrapping around it like a python.

This type of gray magic was not exactly bad or black, but its intent was certainly not good. Even more than black magic, I enjoyed gray the most. It fit me, not good, but not really bad either.

Electricity zapped back at me as the technology resisted my enchantment. A thump pulsed in my head as I shoved at it harder. Heat swirled under my jacket and hat, forming drops of perspiration that dampened my skin. Grunting, I squeezed my lids tighter, trying to keep each syllable clear and directed at its target. My legs shook, the muscles trembling under the pressure.

Lars moved in front of me, grabbing my elbows, taking some of my weight. My magic soared out and fiddled with the technology, learning it, trying to master it. My heart thumped in my ears, each syllable a little tougher to say perfectly. I grunted and Lars gripped me tighter, allowing me to lean more of my weight into him.

Then I felt my power dive into the cables, manipulating their energy.

"Ahhhh." I bit down on my bottom lip. The spell skidded the electricity to a halt, as though a car slammed on its brakes. I sent out another hex, and the lock on the door turned over. "Go. It's down."

Travil and Goran didn't hesitate racing for the door, but Lars still held on to me, his eyes watching me.

"Why are you still here? I said go."

"Do not order me, Ms. Cathbad." His grip dug painfully into my arms. "And you are being quite bossy for someone who is using me as a crutch."

I tried to pull away from him but my legs bowed. Lars reached out and caught me, keeping me from landing on my arse. I took in a deep breath. "I am fine. Thank you."

He lifted his eyebrow in mocking doubt.

I hated that using magic came with such exhausting consequences. Earth's magic let us borrow from her but also made us pay for it. Healing spells restored others but did not replace a Druid's energy. We had no time to wait for me to revive. We had to go now. Though I wasn't sure why, I rushed into a place that might be my grave. I was going to do everything in my power not to allow that, but this plan was flimsy at best. Still, I plunged forward with gusto, not doing anything by halves.

Lars closed the door behind us. The curved windows at the top let in light from the illuminated castle outside. Exit signs and dim security lights led us easily to the room storing the treasures.

Gaudy was the one word I would use to describe the design of the building. With so much gold and marble, I could feel the weight of its décor. Rich colors and motifs loomed over us like they possessed their own power, making me feel small and insignificant.

The brown-and-cream diamond pattern running through the marble floor reminded me of the art piece *Relativity* by M.C. Escher, twisting the pattern into staircases going nowhere. Swirled white and gray marble, trimmed in gold, reached all the way up to the curved painted ceiling. It was beautiful, but far too ostentatious for me.

Lars's men moved through the room, inspecting each case with scrutiny. My gaze landed on the middle case, knowing exactly what they would find in about thirty seconds. The time was now. No going back.

"Sir! Here it is," Goran whispered hoarsely to his master, waving him over. Lars dashed toward him, his eyes glowing with longing. He pulled gloves from his pocket and slipped them on.

The Druid stood all but forgotten by the door. Just as I had planned.

The moment in his office the night of the attack, I understood what I was giving up. I knew what I had to do. Not that I would have ever been given a second chance to raise my daughter. This was a falsehood we both knew he was telling. This was how I would protect her *and* many others.

Inching back quietly, I knew I had only seconds before he touched it and figured out the truth. Distracted, the men hovered around the object under the glass, lifting the barrier around it, not noticing me retreating toward the door.

I did trust he wouldn't hurt Piper. He might lie to her and tell her how awful I was, but I hoped deep in her heart she would sense the truth and find out what really happened when she got older. I wanted her to be proud of my decision and me.

I'd rather never see my daughter again than be a coward. She would eventually realize I was doing the right thing. Guarding not just Druids, but the human race as well.

Keeping the Treasures of Tuatha Dé Danann from the fae was the most important thing I could do. We needed to stop history repeating itself. It was my sacrifice. My burden to carry.

Quietly, I spelled myself to disappear into the

shadows. Lars would try to find me, but I had years of hiding from fae under my belt. I would not make it easy for him, but *if* the time ever came, then I would take my punishment.

The door was so close, freedom just steps away as I reached the doorway.

"Where do you think you are going, Ms. Cathbad?" Magic curled around my bones, stopping me in place like a giant boa constrictor circled around me, bending my ribs together.

Shite! No! My lips parted, a spell struggling to work itself up. If I struck him, I would have only one shot to get it right.

With a *whoosh*, my body flew back, slamming into a wall near him, ripping the air from my lungs. "Why are you sneaking out?" Rage clipped Lars's tone, his eyes flashing.

I couldn't speak or move.

Lars picked up the small cauldron, his gloved hands cupping it like a lover. He blinked, his fingers continuing to stroke the metal. His body went rigid, his green eyes finding mine through his lashes, darkening around the edges.

"This is a fake."

My jaw locked down, though I didn't break eye contact. No pleas of innocence or denial. I had made my bed, well aware of the outcome. His eyes turned black as he realized my conscious deception.

"You. Deceived. Me." He growled so low the floor vibrated with his anger, his olive skin turning milky white. "You dare trick me?"

Neither my body nor my mouth moved an inch, my chin held high.

"You think you can fool me, girl?" He took a step toward me, the bones of his face pressed taut against his skin. As his energy took hold of the room, the air in my lungs faltered. Fury bucked off him like a horse, colliding with me. An invisible hand came up to my throat, tearing me off the ground, digging my back into the wall. My head cracked against the marble and knifed pain through my skull.

"You stupid fool." His energy pushed so hard against me tears leaked from the corners of my eyes. He moved closer, only a few meters from me. "I thought you were a lot wiser than this, Druid. You think you can hold strong against torture? Pain so excruciating you will be *begging* me to take your life?" he whispered hoarsely. His skin was thin, his eyes black, but he balled his fists as though he was holding back.

He crushed my throat further, forcing a gasped cry from my lips. My feet dangled in the air, and the plaster crumbled as he pressed my bones firmer into the wall.

"Tell me where it is," the demon snarled.

My mind began to get cloudy while my legs banged against the wall, trying to break free.

Air. I sought it in desperation as my fingers clawed at the imaginary hands around my throat. Black magic swirled in my gut, building in intensity. I tried to swallow the instinct to attack, knowing if I did, he would learn my other secret and all my cards would be played.

"Tell me," he roared. More magic drilled into my stomach. Agony twisted every muscle into angry snakes, slithering and lashing out at their attacker.

Power popped behind my eyes, lashing back with a snarling bite. Lars stumbled back, his expression warping with confusion. I fell to the floor, the grip on my throat breaking, letting oxygen slip down my esophagus in a burning spurt of fire. When I coughed, bile rose up.

"What the hell just happened?"

I peered up at him, glared, and got to my feet. "You are losing your touch, aren't you, King?" My voice was hoarse but still strong.

"My kindness was clearly wasted. A mistake I will not make again. Not even your sister can help you. This will be painful; I will not lie." His dark, glossy eyes reflected my face as he came a millimeter from mine. "Last chance, Ms. Cathbad."

I locked my teeth, my nostrils spreading with hatred. "I will never let you have it."

"Really? You will throw away a life with your daughter so easily?"

"Let's stop pretending that was *ever* going to happen," I growled. "You won't hurt her. You are cruel but never to children."

"You think you will die a martyr?" His teeth glinted between his lips. "Your little girl will only see how you abandoned her. *Again.* She won't love you more for your 'supposed' heroics. All she wants is for you to choose her."

"Bastard," I croaked, feeling every stab of the truth. All I had wanted was for my mother and father to choose my sister and me too. Yes, what they fought for was important and I understood that. Now. But it had been years before I understood their sacrifices.

A gruesome smile thinned out his already wafer-thin lips.

"You are wasting my time, Ms. Cathbad."

The choices presented in front of me balled in my throat. I was about to lay another card on the table, showing my bluff.

"Tell. Me. Now!"

"I don't know!" I cried out, the truth flying out resembling a bird released from a cage. "I don't know where it is."

Lars went board straight, his breath growing heavier. "What?"

"I've been lying this whole time, saying I knew the location. It was lost decades ago."

I could feel Lars's power, the vehemence of his rage, crowding me like the thick fog outside.

"I'd heard a rumor it was here, but I suspected it was a fake. Someone wanted to cash in on the treasure, as so many do with the Ark of the Covenant." I licked my lips, lifting my head to face the demon.

"Did you think this would fool me?" His boots hit my toes, bending his face to mine. "That I wouldn't kill you the moment I figured it out?"

"What would you have done if I told you right away I didn't know anything?"

"I would have killed you on the spot."

"Exactly."

"You lied to prolong your life only a few weeks?"

"I had a plan. Until you brought my daughter into it."

"You were going to try and escape." He barked a strained, sardonic laugh. "Escape me? How did you think that was going to work? You could never hide from me. And you can't use your magic on me. Remember?"

I stood up as straight as my body would allow, a grin matching his played on my mouth. "Really? Want to test me? I am much more powerful than your ego would like to think." All humor dropped from his face.

This was the last card up my sleeve. I wasn't above cheating. Not when it came to fae. "Black magic. It can be an exceptionally useful tool." I stepped into him. Game point.

"You broke my bind on you?"

"The moment you turned your back." I smirked. "Let me say, it's taken a lot of willpower not to use it thus far." I tipped up on my toes, whispering coyly. "Do not underestimate me, Lars. I can play this game just as well as you."

It had been a hard one to keep back, but I played the long game. There would have been no way to get out of his compound. So I waited.

He stared at me, no emotion hinting on his sunken features.

"Now, I say we call a truce before anyone *really* gets hurt."

"Truce?" The word rumbled like an earthquake, his body pressing into mine. "You really think I play well with others?"

"No. But neither do I," I volleyed back.

A growl filled the space around us, his skin straining so severely against the bones it looked as they would break through it.

His mouth opened as though to say something when a wave of nausea spun my head. Instinctively I reached out, grabbing his arm to keep upright.

When I first met Kennedy, I had lied to her about my visions. At the time, I had not trusted anyone to know she was more powerful than me, chiding her that she should learn how to control them. Envy was not something I usually experienced. But when I'd seen my little sister was by far the more powerful one when it came to full visions, a natural obscurer, the green-eyed demon of envy made its appearance. I had seen our mother get them so badly she passed out. Father didn't get any at all; his family was stronger in healing.

I only got a watered-down version of the element. I stayed in my body, could see everything around me, but it was as though someone layered my sight with a movie film in the near future. I could see both worlds happening, but the one in the future was more transparent and on low volume.

Now the row of dome windows encasing the building shattered, the ghostly debris falling around me. A cry yanked my head to the side. The future figure of Goran buckled over, blood spurting out of his stomach and chest from where several arrows sank into his skin. Travil's body fell like a domino beside him. The room we were standing in filled with strighoul, swinging their weapons at us.

"No." My head lurched around, taking in all I saw.

"What? Ms. Cathbad?" Lars jostled me, snapping me out of my reverie. I blinked up at the solid man before me, into his green eyes that stared down at me. He gripped my shoulders. "What did you see?"

I licked my lip, gathering myself, shoving back the need to lie down. "We're going to be attacked…"

The last words left my mouth moments before the dome windows shattered over our heads, showering us in splinters of glass. Spheres the size of cannonballs cracked the floor as they hit, knocking over displays like bowling pins.

Lars shoved me back down on the floor. I threw my arms over my head when the weight of Lars's form pressed into me, shielding my body from the onslaught. Cries of attack and alarms from the treasury shrilled the air, goose-pimpling my flesh. My hold on the alarms had vanished.

Slowly Lars lifted his head, pieces of the window falling from his hair and jacket.

"My liege?" Goran yelled out from his hiding place.

"Goran." A memory flicked in my head, sitting me back. "Travil. Move…"

Through the open windows dozens of arrows shot into the room similar to missiles. Lars dived over me again, flattening me to the marble floor.

A grunt from across the room told me one had found its target. Just as my vision predicted. More arrows came through the gaps. Another cry of pain.

"Shite." The King shoved off me, seeing what I already knew to be true. Both his men had been hit. Lars crawled forward, hiding behind an exhibit.

"Goran?"

A groan was our only response. I peered around, seeing the two bodies lying flat, four or five arrows sticking out of each of them.

Boom.

The door we came through bowed under the weight hitting it. Shite. They were breaking in. We didn't have much time.

"Can you heal them?" Lars's eyes met mine.

We didn't have time, not the amount I needed to heal both, but I pushed the thought away. I nodded, crawling over broken glass to the two unconscious bodies. Blood dripped from my palms and knees, smearing the floor in red stains.

Boom. Boom.

The door cracked, weight slamming into it, the metal on the handle clinking at my nerves. I hovered over Goran, my hands on his chest where the barbs had imbedded in his chest. Instantly I could feel the darts were made with goblin metal. I yanked them out of his body, swear words streaming through my mind like music.

My arms shook and the chant quavered at the back of my throat as the high-pitched cries from the strighoul right outside clenched my lungs in fear. Healing took a lot of energy, my body the conductor between the earth's power and the recipient. It also took a lot of concentration. Neither was coming to me in steady quantities. Alarms and the pounding of the door ran together similar to bagpipes played badly.

"Shite." I shook my head, trying the chant again.

Only a small dose of the earth's magic clung to Goran., but I only had enough to help them both a little. I moved over to Travil. A handful of poisonous arrows protruded from his gut and neck.

Lars was suddenly by my side, the false idol wrapped in his arms. I understood his logic of grabbing it. Whoever had set the strighoul on us thought we found the real thing. He or she wanted it too.

Leverage.

"Hurry," he barked.

"I'm trying," I snapped.

Boom. Crack.

The entrance to the treasury splintered as howls from the opposing side grew louder. I stumbled over the spell but tried to put everything I had into it, my body crying out with pain.

Travil gasped, his lids bolting open. His stomach and neck were still bleeding badly, but he was awake. I had only slowed the poison from the goblin metal; now their systems had to work out the rest. Most likely they would get very sick with fevers for the next week or so. We had to move before the shock to their systems wore off.

An axe ripped through the crack in the door, gouging an even bigger hole in the wood. They would be inside soon.

Travil was instantly aware of the threat. Rolling up, he struggled to get to his feet. "Sir, you need to run." He heaved, each word a struggle, limping over to Goran.

"I'm not leaving you here," Lars exclaimed.

"Sir!" Travil turned his head, but the resolve in his gaze was solid. "You are the *King*. We protect you. We know the risks and gladly take them. You think he wouldn't kill me himself if he knew I didn't force you to leave?" Travil motioned to Goran. "Do not push me on this, sir. I said run." Travil reached under Goran's arms and lifted him up. Goran groaned, his lids fluttering open.

"Go!" Travil bellowed.

I never had doubt of Travil's or Goran's dedication to Lars, but it was the first time I saw it also went the other way. Pain wrinkled Lars's forehead, his eyes darting between the door and his men. Red eyes and sharp teeth peered through the growing fissure.

Lars tossed the fake cauldron onto the floor. I gaped at him. Even though it wasn't the real thing, he was throwing away the leverage of the fake cauldron for his men.

"No." Lars rushed to Goran and helped him up. "We walked out of the hotel together in Zurich; we will walk out of here as well."

Travil stared at his King and shook his head. "And how the hell are we going to do it this time?"

I couldn't help but feel a stab of remorse. I was the reason they almost lost their lives in Zurich. At the time I would have called it a win, reveling in the fact I took out the Unseelie King as well. Now? I wasn't quite sure which way I felt on the matter. The only thing important was getting away. The sirens wailing in the distance told me our time was up. Threats were coming in at all angles.

"I know a way," I muttered, more to myself than anyone.

"What? Where?" Lars shifted the barely conscious Goran higher.

"Follow me." Ignoring his query, I took off for the far end of the room. When I hacked into their system, I found floor plans and secret exits. I crashed through a private door to another room. My memory flickered back through the blueprints I had studied. One showed stairs going down to a tunnel. Frantically I searched until my eyes landed on a slab of concrete standing out in the sea of marble. It had a name and sonnet etched on it, as though in honor of someone who was buried underneath. I was hoping it was a facade.

Magic sputtered in my veins. I had used so much tonight I could feel the limit of my magic closing in. But a shriek from the next room urged the revealing spell through my teeth. With a hiss of air, the concrete block popped up, shifting to the side, exposing old stone steps going down beneath the surface.

"Find them," a nasally voice shouted from the entrance, bouncing off the walls. The strighoul were in.

"Go!" I yelled at Lars. Travil was barely able to stand, but he kept hold of his friend and moved with Lars. As the men descended the worn stone stairs, a tingle tickled the back of my neck. I looked back.

Far across the cathedral, the shape of a woman stood in the door. Her features were masked in the dark, but I could feel her eyes on me.

I blinked.

She was gone.

An icy chill gnawed on my nerves as I darted around to see where she went. Did I imagine her?

"Druid!" Lars hissed from below, pulling my attention back to our escape. I climbed down the steps, covering up the tomb as I went with the last bits of my magic. Out of my coat pocket, I drew a small torch, illuminating the creepy, cramped tunnel far below the surface. It smelled the same as stale air, decomposing rodents, and feces.

Lars's head brushed the top as he bent forward slightly; the space barely let two men walk next to each other. Lars gathered up Goran, and Travil limped slowly behind, his ebbing energy slowing our pace.

I sighed, went to him, and tucked my shoulder under his arm.

"Get away from me, Druid." His lip curled up.

"Yeah, 'cause this is so fun for me too," I snarled back, wrapping my arm around his torso. "But you are slowing us down."

He wanted to fight me, but one look at his King and he shut up. His pride came second to his leader's safety.

My smirk was hidden in the dark, my hand curling around my true purpose for helping Travil. Scheming and plotting were in my nature now. I always kept my eyes open. Travil was too dazed and sick to notice I'd taken payment for my assistance—his beautifully carved knife he had threatened me with a time or two. The metal felt good brushing against my spine as I shoved it into the back of my pants. It would be weeks before he realized it was gone. If he lived.

Travil and I moved past Lars, taking the lead.

"This better take us out," Lars growled, dragging Goran.

I had the same wish. I really, really hoped the plans were current and someone hadn't sealed off the exit.

"Who the hell is attacking us?" I asked over my shoulder. Strighoul wouldn't bother unless something was in it for them. They didn't care about the treasure, and they would rather capture the King and have him for dinner. Someone was using them. This time it wasn't me. Hiring strighoul was not my finest hour, but in war you did what you had to do to win. "Who knows we are here?"

"You tell me, Ms. Cathbad. You sure they are not still working for you? Is this part of your plan to escape and betray me?"

I shot Lars a glare. "You think if this was part of my plan, I'd still be here with you?"

"Like you said, never underestimate you." He shifted Goran's weight higher on his shoulder, the man's legs all but dragging on the ground. Travil was in only slightly better shape, his jaw grinding in pain. "Use them as a diversion. Make it look as if we are on the same side."

I whipped around, stopping him in his tracks, Travil's form knocked against the wall at my sudden movement and release. He clung to the wall, trying to keep himself upright as sweat poured off him.

"It wasn't me. You can believe me or not, but right now both your men are dying. Every second goblin metal is leaking into their system. If we don't get them out of here and healed, they will die. So...do you really want to fight with me right now?"

Lars and I scowled at each other before he gave me the briefest of nods. I turned back around, taking us down the path in my mind. My flashlight dimly lit the way, just enough to mistake every shadow for an attacker. My body was so tense and jumpy I felt like a jack-in-the-box ready to leap out of the container.

"There." I pointed with relief down the corridor at the sewer exit above us at street level. The tick of water dripping down echoed through the tunnel.

I reached the old stone steps leading up to the exit. The lock took some time to break, but finally we emerged at street level, the night blistering with sirens and commotion, spectators running away or trying to get closer to see what was going on.

Goran's body sagged on Lars similar to a doll. He reduced us almost to a crawl, and Travil trudged like a ball at the end of the chain. We slipped into a dark alley a couple blocks away from the palace grounds.

"Sir, we are slowing you down. You need to flee while you have the chance," Goran muttered.

Lars's lips parted. "I will hear none of it."

Goran pushed away from Lars, falling onto the wall, letting himself slide to the ground, panting. "You have to leave us. Travil and I will go into fever comas soon. We are no use to you. We will only bring you more danger. I swore I would protect you. The best way to do that is for you to leave right now. Take the plane home."

Lars pinched his nose, his shoulders curving forward, as though the weight of his decision was tangible.

"Sir, you know this is the only way."

Lars took a few deep breaths before nodding. "Fine, but you will be leaving me. You and Travil are taking the plane back home. There you will heal."

"No, sir."

"This is an order, Goran," he replied with ferocity. "Ms. Cathbad and I are not done. I do not plan to go home empty handed."

My head twisted to him, my mouth parting.

"My liege." Goran struggled to keep standing. "You will be unprotected."

"I am a demon. An exceedingly powerful Unseelie King with centuries of training. I think I can manage on my own just fine."

Goran wanted to protest, I could see his lids narrowing with concern, but his thread of energy was about to snap.

"Plus, I have a formidable, conniving Druid who specializes in the dark arts." Lars shot me a look. "We will be just fine, right, Ms. Cathbad?"

Clenching my lips, I cleared my true thoughts from my throat and nodded.

Sure. An arrogant, narcissistic king and a hotheaded Druid who dabbled in black magic.

What could possibly go wrong?

~~

Sweaty and exhausted, Lars and I finally got the two injured men on the private jet. Travil tried so hard to stay awake and walk by himself, but it was a pathetic attempt at best. He stumbled and fell over a dozen times, and my small frame was not built to hold up such a beast of a man. The King carried Goran over his shoulder, blood soaking through his designer jacket.

"Get them home, now," Lars ordered the pilot as Melanie and Jessica attended to the wounded men without a word.

"What about you, sir?" the pilot asked.

I never noticed before, but what I thought was styled brown hair was gold, brown, and red feathers. His nose was long and slightly hooked, his eyes a piercing golden yellow-orange, his black pupils huge. A bird shifter. What better person to fly a plane than one who could fly himself?

"I will be staying here." Lars didn't elaborate, putting his hand on my lower back to lead me back out the plane. "Call ahead and have my healers waiting at the hangar."

"Yes, sir." The pilot bowed his head.

Lars rushed me to the stairs. I took a last look over my shoulder. Melanie was crouched before Goran, but her eyes were locked on the retreating King. Desire, desperation, and longing shone in her bright aqua eyes; her lips parted as if she were about to call out for him.

I shook my head with a snort, trampling down the stairs to the ground.

"What?"

"Think someone's got it bad," I teased, flicking my head up back to the closing door of the plane.

The pilot was readying the jet for flight. Muscles along Lars's jaw twitched under his skin as he pulled the rolling stairway from the plane.

The engine started up, and the aircraft curved out of the private hangar, heading for the tarmac.

Gusts of wind snapped the ends of my hair at my cheeks like whips. "What now?" I asked as both of us watched our ride leave without us.

"You are going to complete your mission, Ms. Cathbad." He kept his head forward. "You will find the cauldron for me."

"And how do you suppose I do that? Pull it out of my ass like a rabbit?" I replied evenly, watching the lights of the jet rise up in the sky heading west.

"If that is what you have to do."

I lifted my eyebrows. "There are no reports or leads on the cauldron since it allegedly came here. It might have been destroyed or is truly lost. We have no way of finding it."

"I do not." He lifted his head higher, gaze locked on the dark night. "But you do."

"My family forged it *centuries* ago. And it's been lost almost as long. I have no more of an idea than a person on the street."

"There you are wrong, Ms. Cathbad." I craned my head to look at him. He turned, staring down at me with a glint in his eyes. "What do you need for a locating spell?"

"A locating spell?" I half laughed. "You need a connection to the lost item, to have touched it, and at least know where it was last seen. I have none of those."

He curved to fully face me, a smirk on his face. Acid rose into my throat. What was he thinking?

"You come from the direct line who created the cauldron, the same magic...the same blood."

It felt as though a huge moth was rising up my chest into my throat, the wings batting against my airways.

"You want me to do a blood ritual." It wasn't a question. I knew exactly what he wanted from me. Over the years, I'd heard stories of "witches" or Druids sacrificing girl virgins and gutting animals. All true. The gods were bloodthirsty. To keep in their graces, there had been some animal and human victims over time, especially back in the ten and eleven hundreds. We had become more civil since then. Okay, who was I fooling? We really hadn't. We just traded killings for sexual rituals instead, because the gods were horny shites as well. They loved the energy of group orgies especially.

But what Lars wanted could kill me.

"Are you kidding me?"

His eyes pierced mine as he took a step closer, almost touching me, and his energy roamed over my skin like a drunk with a walker, swerving and rolling on each nerve.

"I think it's the least you can do." His voice was low, but I could feel the threat dripping off each word. "If you ever lie to me again." He lifted his hand, his palm curling around the base of my throat. "And if you even think about escaping..." He reached around with his free hand, clutching the knife slipped underneath my jumper. *Shite.* He knew. I should have realized I couldn't get anything past him. He noticed everything, saw everything. "You thought you could escape me with this? That is amusing." He tugged it out of my pants, skimming the tip of the blade over my neck and down my ribs. Adrenaline thumped in my veins, the space between my thighs tingling.

Breath caught in my throat, his hand pressing down a little harder, the knife poking into my breastbone. Neither of us moved; our gazes latched on each other. Neither of us would back down.

"You know what this ritual entails, don't you?" My voice came out a husky whisper.

"I do."

Shite. Fuck.

"I told you. There is nothing I won't do to get what I want."

That's what I was afraid of.

Chapter Fourteen

Lars

After a few calls to my secretary, whose name I'm sure I will remember one of these times, I acquired a small rental near the Charles Bridge. We could not return to the hotel. It was undoubtedly being observed, though I wasn't yet sure by whom.

Someone who seemed to know my every move.

I hurried the Druid through the cold night to the loft space, Travil's knife tucked in my boot. The dense haze hid our blood-stained and torn clothes from the few tourists walking the bridge.

The statues of the saints perched on the crossing similar to guard dogs, the fog wrapping around them like moth-eaten blankets. Curling up from the Vltava River, these eerie outlines loomed through the mist, so hulking they seemed to be alive and watching us.

The Gothic-style guard gate with its spires and steepled roof rose up at the end of the bridge and stirred the sensation I had returned to the time of death-perfumed cities, when disease eradicated a lot of humans. Dark times for fae as well. Needing to blame someone, humans turned to us, sensing we were different. With pitchforks and fire, groups hunted us as if we were feral beasts, taking pride in putting fae heads on stakes and parading them through villages while they burned our women to death.

Now I was seeing my brother again. Was it because we had been here together when we were young, free, and unaware of the future where the love of a woman would end up dividing us?

I had a sharp memory of Aisling and the day she showed up on my doorstep seeking the King's and my help. She opened her mouth, and I was a goner. I thought I despised her. She was smart, beautiful, strong, and challenged me at every turn. No one else ever had. A fire burned in her, wild and free, and branded me hers. Of course, we both denied it for a long time. Seelie princesses and Unseelie demons did not mix. The penalty of association with a demon was death. The fact she was there to try and stop her sister, the Queen? Treason.

Every second we were together was fraught with danger. And that only made us want each other more. No woman before or after affected me like she had. I resembled a pubescent fae in the pinnacle of his magic and sexual awakening. We couldn't get enough of each other, fucking every moment we could. The more I fought it, the more I fell in love with her. We spent more and more time together, and at night we'd lie naked under the stars, talking about life. Knowing we could not be together for long.

Even when we parted and she went to my brother, our connection never waned. It was like a force field connected us. Our words might deny each other, but our bodies never could.

"Is this it?" Fionna's Irish lilt broke me from my reverie. She twisted the newly magic-proof cell phone in my hand, reading the address my secretary messaged me. This prototype was still being tested, and so far I hadn't found too many glitches. I was eager to get it on the market, letting the world reconnect with those they hadn't talked to since the fall of the walls.

And yes, the money would be nice. It would allow me to grant more funds to Zoey Daniels's Honey House and Dr. Grier for their children's homes and medical research.

I peered up at the numbers on the old neo-baroque building and typed a code into the keypad on the door. The lock unlatched, and the door swung open to a set of stairs. I took them two at a time, flicking on the light switch at the top, illuminating the living space in a buttery light.

Fionna reached the main level and gazed around the room wide-eyed. "Even your getaway apartment has to be meticulous." She snorted, brushing past me to walk in the large corner flat.

I stepped away from her quickly, aware I'd almost acted on impulse at the moment in the hangar when my hand lay on her throat and her gaze challenged mine. My anger at her only mounted the need to punish her...to take her. Hard and unforgiving. My dick stirred as images of me doing just that flooded through. I pinched my nose and took a breath. I had to get myself back in command. I couldn't lose my control.

"Seriously." Fionna ran her fingers over the wood dining table, its metal base glittering under the modern chandelier dripping over it. Each seat surrounding the table was a slim wingback chair. "Ever heard of a Travelodge?"

"A what?"

"Well, you answered my question." She chuckled, tugging off her beanie. The smell of shampoo from her damp locks perfumed the air.

"I am King," I retaliated, as though my answer should resolve the matter. She had no idea how hard I worked to become what I was.

"And you don't let us forget it," she mumbled, unzipping her jacket and tossing it on a side chair as she walked into the family room.

The first floor was mainly the living space. An enormous two-sided stone fireplace divided the dining, kitchen, and the living areas. A modern gray velvet sectional with textured pillows faced the fireplace. Two side chairs, a sleek wood coffee table, and a white furry rug filled the space. A wrought iron spiral staircase took you up to the second level where the bedrooms were. Minimal with a mix of masculine and feminine.

"It is who I am." My skin stung where it thawed. I'd left my coat back at the castle. No DNA would trace it back to me. Science had yet to find a way to register fae chromosomes. "No one should ever forget it."

"Really?" She whipped around. "That's sad. Not even your niece? Or the people who love you?"

"Excuse me?"

"It's a title, not your entire persona."

"With me it is...it *has* to be...my life."

"What about the man? And the demon? How do they describe themselves? What do they want?"

Irritation pricked at the back of my neck, her questions rousing defensive anger. "I don't have the luxury, Druid. My life is to protect my people and run this kingdom."

"I'm pretty sure the humans would like to be a part of that again. Have their democracy back. Do you really think of them when you say *your* people? I think they would beg to differ."

My hands clamped together. *Breathe.* "First, I speak for all people, fae or human. And second, their so-called democracy was a farce. An outrageously corrupt system, where only the wealthiest controlled anything. They weren't free. They just desperately clung to the idea because if they really looked, they would see the truth, and the truth scares people. Most were comfortable with the status quo so long as their lives went on as usual."

She nodded, but I didn't sense she fully agreed with my assessment.

"We need to set up for the ritual." I swept past her, shoving the coffee table back into the sofa. "Is this enough room?"

Fionna bit down on her bottom lip, then cracked her knuckles.

"Don't do that." I tried to ignore the chill wiggling down my back.

"What?" She glanced down at her hands. "You mean this?" Bones popped along her other hand.

"Ugh." I stared up at the ceiling. "Stop."

"Are you kidding me? This is what makes the *King* queasy? Knuckles cracking?" She burst out laughing. "You torture and kill, probably hear actual bones breaking nightly, but this?" She popped her thumb, forcing me to wince. "This is what gets you?"

"It's annoying," I growled. It reminded me of my brother. He used to do it all the time when we were kids, knowing it drove me up the wall. It seemed everything was coming back to my brother lately.

My twin, my other half, my best friend, my partner in crime...and the man I had to kill with my own bare hands.

Chapter Fifteen

Fionna

Flames danced in the fireplace, crackling its warmth into the dark room. The sheep rug was pushed under the sofa, leaving space for us to sit. We'd turned off every light and lit a few candles we found around the house. These now sat in a circle on the wood floor. One remained unlit and sat off to the side, as we couldn't form the circle until we were inside it.

My heart trotted heavily against my ribs. Not a lot scared me about magic, even black magic, but this type of blood ritual was bizarre. And archaic. Honestly, the thought never crossed my mind to try it, and the chances of it working were minimal.

I stood up, staring down at the large candle circle. TV and movies had warped these practices into "demonic" for entertainment value, which really pissed me off. Pagan religion was always twisted from the beautiful feminine power and worship of Mother Earth to satanic ritual. Now everyone associated pagan with the devil, when it was never meant to be that. It showed the power of propaganda and men who feared the strength of women.

No demons rose or were summoned to do my bidding. Why would I need one when I already had one here with me?

The type of blood ritual I was doing would let the gods connect me to my ancestors and find the magic that united the cauldron to me. Believe me, I wish I only had to summon a ghost or demon to tell me its location. That would be easy.

"You ready?" Lars sat back on his heels just outside of the imaginary circle line, his green eyes shining from the firelight.

"Noooo." I shook my head, my voice shaky.

"I won't let it go too far." He rubbed his hands on his dirty jeans, his face serious.

"Why don't I buy what you're saying? Oh right…because there isn't anything you won't do to get what you want."

He held my gaze. "You're right. However, you dying tonight would be more problematic for me."

He understood as I did that if we discovered the location, he would need me to break the protection spell on it. My family connection would more likely open the object to me.

"Lucky me."

"If we were doing the *true* ritual, you would be." A slight smile tugged at his lip.

I blinked. Did he just try and make a joke?

Back when the fae gods first accepted my people, every blood ritual would end with sex. Usually an orgy, believing the energy of the orgasm would be the final gift to the gods. Personally, I thought they added this part so they could have group sex without feeling guilty.

In today's world, some still believed in the "old practice," but most had dropped that part. It would definitely not be included tonight. What he had to do to me was already way past my comfort zone.

Don't think, Fionna, just do it.

I kicked off my boots, trying to keep my breath even as I unbuttoned my jeans. Being naked was normal and natural to Druids. I was far from ashamed of my body. I used to run out in the rain nude all the time near the Cliffs of Moher, freaking out tourists, not caring who saw me. But Lars watching me felt intimate, breaching my walls.

My nerves and heart jumped similar to a kangaroo on caffeine. My throat tightened and I struggled to swallow. Peeling my grimy jeans down my legs, I wiggled out of them, tearing off my jumper with haste. If I did it fast, the less I would notice my nerves or the heat attacking my body like a predator.

His gaze burned into me, but I kept my focus on the task. I undid my bra and slipped out of my knickers. You had to be completely naked within the circle, in your truest form, for this ritual. Basically, what you came into this world with, because you might be leaving it in the same fashion.

My long hair draped over my torso as I stepped inside the circle, sitting down in the center. My eyes finally lifted to gaze at Lars.

Oxygen fled my lungs, as though I had been holding it hostage. His jaw was clamped. Black began to eclipse his bright chartreuse eyes, their intensity squeezing my chest. I had to look away. This was so unbelievably awkward and... *No, don't go there*. It was about to get a whole lot more uncomfortable.

"To join me in the circle, you can't be clothed." I stated the fact as if I were reading a history book.

"I know." He stood, kicked off his boots, grabbed the back of his T-shirt, and pulled it over his head.

My mouth dropped open.

His torso and arms were like nothing I had ever seen. Not in real life. Magazine covers maybe, but even those guys didn't seem to compare...not to the High Demon King.

A tattoo coiled up the side of his upper body and onto one arm. I wasn't expecting someone as controlled as him to have one. The black symbols of two flames set inside a triangle twisted into a gorgeous detailed pattern and crossed his heart to his shoulder. Twin flames. Probably representing his brother. Another symbol for fire twined down his torso, connecting the two together. I didn't know what that one stood for, but they were both freakin' sexy.

He cleared his throat, reminding me to return my attention to his face. A full smirk curved his mouth as he caught me ogling his body.

I rolled my eyes and looked over at the fire. What? I could appreciate an amazing physique, even if I didn't like what was inside it.

He stripped off his trousers, causing energy to rush over my skin and tingle down my legs. Everything was taut and rigid from head to toe. *Everything.* My gaze dipped to the ground, but the need to see him was so strong, looking away was close to fighting gravity. My eyes traveled up, watching him slip out of his boxer briefs.

This was so surreal. Even a few hours ago, I would never have believed I'd be naked with the King of Dark fae, doing a blood ritual. And soon he would be drawing symbols over me with my blood, draining me until I was on the cusp of death.

Did I mention the gods and goddesses were horny, bloodthirsty, and deranged?

Lars grabbed the knife I'd stolen from Travil out of his boot. He smirked at it, then at me. Yes, poetic justice—he'd be using the knife on me I would have used on him.

Lars moved inside the circle, making my line of sight very problematic. "Sit. Please," I grumbled, busying myself with lighting the last candle. "Are you ready?" I was formal on the outside, while everything inside was running and bashing into each other as though I was a burning house.

He got down on his knees next to me.

What was I doing? Was I really going to do this?

"I won't let you die, Ms. Cathbad." He tried to assure me.

"We're sitting here naked, you're going to slice me open, use my body as a painting canvas, and you still call me Ms. Cathbad?" My nerves shot out a snappy laugh. "I think we can drop the formality."

"On the contrary." His gaze dipped down my body, his voice gruff, sending fire through me. "Even more of a reason to keep it." His eyes went back to mine, holding my gaze.

He was right. In that moment I needed to hold on to any bit of convention and reserve I had left. It reminded me this was just a means to an end for him. I was not a person but an instrument to get what he wanted.

I nodded and held a candle out for him. The metal glinted as he ran it through the flame. It was part of the ritual to purify the knife. It cleaned the weapon, but the heated metal cutting into flesh would be even more excruciating.

"Once the circle is closed, the ritual will start. You have any questions?" I pulled my hair over one shoulder, gripping the last candle as if I wanted to strangle it to death.

"No."

"You act like you do this all the time."

He tilted his head.

"Seriously?" I exclaimed.

His lips parted, showing his perfect white teeth. "No."

"Shite, I was starting to think this was what you did to relax."

"Minus the ritual and blood." He lifted one eyebrow. "It is."

I stared at him, trying to decipher if he was teasing.

"However, I do like it the old-school way," he said evenly, but I had no doubt what he meant.

My lids shut, swallowing roughly. My body wanted to follow the old ways too, while everything else in me screamed to be revolted by the thought. He was my sworn enemy. The man I spent years plotting to take down. Except I wasn't revolted by the idea, which made me more agitated.

"Let's get this over with," I snarled, lighting the last candle and setting it in place, the ring around us complete. I took a deep breath and lay down, closing my eyes. A hum developed in the back of my throat before the chant stepped off my tongue, snapping my magic in place.

I had never done this level of a ritual, but I heard it was extremely painful, and potentially fatal.

Couldn't we go to a pub and have a beer instead?

Chapter Sixteen

Lars

Flames reflected in the blade I was holding as though I was about to slice into this creature with fire. Her magic swirled within the circle, stimulating my skin. Every part of me was aroused.

Druid magic was powerful, but it had never affected me as hers did. Whether it was because she was so powerful or because of her use of black magic, the sensation unsettled me deeply.

Music hummed from her like a song, as she called to her ancestors and the gods to help her create the link to the cauldron. Her forehead glistened with the first signs of power being siphoned from her. A few strands of her hair stuck to it, and I had this odd longing to brush them back.

No. *I* didn't; the demon did. I furrowed my brow,

not understanding this reaction. The demon did not care about *being kind*. It wanted power. To kill and fuck. That was it.

For the first time tonight, I really let myself look at her. She was so petite. Granted, she had a full ass, but she was flat and bony everywhere else. Not the type of woman I would ever be attracted to.

Aisling hadn't been curvy either, but I'd found perfection in her tall, lean body. I had craved her like a fiend, and I showed my appreciation to her body.

Fionna's long, shiny brown hair twisted down the side of her neck, covering one breast. Her arms were down by her sides, and her legs parted in a relaxed position.

Usually I didn't even blink seeing a naked woman; most of the time I hardly noticed. Fae were all about being unclothed. She was no different. *So why am I noticing her as if I have never seen a naked woman before?*

Fionna's words popped against my chest, drawing my attention back to her face. The corners of her eyes wrinkled in pain, her chant building aggressively, as the rising of magic pulsed out of her.

"Now." She opened her eyes, breaking from the Latin.

Gripping the knife, I hovered it at her wrist. Her perfect ivory skin would be forever marred by this level of ritual.

"Do. It. Now," she gritted out.

The blade dug into her fragile skin and slid in a straight line, blood pooling out from the deep trench.

Perspiration trickled down into her hair. Her jaw ground together, and a slight hiss seeped between her teeth. Then she started her chant again, her voice thick.

If I were any other man, I might feel guilty for doing this to her, but I wasn't. Too much was at stake.

I cut three curved lines, creating the Awen symbol, the mark for inspiration or spiritual illumination, used by Druids. Harmony between feminine and masculine. Blood leaked from the wounds, merging with each other. I repeated the same procedure on the other arm, her life essence dripping out of her onto the floor.

Her nose flared, tears leaking from her closed eyes. I had to give it to her; she did not cry out, but used the pain to fuel her spell.

Dipping my finger in the blood, I brought it up to her chest. The moment my skin touched hers, a blast of energy surged through my veins, bringing my body to life.

Fionna gasped, her back arched, and her chant stopped the moment I touched her.

The sexual charge spun my head, forcing me to gasp for air. My body's reaction was instant. I had been aroused before, but I could ignore it and think about something else. Now I throbbed, hard as steel. A sudden desperation to use her for release was excruciating.

Over the years, I had become schooled in my reactions and responses. My body did not overpower my will, no matter the pain, sexual need, or magic twisting it. Except tonight. The intensity was nothing I had ever felt. I had to close my eyes for a few moments to regain domination, my demon demanding to act on the impulse, to spread her legs more...

I growled. My desire for power had always kept me in order, even with Aisling. I had let go of myself with her the most, but never enough to misplace my need for power. It was the reason I lost her. However, whatever platform I stood on before was tilting, forcing me to scramble to stay on.

Swallowing, I began to paint another symbol over Fionna's stomach, her breath deepening at every trace of my finger. With the spell in place, she only hummed softly to herself now, probably to distract herself from the pain as her blood flowed freely onto the floor.

I brushed her hair off her shoulder, needing to paint the cauldron symbol on her heart, to tell the goddesses and gods what she most desired. Lightly I guided the tip of my finger over her heart, her nipple hardening under my touch. She huffed, nipping her bottom lip, sending another dose of hunger through me and clotting my brain.

My skin was damp with sweat, the contact with her only raising the intensity instead of lessening it. Each time I painted a symbol on her legs, chest, or arms, my muscles became tenser and tenser until they were shaking. *Want. Now. Take.* The demon howled inside, jumping up and down frantically.

"*Fuck,*" I whispered to myself, my jaw aching from crunching it together.

The humming stopped, snapping my gaze to Fionna, our eyes locked. The demon went berserk.

Lust.

Need.

No. Unbearable need.

She no doubt was feeling the same. Her pupils dilated fully with desire, her chest rising and lowering in shallow breaths. Her lips parted in moans as I turned my attention to her hip, painting a goddess symbol on one, the god mark on the other.

Logic shut down, and I stared absently as my fingers moved lower, trailing softly down to her inner thigh. Out of the corner of my eye, I saw Fionna's head dig into the floor, her lashes fluttering closed, her back arching in pleasure.

What are you doing? Stop.

But I didn't.

Both my palms flattened on her soft skin, skating down the outside of her hips, opening her up a little more to me. I licked my lip realizing I wanted to taste her, to savor her climax on my tongue.

Yessss, the demon hissed while a voice in the back of my head was hollering at me, trying to warn me. I couldn't make out the words or understand anything except my lust.

Her moans turned to piercing wails. Pain. Torture. Pleasure. "Oh gods…please…." Her cries jumbled with pleas. "End this…please…it-it hurts…" Her nails dug into the floorboards, her body bucking against my touch, her legs opening wider for me. Her blood heaved out of her body, turning the small ponds into pools. "Please…Lars…n-now."

We couldn't stop or it would all be for nothing. Not that I even could if I tried, a power taking over me, one I was completely helpless with.

My hands wouldn't stop caressing and smearing more blood over her body. Her shrieks seemed to only incite me to keep going. Greedy to keep touching her, to know every inch, I traced slowly over her stomach to her breasts. Every slip of my skin against hers created a greater desire roaring through my veins. I groaned, feeling heat spread up my torso. I wanted to fuck her. Deep and unrelenting.

Her back arched higher, her head tilting back, her lids shut, tears running down her face.

"Fionna..." Her name came from my lips with ravenous desire. I had never wanted to be inside someone more than I did her. A simple touch and I felt I was about to explode. Her legs spread to let me crawl between them, her body stilling as I slid over her. She let out a whimpering moan, then went quiet.

Her blood coated both of us similar to a Pollock painting. Being drenched in her blood only turned me on more. My cock was right at her entrance, only one word from her and I would thrust into her.

"Fionna." Her first name once again fell from me with ease. She did not respond, and an alarm went off in my gut. I clasped my hands around her face. Even covered in blood, she was astonishingly beautiful. "Fionna?"

Nothing.

I sat back on my heels with a roar, my body straddling hers. "Fionna! Wake up." I shook her, her body moving limply.

"Fuck!" I bellowed, fear clawing up my throat. I leaned over, plastering my ear to her heart.

Silence.

"No. No. No. No!" I had told her I wouldn't let her die. I practically promised. I needed her. She couldn't die on me. My hand swept up her wrists, closing the wounds with my limited healing powers. Druids were by far better, but being King did come with perks.

My palms went to her chest, pushing in, encouraging her lungs to start working again. Sometimes basic CPR was the only solution. I could not bring people back from the dead, no matter what energy I drove into them, because I might overdo it and fry her.

My arms pumped three times, and I leaned over to cover her mouth with my own. A faraway realization was Rez was the last person my lips had touched. And in the last year of our relationship, it became very infrequent. Our relationship turned more formal and comfortable in our roles than passionate. All the other women, I did not kiss. That was my rule.

Tilting her head back, my mouth came down on hers. Her soft lips crushed against mine.

As if I kissed an electrical fence, a volt passed through me, jolting me back with force. My ass hit the floor, crashing through the circle we created, bursting the spell like a balloon. My head cleared, logic and understanding cleaning out the haze as though a hose had blasted through my brain.

Fionna shot up. A scream ripped from her mouth as though I peeled back her skin like string cheese. It raked over my bones similar to chains while chills sprouted up my back.

The cry died away from her lips as she gasped for air, her eyes wild and bright. Blood covered every inch of her, knotting her hair in clumps as if she were a wild beast.

Our eyes found each other's. We both stayed that way for several moments trying to take in what had just happened and at a loss for words to describe it. Okay, *I* was at a loss for words. Fionna looked down at her wrists then the blood staining the wood floor, her voice shaky and soft.

"I wouldn't count on getting your deposit back."

Chapter Seventeen

Fionna

Bloody hell.

It was the only thing I could respond with. My brain couldn't seem to stop looping, repeatedly.

I had been completely unprepared for it. Practices like this were mostly instinct now, and growing up with a witch, not a Druid, my knowledge of them was even more limited. They weren't something you found in books. What I did learn about blood rituals was only a glimpse of what my body and mind went through. Pain. Yes. Someone cutting into your flesh was excruciating, but it wasn't the kind of pain that overwhelmed me. That would have been too easy. A lot less cruel.

Every touch from Lars was so intense and pleasurable it hurt like nothing I had ever known. It became torture. Blinding agony. As though someone was burning me alive inside—and the only thing that would quash the flames was sex. Endless, brutal, consuming, sex. And I'd wanted it from *just* him. My pleas to him were not to end the ritual or my life but to stop the burning inside. To take me.

The goddesses and gods were truly arseholes.

"I'm starting to understand the group orgy thing at the end," I muttered to myself, not able to fully look at the demon. It was still too raw and new. Even though the spell broke and the crushing need had fled along with the pain, it wasn't completely gone. If the blood caking my skin didn't already make me feel dirty, the sensations still flittering inside did.

"Did it work?" Lars cleared his raspy throat. I looked up to see he was smeared in my blood from head to toe. I felt a strange intimacy with him.

I pulled my knees to me, staring at the fresh weeping scars on my wrists. "Yes."

He moved quickly, sitting up. "What did you see? Where did they tell you it was?"

It happened so fast, just glimpses flashing in my brain. A tall lean man in a robe holding a thick tree branch for a cane stood on a cliff too far away to see his face. A river cut through breathtaking landscapes. Rocky green dramatic mountains, the cloudy sky patching the earth in shadows and light. Screaming and death. Pain from the victims pulled me down into the dirt. A small village, gravestones, a cave with a large keyhole opening.

Then the images broke.

I knew the exact place.

"Scotland." I licked my lips, tasting the tang of blood. "The Highlands."

"That is vague. It showed you more than that."

"Glencoe." I rubbed at my head, my fingers sticking to the strands. "Near the village, I think. That's all it showed me."

He stared at me for a long time, assessing whether I was lying. I challenged him, my eyes never leaving his.

"Go get cleaned up," he ordered, getting to his feet. "We'll leave in the morning." He turned and leaned over to grab his high-tech mobile phone out of his jeans pocket.

It felt odd to see my blood covering his perky arse. I did not like it. Not the way my stomach dipped or the way my thighs tightened. It was too personal. This was not a feeling you wanted with your sworn enemy.

Stiff and achy, I got to my feet. The pulse in my wrists pounded against my tender flesh, but the pain was distant, as though it had been numbed. I scaled the stairs, heading to where I figured the shower was, breathing for the first time since "waking up."

I had been on the cusp of death, walking the high wire, falling over. I'd felt the peace and quiet of it. Then it flipped, as though someone shoved a thousand volts in me, and unbelievable agony flooded my body along with the images of places I knew.

Like the cave.

If Lars thought I was going to give over the cauldron at the drop of a hat, he was quite mistaken. I knew there was no point trying to keep it from him completely. He was the King. He would find a way with or without me. I just wanted to get to it first. And I was certainly not going to make it easy for him.

Spiteful? Maybe.

After all he let happen to my people, he deserved to be tortured as he gladly allowed me to be tonight.

~~

The shower was modern, and water rained down on me with massaging taps. I had no soap, shampoo, or conditioner, but my muscles melted under the stream, the water washing away the scarlet stains swathing me. I tipped my face up, letting the flow bombard my face.

"You might need these." A voice came from behind me.

"Shite!" I jumped, swinging around to see Lars on the other side of the glass door. The steam from the shower only slightly blurred his unclothed physique. He reached for the handle, swinging the door open.

"What are you doing?"

He stood there for several moments, staring at me, not one emotion showing on his features. I could feel my chest rising and falling avidly, as if I forgot to feed it oxygen.

"Soap." He held up his hand. Small containers of soap, shampoo, and conditioner lay in his open palm. "They were in the hall closet."

"Thank you." I reached out for them, water trundling over my lips, making me suck them in.

His gaze dropped to my mouth. His body moved closer, looming over mine.

I froze in place, probably resembling a fossilized dinosaur. All thought and feeling vanished.

Lars leaned forward, jumbling my breath and heart in a knotted mess. Was he going to kiss me?

In a blink, his fingers wrapped around my neck. As he stepped into the shower, he shoved me back against the tile. "What the fuck did your spell do to me?"

"Uhhh," I stammered. The soaps dropped to the tile with a ping. He had felt it too? The unwelcome yearning.

"What. Did. It. Do. To. Me?" He growled, his shoulders rising under the drops pelting his skin. Tainted water slid from his form to the tub below.

"I-I don't know." I kept my eyes on him, trying to show no fear.

His thumb moved up the middle of my neck, forcing me to swallow. He wasn't gripping hard enough to hurt, but enough to show me he could. A spell rose to my lips on instinct but was crushed when he pressed himself against me, engulfing me in the sharp, stinging desire I felt earlier.

"Will it go away?" His nose slid up the side of my face.

"I don't know that either," I whispered thickly, my body responding to his without my say.

He let out a deep growl, different to any animal I'd ever heard, but just as feral. The untamed power and magic surging off him bent my muscles and mind to him. I realized then I had never gotten close to Lars's true demon. What he showed was the fluffy one. The real one he hid inside could destroy without a thought.

I was powerful. Strong. I had no idea what I'd been up against. But fear did something strange to me. I liked it. It made me want to fight back. Climb on top of it and declare myself the winner. Regain control.

It turned me on.

Need sprang off me like knives. Tipping my head, my mouth skated over his chin to his lips, sucking off the water on his bottom lip.

"No," he rumbled. He grabbed my face and pinned my head to the wall, staring down at me. I didn't react, letting his primal gaze crawl over me.

His jaw twitched, then he dropped his hands, stepping back. With a snarl, he stepped out of the shower, stomping for the door. "It better be gone by tomorrow."

He slammed the bathroom door behind him, shaking the flat.

Holy shite!

My head fell back against the wall, right where he left me as I pulled in long gulps of air.

What the fuck just happened? What was I about to do?

My legs bowed, and I slid down the wall. Humiliation, anger, and terror skimmed the surface, but shock had yet to let them penetrate the surface.

I stayed under the spray until I shivered from the icy water.

Eventually I got out and numbly wrapped myself in a towel, heading for the first bedroom I saw and crashed. I wanted every minute of the last twelve hours to evaporate as if it were a bad dream.

Chapter Eighteen

Lars

Still wet and bloody, I dressed in my garments and burst from the flat while pure rage punctured my skin like nails. Cold air surged into my lungs, burning all the way down my chest. My booted feet moved me swiftly, with no intended direction.

My wrath reached levels I had only felt at my demon's awakening, a time when I couldn't control my emotions. *Or the beginning of your brother's insanity.* I shook my head, ridding myself of that thought. Even when I found West in bed with my lover, my temper only skimmed the line of true rage. Ember helped keep me grounded, but I had been nowhere near losing control. I knew precisely what I was doing.

Tonight I had almost slipped. I was losing restraint.

I had stepped into the shower with no thought, without understanding why. The compelling notion to kill her had quickly flipped to the need to be inside her. The remnants of the ceremony still clung to us like smoke. The desperation to fuck her had been insatiable. But that wasn't what riled me. I wanted to kiss her, which was a line I did not cross. Certainly not with a Druid. I wanted to destroy her for that. Especially when she challenged my wrath and threats with her own hunger. When her lips brushed mine... It took everything I had to turn away.

"Fuck!" I bellowed into the night, the mist growing denser, concealing me in its icy embrace. The chilly air was not helping clear my head. The desire to return to the flat, to resume what I had walked away from, was painful as if I were being divided in half.

I reached the empty Charles Bridge and heard the water gush wildly underneath, as though it understood my inner turmoil. The tourists and locals were safely tucked in their rooms away from the bone-chilling cold and the seedy monsters who came alive at this time.

Someone just like me.

My ribs knocked into the side of the bridge, and I sucked in a deep breath, leaning over to see the dark depth churning below. My fists smashed against the stone, a long cry of frustration and anger came from my gut.

Get it together. Now.

I had no patience for others being reckless and even less for me.

I pinched the bridge of my nose, trying to center myself. *No more.* My mind kept repeating this, however, I could still feel the pull. My muscles flexed with the urgency to go back, like a baby who had yet to grasp how to control their own body.

Either desire, to end her life or be inside her, was unacceptable. She was essential in getting the cauldron. That was all. The last Treasure of Tuatha Dé Danann was the only thing important.

"Laaaarrrsss." My name whispered over the wind like music.

My shoulders bunched and my head snapped around in all directions looking for the speaker. I didn't see a soul. Silence extended for over a minute, causing me to doubt if I had actually heard anything.

Rubbing my chin, I shook my head. I fastened the last button on my coat and faced the direction of the flat.

"Lars," a woman softly called from behind me, her voice so familiar it stopped me in my tracks.

No. There's no way.

I whipped around to peer behind me. Nothing but thick fog obscured the bridge and its saints in a game of hide-and-seek. A chill drew up my spine similar to connecting the dots.

Seeing my brother had been bad enough.

"Lars?" Her voice echoed in front of me, jarring me forward. This time her voice was clear, ramming my heart against my ribs. My eyes lurched around, trying to make out any shape in the mist.

"Have you forgotten me so easily?" The words danced lightly over to me, echoing off the walls, surrounding me.

I clenched my jaw, circling around to keep each end of the bridge in sight. The need to call out to see who was there sat on my tongue, but I kept quiet. Someone was messing with me. They had to be. The other possibility was not an option.

"Did you know how much I loved you?" Her statement circled around me, crushing in my lungs. "You left me."

Like a dagger straight to the gut, my sorrow and guilt parted my lips. "No," I whispered. Sweat dampened my back and forehead. "You left me."

"I think we both know you had departed way before that. You loved power much more than you loved me," she spoke, sounding closer.

I cleared my throat. "Show yourself."

The lights from the bridge glowed eerily through the fog, my gaze waiting to catch any movement on either side. Through the haze a silhouette of a woman stood, the streetlamp radiating the mist around her similar to an angel, her long hair brushing her hips.

A gasp tore from my throat, my knees bending. "Aisling."

I knew her figure better than my own. My hands and mouth had mapped every inch, memorizing it. The way she held herself was like a permanent blueprint stamped on my heart.

"This can't be..." I muttered, my mind unable to grasp what my eyes were taking in. My feet stumbled forward, my heart flipping around as if it were on a carnival ride. Disbelief could not cover the spring of hope from leaping up my throat.

Could it be possible? Did she somehow survive?

The questions pitched quickly through my head, as reason stood like a wall, blocking each one from venturing too deep.

"Aisling…" I called her name, every step taking me closer to the outline.

A foghorn resounded from down the river, taking my attention for a moment. When I turned back she was gone.

"Aisling!" I bellowed, running into the murkiness, twisting in every direction to find her. "Ash!" Her pet name bounded out of my mouth. I quaked with the need to touch her, to feel her once again. As I spun around, I continued to scream her name, sounding desperate and needy. The fog resembled cream soup, brewing and bubbling up from below.

Her laugh weaved through the dense air, wrenching my head to one side. The laugh bounced to the opposite side, twisting me like a pretzel. My body moved, following her voice as though she was a siren.

"*Ais-ling*," I howled, my desperation expanding throughout ever part of me. Her location switched again. My lungs pumped heavily, pounding in my ears.

"Ash…" I breathed out her name, hoping she would answer me.

A deep chuckle rumbled up to my boots, drilling through the soles. My lungs halted, struggling to let oxygen in. I knew that laugh as well.

"Devlin," I uttered so softy it barely made it past my mouth. As children he had always been the one quick to laugh, to smile. Easygoing and willing to follow me into whatever trouble I concocted. I had needed him far more than he ever needed me. He tethered me to earth, neutralizing my intensity when I grew bored and impatient. When he had become King after Father's death, we had grown apart. My jealousy had contributed.

Aisling brought us together again. At least for a while. Then our love for the same woman destroyed us both in different ways. And the proof of our love ended her.

"Brother." His raspy tone twirled me around, spinning my head. Only twelve yards away, slightly shrouded, my twin stood, his green eyes glowing through the haze.

"Gods." My muscles could no longer hold me up, bashing my knees painfully into the cobbled road. Fear dripped into my veins. "I am going crazy, aren't I?" My lungs grasped for bits of air, fluttering in and out without seizing anything substantial.

His mouth parted into an odd smile. The sensation of seeing my mirror image again was comfortable and strange. It had been so long.

"Yes," he responded, a glint in his eyes. "You can't run from it. From yourself." Then he stepped back into the mist, letting it consume him.

"Devlin!"

Aisling's laugh filled the air, my brother's following right after.

I leaned over my knees and clasped my hands over my ears, the ring of their voices banging around my head.

Long after the hallucinations disappeared, I stayed crumpled up on the ground. The fog coiled around me like ghosts. Phantoms of my past wrongs had come back for me.

Chapter Nineteen

Fionna

Even before I opened my eyes every muscle in my body screamed in agony, dragging me out of my slumber. Stiff and locked in the fetal formation when I fell asleep, I tried to stretch my legs, but spasms cramped down my calves. I groaned into my pillow, rubbing furiously at the back of my legs.

Awareness crept over me similar to an afternoon shadow...a feeling I was not alone in the room.

My reaction was instantaneous, cursing myself for being so careless and not putting a weapon within reach. I normally never slept without a gun under my pillow and a knife in my boot next to my bed.

My back struck the wall as I scrambled into a seated position, ready to respond to an attack. Nothing rushed for me, but adrenaline discharged through my veins, spreading trepidation like a virus.

In the early dawn light, glowing yellow-green eyes stared at me from the chair in the corner.

Anger. Disgust. Ruthlessness.

As if my tongue could taste every emotion coming off him, I pressed farther into the wall, dragging the sheet up to cover my body. I preferred sleeping naked, but in the years since I had become the leader of the DLR, I learned to sleep with clothes, ready to jump up and go in a moment's notice. Last night, I had forgone every rule I had instilled in myself over the years, and now I was going to pay the price for my carelessness.

Lars's hair was wet and sleek, his dark jeans and black jumper brand new. Even in jeans, his power was suffocating. He was a king in denim as he was when wearing suits. But I did notice darker circles under his eyes, as though he hadn't slept in weeks.

We watched each other for a moment. He was stone. Whatever influence the ceremony put on us last night was gone. Long gone.

"How long have you been there?" I addressed him, my hand clamping on the sheet tighter. Instinct was telling me to be on alert. Prepared to act.

He didn't move or even blink.

"You know, it's really creepy watching a girl sleep. Not sexy at all," I said dryly.

Nothing.

"Are you the kind who isn't talkative in the morning?" I wiggled up higher on the bed. "Need coffee before you can function? I get it."

"Shut up," he said so low it rumbled the air. Before I could respond, he pushed out of the chair, his body moving like a predator. "As my prisoner, you speak when I tell you, you eat when I tell you, and you breathe when I tell you."

Tilting my head to the side, my eyebrows curved up, and sucked in air with a theatrical performance. "Oops." I drew in again. "Dammit! Keeps happening."

Invisible hands wrapped around my throat dragging my frame up the wall, as if I were possessed. Air ripped from my airways, but my Druid was fast to step in. Words flung across the room, slamming into the demon.

Lars stumbled back, crashed into the chair, and fell to the floor. I dropped to the bed with force. Barely hitting it, I rolled off the bed to the opposite side as him. It would do nothing to stop him, but it seemed better than to sit down next to him.

A growl erupted from him as he got his feet underneath him. His skin was bleached white. The spell exited my lips in a rush. A bellowed cry came from the demon while his hands clamped around his head in pain.

When he lifted his head, blood dripped from his nose and blackness filled his eyeballs, as he fought against my hex squeezing his brain.

Magic drilled into me like a laser beam, picking me up off the floor, hurtling me across the room. My bones crunched as they hit the far wall, falling to the ground on my right shoulder with a painful crack.

Lars snarled, his cuspids pointy and slightly longer than the rest of his teeth. I had no idea they did that. *Shite*. The demon could also rip into me with his teeth.

Biting my lip against the sharp pain in my shoulder,

I scrambled to my feet, feeling blood trickle down the side of my face from where my head hit the floor.

"We can keep doing this." I cupped my right elbow in my hand, pulling into my chest, my naked body defensive. "Until one of us kills the other."

"You think you can kill me?" the demon sneered.

"Maybe not kill," I sneered back. "But you're not as untouchable as you'd like to believe."

His nose flared.

"Don't mess with me, *demon*. I can go toe to toe with you." It was not a threat but a fact. "It's probably why you let my people get slaughtered. Deep down you don't like the idea another race can actually challenge you."

Lars took a step, his magic pushing me into the wall.

"You need me." I locked on his black pupils. "I *don't* need you."

His boots nicked my bare toes, physically shrouding me in his shadow. "You want to see your daughter again?"

My chin tipped higher to look into his eyes. "That doesn't make me need you," I replied coolly. "It just means you're a sick asshole who will use my daughter to get me to act." My lip lifted. "Typical demon."

"Typical?" He snorted, inclining farther over me.

"Yeah. Standard mainstream demon stuff. Really, for a king I expected more."

"Be careful," he rumbled.

"You too," I challenged, staring at my reflection in his eyes. Naked and clearly physically smaller, I pushed back. He would never make me cower. In magic, I was his equal. And I would never bow to him.

Seconds ticked by. Ignoring the drying blood crusted at his nostril, he breathed in and out, both of us at a standoff.

A ringing flared up from his pocket, like an ice pick to the ears. Lars turned his head to the side wall, breaking his gaze. He shook his head and dug the mobile out of his pocket. His complexion returned to its natural olive as he twisted for the door.

"There are new clothes for you in the bathroom. Be ready to go in ten minutes." He strode from the room, putting the phone to his ear. "Update," he said into the cell before he hit the stairs and padded down to the main floor.

I leaned into the wall, exhaling, still holding my hurt shoulder. I had to admit it had been a while since I'd been so challenged. My skill in Druid magic and the black arts had kept me separate from everyone. Not many fae or other Druids had rivaled me in any way. Lars would keep me sharp. Focused.

The hum of my healing spell warmed my arm as it shot up my shoulder and took the throbbing pain away. It still was sore, but I wiggled it out, feeling my shoulder slip back in its socket.

Lars's voice mumbled from the floor below. This morning had taught me a valuable lesson: not to be caught unprepared. I would be ready next time.

~~

Dressed, I proceeded downstairs. Lars had managed to buy me clothes that fit perfectly: extremely soft dark denim jeans similar to his, a gray tank, and a black, knitted jumper. All of extremely nice quality. At first I was slightly amused, but then I remembered the man had a lot more style than I did. I was a "black stretchy jeans or cargo pants, boots, and old black woolen jumper kind of girl." The epitome of emo style. Or lack thereof. Growing up, Olwyn tended to buy me shapeless tunics after I put my foot down on getting clothes from the Goodwill. I'd rather be teased for wearing a potato sack than something my fellow students had disposed of.

My ponytail bounced as I hit the bottom step, boots clomping the wooden floor without any grace.

"There better be coffee. I get testy without it." I swung past Lars, who sat at the table reading a paper, his leg up on his knee with such nonchalance, as though the incident of a few minutes ago never happened. The way he held himself sang distinguished, refined, and polished. Along with powerful and confident. He made me feel like such a klutz. Even my walk felt gangly and unpolished next to him. But in my eyes it just made him a priss. Did he even have a clue what it was like to fight for your basic needs? King or not, he was a pampered princess.

"Is that what you call it? Testy?" He picked up the cup in front of him, taking a sip. The smell of roasting beans tugged me to the kitchen.

"Next time come to my room with coffee then," I spouted over my shoulder as I beelined for the coffee pot on the counter. If he responded, I didn't hear him, too focused on getting the liquid into the largest cup I could find.

Despite steam warning me the coffee was hot, I slugged some down like a shot. My tongue sizzled as scalding fire dropped down my throat to my stomach.

"Ahhhh!" I waved my hand in front of my face, as though it was going to help soothe the fire inside my mouth.

"Couldn't wait a moment to let it cool, could you?" Lars didn't even lift his eyes off the paper, while I bounced in my seat, panting similar to a dehydrated animal, poking at my scorched tongue.

I glared at him, then quickly said my healing spell before my tongue swelled more. The blistering pain diminished, causing my shoulders to lower with relief.

"Imprudent." He turned the page.

"Narcissistic." I took another sip of coffee, easing back in my chair.

I could have sworn I saw his lips twitch with a hint of a smile, but he cleared his throat, placing down the newspaper.

"I secured a helicopter to get us to Scotland."

"A helicopter? Can it even fly that far? Their tanks aren't very big."

Only Lars's eyes moved, peering at me with contempt. "This is a *special* helicopter."

"Of course it is." My gaze rolled up to the ceiling.

"We'll be leaving soon. There is some breakfast in the microwave if you want it." His chair skated over the floor as he pushed it back and rose. "I have a few more phone calls to make."

I nodded, watching him exit down the stairs and out of the house.

A frazzled laugh hiccupped from my chest as I got up from my chair. We could so easily go from almost killing each other to sitting around and having coffee together, as though everything was fine. I was pretty sure he hadn't slept, but instead he had obtained us clothes and a helicopter to the UK.

Tugging the microwave door open, I barked another sharp laugh. Sitting in the middle was an Egg McMuffin. He'd already been to McDonald's this morning, and it was barely six a.m.

I took a big bite. I never turned down "free" food. Except this wasn't free. It came with a very large price tag.

Chapter Twenty

Lars

"Helicopter? Is that what you call this thing?" Fionna gaped at one of my latest inventions. It was patented from an Airbus H series that was never approved commercially. The fall of the barrier stopped most human manufacturing. Cooper and Cole "acquired" the plans for me. My engineers made a few changes to adapt to the new world, and had it ready faster than I expected. It was one of my pride and joys.

My palms slid over the sleek pointy nose of the machine, stroking it.

"Men." She rubbed her forehead with a chuckle.

"You cannot deny its beauty."

"No." She stepped up to it, running her hand over the smooth metal. "It is pretty."

The helicopter was not the normal egg shape. The front of this one resembled the head of a duck or dolphin. The choppers curved like scythes, cutting through the air with ease. The entire thing was made to race through the sky with speed and efficiency resembling a shark in the ocean or a falcon in the sky.

She peered inside the empty hangar. "Who's flying us?"

I smiled, heading for the pilot's door.

"You've got to be fucking kidding me." Normally when she cussed it sounded cute and lyrical. It was simple to forget the pint-size girl packed a mighty punch. But today it kept taking me back to the moment on the bridge, when I heard *her* again. The woman who would forever haunt me. My chest contracted, the sound of Aisling's voice cutting a fissure in my heart. As much as I wanted to absorb every nuance, it would only give credibility to the hallucinations. I could not allow that.

After the blood ceremony and situation on the bridge, I had walked through the night, trying to get myself together. As King, I could not give myself any leeway. My focus had to remain fixed on the cauldron. The rest I could file away. I could easily put Ms. Cathbad back in her box by the time I returned to the flat. Whatever magic had twisted my disgust into hunger for her, evolved into anger. She was my prisoner. A Druid. An instrument to use to get what I wanted. This morning I intended to put her in her place again.

Slipping into the pilot's seat, I settled in, preparing the helicopter for takeoff. The rotors began to whirl in the air, sweeping Fionna's loose locks around her face. I couldn't help but chuckle, watching her bat and wrangle her strands away from her face. She reached for the door, trying to pull it open.

"Oh. Did I forget to unlock the door?" I yelled innocently toward the window. Her lids narrowed and her mouth tightened, but I could only glimpse her glare for a moment before her hair tried to strangle her again.

"*Lars*," she huffed, wrapping her mop in a bun.

"So tempting." I slipped on my headset, the microphone curving around my mouth.

"I will gladly part ways," she yelled back. "See how well you do finding your dear treasure without me." She twisted to walk away.

I unlocked the door. A haughty smile enveloped her mouth when she turned back around and climbed into the cockpit next to me.

"I think someone needs more coffee." She latched her buckle. "Bit snarky today."

"You seem to bring it out in me, Druid." I handed her a headset.

"Same, demon." She pushed it onto her head, the earmuffs slipping past her ears, making me laugh.

"Here." I reached over. "Lean over."

Her body moved close, and she tilted her head to me so I could adjust them to fit her. I brushed her hair off her face, saving a few strands from getting tangled in the set.

"There," I said, my fingers still wrapped in her receiver. Her brown eyes raked over me from under her lashes.

"Wouldn't it have been easier to take them off and do that?" Her voice came loudly through my earpiece.

I dropped my hands away, facing front. "They fit you exact this way."

Clutching the cyclic and collective sticks and pressing my foot pedals, the helicopter began to lift off the launch pad.

"Holy shite!" Fionna grabbed her seat, excitement beaming on her face.

"Never been in a helicopter?"

She rolled her eyes. "Yeah, sure, I call for one whenever I feel like grabbing some caviar in Paris or shopping in Milan."

I chuckled, wagging my head back and forth.

The helicopter lifted past the building. The sun was breaking over the horizon, streaking the town in buttery yellows, vibrant oranges, and tints of blue.

"Wow." Fionna leaned forward, taking in the view. "Amazing."

"Yeah." I agreed. "I actually don't get to fly as much as I'd like. Mornings like this put everything in perspective."

She glanced over at me with a strange expression clouding her features.

"What?"

"Nothing." She shook her head. "You surprise me sometimes."

I lifted my eyebrows.

"Don't worry, it's not a compliment." She waved her hand, trying to hold back a grin. "I didn't say the surprises were good."

I pointed the helicopter in the desired direction. *Right back at you, Druid. Right fuckin' back at you.*

~~

As we landed, rain dyed the old stone buildings in Edinburgh almost black, giving the city a macabre, enigmatic feel. It felt alive like one of our old fae books where secrets hid behind every door. All you had to do was give yourself over to its thrall and it revealed those secrets. Some you wished you never learned: tragedy, death, torture, schemes, lies, affairs, murder. The best soap opera in the world could never compare to the tales contained in this city. Magic ran thick here, and the façade vibrated with the mysterious stories it held beneath the surface.

However, the city that drew tourists was not the original. That was below, where the seedy dwellings of brothels, the poor or sick, and illegal activities operated until they were closed up. The truth hid below the respectable streets, shops, and homes above.

My brother and I had lived here for many years when we were young men, and those tunnels and seedy ventures had been our lifeblood. Back then, life was good. I missed those simple times.

"You okay leaving your baby there? What if someone scratches it? Or...horror...rubs it the wrong way with a nappy?" Fionna gasped, covering her mouth in false dismay.

"It is in the best of care." Not taking the bait, I flipped through documents my secretary—dammit, what was her name—sent me. I could not neglect my duties at home because I was half a world away.

With Ms. Johnson still vulnerable as Seelie Queen, I had to be diligent in making sure everything was running like clockwork.

"Is that why I had to drag you away, crying and screaming like a toddler?"

I will admit I may have stroked the helicopter several times and tripled-checked the men watching it would take proper care of it. My private hangar in Edinburgh was top notch, but the airbus was brand new and one of kind.

"I'm going to find you slipping out at night to secretly visit it, aren't I?" She turned to stare out the window of the town car as the city rolled past on our way to the hotel.

We'd only be in Edinburgh one night before we'd journey out to the Highlands. A night to get supplies and force her to give me more evidence on where the cauldron was located.

I did not trust she divulged everything to me. The more I learned about her, the more I understood she was a contender in this fae world. Fae never gave over more information than absolutely necessary. It existed in our blood to hide truths and barter in information.

"Probably," I replied absently, skimming the last page of a contract.

She snorted, shifting in her seat. "Are we going to one of your fancy places again?"

"No, I had, uh…" I teetered off, rolling my lips in frustration. "My secretary rented us a private flat near the Royal Mile. One I use when I come here."

"You don't know her name? Do you?" She drew my attention up to her face, her eyebrows curved in amusement. "That's awful."

"I've had many come and go in the last few months," I growled. "It's hard to keep track."

"Sofia." Fionna tucked her hair behind one ear, her head waggling.

"Who's Sofia?"

"*Your* secretary."

I blinked. "How did you know her name?"

"Because I listen and pay attention." She crossed her legs, sinking deeper into the soft leather seats.

"Well, I've had a lot on my mind," I grumbled, turning back to my documents. It was a poor excuse. I used to recall the tiniest of details as though I was Sherlock Holmes. You never knew what was important and what could be used down the road.

My hand traveled up to my forehead and rubbed it roughly. Another sign I had been slipping. Rez's departure could no longer excuse my lack of organization or rush to fill her spot.

The driver, Thomas, pulled the car up to the front of an old limestone row of buildings, a mix of medieval, neoclassic, and English Gothic architecture. Alleyways, called closes, connected to Princes Street and the new part of the city like a labyrinth.

The driver opened my door, and I slid out. "Thank you." I placed my files in his open hands. "Get these back to Sofia."

"Yes, sir." He bowed and shut my door. I turned around to watch Fionna round the back end of the car.

"Wow, opening your door was so tough. I can see why you have other people do it for you." She wiped at her brow.

I pinched my mouth together and gave Thomas a nod. "We won't be needing you again. Thank you."

He bowed, returning to the driver's seat. My palm pressed into the Druid's spine and pushed her down one of the many closes in Edinburgh. She stepped away, glaring at my hand. No, it wasn't my hand but my control over her she was sneering at. "It does not matter if I'm capable of opening my own door or not. Believe me, I feel it is a waste of time. However, I am King. Some things change when you are a royal, especially in public. There are many traditions I'd prefer not to do, but I must."

We walked quietly down the path, reaching the private door. Before I even could grasp for the handle, a familiar plump, fair-haired woman opened the door, curtsying. "Majesty, let me say what an honor it is to have you back."

"Thank you, Iona."

I had found this location years ago, and it remained the perfect situation for my business dealings. Human seers, Iona and Jacob, owned it. They were the types who knew no personal boundaries, but being the biggest busybodies had come in useful. They were faithful to me and would find out all I needed to know, and at the same time they kept my secrets. I learned to look past their overbearing natures and actually enjoy their warmth and energy.

Iona stepped back for us to enter, waving us to enter quickly.

"This is Ms. Cathbad." I clicked my head at Fionna, my hand returning to her lower back leading her in. A subtle hint at who was dominant. Angering her only was a bonus.

Iona's eyes darted to my face then widened, a blush coming over her ivory skin. She clasped a hand over her mouth. "Oh, Majesty, I am so happy for you. We had heard you were recently single, and I told Jacob that just wouldn't do for our King. He's far too handsome and kind to be alone."

"Kind?" Fionna snorted, shooting a bemused look at me.

Iona didn't seem to notice, speeding over us like a freight train. "We were wondering when you'd bring a woman here. Oh, you two look so in love."

"No—" Both Fionna and I started, but Iona bubbled over us with excitement, snatching Fionna's hand, looking more as if she wanted to hug her. "It is such an honor to meet you. I am so pleased you are here." Her words bleated out faster than a shotgun. "Oh, this is so lovely. He's never brought anyone here before. The previous woman he dated never came. So...don't you worry; you must be *very* special." Iona patted her hand. "Gods, you are so pretty too. Tiny. Need to get some good home-cooked food in you." She pranced around, looking as if she didn't know which direction to go, pulling Fionna along with her. "Let me show you around, my dear. I wish I'd known; I would have made it more..." She knocked her shoulder into Fionna's her eyebrows going up and down. "Romantic."

"That's quite all ri—" Fionna's eyes were wide, shaking her head.

"The bathtub is definitely big enough for two." Iona wiggled her shoulders up and down.

"Oh gods." Fionna looked horrified.

"I'll be sure to get Jacob to stop by the shop and get the best champagne. Or do you like Scottish whisky as our King does?"

"Uh—"

"I'll have him get both." Iona swished her hand, leading Fionna up the stairs to the main floor. The Druid looked over her shoulder at me, mouthing *what the hell?* I rubbed my mouth to stop from laughing at her stunned expression. She had been hit by Tornado Iona.

I shrugged, enjoying watching her squirm, and followed them up to the main floor. This three-story flat was a unique mix of extremely old medieval— conveying a feeling as though you were part of the underground world below with cobblestone walls and rounded ceilings—to extremely modern. Sliding barn-style doors and rich dark fabrics and textures decorated the bedroom with a gorgeous chandelier hanging over the bed.

It looked sexy. Sultry. An ideal place to bring your lover for a weekend escape. You would never have to leave the bedroom. But that was not why I chose this place each time. My enjoyment of this flat was a lot seedier.

"It's beautiful." I heard Fionna say when I reached the top. The steep spire of the scorched Scott Monument was visible through the windows, displaying a stunning view of the new town below. On a clear day, you could also see Carlton Hill, but the thick fog hugged close to the earth now. I knew from the bedroom above you could see the castle, High Street, and parts of Princes Street Gardens.

I probably should come back here someday for an actual holiday. Vacation. A word I no longer understood. I had never been good at relaxing. But lately I couldn't deny I felt tired, and I wanted to slow down for a moment.

Fionna finally reclaimed her hand, but Iona was far from letting her go. From experience, the only way to get Iona to leave was to suggest I needed to "get to my duties" and still it would take her fifteen minutes to actually go.

Watching Fionna twitch like she wanted to bolt down the stairs away from this woman, I decided to kill two birds with one stone. Annoy the Druid and get Iona to leave.

"I'm so glad you like it, FeFe." I grinned mischievously at the tiny brunette, taking her hand in mine and kissing the scars on her wrists, knowing the intimacy of these marks would rattle her. "You know there's nothing I wouldn't do for your happiness."

She stared up at me, unmoving for a moment, her muscles rigid as though she had been stunned.

"Aww." Iona clapped her hands together, watching us dreamily.

Slowly, the corners of Fionna's lids tapered, her pert nose flaring. I thought she was about to punch me in the face, when her body relaxed, her lashes fluttering. But her grip on my hand crunched down.

"You are so *good* to me." Sarcasm laced delicately through her words. "Sometimes this doesn't seem real.

As though someone dropped me in a boiling hot *cauldron...*"

I should have known the Druid would come out to play.

Iona's forehead wrinkled in confusion.

"I know, it's as if we're drowning in love, right, FeFe?"

Her fingers dug into my skin painfully. The girl was strong.

"Drowning." She laughed emptily. "That sounds amazing right now."

I brought Fionna's hand back up to my lips, looking like I was kissing it again, and instead I bit the tender spot between her thumb and index finger.

She yipped but covered it over with a cough, yanking her hand away from my hold.

"As you can see, Iona, we're madly in love and looking forward to some *alone* time." I gave the older woman a wink.

"Oh, oh!" She put up her hands. "Majesty, don't say another word. I am gone." She pointed her feet for the stairs. "It may have been a while, but I remember what it's like to be young and in love. You can't get enough of each other."

"Exactly." I turned to watch my old acquaintance flutter about resembling a drunken bee, heading for the exit down.

"You know how to contact me if you need anything. Jacob will drop the whisky and food off later." She hovered by the steps.

"That won't be necessary. We'll probably be *indisposed*."

Iona's cheeks reddened, her hand going to her mouth again. "Right! Of course. Well, you two enjoy. Oh, this is such great news. I am so happy for you, Majesty. And you, Ms. Cathbad. Congratulations to you both."

"Yeah, I'm so happy I could die." Fionna walked the line between snarky and sweet.

"Thank you, Iona. To both you and Jacob." I took a step, trying to encourage her to leave.

"Of course, my liege. We love when you visit." She took one last look around. "Well, okay." Iona waved and took a step down. "Bye."

Neither Fionna nor I moved until we heard the door shut, the tension filling the space between us like curdled cream.

Thud. The old door clicked closed.

Already sensing what was coming, I whipped around, grabbing for the fist directed at my face. Anger burst over her features like fireworks, a low growl rumbling in her throat.

"Now, now, honey. Is that the way you say thank you?"

"Thank you?" Her gaze burned with fire. "How about I show you how *thankful* I am."

"Sounds fun, but maybe later, *FeFe*," I replied evenly, shoving her hand away from me. With speed I wasn't expecting, her other fist smashed into my gut. It didn't hurt, but it knocked me a few steps away.

"If you *ever* call me FeFe again, you are going to find the new way of getting a colonoscopy."

My false demeanor dropped away, my jaw clipping together.

"And if you..." I stepped up, looming over her. "Ever attack me again, you're going to find your lips sewn together and your body in chains."

"Can't take a real fight, huh? With someone who can actually challenge you?" She dared my step with her own, aligning our bodies. "Too intimidating for the handsome, *kind* King?"

"Nothing about me is kind," I snarled, getting close to her face.

She put her hands on her hips, confidence beaming from her steady gaze. "Me neither."

Chapter Twenty-One

Fionna

His energy radiated in waves off him, thumping into me. We held our ground, ready for the other to attack or back down.

We might be here a while.

His eyes slid over me; his jaw twitched as though it were doing jumping jacks. Heat from his close proximity shrouded me, his body intruding in my personal space.

He will not intimidate me.

"No. There is *nothing* gentle about you," he rumbled. My bones felt the vibration of his voice, turning up the temperature inside. He was the perfect representation of the devil, so tempting and delicious on the outside, making you want to sin over and over again, only to find he consumed your soul along the way and left you burning in flames alone.

I was no fool. Handsome men were nothing but trouble.

But when he leaned closer, I found my lungs halting in my chest. His gaze moved from my throat up to my face, the green of his eyes deepening and sparking. Lars went still, and his muscles locked down his neck and his shoulders, his eyes drifting over my shoulder. The temperature in the room seemed to drop, causing my heart to skip in my chest.

"Wh-what?" I turned my head to follow his eyeline. He didn't move or speak. Tension crackled from him to me, itching my nerves and spitting adrenaline into my veins. I broke away from him and glanced over my shoulder out the window.

A stirring at a window of the building over from ours pulled my focus. All I saw was the movement of the curtains, the room too dark to see anything else inside.

"What's wron—?" I turned back around to face him and stopped speaking immediately. The spot in front of me was empty. Lars was already at the stairs, moving soundlessly down to the first level.

"Lars?" I yelled after him, taking after him, stumbling down the steps. "What's going on?"

He didn't react as he reached the small ground-floor landing. He turned to the coatroom next to the front door, flinging it open.

"What the shite?" I muttered more to myself as I hit the bottom, racing over. The tiny space was filled with brooms, blankets, and brollies for guests to use. Lars shoved the stuff to the side, delving deeper into the cubbyhole. I came up to the door, placing my hands on the frame, watching him. Lars jostled all the way to the back, his hand pushing at a section of the wall.

"What are you do—?"

With a hiss of air, the entire back wall swung open, blowing old, stale oxygen over my face. A wall sconce flickered on as a door swished open, lighting a limestone stairway behind the door with a shadowy gloom. It circled around in a spiral, leading below the ground level.

"Holy shite."

Lars traveled quickly, his boots moving down the curved staircase with determination and speed.

"Lars!" I called after him, stopping at the entrance of the hidden door. The hesitation to stay or go lasted only an instant; I was never the girl to stay back. My feet hustled down the rutted stone steps, trying to catch up, the air shifting to a cool, even temperature with every turn I took. A musty, decaying smell wafted up my nose, making it itch. Strategically placed motion lights flicked on as Lars got near, only illuminating the area a couple meters before us.

Lower and lower we ventured under the earth, my stomach bouncing with fear of the unknown, and even of him. Lars moved low and determined, as though he had been programmed with one purpose: to pursue and kill. My mouth stayed pinned shut, sensing the savage demon skimming the surface. I couldn't even tell if he knew I was with him or if he noticed anything but stalking toward his goal.

Finally we hit the bottom of the steps leading into a low-ceiling tunnel drenched in a sharp sour odor. Fire bulb lights along the walls cast an eerie glow on the underground labyrinth, showing life down here was still active. Edinburgh's past underground world was well known among tourists. Many tour companies raked in money leading people through a small part of the seedy world that existed once under the city.

People thought this world had died away long ago. It hadn't. Not in the parts the tourists didn't venture to. And seeing the familiarity with which Lars progressed through, I had no doubt he was or had been a part of it.

Lars stopped abruptly, my frame almost smashing into the back of him. He tilted his head, his shoulders rolling forward as he inhaled sharply through his nose. His movements were slow, jolting, and inhuman, unsettling me even more. His actions were similar to a beast, but he resembled no animal I knew. Shape-shifters had animal-like qualities, but as scary as they were, there still was something familiar, something you could recognize. Nothing about Lars had that kind of comfort. He might growl, snarl, and hunt, but he was nothing like anything I'd ever come across.

A chill shook my bones and dimpled my flesh, as he silently crept forward, becoming one with the shadows. A low growl rumbled from his throat, spiking my heart into overdrive, which thumped loudly in my ears.

"No. Not this time." His lips parted and he hissed. In an instant he was gone, slipping around the corner and down the tunnel before I could even blink.

"Lars!" I took off after him, following a reflex to stay near him. It felt safer with the demon I knew than whatever else could be down here. My short legs stretched, trying to catch up, following the passageway. The lights flickered and dimmed, tricking my eyes at every turn. Curving and veering down another path, I sprinted, holding his name on the tip of my tongue. The desire to call out for him was strong, but not as powerful as my self-preservation. No telling what was down here, what was stalking the underground.

Fear pumped my heart, pushing my legs faster. I had no reason to be afraid. I was no victim, but warning bells nipped at the back of my neck. And though I hadn't seen anything yet, I had no doubt we were not alone here.

My adrenaline flickered, bringing me to a stop, the path twisting and sprouting off in so many ways I had no idea where to go or where I came from. "Dammit," I scolded myself, knowing I should have stayed and waited for him to return. I wasn't even sure what made me run, except his agitation inflicted me with the need to flee. To be with him.

I bent over my knees, sucking in breath.

A tortured howl tore down the tunnel, freezing my blood, catching air in my throat. I jerked my head right and left, not sure where it came from. I hoped I could find the way back to the flat. This place seemed to be out to confuse and displace you, as though it were a giant oubliette.

The sound of heavy boots striking the path reverberated, spinning my attention around again. *Thud. Thud.* My heart slammed against my ribs.

"Lars?" I whispered, his name no longer wanting to stay in my mouth.

Silence. The tap of water was the only noise. Drops of draining water above hit the stone ground, echoing down the hollow channel. I turned back the way I came, creeping to one of the junctions, peering around the corner, my body tense and ready to spit out a spell at a moment's notice.

Nothing.

I prodded my way a little farther, hoping I was going the same way I came. Slinking down the dark corridor, I stayed close to the wall, keeping an eye on both ends of the tunnel. When I reached another Y-junction, a tremor stopped me in my tracks, shoving my heart up in my throat.

A gut-wrenching wail slashed through the underground like a branding knife, quivering the walls with its agony, bending my knees toward the ground. I reached for the wall, chills raging over my skin similar to a thousand bugs.

Something in my gut knew instantly.

Lars.

Panic fizzed up my throat, burning it like acid. "Lars," I muttered, my feet slamming against the ground, darting toward the source of the pain.

I rounded a corner, recognizing the tight tunnel as the one near the door to our flat. A dark mass lumped on the ground, rocking back and forth.

Shite.

"Lars?" I inquired apprehensively, inching up to the figure. The closer I got, the better I saw the man on the old cobble brick. "Lars!" Was he hurt? Something was obviously wrong with him, twisting my stomach in a knot. I ran to him, dropping to my knees at his side, my hands grabbing his face, turning it to me. I sucked in a hiss through my teeth; his eyes were wild and filled with terror and anguish.

My stomach bounced into my throat, my heart batting against my ribs with utter fear. To see Lars terrified was like the biggest security blanket being ripped from you. You always knew you were safe with him. If he was ever scared or sad, he kept it locked deep inside. The King was not allowed to show anything but strength.

"Lars?"

At my voice, he started batting my hands away, his body squirming away.

"Get away from me. You're not real. Stop torturing me."

"What?"

He scrambled to his feet, breathing heavily, his hair tousled, his clothes skewed. His knuckles were cut up and bleeding.

"Let me heal you." I reached out.

"DON'T!" he bellowed, backing away from me until his back slammed into the wall. He bent over, moaning as though his heart was breaking apart. "Please don't touch me," he whispered. "You'll make it real. And I won't be strong enough to fight."

I stood up, moving as if I were locked in a cage with a tiger. "Strong enough to fight what?"

"You," he whimpered. "Do you know how much I want you in my arms again? To choose you this time? I made a huge mistake. I should have picked you." Pain burrowed deep across his forehead, agony etched in his features.

My throat curled in on itself like a terrified animal. Witnessing him heartbroken, vulnerable, scared, and confused reflected the same emotions in myself.

"I loved you so much. I am so sorry. I'm sorry I wasn't the man you wanted to raise our daughter."

Whoa.

You always learned everything you could about your enemy. I knew most of the rumors about him and the dae. I thought Ember was supposed to be his niece, not his daughter. Did they do that to keep her better protected? The daughter of a king would be a lot more valuable to his enemies.

We both had kept our children secret to protect them.

"It would be so easy to let you take me. Forgo everything I've worked for...to finally live in peace with you. Even if it's in my head." He rubbed his palm furiously on his forehead, messing up his hair even more. The impeccable image of the King was lost behind the feral man before me.

"Hey." I eased up to him, taking his hand in mine to stop him. He let out a heart-wrenching cry, his fingers gripping down on me, crushing my bones painfully.

"Ash," he whispered so quietly I barely heard him. With a tug, he drew me into him, his hands sliding up my cheeks, cupping my face. My body froze, oxygen evaporating as he pulled me to him, his lips brushing mine.

Fuck. Shite.

"Lars." I curled my fingers over his, trying to step back, but his grip was firm and wouldn't allow me to budge a centimeter. His nose brushed up against mine; his breath slid down my throat, between my breasts, clouding my mind as my body responded to his touch.

He tipped forward, his mouth barely sweeping over mine. Something deep inside told me if I let him really kiss me it was game over. I wouldn't be able to stop anything after that. And this was wrong. We were wrong.

"Demon." I yanked out of his grip, shoving him into the wall with a thud. "Snap out of it."

His gaze jolted to me, his lids blinking rapidly.

I watched as reality swooshed back in, sharpening his gaze on me until his eyes tapered in a glower. The muscles along his jaw rolled. We watched each other in a tense silence for a few beats. Then he shoved off the wall, knocking me to the side as he strode past me, heading for the entrance. He ripped open the door, stomping up the stairs, leaving me gaping after him.

What the fuck just happened?

~~

I stood in the rancid-smelling tunnel for a full minute, trying to restore gravity to my body. Off-kilter, my head and stomach were swirling as though someone flushed a toilet in my brain.

Every nerve danced under my skin. The actual fabric of my clothes against my skin elicited electric shocks through my body. It itched, needing to be soothed by someone's touch.

His.

I ground my teeth together in disgust, anger firing up my back like sparks, wiping the thought away as fast as it came.

A lack of sex was splitting my brain and body into two directions. One still hated fae, the other clearly wasn't so picky. It angered me beyond belief he triggered something in me no one else had. It made me want to crawl out of my own skin and leave it behind.

Like the King, I could not afford to display any weakness. Not around anyone and especially not around him. My fists balled up in fury at him for causing these feelings in me. I despised him. He was more than my enemy; he was holding my daughter as leverage.

"Fuck you, arsehole," I grumbled, marching for the staircase. My legs bounded up the stairs, each step solidifying my resentment. Tearing through the closet, I slammed the secret passage door and pounded up the rest of the stairs to the main level.

My feet stopped short, air clipping in my mouth. Lars stood with his back to me, his hands on the dining room table, his head dropped forward. His back was rigid, his shoulders up to his ears.

"What the hell was that?" I folded my arms, leaning my weight to one leg.

A muscle popped in his back, but otherwise he didn't respond.

"Ignoring me?"

"Go away," he growled, punctuating the tension expanding in the room.

"No."

"I am *not kidding*, Ms. Cathbad." His fingers dug into the table. "Walk. Away. Now."

"I'm quite aware you have no sense of humor," I quipped. "But I'm not moving."

A noise vibrated from him, pricking the hairs on the back of my neck. My nails dug into my flesh.

"Growl, bite, tear the room to shreds. I don't care. But you are going to deal with me."

"DAMMIT, DRUID!" He swung around with a roar, shaking the chandelier above the table. His olive skin bleached to a translucent color, displaying the veins and bones under his skin. His eyes plunged into blackness. "You want to die?" His body curled forward, his steps eating up the room as he stalked toward me.

My rational side was telling me to run, to hide in the corner and hope the end came fast. My heels only dug farther into the wood floor, my legs locking as he barreled up to me.

"Do you want to die, Druid?" He sneered, his cusped teeth growing out resembling daggers.

I stared up at him, defying his threatening appearance, keeping my expression neutral. "Try it. We'll see how far you get."

His nostrils flared. "Do not challenge me. Not much is keeping you alive as it is."

"Bring it, tough guy. Let's see what you got." I was sure not too many people, if any, had ever challenged him and been able to match his magic. I was not his inferior.

I stepped closer, my folded arms shoving into his chest.

"You're angry at me because I saw there is an actual person under this façade. Is that it?"

His lips thinned, straining against his teeth.

"You want to hurt me because I saw you vulnerable for once?"

"Shut up."

"Who did you think I was? Who have you been seeing?" I pushed into him. "Something is torturing you."

"I said shut up."

"I don't take orders. Especially from you."

"I. Am. A. Fucking. King." His chest bumped into me, almost knocking me over.

"And. I. Am. A. Fucking. Druid." I rammed my hands into his chest, shoving him back with extra force. He hit the table, knocking over two chairs.

His black pupils became bottomless, a spark crackling along the rims. It was a heartbeat, a tick of the clock, when we both reacted.

Magic spilled into the room, as though a hole in the dam finally splintered, gushing in torrential waves. The force of my words and his power ran into each other like two rugby players crashing against each other, shoving us both back off our feet.

My spine throbbed as I slammed into the wall and landed hard on my arse on the wood floor. I was trained to respond instantly, giving the fae no time to attack or muzzle me.

My spell shot across to where Lars was getting on his feet. He sailed back again; the table and his body crashed into the wall with a splintering snap.

My mouth opened to speak when I felt an invisible hand lock around my throat, stealing my words. Pressure entered my head, forcing a sharp cry from me. My knees buckled, and I dropped to the ground.

Panic was a hard thing to control. It was instinctual. It had taken many years to teach myself to overcome it. I dug deep inside, the black magic jumping up and down like an eager puppy wanting to be taken off its leash.

Words grew sharp and strong in my head, magic flowing up. I was the only one I knew who could use black magic without actually speaking. My years living with Olwyn, being outcast and alone, had prepared me for the war I knew was ahead. I was brutal in my own lessons, knowing my challengers would come at me with the force of the earth.

I would come back with the power of my people.

With a snap, the hold on my throat and mind broke away, my lungs drawing in gulps of air. Before I could do anything, energy rammed into me, kicking me like a football into the kitchen, cupboards stopping my momentum, my face whacking painfully into the wood. Blood spurted from my nose, my bottom lip slicing against the hinge.

"You had enough, Druid?" The demon prowled over to me. His cheekbones poked out of his skin, his body filled the room, taking over every molecule. Healing gashes and dried blood covered his face.

I wiped the fresh blood from my lip, smiling as I rose to my feet. "Not even close." Damn, I couldn't deny it; this made me feel alive. Who needed sex? This had me burning with life and euphoria.

Lars's mouth twisted into what could be called a grin. "Good."

Our magic met in the middle again, butting heads similar to rams, tossing us like rag dolls. Furniture fractured as we pitched each other over the room. We were just batting each other around, testing each other's power.

My bruised body shook with adrenaline, firing up dormant nerves. My clothes chafed against my skin, which wanted to be free.

The demon crackled with energy. This was the true man. He played a refined king but was nothing more than a monster underneath. He forced it to hide in seclusion.

"You like this." I gasped for air, brushing back the loose hair coming from my ponytail. Most of it was stuck to the drying blood. "Look at you. You can't deny it. You get off on me kicking your ass."

"Kicking *my* ass?" he rumbled, the vibration shooting between my legs. He tipped his weight from leg to leg, ready to strike.

"Yeah. When was the last time someone really equaled you? Actually challenged the demon? Stretched those muscles?"

"You think you are challenging me?" he quipped but couldn't hide his chest going up and down in heavy drawls.

"I know I am." My eyebrows curved up.

"You haven't even gotten close to the demon." The side of his lip went up in a smug grin, moving closer to me.

I darted to the side, expecting his magic to head for where I was standing. Instead he leaped for me, his arms encircling me, his body crashing into mine, taking me backward over the sofa. The couch rolled with us. My back and head slapped the floor as I hit, knocking the air out of my lungs. His body fell on top of mine, engulfing me.

We both lay there, our breaths the only sounds in the silence. He peered down at me, my reflection visible in his black pupils. Seeing myself so clearly in his eyes rendered me still. My cheeks were flushed, blood smeared on my lips and temple. I looked hungry. Wanting. Turned on.

His mouth was so close; every part of him strained against me, stealing more air from my lungs. His body reacted to violence as mine did. From my hip to my belly button, every inch of him pressed into me. My lord, he was huge. It would be so easy. Meaningless. Two people letting off steam with extremely good hate-sex.

My lashes pressed together, the idea flaming my body painfully. *No. No. Unequivocally no.*

I lifted my lids to see him watching me; he seemed even closer than he had before. His dick twitched against me, and I couldn't stop the sharp inhale, my hips tilting up, rubbing against him.

Every muscle in Lars's body tightened as a low rumble erupted from him.

There was no denying I wanted this. I *needed* it, especially after the years of stress being leader of the DLR put on my shoulders. It would just be sex. Release. Nothing more than a fuck.

My hips moved against him again, eliciting a deeper growl from him. He pushed himself firmer into me, moving with me, the fabric creating more friction. Lust rolled through me with such force I gasped, my brain shutting down. Whatever the consequences, I didn't care. Just feeling him now, I knew it would be well worth it.

His hand moved up my side, pushing up my top. When his skin touched mine, I had to bite my lip. With a tug, he had my jumper off, tossed in the corner. We stared at each other. His skin and teeth were back to normal, but his eyes still were black, reminding me I was about to have sex with a fae.

Not just any fae. The Demon Unseelie King.

I ignored every warning telling me to stop when his hands skated up my stomach, his fingers shoving up my bra, cupping my breasts, his thumbs teasing my nipples.

Oh. Holy. Shite.

My head cranked back, shoving my chest up higher into his hands. Desire flushed my skin, and I opened my legs wider for him to settle in.

I hated him.

He hated me.

It didn't seem to matter.

He moved down, his mouth covering one of my breasts with a moist heat. His tongue flicked my nipple.

Fire.

I had to be on fire.

My body had never responded like this. With one guy I had been keen for, we were so sweaty and horny after a boxing class we barely made it to the locker rooms. But this was as though he actually was driving electricity straight into my nerves. Was it because he was fae? Or was it just Lars?

I blocked the last thought from reaching the analytical side of my brain. Not wanting to think, I shoved his chest until he was on his back, and I straddled him. Tugging his shirt over his head, I leaned down, brushing my lips against his. His hands slithered up, cupping my face.

"No," he whispered. He didn't need to say more. I knew he meant no kissing. Too personal. This was anything but that. I nodded and wiggled down, my hands working the buttons of his jeans. Foreplay was too intimate, a time to learn someone's body and responses. This was about fucking.

He swore under his breath, the need rising between us, our movements growing more frantic. He started wiggling out of his jeans as I tugged mine down.

"Hello?" A cheery man's voice emerged from downstairs. "Knock, knock."

"Shite!" I scrambled away from Lars, trying to get my bra back in place as feet began to pound up the stairs.

"Iona, told me to stop by with a few item—" A gray-haired, round-faced man peeked up from the top of the stairs, his sentence dying on his lips. His wide eyes took us in.

"Jacob." Lars was up on his feet, buttoning up his jeans, his eyes back to green.

"Oh, my liege, I am so sorry," Jacob bumbled, already turning down the stairs.

"It's all right, Jacob. Please, we both know Iona would be more than upset with you if you didn't leave that." Lars nodded toward the box in his arms.

"Oh, right." He turned back around, looking distressed. "Right." He placed the box at the foot of the stairs. "I'll just get out of your way."

Jacob's face turned a deep shade of crimson right in front of us. I quickly snatched up my jumper, tugging it fast over my head.

"Thank you, Jacob. And tell Iona we appreciate her kindness."

"Aye, aye." Jacob waved, taking a few steps down.

"And Jacob?" He stopped and looked back at Lars. "I will pay for the damage. Order whatever you want and send the bill to my secretary."

Jacob's mouth opened as though he wanted to refute the offer.

"No debate," Lars said firmly. "And I apologize for the mess and inconvenience."

A smile grew on Jacob's face. "Och, aye, I remember what it was to be young and not able to get enough of a lass." His eyes wandered the battered room. "Well, maybe not quite like this."

"Thank you, Jacob." It was Lars's way of ending a conversation.

Jacob gave a quick nod and wink toward me. "Glad to see you so happy, Majesty," he said and disappeared down the steps.

When the door shut, I let out a breath I didn't know I was holding. The mood of the room had shifted in only a few minutes. Lust and need turned cold. Anger, shame, and regret took residence inside me. Lars's aura kicked off remorse and disgust similar to a footie player. Keeping my eyes on my boots, I placed my hands on my hips. Awkward didn't even cover it. The clock in the kitchen ticked away at the unbearable silence.

"I need a fucking drink," Lars grumbled, seizing his shirt and putting it back on.

I let out a strained laugh. Drink? Feck. I needed to immerse myself in a barrel of whisky, until all memories and feelings of him against my body washed away.

Lars grabbed keys and started to head down the stairs. "You coming, Druid?" he asked from halfway down the steps.

I blinked in surprise. "Yeah." I nodded, following his trail. I was surprised he wanted to be anywhere near me, but hell if I was going to turn down a drink.

Bruised, crusted in blood, and looking as if we both had the shite kicked out of us in an alley, we headed to the local pub.

The only way to deal with what just happened?

Get shite-arse drunk.

~~

"Another?" The bartender lifted an eyebrow at us. I could feel my body teetering side to side on the barstool, trying to adjust every time the room moved on me.

"Yesss." Lars nodded buoyantly, looking like one of those bobblehead dolls. He had put on a newsboy cap and kept his head low as we sat at the bar, our backs to the room. The fae-owned pub was not something you'd find easily. The small, seedy space was warm and perfect on this drizzly, cold night. A burning fire across the room provided some of its only light. Most patrons had looked curiously at us when we first came in, probably feeling the magic coming off us, especially Lars, but they soon returned to their drinks. If we didn't mess with them, they would certainly stay away from us.

The fae bartender, James, looked back and forth between us. He got cuter and cuter with each drink. He was young with dimples and bright blue eyes. He didn't seem to recognize Lars, but I could tell by his body language and attention on us he grasped the concentrated power coming off him and understood Lars was important and powerful. "You sure?"

I wanted to say no. Not to me but to Lars. The King was not handling the magic-induced whisky as well as I was. Humans would be on their backs with only one or two. Most fae weren't far behind.

I think we were on our fifth...sixth... Hell, I'd lost count. Being Irish and living with Olwyn, I had obtained the skill to outdrink most people. Except her. Even at her advanced age, she could outlast me. We'd spent many winter nights deep in the drink. My tolerance grew so high I would make wagers at the pubs. Time and time again, some brawny man could not fathom a girl, notably one of my size, matching his intake. I frequently walked away with a lot of cash.

My lids fluttered at the memory of the woman who raised me, my heart aching at her memory. Her loss still hadn't sunk in yet. I was truly an orphan now.

The barkeep refilled my glass, the warm, brown, spicy liquor perfuming my nose.

"To Olwyn." I raised my glass in the air, my throat tight. "Death leaves a heartache no one can heal; love leaves a memory no one can steal."

I felt Lars's eyes on me as I cheered to the air and downed the glass of whisky.

Lars's glass went up in the air. I turned to look at him. His eyes were glossed with drink, unable to truly focus on me. "*Aspron páto*," he slurred. I understood enough to recognize it as a Greek toast. He tipped back his glass, and some dribbled down his chin.

"Holy shite, you're *trolleyed*," I snorted, a smile breaking over my face. Could I videotape this? The Unseelie King was pissed off his arse in front of me.

His head bobbed, a grin edging at his mouth, making him look like a naughty boy. "I don't get to do this. Ever."

"What, get shite-faced?"

Lars turned his head, his gaze landing on my face. "Be myself."

For some reason, a pitying sadness nipped at me. Most people would kill to be in his shoes, but it also came with a price. He could never relax or be off. The world, especially now, needed a formidable leader. Strong, in control, and capable. He couldn't show anything less. Fae were too scared and unsure. They needed someone to carry them through this hard time, making them feel safe. He could never doubt or stumble. Be himself. If he even knew who that was anymore.

For once when I looked at him, I saw no barriers and walls. He was just a man. Real and relaxed.

His long lashes were half-mast, his cheeks rosy, and a grin hinted on his perfect mouth. Damn, he was gorgeous. His appearance and power were daunting and impressive, but all I could think of was the feel of his skin on mine, his mouth. The need to have him kiss me.

I could fight the asshole King. But this man? The one slurring his words, laughing, and smiling? I turned away, my tongue grazing my bottom lip.

"What?" He swiveled his chair to me, leaning in. "What is that look?"

"What look?" I cleared my throat, tipping my empty glass at the bartender.

"That." He leaned in closer, and his hand grabbed the bar to keep him from falling all the way over, his presence running over me like a lorry. He reached up touching the creases between my eyebrows. "What went through your head right now?"

"Nothing." I pulled away from his touch and tapped my cup on the polished wood to get James's attention. I could flirt with the barkeep, use him. He was cute and safe. Fae, yes, but he felt almost human compared to the man next to me.

"Liar." Lars leaned in closer, his breath brushing my cheek.

My chest clenched at his nearness. The liquor lowered my defenses. Whatever we started earlier was slinking back around us, but this time it didn't stem from violence. It was pure lust, and I had to defuse it.

"I was just thinking what an annoying wanker you are. Poor rich boy who can't find a room in his mansion where he can just be himself."

Lars's lips thinned, his brows wrinkling. His head bobbed as he scooted back away from me, letting me breathe. "You think money and being raised as a royal prince made my life easy?"

"Easier than most."

"True." He swirled the tiny bit left in his cup. "It also rendered it more difficult. Nothing was simple about my life. Ever. I was not given unconditional love or respect from my parents. It never came free. I had to earn it. And the bar was ever changing, rising, never achievable."

His Adam's apple dipped as he swallowed heavily. "I do not feel badly for myself. I never went without food or clothing. I slept in a comfy bed, not an attic with leaks." He tilted his head to me. I sucked in a gulp of air, his words nudging past my walls. He took a sip. "Like you, Ms. Cathbad, I find out all about my enemy as well."

"I am not ashamed." My chin clicked up.

"And neither am I," he volleyed back. "I may have had money, but you had love."

"I didn't think demons cared about such weaknesses." I gripped my glass, rolling back my shoulders.

"Do you say that because you believe fae are not capable of love? Would it make us too 'human' for you?" He shifted, turning to face me. "Or do you not want to think of *me* as able to love?"

Heat blazed across my cheeks. The Dark Demon King talking about love? No. I couldn't even entertain that idea. I stirred in my seat, feeling pinned beneath his gaze.

"Yes." I peered down the bar, willing James to be done with his other customers and save me.

"Yes to which one?"

"To both." I cleared my throat, looking at him. "It was how I could understand your cruelty to others, to anyone or anything less in your eyes. How you could let my people be slaughtered."

"Thinking of you unable to love was also how you could rationalize your own actions. How *you* could *slaughter* hundreds of fae. If we had no families, no soul or love, it wouldn't matter."

"I was just following your lead."

"Except I didn't harm your people." He slammed back the rest of his drink. "But I won't defend myself. I let it happen. I apologize for my part."

My glass fell from my hand, dropping on the bar with a clatter. People turned to look at us, but I didn't care. "I'm sorry, did I hear you right? Did you just apologize and admit you were wrong?"

He smirked, turning my glass upright. "As much as I despise it, a good leader is willing to admit when they are mistaken. But I do not dwell on the past. It is done. We move forward."

That wasn't so easy for me. I actually was a bit envious of his outlook. The past constantly rode my shoulders, consuming my life with the need for revenge. To honor my parents. Could I ever find peace if I didn't? I never thought what I'd do if that day ever came. My life's ambition was to avenge the Druids. I had nothing besides my anger and hate. But now, sitting next to one of the enemies I had contrived to destroy once, everything felt unstable and unsure. I didn't like either sensation.

"I thought we came here to forget all this shite?" I shook my shoulders, trying to release the dark mood tensing my back.

"Yes, we did." Lars smiled, giving me a nod, tipping up his glass to the barkeep. "I think we need another then." The movement made him sway, and he slipped off his stool into me.

"Whoa there. I think you've had enough." I chuckled, shoving him back on his chair, the odd mood dissipating like vapor.

"I can handle my liquor." He frowned.

"Looks like it."

"You are the size of a pint glass. How the hell are you still fine?"

"My superpower." I winked, earning a deep chuckle from him. His laugh warmed all the bits of me, and a huge smile curled on my face.

James walked toward us at last, his gaze flashing between us, then zeroing in on me. "Another, lass?" He leaned over the bar, inches away from me. He had asked when we first got there if Lars and I were together. We both were extremely adamant in our "no," Lars firmly adding, "She works for me."

Since then, James flirted and stared at me ceaselessly. Tempted? I wanted to be. I wanted to leave

Lars and go home with this guy, to forget earlier. But even while angry with him, my body was so highly aware of Lars it was frightening. And magnetic. With my consent or not, my body inched closer and closer to him. Images of his mouth on my breast, his hands running up my body, kept flickering in my mind. My skin still pulsed with his touch.

"Yes." I practically threw the glass at James. *Please help me drown any additional dirty thoughts I have of this man.* What was wrong with me? This was Lars, the King I had studied and grew to hate with a deep-seated passion. The one just a moment ago I wanted to punch in the face.

Mr. Dimples grinned at me as he poured my refill.

"You can drink." He winked, impressed with my intake. We Irish, and Scots too, prided ourselves on our level of consumption. "I get off work in a bit if you want to get another somewhere else?" He licked his lips. "I have a bottle of whisky over a century old at my flat." The implication was very clear.

He was frickin' adorable. I would squash him.

"Sounds tempting—"

"James, is it?" Lars growled, cutting me off. He sat up in his seat, not waiting for the boy to respond. "Won't your mummy be mad if you miss curfew?"

My mouth dipped open, surprised at the unconcealed sarcasm in his tone. Very un-kingly.

"I'm over four hundred years old," James huffed, his shoulders rolling back.

"Exactly," Lars snorted diversely. "I have furniture older than you."

James looked back and forth between us, raising his arms. "Hey, man. You told me you weren't together. She's smoking hot. And she seemed interested in me too."

Lars's head snapped to me. His black swirled into his pupils.

I blinked, unsure how to respond.

Lars returned to James with a snarl. "She's not."

"I think the lady can answer for herself." James kept his voice even, but a nerve twitched in his neck.

"Let me say it again." Leaning farther over the bar, Lars's back coiled into a ball. "She. Is. Not."

James took one step forward and magic smashed into him and slammed him into the back of the bar. Bottles rattled, then tipped over. Similar to dominoes, they fell and knocked each other over, crashing to the ground, blanketing the room in a mixture of alcohol and magic. James's mouth and blue eyes widened with shock.

Ah, shite. "All right. We're done here." I jumped up, grabbing Lars's arm. He was locked on the bartender, all humor gone from his features.

"Lars. We're leaving now." It took a few tugs before he broke away from James. He pulled out his wallet, took a wad of bills, and chucked them on the counter. With a huff, he twisted and stalked out the door with a bang.

"Sorry." I gave the cute bartender a shrug before running out after the King.

Freezing air pinched my lungs as brutal rain stabbed my skin. The little light the streetlamp gave off did nothing to penetrate the darkness. The only sound was rain and the beat of our feet on the cobble.

"Hey?" I tracked after the huge figure in front of me. "Lars?"

He didn't stop or falter in step.

"Hey, arsehole!" I bellowed, catching up with him. "What the hell was that?" I grabbed his arm, yanking him to a stop. "Lars?"

He stopped but kept his head forward.

"Look at me."

Slowly his head turned, his chartreuse eyes glowing in the dark.

"Are you going to tell me why you just tossed our bartender, ruining all that precious alcohol? You never, ever hurt the liquor."

Lars's lids lowered partway as he licked his bottom lip, staring off again.

"Hello?"

He sighed, looking down at me, swaying like a boat. "Chalk it up to a bad day."

I cocked my eyebrow, my hands on my hips.

"I need you to focus on getting the cauldron, not taking a pubescent boy for a ride, Ms. Cathbad," he stated, only slurring slightly. "Let's go." He stumbled down the alley, knocking into the walls.

I pointed my face up at the sky, letting the cool drops tame the heat of my temper. Lars had to be my greatest lesson in patience and in keeping my hot temper from exploding all over.

He was becoming my greatest test in everything.

~~

If Lars didn't know he was drunk before, the walk home made it clear. He drooped and dragged. Getting him up the stairs took some effort, even with his arm around my shoulders.

"Last one," I grunted, getting him up the final step. A light we left on in the entry wall sent murky shadows on the walls. The rooms looked as though a bomb had hit it, the casualty of our fight, with most of the furniture in pieces.

"Bed," Lars mumbled, leading us toward another set of stairs up to the bedroom. It was a large, gorgeous flat with only one bedroom. I guess there was no reason he would need two. Either he was by himself or his "friend" would be staying with him. His guards were probably on duty or slept on the pullout sofa in the living room, which was now broken.

The floor was mine. I wasn't picky. I had slept on a lumpy old mattress in a drafty loft space since I was nine.

"Wow." I flicked on the light to the bedroom, the elegant space coming to life. A chandelier hung over the gigantic bed, with dark luxurious wallpaper featured on one wall. Every piece of furniture was unique and massive in an antique sort of way. The room was sexy. It made you want to crawl on the bed naked, letting the deep gray silk sheets slide over your body.

"Here you go." I led Lars to the bed. He fell on the comforter with a groan, his body taking up most of the bed. I wanted to relish in his future headache, but fae were fast to absorb alcohol and get through a hangover.

He would probably sleep right through it and wake up refreshed.

Bastard.

He tried to reach down, to untie his shoes, but he resembled a turtle caught up on a rock.

"Damn, I wish I could record this," I muttered to myself, reaching for his boots.

"Don't even think of it." His words were muffled from the comforter.

"Sorry, too late. I already thought of it about seven times tonight." I smirked, tugging his right boot off.

He twisted his head, so he was looking at me with one eye, his gaze sparking with amusement. "I've got to watch my back with you, don't I?"

"That's what I've been telling you the whole time." I grinned, taking off his other shoe and tossing it on the ground. The way he looked at me was so direct I had to turn away. "Okay, you sleep it off. I'll see you in the morning." I took a step for the door.

"Wait." He lifted his head, climbing higher on the bed.

I pretended I didn't hear him, needing to be far away from him so I could breathe again.

"Fionna?"

My feet stopped, my chest falling toward my knees, hearing the sound of my name and the husky, soft way his tongue wrapped around it.

"Yes?" I croaked out, my hand on the door.

"Sleep here. We destroyed the sofa," he said matter-of-factly. I couldn't explain the pang of disappointment in my gut. It felt more of an order or formal request than an offer.

"I promise I don't snore." He struggled taking off his coat, tossing it on the ground with force.

"You're okay with sleeping next to a Druid?" I turned back, mockery drilling my words. "Don't we have cooties?"

He lids narrowed, shaking his head. "Do whatever you want." He sighed, flopping back on the bed.

Walk out, Fionna.

I didn't move.

Seriously, walk out now.

Nothing obeyed me.

"Either get in or go out. Don't fuss by the door; you're making the room tilt."

I barked a laugh, and my toes inched back toward the bed. It did look incredible, as though it would envelope me in cuddly softness. The sound of the rain pelted the window rhythmically. I'd probably sleep like a baby in here.

Screw it. The king-size bed could contain us both without even getting close. I kicked off my boots and tugged off my jeans. "Sorry, I can't sleep in trousers."

"Me neither." Lars exhaled, like he was hoping I'd say that. "I actually sleep naked but thought it might come across as impolite."

I snorted. I'd seen him fully naked already, but still I couldn't help snatch a glimpse of the impressive package contained in his boxer briefs as he pulled off his jeans.

I climbed into the bed and groaned as the mattress snuggled around my form, the sheets sliding delicately up my bare legs.

"Damn, this bed is amazing."

"Only the best."

I leaned over to reach the light on the wall and slid right off the silk sheets and out of the bed. "Ahhhh." I hit the floor with a thud.

A deep howl of husky laughter erupted from the bed.

"Slippery." I giggled and got on my knees, seeing Lars's silhouette in the dark, laughing his arse off.

"Do I need to strap you in?" His laughter ebbed away.

"Possibly." I climbed back in the bed, moving a little away from the edge of the bed.

"I am finding you extremely amusing, Ms. Cathbad."

"Back to Ms. Cathbad, huh?" I rolled on my side, staring at his glowing eyes.

He twisted his head to me. His gaze locked on me. He watched me for a long time, finally saying. "It's safer that way."

"What do you mean?"

"First names are personal, breed comfort and familiarity. Two things I cannot afford, nor should any person dealing with me. This keeps things in their place."

"But I call you by your first name. Most fae don't have last names."

"Fae understand the subtle way we verbalize names. Humans...and Druids...do not."

"Explain."

"What is your response if I call you Ms. Cathbad?" He peered up at the ceiling, his voice formal. "And what is your response when I call you Fionna?" His voice didn't change, but it felt like a zap between my thighs.

My gaze darted above, my tongue slipping over my lips, my chest tight. "Got it."

"With all people, I need to keep up my guard."

I faced him again. "What I saw in the tunnel...?"

I heard his teeth grind against each other. "I apologize for that."

"No. That's not what I meant." The dark may have hidden my blush, but it also created intimacy. "What happened, Lars?"

He twisted his head, facing the window. He was silent so long, I thought he passed out.

"You remind me of someone," he finally said. "Your accent. The way you speak..."

"Ash." I hated the sinking feeling in my stomach, the only reason he tried to kiss me or hooked up with me after our fight was because I reminded him of her. "You called me Ash."

His arm lifted, his hand running over his face.

"You loved her."

"With a fierceness," his voice strained. The emotions I felt under his declaration froze me in place.

"We were the ultimate star-crossed lovers. I couldn't

imagine loving anyone as much as I loved her...but I still let her go. Opted to rise in power instead. She ended up falling for my brother. Their love was sweet and comfortable. Safe. She and I were similar to a tsunami. Breaking each other and everything in our path. When she was killed, my brother couldn't handle it." Lars sucked in a deep breath. "I had to challenge him."

"You mean kill him," I said. I was in awe. Not only was he grieving for her as well, but he had to, by fae law, kill his own brother. What must it do to a person?

"Yes." He adjusted the pillow under his head. "He went insane. I was the only one left in my family. It remained up to me. He was my best friend. The one who kept *me* sane. The last words he said to me? *Aisling was always yours. I'm sorry for falling in love with her. I love you, brother.* And I watched the life drain from his eyes." He cleared his throat of emotion. "Just like my father had to do to his own brother...we both murdered our twins. Insanity runs in our family."

"What?" I lifted my head.

"My uncle was the rightful King, but power went to his head and became a liability. My father, on a pretense of getting away together for a weekend, murdered his brother and claimed the crown. When my father died at war, he had declared my brother his successor."

"But you wanted to be King."

"I thought I did." Lars's Adam's apple bobbed. "But I gave up so much to get it. I'm not sure if I would do the same again. She'd probably be alive if I chose her. I lost the years with her...with my daughter."

I blinked away the moisture in my eyes, feeling similar pain of regret. "Something I know all too well," I whispered.

His head turned to me, our gaze meeting. "Why did you give up your daughter?"

I tucked my hand deeper under my pillow, my chest clenching. "I would say it was to keep her safe." Tears filled my lids. "But if I stayed home with her, it wouldn't have been an issue, right?" My heart had held the guilty secret for so long. The truth was too harsh to face. But I didn't look away, locking on Lars's gaze.

"I craved power and revenge more than I wanted to be a mother." My voice broke and it took me several swallows to continue. "I kept telling myself it was because I wanted a better life for her, which was true. But deep down, I wasn't ready to be a mum. Not the way she would need me. Give up all I worked for? After years of training and being in hiding, I felt my destiny was to be the leader of the Druids. I didn't want that for my daughter, the way I had grown up until I went to Olwyn's. I guess I thought it best for her."

He rolled onto his side, moving closer to me. "Something *I* know all too well." For a moment we stared at each other, realizing how similar we actually were. Two creatures full of regret, who'd traded in love for power.

Saying it, sharing my deep shame with him, lifted a tiny piece of the burden inside.

Lars shifted his head on the pillow, his voice low. "Aisling and Devlin have been haunting me. They're who I think I see." He swallowed. "It's so real... And no one can afford a leader who is not fully focused."

"You mean insane. You're scared you're losing your mind. That it really does run in the family. And now it has affected you." None of these were questions.

"Yeah." He focused back on the ceiling.

Nothing I could say would reassure him, not without sounding false. I hadn't seen anyone, but no doubt something very real was taunting him.

I reached out and placed my hand on his. "We'll figure it out."

His head jerked to me, his gaze scouring me. "*We* will?

"Yes." I nodded, my cheek brushing the soft fabric. "Like it or not, I'm your partner in this."

"If you remember correctly, I said you were my employee."

"Right." A smile parted my mouth.

He sighed, letting his lids close. "Now can you please tell the room to stop moving? It's making me feel unpleasant."

"Just go to sleep."

Lars wiggled deeper into his pillow, all the tension leaving his face. I could almost see the young, carefree man underneath. I moved my head to the end of my pillow closer to him, the impulse overriding everything else. My lashes dropped, letting the alcohol, the sound of the rain, and the warmth of his body near mine lull me into sleep.

He would never know this, but this was the first time I really slept, feeling safe and secure enough to let go.

Chapter Twenty-Two

Lars

I opened my lids for only a second before they dropped again against the harsh morning light streaming through the curtain. My body and mind were relaxed, rejoicing in the first good night's sleep I had in months, if not longer. Every muscle melted into the bed, not wanting to move. I had the urge to curl up against the warmth on one side of me.

Reality loomed on the other side of the thin line, the knowledge I had to get up and prepare for the day. Be a leader. King.

I never needed an alarm to get up. I was always up before anyone. Most times I barely slept at all. But today, for once, I didn't want to lead or handle business. I wanted to stay here.

I rolled over, lured to the source of heat like a beacon, my hand reaching out. My fingers skimmed bare skin, sliding up the curve of a back until it bumped into a bunched-up T-shirt. My eyes popped open to the sight of long strands of luxurious deep brown hair curling on the same pillow as mine.

Fionna.

She slept on her stomach, her face turned the opposite way and her barely covered body so close her leg brushed mine. My dick was awake and wanting, my hands aching to sweep up her curves, to crawl between her legs. The overwhelming need stilled me; if I moved, I would act upon it.

This wild hunger was another thing that had taken me by surprise. It had died away when Aisling did and now had returned with a vengeance.

Why now? Why did it seem to be especially elevated with *this* girl? She was a *Druid*. My prisoner. Was it because she reminded me of Aisling with their strength, stubbornness, and vibrancy for life? They couldn't have been more opposites in looks. Ash was tall, thin, had legs for days, vibrant red hair, and violet eyes. Fionna was muscular and petite with brown hair and eyes. She did have an amazing ass. Perky and round like an apple. One I wanted to bite.

My jaw crunched down at the impulse, and I grew harder at the thought. I pulled my hand away from her skin, running it through my hair. No. This girl would not get the better of me.

In the tunnel I had almost kissed her. I had not been in my right mind. But upstairs when we were fighting? Not once had Aisling crossed my mind. It was also the first time in a long time someone had successfully challenged me. I was used to holding back, not letting the demon fully come out. With her, I let him off his leash. It felt exhilarating. My demon really wanted to play with her, and the more she fought back…

My lids squeezed together painfully. I had to move, get out of this bed. Even sirens and succubi born to entice and seduce had never had this much power over me. And I didn't like it.

Slipping out of the bed, the comforter lifted; my gaze trailed up her naked legs to her scarcely clad ass, and up the curve of her spine to where the T-shirt rode up overnight.

A groan vibrated in my throat. Ignoring the need to crawl back in, I set my determination on the bathroom. Shower. Cold.

My mind had once been stronger. I could dictate my needs, call on Rez when either of us required a release. Or lately, go to a hotel. As the King I didn't have to worry about seeking out sex; it came to me. But it had also been a long time since I had felt this out of control.

The chilly water rolled down my body as I leaned my hands onto the tile, still feeling so tight it hurt. I gripped myself and let images of Aisling float through my head, her smile, the countless times we devoured each other. Lines drew across my forehead, my mind trying to sharpen the memories, but they were hazy, evaporating like trying to catch a cloud. They were replaced by stronger images of my tongue running over a firm ass, waking a brown-haired girl from her slumber before I thrust into her from behind.

It was too late to drive the fantasy from my head; my body reacted to it, my mind going into full detail. My pounding, the way she arched for me, our moans.

"Fuck," I hissed, letting my orgasm roll over me in waves so powerful I fell against the wall. A minute went by before my senses came back to me. Then anger poured in. Crisp, fresh, and fixed. Clearing my head.

She climbed under my skin like a termite, destabilizing me. Destroying my home. I would not stand for it. Nor would I allow the ghosts of my past to dictate my sanity. They were dead and needed to stay where they belonged.

I dressed quickly and moved to the coffee machine. The day was overcast but dry, and a good day to head to the Highlands.

The little Druid was going to lead me to the cauldron. Today. I would not spend any more time with her than I had to.

My future, my kingdom, was my priority. All else were distractions.

Especially stubborn, mouthy ones.

~~

"Do you know how vast this area is? And as gorgeous as it is, it looks the same." Fionna motioned out the car window, her hair still damp and filling the car with the smell of almond-honey shampoo.

My secretary, Sofia…I finally recalled her name…had the car waiting for us the moment we stepped outside the flat. The need for something fast and dangerous was streaming through my veins, but we would have to go off road and possibly sleep in it if things got down to that. The Rover was more than built to go off road. It was not one of those city, pretty ones, but geared for the rough terrain of the Highlands.

I had been here several times, but the landscape never ceased to amaze me. The clouds parted enough to allow rays of sun to strike the hills with colors you only saw in paintings. Emerald greens, caramel yellows, vibrant reds, and golden browns brushed the land with dramatic vibrancy. The majestic glens and rugged mountains, still snowcapped, soared and rolled into each other with the power only nature could create.

Castles and ruins dotted the immense territory like scars, giving insight to the bloody history of the Scottish Highlands. There were many tales of famous Scotsmen fighting the English, but before that this was fae land. The Scots understood the importance of this land, its magic, and fought hard to keep it. Their blood drenched the land, only strengthening the energy on this piece of earth. Even visitors could not ignore the magic saturating the ground similar to the constant rain. Cities held a lot of magic because of the density of fae in them. The land was enchanted, alive, and sacred to fae.

"You think we're just going to roll up to this cave I had in my vision?" Fionna lowered the window, the cool wind snapping at her hair and face. The River Coe snaked on one side, leading us to our destination. "Talk about the best area to hide a treasure. It's as if the land itself is playing hide-and-seek with you."

I tapped my finger on the steering wheel of the Range Rover with irritation. She wasn't wrong; the way the light shadowed and lightened the ridges, it would be impossible to see a cave even if you were staring right at it.

"Then I suggest you have a more detailed vision," I rumbled, curving the car around a corner.

"Yeah, because it works like that," she scoffed, shaking her head. The tension between us was palpable, following us from the flat into the car like a dark cloud.

I looked at her, her forehead scrunched up with annoyance, her legs shifting and wiggling. My lids narrowed, eyes going back to the road. Her feelings were apparent to me this morning, as if I stepped through a smoke screen, reaching the other side where it was clear and sharp.

She was nervous. Apprehensive.

Lying.

Warning curled around my shoulders, then slithered up the back of my neck.

"What is going on, Ms. Cathbad?" I gripped the steering wheel. Why hadn't I picked up on it before? I was letting too many things slide lately, missing what was right in front of me.

"Nothing." She peered at me wide-eyed as though trying to convey innocence.

"You are lying to me," I growled, sparks of anger firing at my nerves. "Why?"

"I'm not lying to you." Her lips pressed together stubbornly. "I told you everything I saw."

I yanked the wheel, the car bounced off the road onto an unpaved path, throwing Fionna against the door.

"Shite!" She grabbed the handle above her head, barely keeping herself from flinging around her seat. I only sped up, the axel whining as we banged and jerked down the side road.

"What the hell?" she yelped.

A grin played on my mouth, enjoying it way too much. Her little frame, even belted in, flapped and flailed about. I prided myself on not being vindictive. My punishments fit the crime. Most of the time I was quite lenient.

Like with West. It had been in my right to kill him. I not only let him live, but allowed him to remain with Rez. As King I was justified to take back what was mine. But I respected and cared about Rez too much to force her to live a life she no longer wanted. He took the punishment as a true fae, and I respected him for it. I even sent my doctors over to heal him. I had been more than fair. And he knew it.

Fionna Cathbad was different. Something about her made me lash out like a five-year-old and revel in making her pay. Especially when I knew she was deceiving me. She was not scared or intimidated by my demon or my title, which was refreshing, and I'd let this sweet-looking girl play me for a fool.

The seat belt jabbed into my gut as we continued to bound down the lane when I felt the energy shift; the murder of so many Scots on this land was like a force in itself. The Massacre of Glencoe was one of the worst. Guests of a clan betrayed and slaughtered all of them in the middle of the night. Treachery similar to that does not go away; it taints the earth with their ghosts. When we were close, I slammed my foot on the brake, folding the Druid over like origami.

Unsnapping my buckle, I hopped out before she got her bearings. My boots crunched the gravel, and I took in a depth breath, my shoulders relaxing. The air even tasted different here. Dense, it sat on your tongue with an earthy sweetness, reminding me of my years in the Otherworld.

"What the hell?" Fionna slammed the door, stomping over to me. Her puffed-up angry kitty act only made me smile. "What is with you this morning? Usually whisky turns people to arseholes when they drink it, not the next day."

"Don't you know?" I peered down at her, ire sitting on the cusp of my tongue, getting so close I watched her swallow. "I am an asshole most of the time. Whisky makes me nice."

"Then let me grab the bottle in the back and shove it up your arse." She didn't move an inch and as usual challenged me every bit of the way. "Presto, happy arsehole."

Most of me wanted to laugh, but my anger bubbled at the surface knowing the wretched little witch had been lying to me. I took a step, bumping her until she had to retreat.

"Tell me the truth, Ms. Cathbad. What did you *really* see in your vision?"

"I told you." She tilted her chin up, holding strong.

"No. You did not." I loomed over, shoving her against a rocky hill. "You are lying to me. I can see it as clear as day. You don't hide nearly as much as you think."

"I am not lying. My vision showed me the Glencoe area. The River Coe. A cave."

"What else?"

"Nothing else."

Normally I didn't touch people, I didn't have to, using my magic instead. I kept it impersonal. However, now I wrapped a hand around her throat. My thumb pressed into the soft spot in her neck. I had to give it to her; she didn't even flinch.

"You know what else I find odd?" My body had a mind of its own, pressing more firmly into her. "I've been around the Queen enough to notice she seems to get visions a lot more than you do. Incredibly powerful ones." My eyebrow hitched up. "But you do not. So far, one of the *only* visions you've had was forced by a ritual..." I purposely let my statement trail off. "Does that not seem strange? From such a powerful Druid, one who brags about her power, with lineage rooted deep in seers?"

Fionna's jaw clenched, a nerve twitching at her temple.

"Nothing to say, Druid?" My voice turned cold and taunting, walking a thin line to danger.

Muscles along her cheeks strained, her nose flaring.

"You know what I think?" I let my power knock into her. "You are *not* a seer." She jerked under my hand, indignation coloring her cheeks. "Not like your sister anyway. You're a low-level one. My cook probably has more talent than you."

"Fuck you." She pushed against my hand, fury flaming her eyes.

"Did I hit a nerve, Ms. Cathbad?" My lips stayed together as I smiled. This was how it was supposed to be. She was not my equal or capable of getting under my skin. She was a criminal. Meaningless. Her life was mine.

"I suggest you tell me everything. Because I think the ritual showed you more than you are letting on. It is not in your best interest to con me."

"Go ahead." Fionna put her hand over mine, squeezing. "End me here. Go for it. Show me what kind of king you are."

I sucked through my teeth, air burning down my throat like flames.

"Come on, Lars, don't be a pussy now." She grabbed my wrist, pulling me closer to her, determination set on her brow. "I don't mean anything to you. After all, I'm a disgusting Druid. Worse than an animal, huh? Why keep me around? The cauldron is somewhere around here. You're a big powerful boy. Find it yourself!"

I gritted my teeth with rage. "Don't tempt me." We both knew I would still need her to break whatever Druid magic guarded it, but I would *never* admit I required her.

"Do it." Her brown eyes drilled into mine, her cheeks rosy with fury. She looked fierce. Breathtaking. "It wasn't as if you were going to keep me around after you found it anyway. I am too much of a liability. Don't you think *I* get that? I understand how this works. So...don't throw my daughter in my face or threaten my life unless you are going to follow through."

"You want to die?"

"No." She responded without any emotion. "But I'm not playing this game with you anymore. Either I'm a partner or kill me."

"Partner?" I scoffed. "When you are the one trying to mislead *me*?"

"Why do you *really* want the cauldron?" She pushed forward until I was forced a few steps back. "Because you know what I think?" Her tiny body came at me resembling a lion. "I think you are scared."

"Excuse me?" I rumbled, feeling the demon itching at my skin.

"You think you might be slowly going insane. That you will turn out like your uncle and brother, and possibly your father if he lived long enough. Everything you've worked for, what you've given up to be King, will be for nothing. You will lose your grip on your throne, on power. Yourself. You will become the enemy of your kingdom and nobody is there to challenge you."

I shoved away from her, my barriers flying up and clicking in place. It felt as though she had reached into the deepest part of my soul, seeing my true fears, things I had never even said to myself.

"If there is no one strong enough to take you down...imagine the damage and devastation you could do." She stayed in my face, not backing away. "Is that why you want all the treasures? Their magic is the only thing you think will save you?"

My head jerked up, my chest rising and falling in sharp intakes.

"Ahhhh." She nodded. "That's it. The stone will use your weakness, but the cauldron counters it. Yin and yang. Keeps you in check. And the four of them give you the magic to stay sane." She folded her arms. "*Or* it will plunge you over faster." She peered up at the sky, her head wagging. "Are you really willing to take the chance?"

"I have to," I uttered quietly without permission from my head. For some reason I felt the need to tell her. Tell someone. "I can feel it coming. I was there with both my uncle and brother. Saw firsthand the destruction of their mental illness. Genocide." I swallowed. "And I am *a lot* more powerful than both of them."

Her eyes tracked me; all her anger dropped away and left fear in its place. Maybe she was beginning to understand the true gravity of the matter. Why I needed the last treasure so desperately.

"I think your sister has foreseen it." I inhaled deeply. "When I warned her an even bigger battle was coming for us..."

"Yeah?" Fionna clutched at the neck of her sweater, tugging at it.

"The war that is coming..." I rubbed the back of my neck, then looked straight into her eyes. "It's me."

Chapter Twenty-Three

Fionna

Shite. Fuckery. Shite.

In one moment everything changed. My entire plan to undermine the King and steal the cauldron, hiding it before he found and killed me, went to shambles.

I wanted to doubt him. Pretend he was deceiving me. But the man who stood before me was open, showing nothing but truth. Fear. He let me see all of him. His vulnerability. He'd admitted to me what he had never told anyone.

My throat thickened, and I had the urge to wrap my arms around him, to tell him it would be okay. But we both knew it wouldn't be. With the treasures, he could turn unstable and reckless, without them he would go insane.

"Fuck." I rubbed my face.

"Exactly my thought, Ms. Cathbad."

"Enough." I waggled my head, stepping up to him. "If we're going to do this, *really* do this, you are going to call me Fionna." I practically stomped my foot.

He gazed down at me, the green glinting in his eyes. "That's the line you draw?"

I tilted my head to the side.

"Fine." He smirked. "*Fionna.*"

Oh feck. I totally forgot the power of hearing my name from his lips. Maybe this was a bad idea. Clearing my throat, I adjusted my weight. "No more lies or keeping things from each other."

His eyebrows darted up.

"Please, I wasn't the only one," I grumbled.

"It is a deal, Ms. Cath...*Fionna.*"

A shiver ran up my spine, moving me about like a spasm. A wicked grin hooked the side of his mouth, knowing perfectly well what he was doing. Emphasizing my name on purpose.

"Could you ease up on that?" I glared.

His mouth split into a full smile, and a million butterflies hatched in my stomach. What the hell?

"What will I do for fun then?"

I can think of a thing or two. The thought glided through my head. Why were all his words vaguely sexual?

"I think it is you with the dirty mind."

My head popped up, my mouth dropping open. "H-how...?"

Lars's face grew serious. "I don't know. Since this morning I've been able to read you easier. Feel you."

"What?" My eyes bugged.

"Are you no longer blocking me?"

My head started to shake. "No. If anything, I was trying to block you more."

"Because you were lying to me?" He studied me, flipping through my pages, examining me.

That was not exactly the reason. I tried to slam the book shut, cut my emotions off from him. I did not want him to see the real reason I obstructed him. He couldn't know the dreams I had while he lay next to me. The feel of his hand skimming my skin this morning as I pretended to sleep. Definitely not my desire for him to slide my knickers down or join him in the shower.

I was actually relieved to walk into the kitchen and receive a hostile welcome. To go back to our corners of mistrust and animosity. Much safer.

"Hmmm." His lids narrowed, as though he could no longer reach in and retrieve my emotions.

"What's our plan?"

"I don't know. You tell me." He didn't move, but I could feel his magic skim up my arms and legs, between my thighs. "Now tell me everything. Do not leave one single detail out, Fionna."

I inhaled, my body insubstantial, like it had left solid ground. I sensed if I reached out, I could also touch his emotions and read them, as if he could mine. No way in hell I was going to do that. I already felt unsteady. Terrified. Unsure.

What I did know? I was going to help him get the precise thing I wanted to keep from him.

I really hoped I meant the cauldron.

~~

Heavy breaths battered my lungs, and my legs and calves burned as we hiked up the crag. The Highlands were deceptively high and extremely tough terrain to hike. However, the views were spectacular of the valley and River Coe gradually curving through the snowcapped hills resembling a snake slowly winding its way through the grass. The spring nipped at the snow, licking away a little more every day. Everything here felt slow and wandering, like it had all the time in the world. The rugged terrain was unbelievably breathtaking. I was an Irish girl through and through, but even I could admit the staggering landscape rivaled my homeland in its beauty. Though as stubborn and patriotic as each country was against the other, there were a lot of similarities. Scotland was once a Celtic nation and had a lot of Celtic culture, history, and traditions with the migration of Irish.

Lars came to the ridge and stopped. He pulled out a water bottle from his backpack, took a long drink, staring over the vista, only a hint of sweat along his temple.

Dripping and panting like a dog, I pulled up next to him, feeling the rare rays of sun on my face. The air was freezing the higher we went, confusing my body with shivers and perspiration.

"Here." He nudged my shoulder, handing me his bottle, his fingers sliding against mine. I had one in my pack, but it would take too much effort.

"Thanks." I took a gulp of the lukewarm liquid, soothing my dry throat. Before we headed up, I filled him in on what I had seen. He knew of the legend of Ossian's Cave.

"Of course. I should have put that together the moment you told me we were coming to this area." He scoured his forehead in frustration. "A Druid named Fer Diorich used to reside up here. A vengeful asshole."

If the stories I read about were true of Fer Diorich, I couldn't deny that. He turned a woman into a deer to be hunted and killed because she didn't love him back.

"And what a better place to hide the cauldron. The blood of those murdered from the battle has made the magic so thick up here no one would be able to sense the treasure. It has been hidden for centuries," I added, excited at soon being the ones to discover this extraordinary object lost so many years ago.

"And if I remember correctly, he was a part of your parents' group." Lars snapped his fingers as the pieces clicked in place. "One of the extremists. Vanished without a trace."

"Wait..." My forehead gathered in confusion. "My parents didn't know anyone by the name Fer Diorich."

"He went by Isaac back then."

"What?" My mouth dropped open. "Are you kidding me?"

"Did you know him?"

Did I know him? An acute recollection filtered into my head of a tall, gray-haired, skinny man, who dressed similar to an old wizard in a wool robe and carried a walking stick. I had found him interesting, different from the other Druids coming over to our house. Ancient. Connected to the earth more than any other Druid I met. He'd bring me gifts when he came to the house, tell me stories. I always felt a connection to him I didn't understand but sensed at such a young age. He was nothing like the vengeful tale of Fer Diorich. He was sweet and kind to me.

"Uncle Isaac? No way. It can't be the same man." I hadn't uttered his name in over fifteen years. "He was so nice to me."

Lars tipped an eyebrow at me.

My mind wandered back through time, recalling the many visits Uncle Isaac made to my house, to my parents. A part of their secret black magic club.

"That's the connection. But how did he get our family's heirloom?" A deeper memory rolled in, my parents and Isaac sitting around the dinner table one of the last nights before they sent me off to live with Olwyn. I had snuck out of bed to listen to the adults talk. The serious nature of the conversation scared me. I knew everything was going to change.

"We're being watched. It won't be long. I need to get Fionna away from here soon. She's coming for us." My mother's face twisted with desperation. Her voice coiled with panic. "It's up to you, Isaac. If she finds it, we're all lost. Please, you have to hide it. Protect it."

My eyes pinged open, looking up at Lars. "They asked him to hide it. I think Aneira was getting too close. They were afraid...my mother asked him to conceal something for her."

Lars pursued his lips. "Then it's time to see if Isaac kept his word."

The trek up to Ossian's Cave was not for the casual hiker and very few ever ventured to it. Even fewer attempted it at this time of year when winter still clung to the earth. World-class climbers could barely make it up the dicey ridges where the terrain was steep and precarious. Lars and I had to crawl over perpetually soggy moss and dizzying drops from the ridge to keep from slipping over.

If we were human, we would never have made it.

Exhausted, dirty, and sweaty we finally got to the keyhole-shaped opening around midday. I wanted to eat fish and chips and take a nap, but there didn't seem to be any pubs for the weary traveler up here.

This needed to be addressed immediately.

Lars stopped, scrutinizing the eight-foot opening. "This is it?"

We could see shallowly into the cave without a flashlight. It appeared lackluster. Just more dirt. Because you had to nearly kill yourself to get up here, it should at least have a sauna and bar.

"Do you feel anything?" Lars removed his rucksack, digging inside for his torch.

"Not anything specific." I sighed, stepping into the cave. "But there is so much magic and death here it's hard to pick up on anything."

Grabbing my light, I moved deeper inside. It went up, but the space inside was only about five or six meters wide, the back wall rocky. I frowned, inspecting the large boulders building up the back. I started spouting a revealing spell.

That's when I felt it.

The moment my words hit the mountain, they bounded back at me the same way a boomerang does, shoving my spell back at me like a whip, and flinging both of us off our feet. My spine hit the dirt as I slid back out the cave, grinding my skin into the gravel before I came to a stop. I stared up at the sky, blinking in a daze. "Owwww."

"What the hell was that?" Lars also lay flat on his back, not far from me.

"A rebound spell," I hissed through my teeth, sitting up. "Something clearly does not want to be found."

"Then we are in the right place." Lars got to his feet, brushing himself off. "Can you break it?"

"Yeah. I think so." I matched his movements. "Now that I know what we're dealing with." I returned to the center of the cave and bent down on my knees, my hands out at my sides, palms open. Shattering another's spell wasn't demanding of the brain but was grueling on the body. It seemed similar to taking your magic and turning it into a battering ram and storming a castle. The magic would fight back, protecting its fortress.

Depending on the level of magic from the user, this could be fast or painfully slow. I started chanting, the swirl of magic sweeping my hair around my shoulders. Normally I preferred to be alone while I carried out a spell, but Lars's presence and magic behind me felt like a powerful battery.

The magic wanted to protect its treasure, but I was surprised how familiar it felt, similar to hearing a song, tasting or smelling something that took you back to your childhood.

It made me remember the man I'd thought of as an

uncle. The hours he'd sit and tell me stories of old. The smoky smell from his pipe coiling in my noise.

The spell didn't attack me back, but it was definitely going to make me work for it, as though he were still trying to train me, sharpen my skills from the other side. Perspiration trailed down my face, my muscles shaking as I shoved my incantation at it with everything I had. I grunted, bending over, gasping for air between words.

"Ms. Cathbad?" I heard Lars, his outline coming beside me. "Stop. You're bleeding."

No pain, no gain. Ignoring him, I leaned forward, barking the hex, my voice growing hoarse. My temples pounded and my limbs shook violently, ready to give out. If I didn't do this now, I wouldn't have the strength to try again for a while.

With a last push of magic, I threw my spell at the barrier, wailing out.

Snap.

With a whoosh of magic fleeing from the gates, stale warm wind slammed into us, pushing me back on my arse. The enchantment shattered, zooming past us out of the cave, leaving the space still and quiet.

I sank forward, crashing into the dirt.

Well done, Fionna. Proud of you, my girl. A man's voice came into my head, flittering out so fast I didn't know if I had dreamed it.

"Ms. Cathbad?" Hands rolled me over, green eyes staring down at me.

"Fionna. Call me fucking Fionna or I'll spell you," I grumbled.

"Okay, fucking Fionna. Are you all right?" Lars whisked away hair sticking to my face.

"Funny." I rolled my eyes, not quite ready to move, my muscles still trembling. "You're a comedian, aren't you?"

He smiled, helping me sit up. "Go slow."

I wiped at the wetness dripping off my lip, the back of my hand streaked with red. Magic always came with a price. Bloody noses were entry-level payment.

Lars dug into his bag and pulled out a granola bar and a wipe to clean my face. "Here, you need energy."

"I'd prefer a shot of tequila and a taco."

"I'll see what I can do next time." He chuckled, his gaze assessing me as I inhaled the nutrients. Compared to what I really wanted, it tasted bland and dry, but it got the job done. He handed me his water to chase it down. "Are you ready?" He stood, reaching his hand for mine.

I wiped my face and nodded, noting how my palm fit snugly in his grip. He yanked me to my feet and without a thought started dusting me off, his hands roaming over my backside.

I should have minded. Stopped him. I wish I could say it was because I was knackered and didn't have the energy, but in all honesty, I enjoyed the feel of his touch. The way he was lightly "spanking" me.

Fionna, you are sick and twisted, I chastised myself, scrubbing off the remaining blood on my face.

He stopped, jerking his hand away, as though he finally realized what he was doing or perceived my thoughts. He mumbled an apology before he bolted away, clearing his throat. Lars strode over to the far wall, gazing up. My eyes followed his, my mouth parting.

"Wow. We really did it." I came up beside him, staring at the opening that had not been there before. The entrance was barely big enough for me to stand in; everything past this was lost in darkness.

"*You* did it," he said, not looking at me. He clutched his torch, flicked it on, and began to climb up the boulders.

I had no doubt we were on the right track, but why did I feel this was just the tip of the iceberg? Whatever lay beyond the entrance was just the first of the challenges ahead. My gut twisted, heavy with foreboding.

I should have turned us back right then.

Chapter Twenty-Four

Lars

Darkness permeated the cool tunnel with only the small column of our flashlight beams paving the way. It reminded me of Greece and searching for the Sword of Nuada all over again. What is it with Druids and fucking caves? This one took us deep into the underbelly of the land.

Darkness or confined spaces didn't bother me, but I was done hunting for these artifacts. *Last one.* I was so near to having them all. *Close. So close.*

The cauldron was one of the most important. The stone needed its companion to work for me properly. As Fionna suggested, I was walking a perilous line. The Treasures of Tuatha Dé Danann could tip me over into total insanity or save me from myself.

I had no doubt they would benefit me. I was formidable enough to regulate their power and use it. I could have no doubt, because the alternative was not an option. I would not become my brother or my uncle.

Fionna's footsteps clipped behind me in pace with my own. We hadn't spoken a word since we entered the cave.

Speaking of losing my mind. This woman seemed to rob me of mine constantly. I hadn't even thought; I just started touching her as though she was mine. I had never been a touchy person, not even with Rez. We kept strictly to business in the day and enjoyed each other at night behind closed doors. We were never the couple to screw on my desk in the middle of the day.

This girl stirred me up so much twice the day before I almost fucked her, and we demolished an entire flat. This wasn't like me. At all.

That kind of passion ended with Ash. There'd been no surface we didn't have sex or place we didn't wreck. But then I was young and foolish, in the whimsy of first love. Time and life had changed me. Now I saw the world for what it was. Love was for the dreamers. The ones who weren't King.

My boots plodded along, descending, and finally gave way to a vast room where the air grew even cooler. Fionna came up next to me, her flashlight scanning the space in jerky movements along with her head.

"What is it?"

"I don't know." She nipped her bottom lip.

Taking in a deep inhale, I felt out the cavern, sensing a blip of magic, but not from a spell or an object.

"We're not alone." I barely got the statement out, before a fire exploded to life near us, igniting the room in buttery light.

"Shite!" Fionna jumped back. Ashes circled around it to keep it contained. By the amount of cinders, it seemed clear the user had been here for a while.

"We have guests. We have guests." A strange voice echoed off the tall, bare wall, coming from all angles.

I jerked my head around. "Come out now," I boomed. Not much could hurt me.

"He wants us to come out," it said.

"He can stuff it," a grouchier-sounding one spoke. "Go back to where you came from. Leave us be."

"Two fae?" Fionna mouthed to me.

I nodded, trying to find where the voices were coming from. I took another inhale, the demon tasting the air. Sub-fae. But whatever it was, it was not a common one. This was unique. Old. Familiar, but I couldn't place it.

"This is your King. Come out now," I demanded.

"King? Toad bucket. I am a king here." The second man chortled derisively.

"Ha! If you're a king, then I'm a dragon." The first one laughed.

"Dragon? Only flames you could create are from your own gas."

"You do realize how stupid your statement is? And stop blaming your gastro problems on me."

The two bickered back and forth, their argument about gas elevating.

"Great. Crazy sub-fae. Probably have been in the cave far too long." I rubbed my eyebrows, irritation escalating with the pace of their row. "I *order* you to show yourself."

"Ooooo. Now he orders us," Grumpy spoke.

"I am not joking," I growled. "I am the King and I mandate you show yourselves to me."

"King you say? King of what? You can be a king of anything."

"Oh, fuck this." I threw up my arms, anger lining my shoulders.

"Seems your 'kingly' powers," Fionna curled her fingers in quotes, "have as much sway with them as they do with me."

"Seems so." I gritted my teeth. "Difference is I really am *their* leader."

"I think we should introduce ourselves. There is a woman present," the nicer one whispered loudly to his friend. "We are being rude."

"Rude! They come into my house without an invite, intrude in my home. And you call me rude?"

"You're a git and you know it," the second man replied. "Come on, Kevin. A *cailin*! We haven't seen one of those in a long time."

"*Cailin?*" Fionna perked up at her native language. *Cailin* in Gaelic was girl.

Great. *Irish* sub-fae.

"Fine. But I'm not feeding them." The one named Kevin huffed. "And they get nowhere near my mead."

"I should speak to your mother about raising you with no manners."

"Go ahead. That potato sack is probably still living."

I growled under my breath, my fingers rubbing my forehead harder. "We are wasting time."

"See, I'm not the only ill-mannered one," Kevin quipped. "Barges into *my* home..."

"Come on, we haven't had guests in over a decade."

I could hear Kevin sigh, giving in. Footsteps crackled over the earth, bouncing through the cave, but I still couldn't tell which way they were coming from.

Fionna moved closer to me. I sensed she wasn't afraid but defensive. Ready to act. I was not in the least worried about some sub-fae.

A short, bow-legged man, no more than three feet tall, with a large nose and beady eyes emerged in the dim light. He wore a tiny Scottish kilt with a "Rub me and see if you get lucky" T-shirt.

"Holy shite!" Fionna's mouth dropped open.

I stared, making sure he wasn't an illusion.

"Aren't you guys extinct?" Fionna gaped at the short man.

"Do I fecking look extinct to you, lass?" This was definitely the grumpier one.

"But...but...you're a leprechaun." Fionna shook her head in disbelief.

"Oh, good on ya. If you want, you can check under my kilt to see I am male too."

"Your name is Kevin?" Fionna tipped her head to the side.

"Ta." He scowled. "What's wrong with that, lass? It's my *mhamo's* name."

"Your grandmother was named Kevin?"

"Yeah. Something wrong?"

"Uh, no." Fionna waggled her head. "It's just...um...not very leprechaun-y."

"Leprechaun-y? What the hell do you mean? Is that a racist comment?" Kevin's chest puffed up as he took a step closer. "Huh?"

"Noooo. Nope."

"What, you think I should be named Paddy or Lucky? Do I fecking look lucky to you?"

"Where is the other one?" I glanced around, ready for an additional man to join him.

"I apologize for my friend. He literally was born in a barn." The other man's voice came out of Kevin's...hand. "I'm Gerry."

"Holy hen's teeth." Fionna's hand went to her mouth. I had no idea what the hell she meant, but I was sure I agreed.

On Kevin's hand was a sock. A sock that had two eyes, a mouth, and a nose drawn from what looked like charcoal. Pieces of hay were tacked on the top to resemble hair.

A puppet. That's who Kevin had been arguing with? A fucking sock puppet?

"How long have you been here?" I asked, keeping my tone low and soothing. I had been partially joking about crazy sub-fae, not realizing how on point I had been. Crazy didn't even cover this.

Kevin's wrist turned to him, the sock tilting its head back and forth. "It's been what? Fifteen or so years now?"

"Ta." Kevin nodded in agreement.

A chuckle came out of my mouth. Fionna whapped me, darting me a look.

"What?" I motioned to the leprechaun. "Are you seriously going to go along with this? He's talking to a fucking sock."

She pinched her mouth together, taking a step closer to Kevin. "I'm sorry for my friend. He forgot *his* manners." She held out her hand. "I'm Fionna. This is Lars."

"Majesty to them," I protested.

Kevin grumbled, but Gerry, the sock, leaped out, kissing her hand with his drawn-on lips.

"We haven't had such a bonny lass here ever. Welcome!" Gerry gushed, while Kevin stood back, his free hand hugging his chest like he was pouting.

"Are you kidding me?" Both my hands rubbed my face. This was even too twisted for me. And I had seen a lot in my time.

"Ignore him. We are grateful for your hospitality." Fionna swished her hand at me.

"Nonsense! We are thrilled to have company," Gerry exclaimed.

"Speak for yourself," Kevin muttered, huffing another big sigh.

"Shut it, Kevin," Gerry grumbled back at his friend, turning to Fionna. "We don't have much, but we have some honey wine."

"I told ya; they ain't touchin' my mead," Kevin barked.

"We are fine. Thank you. We actually came here to find something."

"Ha!" Kevin's head whipped to the sock. "Knew they were here for that. No one just comes to visit, you log."

I swear I saw the sock sigh. What the hell? It was a sock. Not real.

"Can you help us?" Fionna laced her hands together.

"Help? They will tell me where it is *now*." I had no time for this.

"Shush." Fionna glared back at me, her expression telling me to back off, then returning to Kevin. I exhaled and let my head fall back with irritation. "We'd be so grateful for your assistance."

Time was ticking by. People called me "majesty" for a reason, and I had perks of bypassing pomp and circumstance. Normally, I tried to show respect to all, but my patience had expired a while back.

"No. This is absurd. Enough—"

"I said shut it." Fionna cut me off, an eyebrow raised in warning, scolding me like a child. "I will handle this."

I growled, flinging my arms out, and walked a few steps away to tamp down my testy temper. "Fine," I grumbled.

"Do you know about a treasure hidden here?" Fionna prompted. "The Cauldron of Dagda?"

Kevin rolled his eyes.

"What the toadstool sandwich do you think I'm doing here? I like to live in a fucking cave with this arsehole?" Kevin waved his free hand at his "friend." "Let me tell you, it has not been a picnic."

"Me?" The puppet sputtered back. "I haven't been easy to live with? You are the most cantankerous sod. All you do is gripe and drink mead."

"At least I don't fart in my sleep all night," Kevin spat back.

Gerry slowly turned to look at Kevin, his mouth opening, shaking its head in bewilderment. "You are an eejit."

I was starting to like Gerry. "Shit." I pressed my hand to my face. I was already seeing the puppet as though it were alive. I needed to get out of here. My own sanity was at stake.

"Great." Fionna rubbed her palms together. "Do you know if it's hidden here?"

"Ta," Kevin replied.

"Can you tell us where?"

"No."

"What? Why?" I blurted out before Fionna could respond. "Do you understand I am the *Unseelie King*?"

"I understand you're a wanker."

"How dare—" I rushed for the sub-fae as Fionna jumped in my path, blocking me.

"Lars, calm down. That is not going to help us."

I had demons and shifters cowering at my feet, but a three-foot leprechaun was giving me grief? They were known to be assholes, but he should still fear me. My magic guided straight for him, circling his neck with ease.

Kevin gasped, his free hand going to his neck.

"Kev!" Gerry cried, the puppet frantically hovering close to his buddy.

How was he still able to talk? I was choking him!

"Lars. Stop." Fionna shoved her own magic at me, banging into me like a bumper car. My gaze went to her brown eyes, somehow gentle and strong at the same time. Did I never notice their depth? How you could fall into them and drown? They held so much power, and I felt myself ease off, taking a deep breath.

Kevin gulped for breath behind Fionna, but she kept her regard on me, not severing her hold until she watched my shoulders drop. Her hands squeezed my arms, then she spun to the leprechaun.

"Kevin, please. We really need it." She walked up to him, touching his shoulder.

Kevin snarled at her, rubbing his neck.

"He wasn't lying," Gerry said quietly. "We can't tell you where it is."

"Ah." The back of Fionna's ponytail bobbed. "You're spelled."

"That Druid bastard. He tricked us." Kevin spit on the ground.

"Well, that and..." Gerry trailed off.

"Don't." Kevin lifted his lip at his friend.

"Because—"

"Shut up, Gerry."

"Wedon'tactuallyknowwhereitis!" Gerry spit out the

words so fast it jumbled together. He sighed with relief as though he had been holding it in for years.

"But...you said." Fionna straightened, confusion coating her features.

"You asked if I knew the cauldron was hidden here." Kevin pushed up his chin, rubbing his T-shirt.

"Yeah?"

"It's not."

"*Where. Is. It?*" One stride and I was even with Fionna, anger contracting my muscles.

"Can't tell ya."

My molars ground until I heard my jaw crack.

"You think it would be so easy? You'd just walk in, grab a cup-o-tea, and take a treasure as a fecking parting gift?"

"Watch your tone with me, leprechaun." I loomed over him. "I am still your King, and I have the power to destroy you."

"Someone has anger management issues." Kevin continued to rub his belly. "I'm starving. Is it supper time yet?"

"We just ate lunch," Gerry replied.

"Ta. Your point?"

"How. Do. We. Get. The. Cauldron?" My voice boomed around the cave, slamming off the walls.

"With your attitude, I don't feel like telling you." Kevin harrumphed, wrapping his arm over his chest again, and turned his cheek away.

"Tell me now, or I will make you," I fumed, shocked by the little effect I seemed to have on him.

"No," he sulked.

"Yes."

"No."

"Okay, boys. Time out," Fionna cut in, seeing I was about to strangle the fae, and this time I would not back down. "Gerry," she addressed the puppet. "Maybe you could be so kind."

Gerry pinched its mouth together, looking between her and me.

"Ignore him. *I'm* asking. Please. I would be so grateful."

She was working him. Fionna wasn't a patient, sweet person, but unlike me, she seemed to know how to charm him.

I never needed to be. I asked and got what I wanted. Sometimes with a little force.

"Oh, *cailin.*" Could a sock have the power to blush and look sheepish? "For you I would do anything. You are the prettiest thing I have ever seen."

"Thank you."

"I mean, if you want to lose that arse, you can stay here. You have to put up with this sod." It jerked its head to Kevin. "But he's not so bad after you get to know him."

Was I really seeing this? A sock was hitting on Fionna? And even worse, why did I feel bothered by this? Every man in Scotland seemed bewitched by her. My jealousy over the bartender last night was humiliating. Nothing existed between us. She could do whatever she wanted. Ha, who was I kidding? The thought of her going home with the kid almost made me explode the building. My jealousy had turned me rash, foolish, and angry. I had embarrassed myself.

Now I wanted to strangle a sock.

"You're very sweet. Tempting." She gave me a wink, as if she were taunting my actions from the bar. "But we really need to get the cauldron."

"It's a riddle."

"Excuse me?"

"You have to solve a riddle to figure out its location," Gerry clarified.

I groaned, pinching my nose. "The damn Druid made this a scavenger hunt."

"I guess it was naïve to think he'd make it so easy to retrieve." Fionna's shoulders dropped, but then she rolled them back, lifting her head. "Okay, what's the riddle?"

Kevin grumbled to himself then nodded to Gerry.

Gerry cleared his throat dramatically.

"Descend where red water flows.
Treasure will be *found* in the dark ones *round*."

Fionna and I both stared at the puppet blankly. "That was it? Is that all to the riddle?"

"Did I say it wrong?" Gerry whispered to Kevin. "They're just gaping at me like gobs."

"I need a drink." I swiveled, squeezing the bridge of my nose. I paced around the fire, my boots stirring up the dirt.

"I feel as though I should know this." Fionna nibbled on her bottom lip. "Like Uncle Isaac left this just for me. He used to tell me stories and riddles all the time."

I stayed quiet, rolling the riddle over and over in my mind. *Descend where red waters flow. Treasure will be found in the dark ones round.*

"Red waters. Dark one's round," Fionna repeated to herself over and over, until I was about to lose my mind. "Wait..."

"What?" I swung to her.

She snapped her fingers as though she was trying to grasp something. "I don't know, but I feel I've heard this riddle before. Like I know the answer. But..." She clapped her hands excitedly and sat down on the ground, shutting her eyes.

"What are you doing?"

"A memory-retrieving spell. On myself." She grinned, her lids still shut. She started to hum the words of the spell, her forehead crunching down. Magic swirled in the room, her hair flying up around her face. Apparently this memory was buried deep, as her chant rolled to the back of her throat, exertion already dampening her hair.

A thin trickle of blood trailed out of her nose.

"Fionna." I moved closer to her. I understood Druid magic took a toll, but I hated seeing her hurt herself.

She's doing it for you.

"Fionna. Stop. We'll figure—"

A current of magic shot into her like a javelin. Her back struck the rocky ground, as though someone had thrown her down with all their might. Her mouth opened, but no breaths followed. Her eyes flared with fear.

"Fionna!" I dived for her, pumping my magic into her body. I didn't even consider if it would help or not, working off pure instinct. My energy spread out like a thousand fingers, touching and inspecting anything harming her.

She gasped and her hand grabbed mine as she gulped air greedily.

"Are you okay?" I pushed hair back from her face.

"Ye-yeah." She nodded, her lids fluttering. "Could you stop…doing that?"

My energy still roamed through her.

What was I doing? I healed people all the time, but I kept it clinical and unobtrusive. I healed at the surface level. What I had just done crossed the line from clinical into intimate.

I had only done it once before with the first woman I had ever lain with. It had been so intimate and exposing, it felt like we had flayed ourselves open to each other. Every secret, every thought exposed. I was so young and not yet completely in control of my powers. I vowed to never let it happen again.

I swore, jerking back, pulling everything with me.

Fionna closed her eyes briefly, taking a moment before she reopened them, her gaze landing on me.

"The Devil's Pulpit."

"Excuse me?"

"Finnich Glen. That's where it is."

"You know for sure?" I helped her sit up.

"The night he left, he came in my room to say goodbye. He told me the riddle, saying it was extremely important I remember." She dabbed at the blood along her nose, lost in thought. Fear flicked around her eyes. "It feels as if this has been waiting for me...like he knew something before he left."

"What?"

"I don't know." She licked her lip. She didn't say it, but I could see the unease in the lines of her face, almost taste it. "But it is definitely hiding at Finnich Glen."

Finnich Glen. The name rolled around in my head as I tried to recall anything I could from when I used to live here.

"Red waters flow." I tipped my head back with understanding, the riddle clicking in. Finnich Glen was an area with a hidden gulch running through it. They call it Devil's Pulpit now. From ground level, you descended a set of stairs, which they named Jacob's Ladder, to get into it. A mineral in the water there turned the water a rusty color. I had heard about the place but had never been there. Now it was all I could think of. "Devil's Pulpit, here we come." I smiled.

"This time I drive." She narrowed her eyes.

"Good. Get the hell out of here. You've overstayed your welcome anyway." Kevin motioned for the door, stomping away. "I can finally get some peace.

"Bye, beautiful *cailin*. Parting is such sweet sorrow..." Gerry's voice drifted off down the tunnel.

"Yeah, because a decade alone has done him so well." I shook my head. "Asshole."

"I think you found your kindred spirit." She got to her feet, grinning.

"Kevin or Gerry?"

"Please, you are so a Kevin." She rolled her eyes. "I'm more of a Gerry."

"Oh, then you get all the duties my right hand usually does." I winked and twisted on my feet, heading down the tunnel, leaving her gaping at me.

I enjoyed leaving the Druid speechless, even if just for a moment.

~~

I was relieved to exit the cave. The last bit of sun hit the mountain as we trekked back down the peak with the cold air filling my lungs. Not only did we have a lead, but I was free from Kevin and his hand puppet. I'd had my fill of crazy lately.

"I think I'm going to miss him." Fionna rubbed her arms and put back on her jacket that had been tied around her waist. The most tortuous part of the hike lay behind us as we made our way down toward the valley in the chilly wind.

"Which one," I scoffed.

"Gerry, of course." She peered at me like "duh." "I mean, he asked me to move in with him."

I barked out a laugh.

"Don't mock. All any girl wants is a good man who loves her."

"Love?" I choked. "Is it love now?"

"I don't move in with just anybody."

I snickered, peering at her. "But it would be a lie."

"Why do you say that?"

"Because you, Ms. Cathbad..." I planted my feet in front of her, stopping her short, our figures almost touching. "Are not the type of girl who only wants a good man..." Her eyes enlarged and she swallowed. "You want more than that. Much, much more. Believe me, you are not *any* girl."

Her throat bobbed. She licked her lip and suddenly I could only look at her wet mouth, beckoning me like a siren's call. The urge to kiss her infiltrated my mind, freezing me in place.

Her breath caught as though she had read my mind and felt my compulsion to claim her mouth hungrily. The need was desperate, clawing at the base of my neck.

I never liked second guessing myself. I went after what I wanted. However, this was not about retrieving the latest gadget for testing or facing someone who betrayed me. Kissing her was something I should never do. Ever. My hand slid up her cheek, drawing her closer to me. My body defied me, rejecting my firm command to step away.

Her gaze dropped to my mouth, desire smoldering off her, only enticing mine to rise. I couldn't deny my body wanted her. And even against the warnings in my head, I knew one thing. I was going to kiss Fionna Cathbad.

No, "kiss" sounded like a sweet, charming notion. I wasn't going to kiss her; I was going to devour her. Incinerate and ravage her until nothing was left. Of either one of us.

She made a little noise as my fingers dug into the back of her head, lowering my head, our mouths only a breath away. I could already sense if I crossed this line, nothing was going to be the same.

"*Now* I know why you didn't come to my room that night. Seems you already had someone warming yours," a woman spoke from behind me. "A little surprised it's her, I will admit."

Shock jerked me away from Fionna. I knew the brusque accent all too well. *There's no way she could be here.* Except she was. In tight black jeans, boots, and an expensive-looking jacket.

"Margo?" I ground my lips together, trying not to show my astonishment.

"Look at this. Here we are again. What are the odds?" She shook her head in paradoxical amazement, but her gaze still ran up and down me with heated desire. "I *really* think you must be stalking me. I knew you liked me. Or at least want me in your bed."

Fionna snarled, stepping toward her. I clutched her wrist, pulling her back, but deep down pride budded in my chest. I *liked* her getting defensive of me.

"What are you doing here, Margo?" Every muscle was tight and defensive. I could not believe I had not even contemplated Margo being a con artist who'd been playing me since the day I met her in Zurich.

She smiled coyly. "I think you know why I am here. What I want."

"Why don't you enlighten me?" I hadn't seen this coming. I had kept the Romanian beauty at arm's length because I did not trust her. But I hadn't followed through and investigated her. Her blatant sexual attraction to me and her nonchalance about my business affairs clouded my judgment. Now I was paying the price for letting a pretty face slip through. She had been using me the whole time. She knew what I was after.

"What every girl wants." She tilted her head with a smug smile. "A rock on her hand. But I'll take mine extremely powerful, gray, a few inches big, and in my palm."

A sharp guffaw came from me. "You want the Stone of Fáil?"

"Are you asking? How sweet." She hugged her hands to her chest. "My answer is yes."

"Amusing." I folded my arms, relaxing a bit. She was not a threat. "Good luck finding it."

She gripped one hip, rolling her eyes. "Do not treat me as an imbecile, Lars. I know it not only exists, but you have it. I also know you have them all, except the cauldron. You can keep those. I only want the stone back."

"Back?" Fionna spoke, but Margo didn't even glance her way. "It was you. In Prague. The one who attacked us."

Margo's gaze flicked to Fionna, then back to me, a smug grin twisting her lips.

Did this woman really think she could fight me? That she had any authority or chance against an Unseelie King?

My hand covered my guffaw. "How foolish are you? Are you so power hungry you think you can take on the High Demon King? By yourself?"

"No." She slanted her head to the right. "But I could take you on with another High Demon King."

Great. She was certifiably insane.

I couldn't stop my laughter from ringing in the air.

"Does this 'other' High Demon King come in a form of a talking sock too?"

Margo's lids narrowed in confusion. She rolled her shoulders at being the butt of my joke.

When did I start joking? That had never been me. I was always serious and to the point. I glanced over at the woman at my side. Fionna looked back, humor dancing in her eyes, as though she got the joke. What in hell was this woman doing to me?

"I'm glad you can enjoy yourself." Margo put her hands on her hips with a self-assuredness that made me feel as if the joke were on us.

I pushed out with my senses, but was overwhelmed by the density of ancient blood and magic blocked.

"I am getting the stone." She lifted her eyebrows. "I was promised."

"By whom?" I scoffed.

Margo twisted, staring behind her. A man stepped from the trees, a few strighoul behind him. But I barely took them in as all my attention was on the man.

Tall, olive complexion, dark hair with yellow-green eyes.

Fionna gasped. At least I wasn't the only one seeing my twin. I felt a bit of relief this was not a hallucination. Then quickly the thump of my heart throbbed in my ears as the figure grew closer and closer. Unable to move, I stared at the ghost coming to life before me.

No. There's no way. It can't be true. He's dead. I killed him.

Devlin reached Margo's side, wrapping his arm around her waist with the intimacy of a lover. "Is this form too shocking?" My brother's voice rang through the air. "Well, then you might prefer this."

In front of my eyes my brother's face dissolved, reshaping into another's.

"Holy hell!" Fionna clasped her hand on her mouth, staring at my previous love.

Aisling. A see-through gown draped off one shoulder; my eyes drank her up, taking in her shiny long red hair and beautiful face. The birthmark, the one I had kissed so many times on her shoulder, wasn't there. In the light of day, the tiny details I knew well were missing.

"Not sure this form is working anymore. Looks like you might have moved on." Aisling motioned to Fionna with a pout.

"Stop," I growled.

"Okay, fine. You were never any fun." Aisling's voice and beauty dropped away, a man's face procuring her place. "Even as a child."

My body jolted back. "No." What I saw had to be another phantom, more torment being played on me. I knew his face so well.

"I'm hurt." The apparition stepped forward, a vicious smile parting his lips. "Aren't you happy to see me?"

I swallowed, my brain still trying to understand.

The man's eyes glinted with joy, relishing in my suffering.

"Hello, nephew."

Chapter Twenty-Five

Fionna

What the hell is happening right now?

I had just seen a man turn from Lars's carbon copy to one of the most beautiful women I had ever seen. In my gut I knew it was Aisling. Lars's reaction to her left no doubt. But that was not who stood before us now.

This man was tall and built similar to Lars, skinnier, with a longer nose but the same chartreuse eyes and olive skin. His long jet-black hair was pulled back in a ponytail. He had on well-worn beige cotton trousers and a matching button shirt, which was open halfway down his chest. He looked more like a man on a spiritual retreat than a threat to Lars. But I detected formidable magic under the tattered clothes.

Silence eclipsed the countryside, as if every living creature was holding its collective breath, including me. My head snapped between the two men; their looks were so similar, there was no doubt they were related.

"No." Lars shook his head. "No. This is not possible."

"Why? Because I have been supposedly dead for the last three centuries?" The man spread his arms. "Well, as you can see, my dear nephew, I am alive and well."

"H-how?" Lars sputtered, the shock still swirling in his eyes.

"Because your father was spineless. He was a sentimental fool," he sneered. "He didn't have the guts to kill me. Instead he let me rot in a prison he created, gradually draining me of power and life so he could take my place."

Lars pinched the bridge of his nose, shaking his head in disbelief.

"To protect himself from guilt for killing his twin, he cursed me to a fate worse than death," he spat, his handsome face twisted up with fury. "He took my throne and played the part of the King, but he *never* was one. Just like you and your brother. Not one of you has ever been the rightful King."

"Ah." Lars's head tipped back, his chest expanding. "That is why you are here, Stavros. It was you this whole time."

"Took you long enough to figure it out." Stavros clapped his hands together mockingly. "I left you so many clues pointing to me. I was starting to get bored playing all by myself. Oh, and with Devlin...and Aisling."

Lars scoffed. "Right. Your gift was to make yourself look and sound like others."

I had heard of only a few demons able to do that, exceedingly powerful ones. It didn't bode well for us.

A smile split Stavros's mouth.

"It always came in handy. Your father and I used to torment people growing up. He was disappointed you and Devlin didn't inherit it." He clicked his tongue in shame. "But how fun for me to watch you crumble under the images of your dead lover and brother. Those were the best days." He sighed dreamily.

"At least I know I'm not the crazy one here." The shock was gone. Lars stood tall again. "It was Father's mistake for not killing you. But your time as King is over. Go back to whatever hole you dug yourself out of. You have no power anymore."

A cackle broke from Stavros's mouth. "Oh, nephew, your naiveté is precious. Do I have to explain to you how this King thing works again?" He took a few steps closer, and Margo moved with him. Alarms of danger lit my nerves. "There can only be one King at a time. And guess who the rightful one here is?" He pointed to Lars then himself. "You? Me? Oh, *sorry*. You weren't picked. Terrible break. Try again later."

"Take another look, Stavros. I don't think you really want to challenge me. I am far more powerful than you ever were."

"Oh, darn, you're right. Guess I'll go home now." Stavros snapped his fingers. "Came all this way for nothing."

A grin spread on Margo's face; she was clearly enjoying the scene. I did not let my guard down for one second. Instead, I held a spell behind my teeth, waiting for the gates to open. She would be my first target, and by the way she stared back at me, I was hers.

"Do you know how long I've been free?" Stavros rubbed his chin, reminding me so much of Lars. "The day your father died, my prison was lifted."

"What?" Lars countered. "But father died over a century ago."

"Lots and lots of time to build myself up again, create an army. This is just a little taste." He motioned behind him. "And when rumors came floating my way the King was on the hunt for treasure..." Stavros winked back at Margo. "Well, let's say I suddenly missed my family so much, and you were always my favorite."

"No, I wasn't."

"Oh right, it was your brother." He clicked his tongue. "So easy to confuse you two. I guess not anymore." He laughed mechanically. "Because one of you is dead. At least you had the gumption to actually kill him."

Lars's mouth pressed together, his hands rolling to fists. "So you want to take the Treasures of Tuatha Dé Danann, kill me, be King again, and become a tyrannical dictator of Earth. Is that your plan?"

"Well, it wasn't, but damn it sounds good. I like your plan better. Do you mind if I steal it?" He pointed at Lars. "Thanks, so kind. You were always full of great ideas."

"And you were always full of vanity and psychosis." Lars pulled at his sleeves, a sign he was growing irritated. "My father was the one who ran the place, kept you in order. Just because you were King doesn't mean you should have been."

Stavros inhaled, all humor dropping away. "Neither should you, nephew. You never earned it. Because your father never killed me, it is still technically mine. I am back, *claiming my right*, and there can only be *one* King. The laws of the dark will make sure. You will grow weak as I siphon back your powers...unless I kill you and just get them faster."

"You can try," Lars rumbled, leaning forward.

"I don't need to try. It's finally just you and me, son, and I will get what is mine." Stavros gestured between them. "The strighoul and the hot-ass fighter here are really only for looks."

"You sure talk a lot for someone so desperate to fight," Lars snapped back. "And the Druid next to me isn't just for looks. I could let her take you down."

I looked at him, a grin hinting on my lips, warm fuzzies bouncing off each other in my chest. "I'd be happy to, but I don't want to take away from your family time."

"So thoughtful." He winked at me, our gazes latching on to each other.

"Hello?" Stavros waved at us. "Me here! Remember?"

"Still here?" Lars faced his uncle with a frown.

"That pretty little witch is going to be the first thing I kill. Just so you can watch another one of your lovers die."

"Witch?" My eyebrows shot up.

"Please, the gods only gave you a new title and some

parlor tricks. You can't play with the big boys, dear."

My head spun to Lars. Was he serious?

A knowing grin tipped the side of Lars's mouth, as though he were looking forward to me putting Stavros in his place.

"If I had a beer, I'd ask you to hold it right now." I inched forward, fury boiling my skin.

"Whoa." Lars tugged me back, his lips nipping my ear. "You'll get your chance. Don't show your hand yet."

I grumbled but knew he was right. I needed to come in when they wouldn't be expecting my level of power. Clearly Stavros was from the old school, where fae thought of Druids as fleas biting at fae ankles. Annoying and irritating, but nothing to worry about.

Just wait. This flea was about to draw blood.

"Give me the cauldron. You know this is not going to work out in your favor." Stavros inched closer, his hand reaching out. "No?" He sighed heavily. "I suppose that would have been too easy. Very undramatic and lackluster."

"You were always better at theater than you ever were as King."

"Ouch." Stavros placed his hand on his heart. "That hurts."

"You want the cauldron?" Lars's body rolled forward. "Come and get it."

The pause was minuscule before both men lashed out, energy exploding in a rainbow of sparks as it crashed into the other's. They both flew backward across the field.

My gaze vaulted to Margo, whose hand was already on the sword at her belt. Our glares narrowed on each other.

"Guess I can warm up with you." She exhaled. "But what will I do after the thirty seconds?"

"Bleed into the grass."

Our bodies moved, leaping for each other.

Time to steal Ms. Romania's crown.

Chapter Twenty-Six

Lars

My magic wrapped around my uncle's throat like a noose, dangling him in the air as he did me, both of us staring each other down. I had fought extraordinarily powerful opponents and some who challenged me: Aneira, even the little Druid. But I could feel the difference in their magic, sense the weaknesses where I could find upper ground. This felt as though I was fighting myself. Any crack I could find in him, he could find in me.

Digging deep, I threw my power at him, flinging him yards away into the muddy dirt. He barely came to a stop when a whip of magic lashed back at me, slicing across my abdomen. Searing pain burned my muscles, forcing a bellow from my lips.

"We can do this all day, nephew." Stavros stomped back, his black eyes pinned on me, and a smile curled his face. "And with every hit you send my way, I will absorb your magic…and you will be drained of it."

I bent over, a growl snapping my teeth. Two Unseelie Kings had never lived at the same time. No precedent existed. However, I sensed he was telling the truth.

He seemed to be growing taller, more confident with every magical punch I gave him, while I could feel fatigue weighing my shoulders down. Could he steal all my power back now that he had come to claim his throne? In the eyes of the Dark law, he was the rightful King.

I was the fraud.

A strike of energy bowled into my chest; my body twisted in the air and landed with a crunch on the rocky terrain. My face scraped against the ground, tearing flesh.

Every bone throbbed as I tried to get back on my feet, slinging my magic back at the man I had grown up hating. His slender build hurtled into the side of the mountain, rocks and debris crumbling to the ground around him as I pinned him into the solid surface.

"You want the cauldron so bad? You're going to have to try a little harder." I spit out blood, rolling back my shoulders. The thought of him regaining his seat and claiming the Treasures of Tuatha Dé Danann as his own chilled my soul. Was this how Fionna felt about me obtaining them?

"I want the throne. The treasures are just a bonus." He croaked over the pressure on his throat. A trickle of blood leaked down his forehead. "Thank you for doing all the footwork for me. I appreciate it. Too bad you won't live to see what I will be able to do with that kind of power. But you know how it goes. Only enough room at the top for one of us."

"Yeah, too bad." I growled, crushing his throat with magic hands. "Our family has always been so close." My brother and I actually were. Rare for demons. Killing him was the hardest thing I ever had to do. My father had never liked his twin, but he couldn't destroy him.

Daggers of pain shot across my head as I hurled more magic at Stavros, my lungs grappling for more air.

Fuck. I was getting tired.

Stavros coughed a strained mechanical laugh, his face relaxing as though he were at a spa. "Keep fighting me, son. It feels amazing."

Fighting him only enhanced his magic and weakened mine. For the first time I could remember, I didn't know what to do.

Clangs of swords and shouts from across the field finally broke in, shooting my gaze to the other fight going on around us.

Unfathomable terror filled my chest and almost dropped me to my knees.

Fionna.

My eyes raked the open space, trying to find her, anxiety curling up in my throat. It was like being shocked awake, emotion firing up my veins.

If anything happened to her…

My gaze finally landed on the petite Druid, my mouth parting.

She stood with her arms open, air fuzzy around her as if she were in a bubble. Margo and a handful of strighoul surrounded her. But they weren't fighting her. They were protecting her, clashing against the other strighoul attacking.

Black magic.

I was highly aware she could do this, but seeing her true power—the ability to shred fae of their will and use them as puppets—and more than ten of them? I had vastly underestimated her. But the closer I looked, the more I spotted the strain on her face, the blood pooling from her nose and leaking from her eyes. Death danced on the edges of the barrier, ready to jump.

She was killing herself.

"Fionna!" I bellowed, ripping my magic from Stavros, reeling it back like a fishing rod. Stumbling with exhaustion over the rough terrain, I scrambled to the Druid.

Halfway there, magic shot into my spine like a bullet. I sailed forward and landed a few feet from her, feeling every bump and jostle in my tired bones. My body wanted to curl up and sleep, give in to the lethargy, and replenish. But my ego did not understand the depletion. Not this fast, nor this easy. My mind would not give up.

I clawed the dirt, picking myself up. Fionna still stared forward, oblivious to my presence, her forehead frowning with determination. Blood covered her face and clothes, the stream growing heavier with each passing moment.

Her soldiers continued to fight for her, their faces void of emotion, similar to robots.

"Fionna, stop!" I yelled.

She didn't react at all, capturing one more strighoul in her web.

Any more and it would be too much. The energy it took to bend just *one* mind to your will was immense. Multiply it by twelve or fifteen. The resistance they flung back at you, and the focus you must maintain to keep each in play.

"Fionna. Stop. Now!" I tried to wiggle my magic into her sphere to stop her, but it rebounded against her magic shield. I stumbled back. At the sound of a deep laugh, I spun around.

"Not even your witch listens to you." Stavros strolled up toward me. "What kind of King are you when a lowly Druid doesn't even respect you?"

"Fear is not the same as respect," I snarled, wiping blood from my lip. "And what kind of man *or* King needs to have people tremble before him to make himself feel powerful? That's not a real King or man."

"And look at what your lack of leadership has brought the world. Look around, nephew. The world is at war because of your leadership. Humans are killing fae with no repercussions. Even fae have lost their way. People need laws, to know their place." He lifted his hands, his skin thinning to almost nothing. "Including you."

Invisible hands wrapped around my throat. I could not breathe. My feet swung as I went up into the air, my hands going to my throat. How many times had I used this same magic on others?

Fight. Fight back, I shouted at myself, but with every struggle, energy dripped out of me, siphoning to Stavros as though we shared an IV.

Spots dotted my vision, my muscles falling limp as more compression crushed my throat. My lids lowered; my vision was now black. I had never imagined dying. I was always ready for it, but I never gave any thought to the particulars.

Now as my life slowly drained, it wasn't Devlin or Aisling I thought of—most likely I would be seeing them soon enough. Ember was my first thought. I wished I had told her I loved her. I wanted to see my daughter one last time. And lastly, I thought of *her*. The Druid who had bounded into my life, literally knocked me on my ass the first time I met her, and completely flipped my world upside down.

"Noooo!" a voice screamed in the far distance, barely carrying into what was left of my conscious mind.

I turned away from it, floating in silence and calm, letting it take me where it wanted. Peace. Is this what it felt like? I felt neither asleep nor awake. Just there without worries or concerns. It felt amazing.

Then, as though someone had flipped a switch, I was flung from the serenity, spinning out of the dark cocoon into the blinding light. I hit the ground, air flooding my chest with a choking gasp. My lids popped open. I inhaled as much oxygen as my lungs could take, trying to stop the sky from spinning over me.

Slowly, I rolled onto my knees, coughing and wheezing. My gaze shot around, but it took a moment for understanding to connect to what I saw.

No one attacked me, and no sounds of a conflict filled my ears.

At last I spotted one form standing in the field, her back to me, the wind whipping her dark ponytail around.

"Fionna?" My voice sounded weak as I stood. She didn't respond. I took a few steps, noticing lumps lying across the land. Bodies.

"What the...?" Strighoul, Margo, and even my uncle lay unconscious at her feet. I could sense they were all still alive but knocked out cold. This level of power was astonishing. Unprecedented. She had done it to save my life. "Fionna, what did you do?"

Her head jerked, twisting to me. "Lars?" she whimpered.

Terror stuck in my throat. Her eyes, nose, and ears were no longer bleeding red. Black ooze streamed out of them in surges. Death was the payment for the use of dark magic.

"I can't see." Her legs wobbled under her weight.

"Fionna!" I sprinted, reaching her as her body collapsed into my arms, her head falling back. "Do not die on me, Druid." I could hear the panic in my voice as I placed my fingers at the pulse on her neck. It was light but still tapped against my hand. For now. She didn't have long. I had to heal her. Soon. And I was aware it would take a lot more from me than normal to fight against the black magic. It would make us both vulnerable and weak for a while.

"Stay with me." I lifted her up, her limp frame dangling in my arms.

I peered down at my uncle. He should have been my concern, my only interest, using the last of my magic to kill him. But he wasn't. All I could think of was the tiny woman in my arms. She was going to die.

I rolled her into my chest, stepping over my uncle, and carried her away.

Chapter Twenty-Seven

Fionna

Warmth flamed against my skin. The sound of crackling fire encouraged my lashes to open. Shadows and lights flickered on the rock above my head similar to shadow puppets. I blinked again and turned my head toward the heat. My sight took in Lars crouched in front of a fire, the muscles along his bare back clenching as he poked at the blaze. His shirt hung on a rope, drying over the open pit.

We were back in the cave. Kevin's home.

My memories of the last few hours hurtled back into my mind, recalling the magic that surged through my bones. When I saw Stavros killing Lars, my brain shut off and my magic took over. I had used black magic a lot in my life and learned where my limits were and how many fae I could control at one time. Yet I had gone way past my boundaries. And I only grew hungrier for more in that moment. I couldn't stop even though I knew it could kill me.

And when I saw Lars dying, his life dwindling out, filling his uncle, I lost it. Power I'd never felt before came blasting out of me. It took over my brain and insides. My body barely contained the energy.

I should be dead. My hand went to my stomach. Foreign magic filled my insides, wrapping around my muscles like a blanket, numbing me of the pain I knew I should be feeling.

Black magic didn't come without a *huge* cost. The price should have been my life. But it wasn't. And I knew it had to do with the man by the fire.

Pushing myself up to sit, the bundles of grass and blankets under me lulled me to lie back down. I watched Lars, taking him in.

He saved my life. *And you saved his…*

"Hey." My voice cracked, blending into the sputtering blaze.

Green eyes flashed at me, then back to the fire. Muscles along his back tightened, responding to my presence, but he didn't speak. A dense silence strung between us in which I stared at the designs the flames created over the cave.

"You..." I cleared my throat. "Saved my life?" It came out more of a question than I wanted.

He huffed, standing to his full height. "You saved mine first. Just repaying the debt."

"Ah." I nodded, disappointment pouring down on me like a waterfall. "A debt. That's all it was."

He shifted around, his eyes blazing, but his shoulders slumped and he stumbled with fatigue. "What do you think it would be, Ms. Cathbad?"

I ignored his response, observing the dark circles under his eyes, the exhaustion haunting his brow.

"Lars…" I got up, moving to him, my hand reaching out for his face. He turned his head but didn't jerk away when my thumb brushed over the deep purple ringing his eyes, my hand cupping his face. My lips pinched together, trying to hold back the shock at seeing the King look depleted and withdrawn.

"Did I do this to you? By healing me?"

"No." He swallowed, not looking at me.

"He's taking your powers." The pad of my thumb swept over his cheek. "And you still used your energy to save me. Why?"

His jaw rolled, his gaze finding mine, burning me as if I had stepped into the fire.

"Look who's up." A gravelly voice came from behind me. "Finally."

I swung around, dropping away from Lars.

Kevin strutted up, his lips twisted in a snarl, his arm dressed with the sock, Gerry. "Sleep in my bed, burn my wood. What? You moving in with me now?"

"You are a daft idiot, Kevin." Gerry shook his head. "It was just getting good."

"What the fuck you talking about?" Kevin glanced with confusion between Gerry and us.

Gerry sighed heavily, rolling his head back. "You really are 'special' as your mum suggested. How have I put up with you for so many years?"

"Don't be talkin' to me that way, you ungrateful wanker," Kevin growled at his hand.

"Don't remind me of that." Gerry shivered.

"It happened once." Kevin flung his other hand against his leg.

Gerry slowly turned to Kevin, looking as though he was rolling his lips together.

"Okay. Twice...maybe three times, but you didn't complain the last time."

"How can I complain when my mouth is blocked from talking?" Gerry swiveled to us. "Not much though, his dink is as big as his brain."

"Wow." I scratched my temple, trying to block the images from appearing in my head.

"Glad you're well, *cailin*." Gerry nodded toward me. "I was so worried when he brought you in. You looked dead. But now look!"

Kevin scoffed, rolling his eyes. "Great. Eating *my* food, drinking *my* swill."

"He's the King. Show some respect!" Gerry shot over at the leprechaun.

"Well, get out...soon, *Your Highness*," Kevin grumbled, moving back down the tunnel.

"He really means well, Majesty." Gerry's reply echoed down the passageway, disappearing into the dark.

"No. I don't. Don't tell me what I feel!"

"You wonder why no one likes you. Because you're a grumpy ole' git. A bollix!"

"And you're such a lickarse."

Their voices argued back and forth until they trailed off into nothing.

"Is it strange I'm growing fond of Gerry?" Lars muttered, forcing a small chuckle from me. "The leprechaun is a bastard."

My head bounced with humor. It was easy to start thinking of them as two entities.

"He's right about one thing." Lars reached around for his shirt. "We need to go. My uncle's still out there, which means he could find us."

"Lars, look at you. You are barely standing." I motioned down him. "You will be no good if we run into them again."

"Fionn—"

"Don't Fionna me." I shook my head, pointing to the bed on the ground. "It's your turn to rest."

His mouth opened to object.

"I'm not taking no for an answer." I tipped up one eyebrow. "Do not challenge me right now, Lars. I will win."

He let out a small scoff. "I am beginning to see that."

"Then we might actually get along." A smile curled my lips.

He stood close, staring down at me, his gaze fierce on my eyes, heat sparking in his.

My breath caught, sensing every molecule of him move toward me, as though he were actually touching me. Every muscle tightened, not letting me move. Except my chest. It fluttered and banged with a mix of fear and desire.

His energy glided over me, consuming me whole. But I sensed the cracks in it through which his magic leaked. The longer Stavros lived, the faster Lars would die.

"Let me try and heal you," I whispered, my fingers ghosting the skin of his torso, following the tattoo on his side.

"No. What ails me won't be fixed by magic," he replied huskily. "You need to heal yourself. I've only mended you a little, then numbed it. It will start wearing off soon."

"I knocked Stavros out." I swallowed, staring at his ink. "Why didn't you kill him when you had the chance?"

Lars's silence drew my chin up. He watched me intently, his head tilted, as though he were thinking, *"Don't you know why?"*

Fireworks exploded in my chest, emotion almost knocking me over. He had chosen me.

His chest and hips pressed into me, his arms staying at his sides. I nipped my bottom lip, choking back the rush of need I had for him. My fingers glided up his arms, thankful no clothing impeded my curious hands.

He let out a breath and shut his lids when I skated over the tattoo on his heart.

"What does this mean?"

"Warrior, leader, protector…and lover." He spoke low and husky. "One of the twin flames represent my brother, and the other flame is for my lost love. Her power was fire"

"Oh." I tried to swallow back the sudden lump in my throat.

"They are there to not let me forget."

"Forget what?" I whispered.

"What I have right in front of me." He leaned in closer, his breath slinking down my neck. My heart slammed into my chest as his head dipped even closer to my lips.

And closer. But he didn't stop.

"Shite! Lars!" I wrapped my arms around his waist, trying to hold him up. His legs bent as consciousness seeped from him. I grunted, holding on tight as I dragged him as best I could to fall onto the grass bed. I lowered down on my knees next to him. Not even hesitating, a healing chant pelted from my mouth.

Snap.

Like a band breaking, Lars's magic morphine on me surrendered and sharp pain stabbed through me.

The spell died in my mouth, and I bent over, taking in a shaky breath. A tickle at my nose towed my fingers above my lip. Black liquid stained my fingers.

Shite.

I needed to fully heal myself, but something stopped me from greedily taking energy for myself. My gaze landed on Lars's profile, his scruff reflecting in the firelight. Gray hair now sprinkled his sideburns. I reached out, needing to make sure my eyes weren't playing tricks on me.

Gray hair.

He was aging.

Fae aged so slowly it appeared almost nonexistent. He was far from those years.

This was because of Stavros.

Fury burned up my spine. *He will not take Lars from me.*

I pushed my palm into his chest, then into my own. I had never tried this, to attempt a dual healing. I had no idea if it would even help him, but I had to try. We both needed to be restored. It was not one or the other.

We were in this together.

~~

When I woke up again, the fire was down to embers, the chill in the cave creeping over me. I shivered and nuzzled closer to the warm body next to me. The arm wrapped around me tugged me in, forcing me to peer up at Lars, his eyes glowing in the dusky glow.

"Do you feel better?" I asked, enjoying the nearness of him far too much.

"I do," he responded. "But you shouldn't have wasted your energy on me."

"I didn't waste it."

"It was…if it can help you more. It's only a temporary fix on me." His fingers reached out, tucking a strand of hair behind my ear. "I am dying, Fionna. No Druid magic can fight against the laws of the Dark."

I propped on my arms, looking down on him. "Watch me."

"You will never pull a stunt as you did earlier again."

"Excuse me?"

"I believe I was clear."

I cocked my head. "And I believe I was clear when I said no one tells me what to do. You do not get to order me about, Lars. I am my own person. Not your underling."

"You don't want to be under me?"

I sniffed in a gallon of air, his implication spinning my head like a carnival ride. Was he messing with me? He wasn't really one for being playful. My lids narrowed on him.

"That a no?" A glint flicked in his eyes. Wow. The arsehole was taking the piss.

"Fuck you." I batted his arm.

He grabbed my wrists in a blink, pulling me closer to him, ire flashing over his face. "Be sure you are ready for that response before you say it again."

Like an animal stunned by headlights, I locked in place. Frozen.

"You almost died in my arms for the stupid thing you did." He sat up.

"I saved your life."

His hand covered my mouth, and he inclined toward me. "I need you, Druid." A beat of my heart pumped before he spoke again. "I need you to be at your best. To break the spell on the cauldron. I trust you to carry it. Stavros will come for me first. I need you to run. Get it and the other treasures as far from Washington as possible."

Tears stung the back of my lids. He had given up wanting it for himself. He trusted me to do the exact thing I had originally planned. I shook my head, his hand still over my lips.

"Yes, Fionna. You *must*," he said firmly. "Get your daughter and run to Budapest, anywhere in the Eastern bloc. They are the only places safe from Stavros's control when he becomes King."

I pulled away from Lars's hand. "No. I'm not going to let you die. We will kill him. Together."

"You don't get it. The more magic I use on him, the more he grows in power. It's the law. There is only one King, and he is the rightful ruler." He ran a hand over his messy hair. "Don't worry. I am too egotistical to just give in. I will fight. To the death. However, if things go badly, I want you to do this for me. Do not hesitate or look back. Just run."

My throat braided together, and I struggled to swallow, staring down at the weaving in the blanket.

His fingers slid up my jaw, tipping my head up. "Please."

My lids fluttered with moisture, my head slowly moving up and down.

"I will."

Chapter Twenty-Eight

Lars

The dawn hadn't even broken over the hills when we set out. We made the car ride mostly in silence, my attention on the rearview mirror. I sped down the narrow roads in my hurry to get to Finnich Glen.

Fionna stared out the window. The rolling hills and jagged peaks were lost in a canvas of darkness, the side of her face only highlighted by the glow of the dashboard.

I was serious when I told her to take the cauldron and run. Before Stavros, my main concern had been to remain King. I'd been thinking of myself, of the monster I might turn into, picking power over any other option. Now that it could all be taken from me because of some ancient law, not even the satisfaction I wasn't going insane helped ease my mind.

Now I wanted Fionna to do the precise thing she was probably going to do in the first place: hide the treasures from the Unseelie King.

A knot formed in my throat at the thought. Technically, I was still King, but I could feel the end coming with every breath. Soon all I worked for would be gone.

My first thought, even before my kingdom, was my family at home. Ember. The dark dwellers. As soon as I could get service again, I had to prepare my compound for what was to come.

To show his dominance, Stavros would probably take over my house. I would never allow Marguerite, Nik, or Alki to be his slaves. Nor my men. He would definitely want to use Ember; she was too powerful for him to ignore. They all needed to get to the Seelie castle and fight him with the Queen or follow Fionna east and go into exile.

"I'm hungry." Fionna crossed her legs, shifting in her seat, her face still turned toward the window.

"Well, I'm sure there's a McDonald's around the next corner." I scoffed, staring out at vast emptiness, no streetlamps or civilization nearby.

She turned and gave me a derisive glance. "Funny."

"I seem to be lately."

She snorted, shaking her head, her ponytail brushing the headrest.

"You know I need food and coffee."

"Don't I know it." I grinned, recalling her crankiness in the morning.

"Just warning you."

"We have to obtain a powerful treasure before the rising King gets it and destroys the world, but I'm sure even he would understand I need to feed you first." I glanced in my rearview mirror again, checking for any following cars, any sense of magic. Nothing but blackness draped behind us, like it had since we departed. Not that I was letting my guard down for a moment. "He'll wait."

She tried to fight the smile wobbling on her mouth. "Fine."

"Oh, no. I am genuinely more afraid of your stomach than him." I hit the GPS, finding the nearest town.

"No, really. You're right. We have to get there." She nodded.

"It can wait ten minutes." I zeroed in on a village twenty miles ahead. Hopefully a bakery or grocery would be open by then.

Fionna faced me again, analyzing me. I could feel her gaze creep over my skin.

"What?"

She didn't respond, just kept staring at me. Finally I had to glance over. Her expression commanded my hands to strangle the steering wheel. Emotion swirled in her eyes. Confusion, sadness, and hunger. But not for food.

"What is it?" I asked again.

She broke away, wagging her head. "Nothing."

I can't say what possessed me, but with one eye on the empty road, I reached out for her face, cupped the back of her head, and turned her back to look at me.

She briefly closed her eyes and leaned into my hand.

"Everything is going to be all right."

"No, it won't." Her pupils reflected the liquid developing behind her lashes. "And don't lie to me or pretend it will be."

"Just get your daughter and the treasures to the eastern Europe countries. I know you can survive. You are so strong and will do what you have to do to protect Piper."

"That's not what I was talking about." Her voice was low and hoarse. Her meaning shot into me like a dart gun, returning my hand to the steering wheel.

"Fionna," I rumbled. My heart thumped in my chest, wanting her to touch me, to tell me what she really meant. However, it was futile. Whatever the significance of her statement, it was impossible, especially now.

She groaned, twisting to stare out the glass. "Now I wish you would call me by my last name."

"I wish things were different." I was never one to shy away from a tense subject. "But it is not."

"Do you?"

"What?"

"Wish things were different?"

"It's not." I pressed my lips together. "No point even considering the idea."

"Yes, there is." She pressed on. "Just for one moment say we weren't on the road to get the last treasure, and you weren't being robbed of your throne from your uncle...what would you want to be doing right now?"

"I am not playing this game."

"Yes, you are." Her eyebrows condensed, leaning closer to me. "For once let yourself pretend in the possibility of 'what if.'"

"Why?" I snarled, my voice rising. "What good does it do anyone?"

"It gives people hope. A reason to believe there is more than tragedy and sadness in this world."

"It is foolish to believe anything else."

"Why?" She matched my tone. "What would happen if you gave in? You're a man who thinks of all possibilities and outcomes. Why can't hope be one of them?"

My teeth ground.

"Tell me!"

I growled, snapping the wheel, pulling the car to a stop on the gravel in the parking lot. I whipped toward her, leaned over the console, and grasped her by the back of the neck.

"Because I once let myself hope and believed the rumors were wrong. When I found out the only thing I loved in the world was taken from me by her sister all because of me, because of what we created together..." My skin tightened along my cheekbones, the demon railing behind its cage, though it didn't want blood. "It broke me." I swallowed, the nearness of her mouth almost compelling me to do the actual thing she asked. "I won't do it again."

My fingers slid up the back of her neck, producing a jilted inhale from her. "And what I want to do? I could drown myself in the what-ifs. In all the possibilities..." I inclined even closer, her breath skimming my lips.

"What do you want to do, Lars?" she whispered.

I wanted to kiss her. Fuck her. Hard. Fierce. I wanted nothing more than to pull her into the backseat and thrust into her till our bodies gave out.

"I want what I can't have." My nails dug into the back of her head, her chest rapidly moving up and down. "Something I should never have wanted because it is far too dangerous for me to possess."

Her parted lips were far too tempting, and I felt my willpower breaking down, crumbling to dust before my eyes. My eyes dropped to her mouth, my own aching to tug on her bottom lip. My tongue wanted to explore her mouth, her body.

"You're talking about the frickin' cauldron, aren't you?" Her jaw locked, her head turning away from me, a wall building back up between us. "Figures." She snorted, grabbing the door handle and slipped out of the car, marching toward the bakery where I parked, her ass wiggling with determination to get away from me.

I let out a ragged breath, almost grateful she had read my statement that way. I was about to cross the line, not even caring about the consequences.

"No, Druid. I was most certainly not talking about the cauldron," I said to myself, getting out of the car.

The treasures I could handle. I wasn't afraid of much, if anything. What I felt for the pint-size Druid? She terrified me.

I was trying to fight her, fight whatever I was feeling. But the fence I was walking on was crumbling before and behind me.

One more shove from her and I would fall.

Chapter Twenty-Nine

Fionna

I stuffed the egg croissant in my mouth, downing it with a gulp of coffee. I kept my gaze pointed on the stormy morning eclipsing the landscape. Gray skies blocked all sunrays from touching the earth. The clouds grew darker and angrier as bolts of lightning danced across the sky before us.

Just like my mood.

At first I was pissed at him, but soon it turned to humiliation. I wasn't a what-if type of person. I'd let those pipe dreams fade with my youth. But my need to hear him say a possibility existed, that there was hope, backfired in my face. How hard was it to say *he wanted me*? The phrase crossed my brain, making me cringe.

If I had left it as he asked, I'd be able to turn my face his way every once in a while. Now the dim, drizzly day was the most interesting thing in the world. I ate my breakfast without even tasting it, which irritated me more. I was just a frickin' happy ray of sunshine.

Lars sighed again, his annoyance ramming up against mine. The tension in the vehicle divided the car into two different compartments, except I sensed every breath, every twitch of his muscles. The deep masculine scent of him skulked over the coffee aura, slinking up my nose and tormenting me.

Damn, he smelled good. The scent was hard to describe: creamy, rich, dark, a little sweet, and sexy. It was multilayered and complex. Similar to him. And it drew me to him like sheep to grass. That might not seem fierce, but it is if you were the pasture. Lars was lush green grass to me right now.

Why weren't we there yet? Two hours felt like centuries. The tip of my fingers tapped impatiently on the top of my empty coffee container. From my peripheral, I watched Lars's shoulders hunch up to his ears. I grinned smugly out the side window.

"Stop."

I ignored him, tapping louder.

"Stop. It."

"Stop what?" With my other hand, I started cracking my knuckles, popping each finger. Yes, I was taunting him, but I didn't care.

"*Fionna, I swear.*" He curved the car into a small, empty unmarked lot next to a three-way intersection. We were out in the middle of nowhere, surrounded by nothing but fields and hedges. Only one house sat directly on the corner. This early, the area was empty and still.

"What?" I cracked my thumb, the pop echoing off the metal, and finally rotated my head to him. "What will you do, Lars?"

He hit the brakes, gravel flying everywhere as he stopped the car. He barely turned off the engine before he jumped out of the car.

I tracked him in the rearview mirror, his back curled forward with fury. It should have scared me but it didn't. His temper worked on me like a magnet. Similar to a ram, I grew excited to strike against him. Challenge him.

He yanked on my door, flinging it open, the door groaning with the exertion. He grabbed my arm, ripped the empty cup from my hand and chucked it on the car floor. He dragged me out of the Rover, shoving me up against the side, stealing air from my lungs.

"When I say stop, you stop," he ordered, his green eyes burning into me. I knew we were no longer talking about the coffee cup or cracking my knuckles.

"No." I lifted my chin.

A growl came from him. "Do not push me, Druid."

"Why, because I won't do as you say?" I shot back. "Sorry, *Your Highness*, but you don't always get your way. I am no one's subordinate." I shoved at his chest. His olive complexion faded. "For your whole life everyone has done what you say, met every demand. Do you even know what it is to be challenged? To not get your way?"

"Yes." He gripped my arms tighter, his presence over me growing more intense.

"When was that? When you were an infant?"

"Try right now."

"And you hate it." I nudged him, muttering a spell that made him slip over the gravel a few feet. I walked toward him, my shoulders rolled defensively. I sensed his contained anger slipping. Most people would stop, back off. I wasn't most people. "And *love* it."

"That is the problem." He lowered his head, prowling back for me, a slight pressure circling my throat, pushing my back into a field gate, speeding up my pulse. Though I could easily break it, I didn't.

Lightning cracked across the sky as though the weather felt our intensity, igniting the air with electricity.

"And what problem is that?" Drops of rain hit my head, slipping down my neck.

Lars stomped up to me, both of his hands gripping my face roughly. "Because every time you defy me," he seethed. "I want to *fuck* you instead of *kill* you."

My airways shut down, and my chest faltered under the rush of heat cascading down my body, especially between my thighs.

We stared at each other, his eyes flickering a deep green, as though he was barely holding on to the man. My gaze dropped down, taking in the way the rain plastered his shirt to his torso, defining every ripped ab underneath the cotton. My eyes kept going down. *Shite.* His jeans could barely hold him in. His excitement only sent mine soaring, my cheeks flushing with heat.

At my reaction, the force around my neck dropped away, but his fingers dug into my scalp, igniting fire down my spine like a line of burning hot wax. Desire circled us in thick syrup, sticking to every inch of my skin and weighing down my lungs.

I knew what this was going to be. Merely sex. It had been so long. I may have been fine alone and being single, but I missed sex. I longed to lose myself and feel the desire to feel ecstasy along every nerve. Hopefully this would end whatever I was feeling. Get him out of my system. It worked for most of the guys before.

But this is a demon king. Stop now! My conscience screamed at me. He was my enemy in every way, but the wrongness of us only fueled my need to feel him.

"For once you are going to submit to *me*," he growled in my ear. I wanted to contest his statement, battling the notion I would *ever* submit to a fae, but when he yanked my head back with one hand, his other pulling at my jean buttons, the words dwindled away.

Open to any car passing by, he unzipped my jeans, letting his fingers skim down my stomach. "Get the fuck out of my system, Druid." He gritted his teeth in anger as he rubbed his hand over the fabric of my knickers.

"Same, demon," I seethed back, pushing into his hand; the need for him to touch me deeper clouded any thoughts. His eyes flashed as his hands grabbed my hips. He turned me around to face the fence. Lars placed my hands on the slippery rail of the metal fence and roughly tugged my trousers down over my hips.

Rain poured down, slicking our clothes and hair with shivering cold, the precipitation only slightly easing the heat building inside. Cars rumbled in the far distance, heading down the lane. Inhabitants of the house across the street could look out their window and see us.

I only shivered in anticipation. Who would have thought I'd get an adrenaline rush from being watched or caught?

My breath was ragged as I curled my hands around the fence, arching my back. Rain and cold air slithered over my bare skin, feeling like more hands wanting to pleasure me. His fingers plunged into me, encouraging my body to respond. I gasped as he moved quicker, going deeper.

He made a deep noise as another shot of lightning cracked over us, the hairs on my arms standing up. The way he stroked me, I realized he had complete control of my body. I would let him dominate me, take what he wanted. Over and over again.

I heard his zipper, then I felt him drag himself along me. I cried out, swear words ripping through my teeth, one right after the other. The vehicles were progressing closer, the rain plummeting down on us, whipping my hair. He rolled my ponytail into his fist.

He bit at my ear, causing me to whimper. "Only once."

I nodded. He could have said anything and I would have agreed. Druids didn't go long without sex, but I had conditioned myself and had gotten used to denying my sexual need. Not many men I'd met had really tempted me.

Until now. Until him.

"Fuck me now," I demanded. "Put me in my place, *King*."

His chest vibrated, yanking my head back. He removed his fingers, the emptiness only brief, before I felt the tip of him. I clawed the chipped paint on the fence, pushing back into him. Then he thrust into me, forcing a loud cry from my lungs. Electricity zapped up my spine, dotting my vision and sparking along my skin. *Shite. Fuck. Shite. Fuck. Shiiiiiiiittteee.*

He bellowed out garbled words, his grip digging into my hipbones.

Nothing could have prepared me for how he would feel. Not anything. Nothing I had experienced in life had felt this good. Even the slight pain from his size was exhilarating.

He moved deeper, growling as he picked up speed. I made noises that would have put the stewardess on the plane to shame. I had made fun of her. Now I understood there was so much sensation you couldn't hold it in. It had to break out. He was almost too much.

Almost.

I matched his ferocity. Pushing back, matching the savagery of his thrusts.

We were punishing each other, unleashing all the anger, hate, and desire we had felt and wanted the other to be reprimanded for. It was hate-sex. Nothing more.

He took my hands a rung lower, bending me farther forward and plunged deeper.

Holy shite. I gripped the railing, feeling the pulse of my orgasm start. I never wanted this to end, but at the same time I chased after the climax like a fiend.

"Fuck, Druid." He slammed in harder. "You shouldn't feel this fucking amazing."

I couldn't even respond. Was there lightning in the sky or merely the electricity tearing off our bodies?

The pavement of the road rumbled with an

approaching car. We would be seen any moment, but I didn't care as my climax scaled my torso.

Sensing the approaching vehicle, Lars pulled me up, pressing my back to his chest, getting somehow deeper. His hand reached around and rubbed me as he bit down at the sensitive skin behind my ear.

"Fuccccckkk!" My body broke apart and gripped him like a vise. I screamed, air ripping from my lungs, as my system was crushed by the delicious orgasm. I didn't want it to stop. Surges and waves rolled through, taking me so high I no longer existed as a singular entity.

I was Earth. Sky. Every color. Sound. Every living organism.

And nothing.

I heard him bellow behind me, felt him throbbing and emptying inside me.

Gradually, I floated back to earth. I couldn't move or speak, our breaths in sync, his chest plastered to my back. The rain sprinkled down on us.

Reality started to slip in, but my brain was not ready to accept I'd just had sex with a fae. Incredible sex. Mind-blowing, earth-shattering sex.

On purpose.

If I was going to break a rule. I really went for it.

Shite. What did I just do?

Chapter Thirty

Lars

Every expletive roared out of my mouth as I released inside of her so violently I had to reach around and grab on to the gate to keep upright. I didn't swear much before; it did not suit a king. However, since I met her that had changed. Now I was hollering the words out, stringing them into full sentences.

I had left the bakery determined to keep the focus on our mission, berating myself I had let her weaken me. She should have been nowhere near capturing my thoughts besides how she would break the spell on the cauldron.

My resolve lasted for about two and half minutes. My gaze kept drifting to her mouth, how it moved around her sandwich, how she licked her lips to get the drops of coffee from them. In her anger at me she'd held her chin high and pointed toward the window, as if we'd had a lovers' squabble. The way the Druid, even silently, could oppose me at every turn turned me on. I wanted to fight back, smash the silence and fill the car with her moans.

When she started tapping the lid of her drink, cracking her knuckles just to irritate me, it drove me over the edge. The tension in the car exploded, crumbling the last of my willpower, and the demon took the reins. It wanted her and was not going to let me get in the way anymore.

Demons were not known to be refined or respectful, which is why I kept it far from whomever I was with. It lived to claim and destroy.

After Aisling, my demon went into hibernation, no longer caring enough about a woman to show itself as passion. Since the moment Fionna stepped into my life, the demon had been dancing below the surface, aggravated and restless. Clawing. Wanting. Edgy. Angry.

A strike of lightning zigzagged to the ground, striking the field near us. Electrical energy prickled my skin as I pumped into her the final time. I bellowed as she pulsed and tightened around me. Pleasure tore through me. My mouth locked open in a groan, ecstasy freezing me in place.

Gradually reality dotted my sight. My muscles retracted, going limp, my head fell back. I swear I felt the demon sigh contently, curling back deep under my skin like a sleepy lion.

Happy. Relaxed. Completely satisfied.

Suddenly I felt something I hadn't in decades...utter peace.

Yet even this was different from how it had been with Aisling, as if all my life I had been searching for something. And I finally found it. Even the storm had eased as though we were the ones causing it.

Could our magic be so intense together?

That only happened when...

Fear immediately sprang up, my heart thumping from exertion and terror.

No. My brain instantly denied. *Absolutely not.* She wasn't anything than another fuck. Nothing more.

The hand resting on the gate slid up her neck cupping it angrily as I leaned into her ear.

"Never again, Druid," I snarled. I tried not to think about the fact I was still inside her. Truth was I didn't want to pull out or away, even with the impending vehicles about to pass by. Actually, it only made me want to start again. To claim her like some caveman.

I growled with annoyance about to demand that she understood where we stood, when I sensed eyes stabbing the back of my neck like a fork. I curved my neck, still holding Fionna close to my body.

A woman in the house across the street stood at the window, one hand on her hip, the other shaking at me, her mouth moving as if she were telling me off. I was reduced from grown man to horny teenage. "We've been caught."

"What?" Fionna turned her head the same way. It took her only a few seconds before she started laughing, her body vibrating with humor, which only made me grow hard inside of her again.

She hissed, gripping the fence.

A truck pulled up to the stop sign. I planned to be gone by the time it passed.

Reluctantly, I pulled out, zipped myself back in, hauled up Fionna's pants, and grabbed her arm, speeding us through the gate and down the path. By the time the truck fully passed the house, we would be gone. To human eyes we'd move faster than a blink. The woman would likely be standing there wondering if she imagined us.

"Damn. Let a girl zip her trousers," Fionna grumbled, buttoning her top button once we were safely in the trees.

We both stopped and stared at each other, as though realizing what we just did. Maybe I really was going mentally insane. I had never been so reckless and impulsive. This was by far the most irrational I had been in a long, long time. When you're young, you chalk it up to learning, pushing your boundaries. I was far too old to be this imprudent. I pushed up my sleeves, annoyance burrowing into my head.

"I think it's best...we just forget that little incident." Fionna rubbed her sweater down flat. "Pretend it never happened."

"Yes." I nodded. "I think it's best."

Awkward silence clipped down around us, chewing on the air like a rat.

"Well?" She raised her arms, twisting back for the car. Her eyes wouldn't meet mine.

"It's this way." I motioned down the trail, forcing my gaze to stop roaming over her mouth, tracing her lips. Her neck.

"Oh. We're here?" Her brow furrowed, peering around.

My head bobbed in response. There was no real parking lot or signs, the spot still trying to stay hidden from the general public.

"Okay. Then let's get to why we're here. Find the cauldron." She took determined steps forward, reaching Jacob's Ladder. The glen, which was once called Ashdow, was a gorgeous chasm carved through old red sandstone, reaching heights of over seventy feet and some widths only ten to fifteen feet. Dramatic and magical, it was surrounded by farmland and rolling green grass. Tucked deep in the land and bordered by dense twisted trees and scrubs, you would never know it was there. A true hidden treasure.

According to local lore, the gorge was a secret meeting place for the ancient Druids. My skin thrummed with their magic, which swirled off the surface of the river, as though they were still there communing with nature.

Each step down the treacherous, uneven stone steps, slick with rain, mud, and leaves taunted you like an obstacle course. If you could safely reach the bottom, you were awarded the enchanted scenery soaring up around you in dramatic fashion. Nature's theater.

Halfway down the steep staircase, Fionna's hand gripped the back of my shirt, holding on for dear life as her boots squeaked over the slippery, worn steps. It would be so easy to slip and fall down the steep ravine.

Nearing the bottom, I heard the sound of rubber sliding, her boots losing their grip on the surface. Her arms circled my waist with a cry. Halting, I reached around, tugging her into me, keeping her steady. Her physical weight against me was nothing, however, the heat from her body pressing into mine, and the feel of her hands fanned out on my stomach carried the weight of a boulder against my back.

The demon awoke with a start.

Shit. I wanted to fuck her again.

She didn't move, as though she could sense my thoughts.

"You all right?" I tried to speak evenly, but a roughness pulsed my words.

"Yeah." She yanked her arms back, clearing her throat. "Fine."

I stepped onto the ground and moved away from her. Her nearness stirred my blood to a boil, as if she had put me in a cauldron and let me cook. Clearing my throat, I refocused on the terrain around us.

It was even more spectacular than it had been from above. Nature's own magic coated every rock and tree in deep green moss. Ferns and roots from trees above dangled down like ropes, curling and twisting overhead or alongside the jagged walls. Red water trickled through the gulch, carving out its own trail, crafting an old-world sense of peace and ambiance, a slice of the earth that had not been touched the industrial age or modern technology where pure magic still existed. And somewhere hidden here was the last Treasure of Tuatha Dé Danann.

My gaze shot up to the top of the stairs, paranoid

Stavros was following us, that I would lead him straight to it, picked at my skin the same way a vulture did. I had no idea where he went, but I knew he was far from done with me.

But no magic was felt. Not Unseelie King magic. I would feel it, sense my own magic thrumming off him.

"You probably will perceive it before I do." I turned back to Fionna, motioning for her to take the lead. She stepped past me, looking forward. My sight landed on a deep reddish-purple bite on the side of her neck right above three nail marks. I reached out, grabbing her shoulder. "What's that from?"

"You."

I inhaled through my nose. I didn't remember biting or clawing her. Fuck, I *had* lost control. I let the demon slip through.

"I apologize," I replied stiffly.

"Don't." She curved back to look at me through her lashes. "I enjoyed it."

The demon flooded forward, sharpening my senses. I knew my eyes had gone black. He wanted to conquer and take.

Her nose flared.

It happened one time. That's it. I closed my eyes, man and beast fighting for control. The demon would not rule me. I breathed in and reopened my eyes, stepping away from her.

Fionna gulped, her gaze drifting forward. "Let's go this way." She headed down the gorge. It had been unknown, a secret place only locals and old legends talked about, until a TV show used it. Now the place could be crawling with tourists who were on a mission to discover the gem themselves. The weather this time of year thankfully kept the sightseers away.

We were already wet from the rain, but stomping through the river and climbing over fallen debris drenched us in water and mud. Her tight jeans fit her like a second skin. My notice drifted more than once to her backside as she scaled objects, and my body responded as the wet jeans stuck to her ass and legs.

Shit. I was in trouble.

And a liar.

I said only once, but no doubt once was not going to be enough to my demon. Somewhere inside I knew two or three times wouldn't be either.

My demon had a taste and it marked her.

Now nothing could stop it from completely devouring her…if she'd still have me.

~~

Every once in a while, as Fionna moved through the gulch, she would close her eyes and chant a revealing spell.

"Isaac really made sure the cauldron's magic was concealed." She frowned, her hands on her hips, her body slowly spinning around, examining the ravine. "I mean, how many fae have passed by here over the decade and no one sensed it was here?"

"You really don't feel anything?"

"What do you think?" She cocked her head, glaring at me. "That I'm still trying to trick you? Take it behind your back?"

"I can't say it hasn't crossed my mind," I replied sharply. "You'd love to say you outmaneuvered me, right? Bested the King?"

"Sod off, demon," she barked, swiveled around, and proceeded down the gully. "Everything is always about you, isn't it? Your ego can't see past its own reflection." She stopped short, whipping around to face me, forcing me to stumble back. "Believe me, I haven't spent my nights dreaming about you. Or how to outsmart you. I wouldn't have to put that much effort into it."

"Now who is the egotistical one?" I regained my footing on the mossy rock, though too late for my feet. My boots were saturated with river water. "And who said anything about dreaming about me?"

Exasperation flashed in her eyes, a blush spotted her neck and cheeks, revealing more than she wanted.

"Really?" I rubbed my chin with smugness.

"Fuck. You." She turned to stomp away, but I grabbed her arms, shoving her against the narrow wall of the gulley. Fire shot from her eyes, but I could feel her body curve toward me, her chest moving frantically for air.

"What did I tell you about that?" My words came out gruff, but I could feel my body opposing my need to keep this woman at arm's length. It was no longer just the demon who wanted to be inside her again. And she knew it. It was difficult not to. It throbbed, chafing against the wet denim, pressing into her.

We didn't move, our breaths syncing. Her eyes watched me defensively but smoldering with heat. Then something shifted as though I could reach out and touch her thoughts, understand every nuance of her facial reactions. Her soul hovered close to the surface. If I wanted, I could have breached it, dived in and seen what really made her tick.

The longer we stared at each other the more I felt my layers and protective shields also peel away. I needed those safeguards in place. It was the only way I could survive in the world, and as King, my life depended on it.

My feelings as a man did not matter. I kept them locked away, hidden from my enemy, even myself. But Fionna's inscrutable brown eyes seemed to strip that all away, exposing me.

I detested it.

"Stop," I snarled, gripping her arms tighter.

"You get out first, demon." She shoved back, plunging into my head and soul. I could feel her, intruding on my space, and damned if the demon didn't just sit back, acting as a welcoming host, offering her a cool beverage and appetizer, wanting to show her straight to the bedroom.

"GET OUT!" I bellowed, ramming my walls back up and tossing her out. Before she could even respond, I crashed into hers, shredding her mental walls like an animal. I didn't so much want to know her true thoughts as to give a dose of what her invasion felt like. I prodded forward, ready to be attacked, but all I felt was warmth, power, and exquisite pleasure encompassing my presence. I heard the moan come out of my mouth. Sex was amazing, but this was on another plane. Pure bliss pulsed through me.

To a demon this only meant one thing. If you didn't know it before, sex usually established it, locking it in place. We could have a thousand partners and never experience it. Once in a lifetime, your demon found its perfect match.

I already had found mine a long time ago.

She was dead.

I should never experience this again.

"Oh gods..." Fionna groaned, gasping for breath as if she were about to climax.

She felt it too.

My demon wanted to stay, but I didn't. Fionna was not supposed to be a mate. Aisling was the love of my life. Death was not supposed to change that. I had accepted it. It actually kept that part of my life simple, neat, and easy, while the rest of it remained constantly in chaos. I liked my life the way it was. I didn't need some pint-size Druid messing it up.

I jerked away from her, tugging at my demon to retreat. My spine hit the opposite side of the slender ravine, gasping for air.

The rush of the creek at my ankles filled the space between us. Time ticked by, my muscles twitching with the experience. My demon growled inside, perturbed at me for stopping.

"What the shit was that?" Her voice barely carried over the babbling of the water.

Starring down the gorge, I set my jaw. I had full control here. "Nothing."

"Bollocks." She splashed through the creek. "Tell me what just happened wasn't normal, right?"

"Normal?" I huffed with amusement, facing her. "No, it certainly was not *normal*."

She licked her lips, gazing down at the moving water, her forehead crinkling.

I wanted nothing more than to wrap my arms around her. Hold her to my chest. Protect her. Feel her against me. My fingers pinched the bridge of my nose, breathing through the urge.

"Well, whatever you did." She cleared her throat. "It showed me a vision of the cave where the cauldron is."

"What?" I dropped my hand.

"About two hundred meters that way." She pointed back where we came. "We passed it."

My head jerked back down the ravine, all awkwardness dissolving instantly. "Seriously?"

She waved her arm for me to follow.

"Lead the way, Druid." I grinned. "I will follow."

Yes, you will. My demon smirked at me. *Like a puppy.*

Chapter Thirty-One

Fionna

My limbs couldn't stop shaking; even my brain was wobbly. Whatever had happened between us was so frickin' intense I couldn't seem to find steady ground or breathe enough air since he pulled away.

Nothing my arse. That was the opposite of nothing. Only his hands touched my arms, but I had felt him everywhere. He filled my body and mind, rubbing against every nerve like a cat. He invaded my veins, my soul, sending such brilliant desire through me I thought I would implode. And I welcomed him, letting him penetrate as far as he wanted, as though he owned the place. It should have been invasive. Violating. And it was the opposite. I had liked him there, rolling and running around similar to a dog in a park. I had felt safe and happy.

And now I was cold, empty, and forlorn.

I detested those emotions. The only thing keeping my temper in check was the fact, at the height of—what do you call it?—inner orgasm, images of the cave flashed into my head.

I siphoned all my energy into that, emptying my head of the rest. Cauldron. That was why we were here. The goal and focus. Not the multiple orgasms he'd already given me today.

"Here." I held out my hands over what looked like a solid rock wall. The buzz of energy was so well guarded I could see how we passed it the first time. The magic and energy of the entire place was the perfect disguise.

"Here?" Lars gazed skeptically at me.

Without thinking I grabbed his hand, taking it up to the stone, holding mine over it. "Do you feel that?"

His chartreuse gaze drifted up to mine, looking between my eyes. "Yes. I do."

Shite. I did too. Wait, what were we talking about again?

Clearing my throat, I dropped my hand away. I was normally not nervous around men, but feck if Lars didn't turn me into a prancing goat, bopping all over like a Muppet.

My fingers returned to the rock, and I closed my eyes. Magic protecting the rock zinged up my arms as though it were excited to see me.

"Can you break it?"

"Shut it," I muttered, trying to find my center, getting settled in it. The moment the spell cascaded over my teeth, I sensed Uncle Isaac's magic. When I was a child, he seemed so formidable. A legend. At age eight, I could never have dreamed of achieving his level of magic. Yet not only had I reached his level, I surpassed it, which had me doubting myself for a moment. It couldn't be this simple. He had to set up a trap behind the spell, but I searched and found nothing, his spell easily giving into me.

"Good job, Ms. Cathbad."

My lids popped open to see the solid wall was only an illusion. A cave entrance hid behind hanging roots and weeds, the opening narrow and dark.

"It felt too easy." I frowned.

Lars jumped up on a boulder, holding out his hand to help me up.

"Isaac was deep into black magic. My parents trusted him to hide it from the Seelie Queen. It was kindergarten level."

"You're exceptionally powerful, Fionna." The sound of my name on his lips gave me gooseflesh. "You have far surpassed the teacher."

"Perhaps." I still felt itchy, ready to react as we stepped into the cave. The low headway gave way to a massive cave.

Lars tugged a torch out of his pocket, flicking it on, taking steps deeper into the cave. But as soon as we turned the first corner, daylight streamed down from an opening above, igniting a milky pool of water in the middle of the cave, similar to a spotlight.

Magic hummed around the cave, but it seemed to greet me instead of block me, brushing up against me as though it were happy to see me. *Strange.* It felt way too familiar. I knew Isaac, but his magic shouldn't feel this intimate. This wasn't similar to the magic I broke through to get in here.

I moved in deeper, looking around the cave. Something wasn't sitting right with me. This shouldn't feel like this.

Fionna.

I inhaled hard, scanning for the source. *Did I just imagine my name being called?*

"What?" Lars followed my gaze over the room.

"Nothing. But I swear—"

Fionna. This time I had definitely heard it. I took a step closer to the pool. *Fionna.*

"There." I pointed to the water. "It's in there." I heard it calling me. It knew me.

I foresaw you coming, Fionna. I jumped, the voice even stronger. A male voice. One I recognized from childhood.

"What's wrong?" Lars touched my arm, but then I no longer saw or heard him.

A ghost of a man stood across the pond, hovering at the edge of the water with long white hair, brown cape, and walking stick.

"Uncle Isaac?" I stepped closer to the mirage.

I've been waiting for you.

"Waiting for me?"

The riddle. I placed the memory inside you. It had been waiting for you to reveal it. To recall the night I told it to you.

Now I understood why getting in the cave and solving the puzzle had been so easy when I knew it shouldn't have been. Isaac had made it for me.

I took some of your blood the night I left. This spell is you, Fionna...not me. My purpose was merely to put it in place for you. This was always your destiny. Your fate to play out.

"Play out? What do you mean?"

I could never tell your parents what I had envisioned for you. What I saw in your future. It would break their hearts, and your mother already pictured their lives would be ending soon. I wanted them to go in peace thinking you and your sister were safe.

"What are you talking about?"

Isaac's expression grew weary; his shoulders sagged with sadness. *You will die here, Fionna.*

"What?" My hand went to my stomach.

The cauldron needs you, your strength, to fight what is coming. This is your destiny.

"W—what is coming? Why me?"

I do not know. I am merely a shade of my human self. I only know what he did. Isaac's ghost flickered, the illusion dimming.

"No." I reached out for the specter. "Don't go. Tell me whatever you know."

I am sorry, my dear girl. You know how fond I was of you. The moment I met you, I knew our lives would always be linked. I didn't know how until the day your parents handed me the cauldron to hide. Then I saw what was to be. I died to hide it, and you will die to protect it. I wish things could be different. But we were meant to keep the treasures safe, out of hands that will only use it to destroy, whatever the costs. I fulfilled my part. Now it is your turn.

"No…"

You cannot fight fate. The vision has already been prophesied.

With his last words, his image faded away, becoming the rays of light filtering down, glittering on the water.

"No. No…" I shook my head, stepping forward. "Isaac! Come back." But I knew it was too late. He would not be coming back.

"What?" Lars's fingers wrapped around my arm and turned me to face him. "What just happened? What did you see?"

Obviously he had not seen or heard what I had.

"I…" I peered over at the small pond, my brain registering what Isaac had told me. It was true; my gut seemed to understand this before I wanted to. The cauldron waited for me. Similar to a strighoul it wanted to use me, consume all my magic for itself, to defend itself against something. What? I didn't know, but it needed the same blood, the same magic, that first produced it. A Cathbad.

"I really hate those treasures." I tried to joke, but a sob crammed my throat.

"Fionna." Lars's voice was demanding and deep. Warm hands cupped my face, bringing me to his chest. "Tell me what is going on."

"Do you know why we found it so easy to get in here?" I gulped, trying to get past the knot in my esophagus. "It's because the cauldron has been waiting for me."

"I do not understand."

"Isaac...he knew I'd be coming here. Foresaw it. He designed the spell so I could pretty much walk right in and take it."

"Well, that is convenient. Finally something positive for us."

"No. You don't understand." I choked, my head falling into him, wanting to crawl inside and let him protect me. I could already feel the pull to the object. The hold on me grew stronger with each passing moment. The cauldron knew I was here. It wouldn't let me go now.

"What aren't you saying?" Lars pulled back, searching my face. Dread twisted his features into anger. "Tell me now."

I inhaled, rolling back my shoulders, turning my shock and terror into determination. Isaac was right: you couldn't fight what was already foretold. You could only control how you did it. I would go with my head held high. "I have a purpose."

Lars pursed his lips, his eyes weary, ready for me to continue.

"I won't be leaving this cave."

Chapter Thirty-Two
Lars

"I'm sorry?" I tilted my head, one eyebrow curving up.

"I'm going to die, Lars." She glanced away, licking her lip. "Isaac's vision saw my life was meant to protect the cauldron. It needs my magic. Cathbad magic. I failed to defend the spear. I will at least do this right."

"No." I growled, ire twitching my muscles. "You are being ridiculous, Ms. Cathbad. No one is dying here. Certainly not you and not because some old ghost said so."

Fionna shifted back, her head shaking. "It doesn't work like that. It already knows I am here. You can't change fate."

"Like hell you can't." I roared, rage itching the muscles in my legs to move. "Your sister changed a vision, why can't we?"

"It's different." She bit down on her lip as if she were in pain.

"The FUCK it is!" My demon smashed against the thin barrier. The desperation and fear coursing through my veins only heightened what I experienced earlier with Fionna. I could lie to myself all I wanted, try to pretend it was nothing more than lust. But the fact became blindingly clear. Fionna Cathbad was mine. Mate. I had linked with her. I was not going to lose her. Not now. Not ever.

"Stop." She put her hands on her hips, defining me. "This is not your decision, is it?"

"Do not test me." I stomped up to her, wrath crackling off me. "I will carry you out of here over my shoulder if I have to. The cauldron be damned."

Fionna wrenched backward, her eyes widening. "What?"

"Fuck the cauldron. Fuck it all." I countered her retreat. "It can stay buried."

Her lids blinked slowly, her mouth parted. "Are you serious?"

"Don't I look serious?" I tugged her to me.

"You would give it up?" Disbelief defined her features. "For me?"

"Yes." My fingers squeezed down on her wrists. The answer slid off my tongue so fast and easy it should have startled me. It did not. I only felt more determined to make her see how foolish she was being.

Tears filled her eyes and she shook her head, a pained chuckle coming from her mouth. "This is so my luck," she muttered.

I was about to ask her what she meant when she snapped back to me, her legs going still, her chin high.

"Whatever I feel for you. Whatever could have been...it's too late." She pulled from my grip, her teeth grinding together, beads of sweat dotting her hairline. "You may not understand, but I have to do this. It calls to me. I have to go to it. We're linked. My soul understands this...even if my heart does not."

"No," I snarled, grabbing for her, cupping my hands tight around her face. "No."

"It's too late, Lars." Sorrow shaded her eyes like clouds. "The moment I stepped into this cave, I sealed my fate. The cauldron won't let me go."

"What do you mean?"

A flinch of pain creased her brow as she bowed forward.

"What the hell is going on?"

"It's the cauldron..." She grunted, holding on to her knees. "It is getting impatient."

"It's doing this to you? Causing you pain?" I looked at the pool of water. My sight zeroed in on the streams of light coming down on the water. I dug into our connection, exploring the newly minted bond. That's when I saw the light beams stretching to her, wrapping around her like cobwebs.

Fury sizzled off me. I wanted to combat the snares tugging at her. But my hands came up empty.

"Lars. Stop. You are only making it worse." She bent over her legs, taking shallow breaths.

For the first time in my life I felt truly lost. Confused. Scared. Unsure what to do. This was not something I could fight. "I'm not letting it take you." I came back up to her, gripping her neck in my palms. "I will not allow it."

"For once, Lars..." Her lips twitched with humor. "You have no control over something."

The demon was going crazy, about to explode over the room and destroy everything in its path.

Mine. Mine. Mine. With the first inkling of true understanding, I knew if she died, I would not recover. Like my brother when Aisling was murdered, I would lose myself. The demon would not allow me back in control. It would only want to rain a reckoning down on the earth.

"Holy fuck." I twisted away, running my hands furiously over my head. My heart thumped in my chest, air strangling in my lungs. I was not expecting this. It felt completely out of my control and went beyond anything I thought myself capable of, even though we were still practically strangers. Deeper emotions were there and more powerful than I ever could imagine, coming so fast and brutal, it was swallowing me up. Women were by far the stronger creatures. Similar to Aisling, Fionna faced her death with strength and fierceness, not even questioning her sacrifice for the greater good. While, like my brother, I would fall apart and let the demon take over, raging vengeance to guard against the heartbreak.

Aisling had been my soul mate, but I did not dissolve when she was murdered, my brother did. He was the one who lost his mind and wanted to destroy the world.

I jumped headfirst into my work to forget. Became regimented and meticulous. However, this time I knew my demon would not recover. The Druid had gotten under every inch of my skin, moved into my soul without my knowledge, taken over.

If she died? Hell would pour down on earth.

"Lars, promise me, you will get out of here. Get far away from your uncle. My daughter...she needs you. Please. I need to know she will be taken care of. Loved."

I whipped around, my jaw set. "Your daughter will want for naught; I promise you."

Fionna inhaled, agony tearing over her face. "I don't care about material things. I want her to feel *loved*. Safe. Have a family."

"Then you fucking fight." My fists balled up. "Because your daughter needs you. And so do I."

A single tear escaped, sliding down Fionna's cheek. I stepped back up to her, my hands reaching for her face again. "You hear me, Druid? That is an order from your King."

"You're not my King," she tried to tease, but pain ground her teeth together.

"Not true." I tipped her face up to mine. "I am certainly yours." I didn't give her a chance to respond, my lips smashing down on hers with the force of my pain and passion pouring into her. My tongue parted her lips, deepening it, marking her as mine.

I felt the significance of kissing her in the marrow of my bones; our connection earlier would not be disregarded. She was mine.

You got it, fucking cauldron? She is mine. You cannot have her.

I bit her bottom lip, sucking on it, tugging it between my teeth. She moaned, clutching the back of my head, pulling me closer to her, our mouths hot, desperate, and needy. Our attraction to each other had never been a question, but now I felt our souls latch onto each other, deepening the desire and need. Her mind and heart claimed me, owned me. She was my equal in every way.

The nice ass was just a perk.

Fionna hissed in pain and drew away, bending over, coughing, and seizing for air.

"Fionna." I reached for her, rubbing at her back.

"It's getting worse," she hissed, squeezing her eyelids together. "I have to do this now."

She went on her toes, her soft lips covering mine, quickly but held every word she wouldn't express to me. Nothing more to be said. Words were pointless. She had to go forward.

Gulping, she turned for the pond, stepping up to the edge.

I stepped up next to her, lacing our fingers together. And so would I.

"What are you doing?" Her eyebrows crinkled together, staring down at our hands.

"What does it look like, Druid?" I said evenly. "I am coming with you."

"No. Lars—"

"The hell I'm letting you do this alone." I clenched her hand tighter. "We're in this together, right?"

"Lar—"

"Three." I jumped into the water, pulling her body with me, giving her no say in the matter.

She wasn't the only exceptionally stubborn one here.

~~

Our heads bobbed back up to the surface, and her eyes filled with shock and wonder.

"You *are* insane." She slicked back her hair, her legs kicking around mine.

"Seems so. Especially around you."

"Lars…I can't…"

"I do not want to hear it. I am coming with you. You have no choice."

She pressed her eyes closed tightly for a brief moment, before her warm eyes found mine.

"Okay, but once we have it, you have to let whatever happens, happen. Do not intercede."

"Of course." *I will not.* I did not lie, just didn't finish my sentence out loud.

We bobbed in the small pond. I had no idea how deep or what situation we'd find the cauldron in. Fionna's lips started moving.

"What are you doing?"

"Spelling us so we can breathe underwater for a time."

"How long is 'a time'?"

"Last time I used it was when West tossed me off a cliff into the ocean. But it lasted only for a couple of minutes. I don't know how long it actually lasts."

"Great. Sounds exciting." I never liked going into situations where I didn't know the outcome, but because of my weeks with Fionna I had been getting used to taking things as they came.

Fionna finished her spell and dipped below the water.

I took a last breath and dunked my head after her. *Here we go.* Panic immediately made the demon jump up and down. I didn't want to breathe in, fearing I'd fill my lungs with water.

"Relax." Fionna grabbed my arms, popping my eyes open. Light from the surface broke in, her face glistening as her hair billowed around her. I could see a thin bubble around her head. "Take a breath."

Inhaling through my nose, I found oxygen readily entering my lungs. "Impressive."

"A Druid trick." She grinned smugly, knowing no fae had magic similar to that. Either you were born to breath underwater or you weren't. We could not change our stripes.

She clicked on her flashlight and began to swim down into the darkness. I couldn't fight the tightening in my gut, the bad feeling descending as I followed her down. I was aware enough to know obtaining the treasures came with costs, to those who had obtained them for me and even for myself. But it had not been enough to stop me from perusing them.

Nothing else had meant enough to me to stop. I could no longer say that.

Her beam of light went down for about twenty feet before the bottom of the rocky lagoon could be made out.

"Do you feel it?" I swam up next to her, clutching one of the boulders.

"Yes." She nodded. "It is happy I'm here. It's been waiting a long time."

Fuck you, cauldron. I've been waiting a long time for her too. The thought rushed through my mind.

"It just said *too bad*." Fionna wiggled her head with confusion. "I don't know what it means."

Shit. Had it heard me?

Fionna's head jerked to mine, her eyes wide. "It said yes, it can hear you. It understands your intentions and will fight you. What does it mean, Lars? What are you planning?"

Fantastic. Like the Stone of Fáil, the cauldron could penetrate your thoughts as well. Get into you head.

"Nothing."

"It just called you a liar." Fionna pressed her mouth together. "I thought we went through this. For once you have no say in something. Deal with it."

I won't just let you have her, I said to the cauldron, not responding to Fionna.

Yes. You will. A voice stirred in my brain. Ancient, old, and genderless. *You are not supposed to be here. This is not your fate.*

I tried to empty my head of thoughts, of anything past the present moment.

"How do we get it?" I asked.

"Give me the knife." She pointed to my boot.

"Why?" My hand went to it, blocking it from her reach. "What are you going to do with it?"

"Lars, don't make this more difficult." She frowned, holding out her hand. It was the same knife she stole from Travil. The one we used in the blood ritual. Now it would be used in another blood sacrament. "It needs a taste of my blood."

I stared at her.

"Do not make me put a spell on you." Annoyance flashed in her eyes. "Because I will if I have to."

"Fionn—"

She shoved at my hand, her fingers wrapping around the handle of the knife, which she ripped from my shoe. She didn't even hesitate before she sliced at her wrists. Red blood wafted out from her wounds, like smoke clouds, mixing with the water until only tendrils remained.

Ever muscle in my body tensed with anticipation and fear. Waiting for what was to come brought a slow agony. The beat of my heart thumped away the seconds.

A glow began to surround Fionna so softly at first I thought I was imagining it. But it continued to grow, as did the pressure of magic throbbing against my skin. The more blood poured from her, the brighter the light became.

The cauldron was siphoning her energy the same as a battery did, taking for its own. A blood sacrifice was some of the most powerful magic you could create, especially self-sacrifice.

Fionna bent over, a cry tearing from her lips, the magic growing, pounding down on us, pinning me in place and burrowing painfully into my bones. Her blood continued to pour from her arms, hazing the water. Her expression twisted with pain, and a sob parted her trembling lips.

Stop this! My demon screamed at me. *You can't let this happen. You can't let her die. She's ours!*

I felt my teeth grow, tearing at my bottom lip as I growled. Anger staked between my shoulder blades. "No," I rumbled, trying to move closer to her.

It happened instantly, as if Rimmon had barreled into me. Magic slammed into my chest, rolling me back through the water, zapping my muscles with blistering hot lava. I roared, the agony shredding every nerve.

Leave her be, demon. This is her fate.

"No," I spat back, my fingers digging into the gravelly bed of the pool, trying to move to her. Energy pinned me down.

She must sacrifice because fae couldn't leave us alone. You lust to be the most powerful in the world. This is why she is going to die. I would not have to censor the Stone of Fáil if you let us be. But now I feel it is out there. My destiny is to go to it. All you have to blame is yourself.

The truth of its words constricted my chest, but I had no time to repent or feel guilty. Fionna was dying before my eyes, her body limp and falling into the rocks, the cauldron taking more of her life every second. The glow around her pulsed but was now dimming quickly. If it went dark, would Fionna be dead?

"Fuck off." Pain shot up my fingertips and my legs as I shoved against the power holding me down. My muscles shook, only moving forward a few inches. My demon was frantic and crazed inside me as it tried to reach out for her. The cauldron kept a bubble of magic between us.

The light around Fionna flickered, diminishing down to a nightlight's brightness. The spell allowing us to breathe underwater thinned, permitting barely a trickle of air into my lungs while the energy of the magic was directed to a spot between the rocks, thriving with life and light.

Panic squeezed my heart, ripping a cry from my throat while I dug deeper into the dirt with my toes.

Your sacrifice for her, insignificant demon, will only make me stronger.

I wasn't insignificant or ordinary. I was one of the most powerful fae in the world, even with drained powers. I was the fucking High Demon King. No mixing bowl was going to take from me. Nothing and nobody took from me. Ever.

The demon roared, shoving the man part of me to the back. My usual instinct was to fight it, to not let the demon take me over, but this time I let go, allowing it to fully consume me. Frivolous emotions fell away, allowing room only for complete and utter power and conviction. My sight sharpened on the Druid, her life barely humming around her. The demon bellowed, shaking the underwater cave, shoving itself into the magic keeping it away from the woman it loved.

My magic is different, demon. You cannot beat me.

Watch me. Energy exploded from me, wild and unrestricted, it held nothing back. Like a cannon, it barreled toward the light, slamming into it, breaking apart over the protective surface the cauldron held around itself. It swayed a little.

The demon leaped for the barrier, grabbed the knife settled into the dirt next to Fionna's body. Very little blood escaped from her wrists anymore. Her chest shuddered, then the light went out. The spell broke that allowed me to breathe, and water rushed into my mouth.

The demon understood it could not fight the cauldron with brutal strength. It would have to surrender. Willingly. A selfless act for what it loved. The ultimate sacrifice.

Fionna's skin and blood still clung to the blade, but the demon didn't even hesitate as it sliced my wrist, mixing our essence together. Even the tiny bit of Fionna's blood was life to me, taking her in as mine. If I breathed, she breathed. If she died, I died.

The moment I felt her inside me, energy expanded around us, the pressure so intense, it crashed my bones into the rocks.

Noooo! Do you realize what you just did? The cauldron's voice filled my head with a cry before everything exploded, tossing my body up to the surface.

Gasping for air, I breached the water, filling my lungs in great heaves.

"Fionna?" I sputtered, hoping she had been pushed up as well. However, she was nowhere near me. Panic clawed at my chest as I tugged another pull of oxygen, diving below the surface. My lids blinking through the murk, the light from the cauldron was gone, making it almost impossible to see. But the farther I swam, I spotted a stream of light from the flashlight, letting me get my bearings.

Fionna? I screamed her name in my head. *Fionna!*

No voice or sound returned, but similar to a rope, the connection tugged me farther down, my arms cutting through the water, taking me right to her. The blood magic I'd created between us wouldn't last for long. The intensity too much to keep up. She could still die if I didn't reach her in time.

Fuckfuckfuck.

At the bottom, between two rocks, a metal object about the size of a large soup bowl lay on her chest, pinning her to the earth. Her face appeared colorless, her body lifeless.

The cauldron, too, felt dead and lifeless, like an ordinary dish.

Terror blurred all thoughts except getting to her. My arms swept around her form, seized her in my grip, the treasure tucked into her chest. I shoved off the ground, my legs frantic and kicking and my lungs already straining for more air.

Like a missile, I headed straight up, not looking down at her. I couldn't focus on anything but getting us above the line of water.

Air.

It was so close.

Dots filled my vision, my lungs grappling. Aching. Demons were not meant to hold our breath for long. Water wasn't our domain.

Rez's powers would have been extremely helpful right now. Her magic, which I ripped from her, was sitting in my vault waiting for the day it would be returned to her. It was her punishment for betraying me. For having an affair with another while still in my bed.

It had been my fault. The moment Ember entered my life, Aisling had come with her, stirring up old emotions and feelings. I pushed Rez away. I didn't love her. And she deserved more.

The moment I started to think I deserved more as well...it was being taken from me. It didn't stop the gut-wrenching terror at the thought of losing Fionna.

With a last kick, my head broke through the surface. Wheezing for breath, I tossed her body up on the dirt with no grace or ease. She flopped on her back, the cauldron rolling off into the corner. I pulled myself out of the water and scrambled next to her body.

We had been in a similar situation. During the blood ritual, she had put her life on the line for me, for my need to obtain the treasure. How could I not see then how unbelievable amazing and strong she was?

My magic shoved into her as I tipped her head back, opening her mouth, feeling her neck.

No pulse.

No. I cannot be too late.

My palms slammed down into her chest, pumping, before I covered her mouth with mine, trying to fill her lungs. I resembled a robot working methodically. Over and over again.

"Fionna. Please." The words came pleading out of me. Every second she didn't respond stripped the demon of its shell. Very little was holding it back. Fury stacked like blocks, ready to tumble down and crush everything in sight. "You will not die."

I pressed at her chest again, peering down at her unresponsive and ashen face. She was so beautiful.

Once full of life. Stubborn and obstinate, challenging me every step of the way.

"No." I curled over her. "You're supposed to fight. For Piper. For me," I spat through my teeth. "You are not giving up." I would not take death for an answer. The vision never counted on me. I would not let it win.

With every ounce of energy I had left, I blasted into her body, trying to jump start her heart.

No reaction. No pulse.

She was gone.

My head fell back, screams tearing out of my throat, the demon thundering through me. Like a slow crack of ice, the demon splintered away from the man, my howls shaking lose debris off the walls. Brutal wrath gripped my chest.

I was rage.

Cruelty.

Pitiless.

I was adrift with no anchor.

All my anger and pain zapped down my arms, needing to get out of the small cage of my body. As though a sonic blast went off in the cave, energy rammed everything in its path. Large chunks of rock and earth tumbled down, crashing and breaking over each other.

Mirroring what I felt inside.

Chapter Thirty-Three

Fionna

My lashes flung open as water hurled up my throat. My body fought to purge and inhale at the same time. Hacking coughs shredded my chest as my body twisted, vomiting onto the ground.

I was alive. I shouldn't be. I had sacrificed myself for the cauldron.

Spewing out the last bits of water, my stomach and lungs spasmed from the assault. Inhaling slow and evenly, the burn eased as I muttered the paltriest of healing spells, the best I could manage.

His presence hovered over me, looming and heavy. I kept my gaze on the ground, my skin prickling with awareness.

I had been in darkness, floating away to death, but he had come for me. I knew it was him, the feeling of his essence, the demon, surrounding my soul like a blanket, protecting me.

A cry pierced through the darkness, charged with pain, grief, anger, and...love. It surged at my soul, flinging me back to my body. To him.

Olwyn was the only one I let myself love after losing my parents. I didn't give myself a chance to love Piper when she was first born. I couldn't afford to. That kind of love was so deep, pure, and unconditional, it would have broken me. The same fear came back with Lars. He could annihilate me.

His silence was violent, mutely teeming down on me, coercing me to peer over my shoulder at him. He sat back on his heels, his face void of any emotion. His eyes were black.

"Lars?"

"Don't," he rumbled, motionless.

"What's wrong?" I scouted the cave, spotting the cauldron in the corner. No magic shifted off it. "What happened? What did you do to it?"

"I broke it." He rose and spun toward the opening of the cave. He halted at the entrance, his hand striking the wall, his chest moving violently as he breathed in and out.

Tucking my feet underneath me, I hoisted myself slowly up, my muscles wobbly and my head light from the blood loss and lack of oxygen.

"I'm sorry." I walked over to him. "I know how much you wanted it. Maybe it just went quiet."

"Silence, Ms. Cathbad," he growled, his voice clipped and formal.

"Are you kidding me? Are we bac—?"

Lars swung around, grabbing me by the shoulders, pushing me into the wall, his hand covering my lips.

"I said I need a moment, Ms. Cathbad." His black eyes reflecting me, his voice and expression strained. "The demon is fighting me right now. And I don't give a *damn* about the cauldron."

I nodded, staring up at him, the brightness from outside striking his face in distinguishing soft and hard lines. He inhaled, a tint of green returning to his eyes, glinting in the light, his full lips pressed together tightly.

Man.

Monster.

Both there, fighting for dominance.

Shite, he was beautiful. Magnificent and frightening. Savage and refined. Brutal and gentle. He was everything and nothing. Lars could never be defined or put in a box. He just was.

We stood silently, watching each other. He flattened his tense body into mine, his heat burrowing through my damp clothes. His frame encompassed mine, shielding me from the world, my back digging into the rocky cave wall.

There were so many reasons we should grab the cauldron and run. Get far away from Scotland. But all I could focus on was him. The demon. The man. The feel of him ghosting between my legs, reminding me how incredible he felt inside.

I didn't need a memory. Lars's magnificence was pushed against my hip, my hormones tripping and flailing around like a drunk person. My breath struggled to wiggle out of my esophagus, a flush that unceremoniously climbed over my body, heating me in ways I had never experienced. This time it knew how he could make my body feel.

Fear and desire fought for supremacy. I should have known he wasn't someone you shagged and walked away from.

He ruined.

He took.

He gave.

He destroyed.

And you would beg for more.

Lars's muscles constricted against me. His lids narrowed, his eyes drifting down to my mouth. No doubt he had picked up on my emotions. Coming so fast, they essentially shouted from every pour. I couldn't hide from him anymore. Not since the moment outside. He was everywhere inside me, slipping into the darkest corners of my soul.

"You saved me," I whispered. "Again."

He didn't say a word, his gaze penetrating and puncturing my lungs. My chest locked up, almost suffocating from the intensity, remembering how his lips felt on mine. Lars had *kissed* me.

He seared himself like a brand through my veins. Now I understood. He was heroin. He was mine.

He leaned farther into me, puréeing my brain into mush, stealing oxygen from me. His wet hair was wild, asking for my fingers to run through it. I loved his usual faultless appearance was rugged and unkempt.

I could see the demon right at the surface, the wildness. Lars appeared to be trying to lock it back up. He didn't seem to understand I was not scared of the demon. He had protected me, been with me.

"I know we both said only once," I breathed.

"Fuck what we said." A sound similar to a growl erupted from his throat, our breaths dancing together in a rapid rhythm. The intensity of the moment only increased the throbbing between my legs, my need rising like bread in the oven. His head tipped into mine, bringing our lips only centimeters a part. Logic and reason seeped out of my head as his breath tickled down my neck.

"Fionna." My name came out in a rumble. Raw and hungry. It undid me. I wanted to hear him say it again. Scream it. Claim it as his.

"Okay, maybe twice." I gasped as his fingers brushed my stomach, his touch burning my skin. "Then we'll be fine. Get each other out of our system." I lied through my teeth, knowing I would never have enough now. Whatever he did to me earlier, he possessed my soul now. It was his.

My wet clothes hung on me like weights, my skin itching to get them off, to feel his skin against mine.

His fingers curled around the bottom of my shirt, ripping it over my head before I could blink. "Fionna." His hands slid up from my stomach to my breasts, skimming below my bra, pushing it up to expose them. "There is no number we're ever going to reach. And there is no getting me out of your system." His thumbs moved over my tender nipples. "Nor you from me. I almost lost you. I won't again." Air caught in my lungs when he leaned over, his warm mouth taking one breast between his lips. Resembling a lion leaping for its prey, my body roared, flaming to life, desperate and brutal, ripping away anything sensible or human.

I was need. Desire.

Lars's eyes flashed so bright they glowed in the gloom of the cave before blackness started to seep back into the corners. His demon form took over the polished man he clung so tightly to. He was neither animal nor man, but something so much more primal and savage. Ancient and unrestrained. Primal and basic.

My fingers fumbled for his damp shirt, tearing it over his head. It landed on the ground with a heavy wet splat. My hands grabbed at his pants, desperate for what was underneath. His pants fell to the ground, and he kicked them off along with his boots.

He stood in his boxer briefs. I tried to swallow the dryness coating my throat. The King was indeed granted greatness in every way.

He moved toward me. I put out my arm to stop him from coming closer. He growled, his almost black eyes looking down at my hand, then back at me.

"I want to see you," I growled back at him.

He watched me from under his eyebrows, danger looming at the surface, fear and lust spiking up my spine.

"Now," I ordered. He breathed in, snarling, every taut muscle contracting at my demand.

"I am not a man you can order around." His voice vibrated the packed dirt underneath my feet.

"I wasn't asking the man." I held the demon's gaze, not backing down. I knew he didn't show the true demon to others often, not like this, but I wanted to break his rules. To push further.

The air pinched with peril, his shoulders curling, as if he were ready to attack. Water trailed down his taut muscles.

I dropped my arm and pushed off the wall. Predatory eyes watched my every move. I unhooked my bra, letting it drop off my arms. He growled. I didn't stop; my fingers went to my jeans, undoing them. His nose flared; his olive skin turned white. I kept my attention on him as I wiggled out of the sodden fabric. They clung to my skin as I shoved them off and kicked out of my boots. My knickers were the only thing left covering me.

I lifted an eyebrow, conveying it was his turn.

His tongue slid across his bottom lip.

For feck's sake. This man didn't even have to touch me, and I was burning to death. His thumbs hooked into his briefs, torturing me by slowly tugging them off. Then he straightened up. This time I really let myself explore every inch of him.

I was lost.

Ruined.

"Let me see you," I muttered, taking a step closer, trying to not sound as breathless as I was.

He let me move to him, staying still.

"Please." My hand skated over his chest, curving around to his arse. I was so screwed. This man's body felt similar to heaven under my fingertips. Actually seeing him naked, feeling his ripped muscles under my palm, was like a spiritual experience. My fingers moved back around, sliding down until my fingers brushed him. His spine jolted along with his dick.

I let out a needy groan, trying to wrap my hand around him.

A roar trembled the cave, and my body lifted off the ground as he picked me up. I wrapped my legs around his hips, as he slammed me back against the stone wall. Bits of dirt and rock crumbled in pieces to the ground. A thin layer of fabric was the only thing keeping him from sliding in. He pushed himself against me with a snarl, producing another weighty moan from my lips.

"Fionna." He rasped out my name, his hands clasping the sides of my face, slipping one hand to the back of my head and tugging. I wanted him *now*. My lashes lifted, answering his call. He stared at me for a moment. Long, lean fingers dug into the back of my head. At the flick of pain, pleasure sprinted through my senses.

I bit down on my lip, fighting my need from vocalizing itself. His pallid skin thinned till his bones stuck out, like parchment paper. His body shifted, and I felt as though he took up the entire cave, his eyes pits of blackness.

He slid his thumb across my bottom lip, and my heart thudded violently against my ribs.

"Is this what you want?" His voice was low, vibrating through my body. Daggered cuspids jutted from the upper and lower teeth, the man dissolving, the face and body of a demon appearing before me. I had seen versions of it, but never the full demon. It was designed to terrorize, petrify.

Not me. "Yes," I whispered. "I want you to fuck me like this."

He didn't blink or move. His body went still. "Lars?"

He sucked in a gulp of oxygen. Without warning, his fingers pulled me to him, his mouth finding mine, savagely devouring me.

Fire. I was sure actual fire shot up my spine and melted my insides.

Lars did not simply kiss. He consumed. He injected me with the same desperate response. His lips parted mine; his tongue deepened our kiss. His hand twisted into my hair, digging into my scalp. His daggered teeth dug into my bottom lip, sending me over. My tongue slipped between his teeth, demanding more from him.

With speed I wasn't ready for, he tore me from the wall, laying me on the damp ground. His lips never leaving mine.

Even if the basic shape remained of a man, the King was gone. The power and weight of his true self filled the space with energy.

Magic licked at my skin, as though I had a dozen people caressing, kissing, and pleasuring me at once. My head tipped back and I moaned, then I ran my legs up the back of his thighs, encircling them tightly around him.

I had experimented a little with drugs, sex, and erotic spells in my life. Nothing. I mean *nothing* could even come close.

His hands ran down my body, and I practically orgasmed right there.

"I don't want to hurt you." He started to lift off me. I knew he was talking about the demon harming me, not the sex.

My legs strangled his hips, keeping him in place.

"You won't." I brought my hands to his face, pulling him back, nipping at his bottom lip. "But if you stop, I might hurt you."

A smirk flicked up his lip, making him resemble a snarling monster.

Yep. I was completely messed up. Because I only found him hotter.

His mouth crashed back into mine, his fingers slipping down to my underpants.

"Don't rip—"

Too late. Lars shredded them with one tug.

"Thanks. Now I have no pants left." I smiled against his mouth, my tongue dragging up one of his sharp cuspids.

"Good." He kissed me again, then went back on his knees. He bent over, biting my inner thigh.

Holy shite. Holy fucking shite.

A thousand magic hands rubbed at my nerve endings, his blistering magic spreading inside my body. I laced my fingers into his hair as he slid his hands under my ass, lifting me to him. I curled back, the wind blowing into the cave slipping over my bare skin.

His tongue slid through me slowly, a guttural noise reverberating from his body into mine, blasting my body with pleasure. His grip tightened on me, moving his mouth in deeper, devouring me.

"Oh. My. Gods!" I screamed, bliss running up and down every nerve, expanding through my skin, shuttering my muscles with overwhelming sensations. My hips bucked against him, needing him closer, even as his demon spread through my body, our connection webbing us together until I no longer felt the difference between us, only heightening the ecstasy.

A raucous cry wrenched from my throat.

I wasn't particularly noisy having sex. Or so I thought. Clearly I hadn't been with the right people to inspire that side of me.

When I thought I couldn't take any more, he nipped down, using his sharp teeth just enough, and my world exploded into brilliant fragmented light.

I was left floating away, as if I were nothing more than dust.

Very happy dust.

Chapter Thirty-Four

Lars

As her body responded to my mouth with moans, arching to my touch, desire for her consumed me. How could so much life be contained within her petite package? She exuded fierce strength, energy, and light, but also deep darkness, which I was drawn to like a fiend. My demon pawed and clawed to be deeper inside her, to intensify the link between us. It knew what it wanted and nothing was going to dislodge it from her, from wanting to be inside her. Forever. It had known for a long time, just waiting for the man to catch up.

Those few minutes when I thought she was gone cleared out all the nonsense, forcing me to see what was important. I let go of the past and jumped to the here and now. Aisling would be happy for me. She would not want me to wallow in her memory. No more ghosts haunted me. Nothing but desire for the woman below me.

I wanted to taste every inch of her skin, to consume her. I felt as though I had awakened from a coma. As though I'd been starving for years and now I was ravenous, with no end to my hunger. My veins blazed with life under the intensity of my craving.

I let my tongue drag over her again, savoring the taste of her. Fionna shivered, as I moved slowly up, taking my time exploring her body. She had shattered all my rules, and I only wanted more. More of her taste, more of her groans, more of her mouth on mine.

I crawled up between her legs, covering her lips, breathing her in. Her legs curled around me, her hands tugging my face closer, our lips devouring each other. I pulled back to look at her. Her gaze burned into me, her thighs squeezing my hips before she twisted, rolling us over, to perch on top of me. She arched her back, and I stroked the hot skin between her breasts.

Something stirred inside as I looked at her, an emotion I had only held for one other woman. I didn't let my mind touch it, focusing on how to make her scream again.

"It's probably a little too late, but you're safe with me." The spell from the tree fairies stayed until you went back and un-spelled it. I wanted no illegitimate children out there.

"Me too." She put her hands by my ears and kissed me.

"Really? You hate fae." My hands ran up her backside, kneading her plump ass. Druids could not use normal birth control. They were strong enough to hold fae babies. And fae sperm turned human contraception into dust.

"Yeah, but I'm no fool. I know how fertile Druids are..." She tapered off. "And how some fae look at us as breeding vessels."

"Ah." The reality of her words sank in. The fear Druid women constantly had to live in. She had done it to prevent pregnancy from rape. Fuck. Druids, fae, humans—it didn't matter; we all had our monsters.

I brushed loose hair off her face and tucked it behind her ear. She leaned in again, her lips brushing mine. "Now, fuck me like you are trying to break the fairy spell." She reached back, tugging the band from her hair and let it fall loose down her back.

A roar of desire went straight to my dick. She made a mischievous grin in response and grasped me, directing me inside her. She slowly sat back down, taking me inch by inch.

"My gods." My nails dug into her ass, my lids crushing together. Seriously, was it the connection that made it feel so different? Sex was sex. Sometimes it felt better than others. Sometimes even incredible. But this was on a new plane. And nothing and no one would be able to compare to how amazing she felt.

Fionna rocked forward, gasping, her head falling back.

"Put me in my place, *Druid*." I grunted through my teeth, my hands encouraging her to move faster.

She paused, looking down, her eyes wide. Then a smile spread over her face. She understood. I was giving up power to her, sharing it, letting her do what she wanted. I had never done that. Ever. Even with Aisling, I would not give up control. I was too young and egotistical, thinking it made me weak.

357

Fionna and time had changed me.

I had found my match.

~~

We needed to leave. I understood the peril we were in. Nonetheless, I couldn't seem to actually get myself to move. Fionna rested on my chest, her fingers trailing over my body groggily.

My back must be scraped and gouged with pebbles, but I didn't feel a thing, especially when she twisted around, riding me backward. There wasn't a position I hadn't tried in my time, but with her I hit climaxes so ferociously I lost myself.

"I know we should go," she muttered against my skin, propping her chin up on my ribs.

"Yeah." I stretched, folding my arms under my head. "We should."

Neither of us moved.

A wicked smile grew on her mouth. I had always thought of her as attractive. No matter how much I disliked her, I could not ignore her beauty. But I didn't see how unbelievably breathtaking she was before. I had not yet been privy to the love she kept deep in her heart, reserved for only a few, as well as her strength, independence, and intelligence. She stripped the solid ground out from beneath me, overturning my world.

The bond between us was rooting itself deep. I hadn't been looking, nor had I wanted a "mate." But I couldn't go back now. My demon had decided, wrapped itself around her, claws imbedded, and it wasn't going to let go. Ever.

And despite her independence I could feel her soul brush against it, and it purred just as loud as my demon.

They were happy. The human parts of us might rear against it later, panicking over the sudden relationship. However, not yet. Her smile widened wickedly before her tongue glided over my chest, her eyes still on me. The simple act inflamed the nerves along my limbs, bringing all of me back to life.

I was already semi-hard, but as her breasts grazed me as she kissed my stomach, I was ready once again. I sucked in air as her tongue slid lower, licking along the inner edge of my thigh.

A groan shook the cave when her warm mouth wrapped around my dick. I dug my knuckles into the dirt. One of her hands wrapped around its base, the other cupped my balls.

"Fuck!" My hips hitched up. My reaction only incited her to go faster, to take more of me. The back of her throat rubbed my tip, forcing noises to huff out of me, my balls tightening. Sweat beaded at my forehead, my fingers finding their way into her hair. "Shit...Fionna." I could feel my orgasm already burning up my spine. Then she started to hum. The vibration tore more swear words from my mouth. I was about to go over.

"Stop." I tugged at her head, not wanting to lose this bit of jurisdiction. Especially if she didn't want that.

She peered up at me. An impish look twinkled her eyes, and she did not back away. If anything, she dived in with more enthusiasm, as though she wanted to rob me of every bit of restraint I had left.

Fuck it. She could have it.

My hips pushed against her as I let her take me over the edge. My head tipped back and a roar pierced the space, not sounding anything like my usual voice. She took all I gave whether I was a demon or king. She might be small, but she was more than my equal. This woman could break me.

Instead of feeling fearful of her grinding my dominance into ruins, it turned me on. I felt free to finally be completely myself. I reached down, tugging her back up, already needing to be inside her. I roughly flipped her onto her back. I was feral and full of uninhabited passion.

Her eyes flashed with desire at my violence and need. I pushed one of her knees over my shoulder and plunged into her. Her lips parted in a gasp, my hips already slamming into her with unrelenting depth.

The woman who had just been in control of me was now lost, gasping and clawing at my skin, screaming for more. Her cries, our slaps of skin, my grunts took over every molecule in the air, making it ours. I had no fear of hurting her as I thrust deeper into her.

I gave.

She took.

Greedily.

My next climax was coming fast, but I would wait for her. Her moans told me she wasn't far behind. I slid her legs to my waist and drew her to sit up, both of us facing each other, burrowing in even deeper.

"Oh gods! Lars!" She tightened around me, encouraging me to pull the solid ground from her feet as well.

Again and again, I slammed into her so deeply, we both cried out. Her body spasmed and she clutched me.

"Now, Druid," I demanded. "Fucking come for me."

Her body responded, seizing around me intensely. I had never felt anything so good in my life.

I exploded inside of her, hot and claiming, bellowing loud, relishing in the feel of her. My mind blanked out for a moment as her nails dug into my back, and she groaned and panted. Another wave crashed into me as her body clenched down on me again, taking us to back to the ground. My muscles were too weak to keep me in a seated position.

We both stayed frozen as we came down, breaths heavy and panting.

"Holy shite, demon," she whispered, her expression dazed.

"Second it, Druid." I placed my elbows on either side of her face, kissing the tip of her nose, not ready to leave her body.

She inhaled deeply, but instead of slowly relaxing, her body went rigid, her eyes glazing over. It was the same vacant look I remember seeing in Prague, when she was having a vision.

"Fionna?" I clasped her face.

Her mouth parted to speak, panic creasing her face.

"What? What are you seeing?"

"St-Stavros," she stuttered, blinking. "They found us."

~~

How did he keep finding us? I could only sense his

magic if my uncle was close. I was pretty sure it was the same for him. I had no time to contemplate the how; I was more furious with myself for letting it happen. Something a king should never do—let his guard down.

"How soon?" I sat back, reaching for our clothes.

"Well, well, well…" Stavros's voice echoed from the entrance. Light from a torch ignited the shadowy cave. Instinctively I stood, still naked, and stepped in front of Fionna, my back tensing defensively. My uncle and Margo stalked into the cave. He set a filled sack down near his feet, but my attention was pulled to Margo. Her gaze voraciously devoured me as she nipped her bottom lip, desire sparking off her in electrical flurries. I only smirked at her. She could look, but she would never have.

Stavros grinned haughtily, his gaze dancing back and forth between Fionna and me. "You *really* do take after me. Your father was way too uptight and highbrow to fuck someone of lower standing, but what else are they good for, right? And when the demon needs to feed, you feed it. Right, son?"

"I am nothing like you." I put my arm out, already anticipating Fionna's response to want to attack Stavros.

However, the Druid only laughed, pulled on her jeans, and slipped her sweater back on. She stepped up alongside me. "Bigoted relics like you are only good when they're dead and take the past with them."

"Oh, pet." He clicked his tongue, shaking his head as if she were the one who had no clue. "You don't see I am the past and the future. The people will be grateful to have me ruling them. People haven't progressed or changed, no matter what you'd like to believe." He turned his attention to me. "And deny all you want, Lars. You've always been more similar to me. Driven and focused on what was genuinely important, which is power. It's the only mistress truly worth having."

I ground my teeth, hurriedly getting back into my jeans. Yes, power had been my first mistress, even when I had Aisling. But I had always felt empty and hollow just below the surface, if I'd only let myself realize it.

I longed for family. Though Ember was now part of my life, she was long past needing me and had her own life to lead. Besides, she was usually off on some other continent, and I barely got to see her.

I had people in my household, but I always kept them at arm's length. I hadn't even allowed myself to be close with the woman sharing my bed. I had considered it weak to need or want someone.

"Looks like your *true* mistress wants to come home. Where it belongs." Stavros stretched out his fingers, indicating my king powers, then looked over at Fionna, raising an eyebrow. "Maybe both of them would. I wouldn't mind getting a taste of a Druid. Especially that one."

Rage ceased every thought, ripping the demon from his gratified slumber. He didn't hesitate, snapping my daggered teeth. I stepped for my uncle.

"Lars! No." Fionna grabbed my arm. It took a couple tugs before I looked at her, snarling. "He's trying to goad you. He wants you to use your powers. Don't give him the satisfaction."

Her deep brown eyes were filled with concern and strength, and I anchored myself to them. The demon simmered down, withdrawing. She was right; if I used my powers he would only siphon them off me, growing stronger. I had to stay in control.

Stavros's laughter filled the cave. "Wow, I see who has you by the balls. A Druid and a demon together? Never thought I'd see that happen. But you can never choose who you love, right?"

"We don't—" Both Fionna and I started.

"Please." Margo scowled. "You both are drenched in it. Believe me, I've seen it before. Pathetic. What a waste. We could have had some fun." She shook her head sadly, as though I were the one missing out.

"Sounds as though someone's been scorned before." Fionna tipped her head. "What? You wanted him, but he fell in love with another? Hmmmm, that's shocking."

"Shut up, witch."

"I guess we didn't learn our lesson the last time. Want me to show you again, puppet?" Fionna wiggled her fingers.

Margo snarled, lunging forward. Stavros reached out and grabbed her arm.

"Last time you didn't have to play with the big boys." Stavros grinned. "I think it's only fair *I* give you a go." He winked. "Let's see how long your boyfriend can stand back and watch you fight his battles for him."

A rumble erupted from my chest, but Fionna's hand squeezed mine. If I fought Stavros, he would drain me. But I also couldn't let her fight in my place.

"Yes. You. Will." Her voice came into my ear, strong and indisputable, as though she had heard what I was thinking.

"Fionna," I grumbled, turning to look at her.

"What?" Her eyebrow curved up. "You don't think I can handle him? I'm not strong enough? Because I'm a girl or a Druid?

Warning. Warning, my brain chanted. This was a no-win situation for me. "I completely believe you can take him on." I licked my lip. "I just don't like being the cheerleader on the sidelines."

"Well, get those pom-poms ready, sweet cheeks." She slapped my ass. "I want to hear your best cheer. Oh, and if you want to change into a tiny little skirt, I'm not opposed to the idea." She hit my butt again and stepped past me, leaving me with my mouth slightly open. "Bring it on, Team Asshole; Team Druid is going to kick your arse."

Stavros's head fell back with laughter. He wiped at his eyes. "I'm really starting to like this girl." He spoke to me, shaking his finger toward Fionna.

"Let's see if you feel the same when you're flat on your back, fighting for consciousness *again*, uncle." I folded my arms, setting my legs out wide. I had no choice but to watch this play out. The moment I felt she was over her head, I was in.

"But only you, Stavros. Fair fight." I nodded at Margo.

"But of course." Stavros placed his hand on his chest, his eyes wide as though I'd offended him. "I always play fair."

I scoffed at the blatant lie. Demons didn't tend to like fairness.

I would also do what I needed to keep Fionna safe.

Chapter Thirty-Five

Fionna

It was doubtful Stavros knew the meaning of fairness, nor did I think for one moment he wouldn't play dirty. Bring it. I liked it dirty.

"Even though I think this will be easy, I always make sure I have a little extra luck on my side." Stavros winked at Margo, whose lips parted in a wicked curl. She squatted, untying the bundle Stavros had laid at his feet.

"Having the luck of the *Irish* never hurt." Stavros's eyes flashed, his grin widening. I felt Lars stiffen next to me at the same time a muffled grunt emerged from the bag. My stomach sank into the mud. "And a little incentive on my side."

Margo tipped over the bag and emptied its contents onto the cave floor as if it were trash.

"No!" The word popped from my mouth before I could even think, and I stepped forward. Lars clutched my arm, holding me in place. Fury and fear fluttered like moths in my chest.

Tied and gagged, Kevin lay on the ground, blood dripping from his temple and mouth. His face was beet red with anger, and he hissed garbled words at Margo and Stavros.

"Want this?" Margo snickered. She tugged Gerry from her back pocket and dangled it over the bound leprechaun.

Bitch.

"Leave it to the Druids to put a sub-fae in charge of one of the most powerful objects on earth." Stavros put his hands on his hips, shaking his head. "It wasn't hard to get him to tell us where you were headed."

I scoffed. "One you weren't even clever enough to figure out on your own. You forced him to lead you here." My hands formed fists. "You don't need him anymore. Let him go." For so long, I thought I hated *all* fae, but it wasn't all fae; I hated the self-appointed superiority of the supposed high fae.

As Kevin wiggled on the ground, still fighting back, trying to reach his friend and not showing the cowardice I had seen in so many high fae, I felt proud. He and I were more equal than not. We might be inferior to them, but you should always watch out for the underdogs. We had more to fight for.

"Keeping him tied up is for his own good." Stavros circled his finger by his head. "He's crazy. He thinks a sock is *real*," he whispered. "But I guess if I was locked in a cave by myself for what seemed like centuries...

Oh wait. I was. By my own brother."

"And Kevin is far saner than you." Lars kept his defensive stance, ready to react.

"Oh, nephew. Are you actually growing fond of your little pets?" He glanced between the leprechaun and me. "Calling them by name and treating them as though they mean something? Sweet, but it only shows how far you have already fallen." Stavros stepped up to Kevin and kicked him. Kevin thrashed and tried to get to his feet.

I chewed my bottom lip, trying to not react. It was what Stavros wanted.

"They have a place. A duty to serve us." Stavros leaned over and ran his fingers through the blood on Kevin's face. "His job is over."

Without Stavros even touching him, Kevin started to gasp for air, clawing at his neck.

"Stop!" I yelled.

Stavros flicked up an eyebrow and winked at me. Margo's laughter pealed out through the cave as the leprechaun fought for life.

Color drained from my peripheral vision. Magic flew out of my mouth like bullets, blasting off the walls and bounding back. Lars's form went flying back, and not one part of me felt bad. He needed to stay out of this. I had to protect him too. Another step, and Margo's frame crashed back into the wall of the cave, where she knocked her head sharply against the stone. Her body fell limp to the ground.

"Just you and me." I took a step toward the old King.

"Sounds utterly sinful." Stavros licked his lips, rolling his shoulders back as though he loved the thrill of the fight. He released Kevin's body, and it crashed to the ground. He lay there, motionless, but I spotted a slight flutter in his chest. He was still alive.

"Give me the cauldron, Fionna. I'll let you live. I could always use someone with your spirit."

"Go fuck yourself."

The shadows disguised the now broken treasure. One of the most powerful antique objects in the world and of course we broke it. Leave it to me.

"Then my only other choice is to kill you. Slowly. In front of my people to show what happens when you don't fall in line. And especially to any other Druid thinking they can challenge me. Like your sister. The Queen will be fun to tame."

A snarl rose from my throat.

"Let's say with an audience of thousands, hmmm? Killing you two will be my greatest performance. Your deaths will strengthen my seat on the throne. People need to know how powerful their real King is."

He wanted to use us to instill fear within the masses, so they would not up rise. Lars and I would be a powerful statement: a king strong enough to kill both an Unseelie King and a high Druid.

"If you touch her…" Lars moved, his anger blistering down his spine in bright reds and blacks.

"You have *nothing*. Nothing to threaten me with." He whipped around to Lars. "I am so much more powerful and smarter than you ever dreamed. Do you know how long I have been planning this?" He stepped closer to his nephew. "You think I just twiddled my thumbs in the hole where I was trapped for decades? I've been infiltrating you, your mind, your business…your *own* people."

Lars's lips fluttered, and he panted.

"You made it so easy to get into your compound. The day I heard you were on the hunt for a new secretary…well, it didn't take a genius to find a way in. Straight through your front door."

Lars's jaw fell open, and his eyes went black.

"They were all spies for me. Every one. The little raccoon shifter was my favorite. Glad you kept her."

Now it made sense how Stavros seemed to be always on our heels. Whenever Lars called to set something up for our trip, Sofia the secretary would disclose the same to Stavros.

"You got rid of them all before they could find out where you were hiding the other treasures. Except dear Sofia." Stavros peered down at his watch. "The raccoon is a particularly good thief."

I could feel Lars's rage as it seared through his body. I had only a split second to assess the two men. Lars was going to attack, and in doing so, he would give his uncle the very thing he wanted. I would not let that happen.

Black magic flowed from my lips, directly at Stavros. Slashes appeared across his chest, and he sailed back into the dirt. He hit the earth but popped back up in a blink, his shoulders shaking. It took me a moment to realize he was laughing.

"Is that all you've got, Druid? This time I am ready

for you." His chartreuse eyes met mine, humor dropping away. "You think you can kill me?"

As powerful as Druids were, we couldn't kill fae royalty without one of the Treasures of Tuatha Dé Danann. This is why we designed weapons to be able to do it. For us non-royals, whether fae, Druid, or human, the only way to kill a royal was with two specific weapons: the sword could kill a queen and the spear could kill a king. I had neither.

"I may not be able to end you, but that doesn't mean I can't take you out of the game and then have him kill you." I jerked my head toward Lars.

A garbled noise came from the ground, pulling our focus. Kevin was awake, trying to get through his ropes.

A malicious smile grew on Stavros's face, dropping my stomach to my feet. His intention was clear.

Time put my muscles in slow motion, while it sped everything else up. "Noooooo!" I reached out, but Stavros drew out a knife, slicing the leprechaun's throat before I could even take a step. Blood gushed onto the floor. Kevin's eyes widened, looking up into mine. He blinked, then slumped to the ground, his life cascading onto the dirt.

"Sub-fae are only good as servants, slaves, or dead." Stavros tossed Kevin's body to the side with a snort.

Color drained from my sight, grief and rage scooping out of my soul, turning off every emotion except anger. My vision narrowed on Stavros.

I was my magic, which was black and angry. Power encased me, billowing through every nerve and muscle. My curse sped toward him like a freight train.

Kill.

Death.

Destroy.

With a crack, my energy clashed against him, burning his flesh with a sizzling pop. He roared in agony and slid backward. He snarled as he tried to step forward, the spell loosening around him, becoming whiffs of smoke. Before I realized what was happening, his magic blasted into my head, chucking me backward. Pressure slammed against my brain, squeezing it. *Shite.* He could break through my magic. *Only* Lars had been able to do that.

Stavros now had Lars's kingly magic.

Anger heaved through my lungs as I shoved him out, easing the crushing torture in my skull.

Bones poked out from the tears in his torso where my spell had struck him. The stench of burnt flesh reeked, and I thought I would gag. His eyes turned black. He growled, shooting magic at me again. Magic wrapped around my throat, pushing down, blurring the spell in my head.

"Fionna!" At Lars's voice, my eyes popped open, and I rammed my magic at Stavros. Claw marks cut across his face and stomach, slinging him like a doll to the entrance of the cave. In my periphery Margo rose to her feet, and I sent my magic at her. She tugged the sword out of its holster and sprang at Stavros, under my thrall. Stavros rolled, getting out of her way.

I could feel thick goo sliding from my nose and eyes, fatigue burrowing into the back of my head. Death fluttered around the edges, waiting to see if this was the time it finally got to claim me.

Stavros stood again, though with less enthusiasm. Pressure once again wrapped around my head and throat. My knees crashed to the ground, breaking my hold on Margo.

With my heart pounding in my ears and dots blurring my vision, I grappled for air. Last time I attacked him, I had caught him off guard. This time he was ready and fighting back with everything he had.

Death hovered, curling around my shoulders. Black liquid spurted from my mouth as I fought against Stavros's hold

A roar I felt more than heard crashed against the walls of the cave and inside my soul. I fell onto my side, as Lars leaped for his uncle.

No, Lars. Don't.

The thought wafted past, but I could do nothing to stop him. Lars tore Margo's blade from her hand as she came after him, no longer under my thrall. His back flexed, all the muscles working as he drove the blade toward her. She slipped to the side to get away from his deadly blow, but the blade pierced her arm. Margo's screams filled the cave. Lars dug the sword so deep into the stone wall, pinning her in place. Her blood poured onto the ground.

Stavros ignored them, taking another step toward me with a gleeful grin on his face. A blood vessel popped in my eye, my lids drifting closed, air no longer moving through my lungs. Blackness ate up all time and space, my body giving in to it.

Then, as if someone kicked me in the chest with steel-toed boots, pain raged up my spine; the pressure lifted, flooding my lungs with oxygen. I gasped, taking huge gulps of air as painful coughs stung my esophagus.

My vision cleared to see Stavros standing over Lars, his body twitching and limp.

Noooooooooooo.

I stumbled up to my feet, swaying.

He was dying. I could feel the edges of his soul slipping away from me similar to threads pulling away from a sweater.

Fuck. No.

Black magic sang from my mouth and struck Stavros in the back of head. He lurched to the side, and I gave him no time to recover. I spotted the handle of the knife I had stolen from Travil in Lars's boot. I vaulted for it, grabbing it. Fury overtook me, everything gray. I didn't even think. The tip of the blade tunneled into Stavros's eyeball as if it were butter. Blood sprayed over my face as he teetered to the side screaming in pain. His mouth gaped in disbelief as though he couldn't believe I had bested him with something simple as a knife.

A strange cry belted from my lips, twisting the weapon in deeper, spewing the only spell I could muster. His frame flew up into the air, his neck twisting as my magic snapped it with a chilling crack. Then his body crashed down to the earth.

I gasped, energy crumpling me to the ground like I was a doll. Clots of tar-colored blood seeped from my nose and hacked up from my lungs, dropping into the dirt. I grappled for breath, to stop my lids from shutting and to keep awake.

Lars.

I turned my head to see his limp body motionless on the ground.

"Lars?" I croaked, crawling over to him, passing Stavros. To everyone else Stavros would appear dead. But I knew better. I could take him out temporarily, but not kill him. Lars had to do that. Stavros was not my worry right now as I made my way to his kin.

"Lars." I clawed myself to his side, reaching for his face. His complexion was ashen and covered with blood. A big streak of silver ran through his dark hair. "Lars?" I pressed my palms against his chest. A slight fluttering told me he clung to life. "You do *not* get to die on me either. Not now. Not ever." I closed my eyes and felt the weak pulse of my own magic barely beating there. I didn't care. I would find a sliver of something for him. Not even a question.

Every joint and muscle throbbed with exhaustion. Ice picks of pain stabbed behind my eye, at my temples, and in my ears, as I forced a chant to fester on my tongue. I gurgled and stumbled over the words, trying to spit them from my lips, pushing whatever energy I could into him.

It didn't take much before the edges of my vision started to darken and blur. I had taken so much today, the backlash from earth's power on my body was splitting me into pieces. A whimper rose from my chant as I pushed on.

I would not lose him. He was mine. He saved me from death, and I would do the same for him, even if I dragged him back from the beyond kicking and screaming. He could hate me, but at least we would be together.

If he died, nothing would stop Stavros, but if Lars lived, we had a little hope. Now Stavros would strip Lars of all his imperial power. He could die now. He could be killed the same as all other fae. I would not, could not, let it happen.

I grunted through the piercing aches ricocheting along my nerves, dumping more magic into Lars.

"Fionna. Stop." I heard a breathy whisper. I opened my eyes. Only a slice of green showed beneath his lashes, but it was enough to produce a sob of relief.

"Oh my gods..." I reached up cupping his face, falling into him, my limbs shaking violently. "Damn you for scaring me. Don't ever do that again."

"Yes, ma'am." He tried to smile, but it appeared more a flinch of pain. We were both so far from our best, but we had to move. The new King and his mistress would not stay down for long.

"We have to go." I tried to assist him, his strength hanging on by a thread. "Help me!" I shoved my shoulder under his arm, trying to get him to his feet while struggling to stay up on my own. The desperation in my tone sounded shrill. He tried a couple of times to get to his feet, without much luck. It assaulted my soul with heartache to see him so feeble. The *great* King. His vulnerability scared me more than anything. He would eventually heal and get better because he was still fae, but his royal magic was gone.

Stavros was the true King. Lars was nowhere near being able to challenge anyone right now. We had to run while we had the chance.

Once on his feet, I leaned Lars against the wall, his eyes never leaving Stavros. Emotions I couldn't decipher moved across his face. Margo had passed out from her own blood loss, still fastened to the wall. The whole cave was a bloodbath.

Sweeping up the cauldron, I shoved it in my small bag. Even though it was nothing more than a beautiful decoration, I still would not leave it for Stavros to find. It came from my bloodline. If it belonged to anyone, it was me.

My gaze wandered to Kevin's dead body. His mouth and eyes hung open. We couldn't carry him out of here. Or try to bring him back to life. I was void of even a trace of magic. It would take me awhile to replenish all I took.

"Fionna, what are you doing?" Lars hobbled for the exit, his gaze snapping to me as I scampered back for the leprechaun.

"If he's going to stay here," I snatched fabric from the dirt, "he's not going to be alone." I stepped to Kevin's body, squatting over him. "You will be missed, my friend." I clutched his fingers and slipped Gerry onto his hand. "Both you and Gerry." I bit into my lip, trying not to cry. Bending over him, I kissed his forehead. "Goodbye, Kevin." He would at least be with his friend in death. "Goodbye, Gerry."

I bolted to my feet and reached for Lars's arm. "I'm fine."

He nodded. "Let's just get out of here."

I gave Kevin one last look before we plunged back outside. The dreary day spit down on us as we made our way back through the gulch.

~~

Magic thumped at the back of my neck as we made our way up the slippery steps. A sinking sensation in my gut moved into my chest, as if the two were connected by a rope.

"What?"

"You don't feel that?" My eyes and body were unable to settle on one place.

"No," Lars growled, ire wrinkling his nose. "Is this what it's like to be common?"

"You're alive." I rolled by eyes. "Deal with it."

His huff was half laugh and half fury. This had to be a huge change. Lars had never been ordinary. The moment he was born he was meant for greatness.

I took a few more steps, breathing in deeply, the sounds of rain pattering the leaves and ground. No birds or any other noise.

Something was off. Wrong.

A high-pitched howl tore through the air, the same way a lone wolf sounds, sending chills down my body. My wide eyes met Lars's. We both knew. It was no wolf.

"I really wish it was." He seemed to understand my thoughts.

Run! He seemed to scream into my soul. Adrenaline was the only thing moving my body as I whirled it around and tore down the trail for our car.

Cries of battle surrounded us like an out-of-key concerto, building up in a chorus to kill. The rustling of movement, of weapons being pounded on the ground, clashed in rhythm with my heartbeat. The strighoul cried out as they came for us. Their shouts and stomping feet rattled my bones, making it even harder for my legs to sludge through the dense mud.

Lars's energy was worse than mine. Our bodies were on the verge of collapsing, but we both tried to move faster up the stairs.

The storm clouds moved in and blocked the sunlight, bringing an artificial night.

"Fionna!" Lars screamed when we got to the top, terror snaking through his voice. I twisted to look at him.

Wham.

My body went flying, my bones cracking as I collided with a tree, hitting the ground with an aching crunch.

A strighoul bayed and jumped on me, its sharp teeth snapping for my neck. "You will be so juicy. Tasty Druid. Tasty, tasty treat," it cackled. I gagged at the fetid scent of it. I was so dizzy and tired that my magic reserve had dried up. Black magic didn't naturally protect, not as Kennedy's did, because she was a natural obscurer. The rest of us had to create it, which used far more energy than normal magic.

The strighoul's claws dug into my arms, pinning me down as it bent over with its mouth open wide to chomp down.

Hands wrapped around the strighoul's throat with a vibrating growl, snapping its neck. The form went still above me, its body going into shock. Wrath pulsed from the man standing over me. He flung the body to the side, his eyes black with rage, his shoulders hunched in a feral stance.

He might not be a king, but damn, the man was still all demon.

"That was hot."

Lars's eyes tore away from the monster on the ground, finding me. He huffed, shaking his head. I could feel the warmth from his demon. It liked I found it sexy. It no longer had to hide or pretend to be what it wasn't.

Lars reached out to grab my hand when another strighoul leaped out from the bushes, plowing into the demon, scratching and tearing at Lars's flesh.

"No!"

I bounded to my feet when another cannibal sprang onto my back, wrapping its arms tightly around my neck, cutting off my air. Every second another one came for us, outnumbering us with unbeatable odds similar to hyenas fencing in their prey.

This couldn't be how we ended, when we had made it so far. But the lack of air and energy weighed down on my brain, keeping me from fighting back.

Teeth sliced into my neck, and my knees buckled me to the ground. My vision blurred. I couldn't even feel the pain I knew had to come with it, as though I were already departing from my body. My lashes flickered to Lars one last time. All I could see was blood and black eyes staring back at me before my face smashed into the ground.

~~

Bang!

Blast after blast shot out over the air, drilling into my conscious, but I didn't give much thought to it. A strighoul screamed and the heaviness weighing me down suddenly lifted, letting oxygen whoosh into my lungs. I gulped in, inhaling particles of dirt and mud.

Voices and pounding feet moved closer to me, but I still couldn't lift my eyes.

"Shit," a voice yelled, and a sense of familiarity tapped at my brain. "They're here! Quick. They are both hurt."

"Fuck. Fuck!" Another husky voice joined the first. "What the hell happened? What's wrong with him?"

"I don't know, but I can feel it…his power is gone," the first replied. "Go, check on her. I'll get him."

Rustling sounded next to my ear. A hand rolled me over, then went around my neck, pressing into my wound. His touch flinched my lids to unlock, sucking in a pained breath.

"Druid." A man hovered over me, wiping the muck from my face. "I want my knife back," Travil snarled down at me.

A ghost of a laugh parted my mouth, relief flooding down on me like the rain.

"Lars?" I croaked. Slivers of throbbing went up my neck. Before Travil could even speak, a voice bellowed over to me.

"Fionna? Where is she?"

Travil lifted his eyebrows and glanced over his shoulder. "She's right here, my liege." Travil helped me sit up. That's when I saw the carnage around me. Strighoul scattered the ground like leaves, bullet holes through their heads or hearts. Blood, brain, and matter doused the ground with a layer of fluid.

"Fionna?" Lars pushed past Goran, hobbling to me.

"I'm fine." I rose to my feet, Travil held me steady as I made my way toward Lars. We met halfway, his hands sliding up my face, his gaze searching me over.

"I'm all right, Lars," I reassured him again. He continued to stare into my eyes, his hand trying to stop the blood oozing from my neck. I didn't even have the strength to heal myself. He also had been bitten, but he didn't seem to be concerned about the blood coursing down his neck.

"Someone get me a clean cloth or shirt. I don't care," Lars yelled to his men. In a beat, Goran ripped off his T-shirt and handed it to Lars. Lars rolled it into a ball and plastered it to my neck. "Hold it there until we can clean it out."

I nodded, cuddling the shirt to my wound.

"I swear, Druid," he mumbled, glowering for a second. "You will be the one to make me go insane."

"I hope in the good way," I whispered, feeling the stunned stares of his guards all around us.

"We both know you already do that." His hands worked farther back into my scalp, stepping closer to me. "I know you are powerful and can fight, but know I am still going to want to protect you and keep you safe. Okay, Druid?"

"Same, demon."

He clutched my head, pulling me to him, his mouth finding me. His lips parted mine. The kiss forced me to brace my hands against his chest to keep my knees from collapsing. Consuming and passionate, he tore me from earth, sent me high above the clouds. But this time it went all the way down to my toes, shaking the ground with the words he didn't say, but I felt them all the same.

He loved me.

And he didn't hold back, kissing me hungrily, not caring his men gaped at us.

I had never told a man I loved him, and I wasn't ready to say it out loud now. But it was there, the sensation prickling the back of my mind. I declared it back to him with my mouth; the rest of the world be dammed.

Fionna Cathbad, a staunch fighter for the DLR, was in love with a fae.

No...I was in love with Lars.

Chapter Thirty-Six

Fionna

"They are safe, sir. The room is secure," Goran confirmed. "Sofia never got close. Travil caught her trying to sneak down to the lower levels. We both had been watching her for a while. I never trusted that raccoon shifter."

"Glad you are recovered and I have you looking out for me." Lars nodded to Travil and Goran as we walked through the hangar to the jet waiting for us, still covered in gore, blood, and mud. "Especially when I was not at my best."

After they had caught Sofia, they "coerced" her into telling them the plan. They sent the jet over while they went through the otherworld doors to get to us on time. I didn't want to know how they obtained the information from Sofia; I was just glad they did.

Lars gave them a brief rundown on what happened with his uncle. He hated to acknowledge he no longer had the power he used to, but for his protection, they needed to know. Travil and Goran were faithful to him; I knew that in my gut. They would do anything to protect *their* King, and they would have to, even more now. The fight was far from over.

Lars no longer had the magic of a King, but he still held himself like one. His command would remain unquestioned by his men. It was everyone else we'd have to worry about.

"It seems you are back to yourself, sir." Goran's stopped at the bottom of the stairs, his gaze slipping to me.

Lars's eyes followed, clicking with mine. "I am."

The last time they saw him, he was talking to ghosts and battling his demon. Now that I could feel the demon, I knew it felt content and happy.

"I am glad for you, my liege."

Lars nodded, lacing his hand through mine, and took a step up the stairs.

Two women stepped out on either side of the entrance, curtsying slightly. The blonde gazed at him through her lashes as though he were her last meal.

"Oh. Hell. No," I muttered, my shoulders rising toward my ears.

Lars stopped on the step above mine and turned around with a shite-eating grin on his face. He squeezed my hand tighter. "What?"

"Shut it." I glared up at him as he widened his smile. "You love this, don't you?"

He set his mouth, trying to hold back the laugh I could see in his eyes.

Smart boy.

"She's not staying." I moved past him up the stairs, letting go of his hand. "Next one is old and male."

"You think that would stop me?"

My lids tapered into slits, a chuckle bursting from his lips.

"You can hire the next one if it makes you feel better."

I snapped back to look at him. Was he serious? "Really?"

"You can re-staff the entire house. I don't care."

I looked closely at him to see if he was sincere. He tipped his head, his green irises holding steady. I could feel his emotions as clear as day.

"Shite," I whispered, feeling the true impact of his offer. We had fought our feelings for so long. When we finally gave in to them, they were way ahead of us, knowing what we should have weeks ago.

"Except Marguerite. She's a deal-breaker."

"Oh, I'd get rid of you before I'd get rid of her," I teased. "And that hot incubus. He stays."

Lars chuckled, shaking his head, his eyes glinting with humor.

As a Druid, I didn't grow up believing in "mates," not the way fae did. But I couldn't deny it was exactly the word my soul conjured up when I looked at him. He was it. The only one I would ever be happy with. And if I had been more willing to see it, I probably would have noticed it the night he stepped into my world in Ireland, the only person able to challenge me.

"You are also stuck with me," he replied. He cupped my face, standing even with me.

"Is that how you see it?" I raised an eyebrow. "You're *stuck with* me?"

"No, but I am hoping to be stuck deep *in* you in about five minutes."

I inhaled, lust rushing over me. He leaned in, kissing me hard. Both stewardesses gasped behind him. I'm sure they were shocked. I had started this journey as his prisoner. Now if we used handcuffs and rope, it would be for fun.

A Druid and a demon. We might be making history.

"Now get up those steps and into the shower before I carry you there."

"I'm going to be *extra* loud."

"Yes, you will. But it will have nothing to do with trying to make her jealous." He grabbed my hip and turned me to head up the stairs. I raced up, passing the sylph, the jealous air fairy. She glared at me, rage bursting from her eyes like lasers, but I didn't care. I was too excited to get under that stream of water.

When I entered the back of the plane, I stopped, causing Lars to ram into the back of me.

"What?" His hands slipped around my waist.

I blinked back the tears. On his desk in the office sat two hamburgers, fries, and milkshakes.

"Feck. You know a way to a girl's heart."

"I thought you might be hungry. And before you ask, yes, they are both vanilla."

I touched my chest, snaking around to face him. "Where's yours?" I teased.

"You think I'm going to eat that crap again? Marguerite sent roast beef sandwiches. To die for."

"Nice, feed me the garbage while you feast."

His eyes flared, his foot slamming the office door shut. He lifted me up, wrapping my legs around his waist. He walked us back to the shower, then stripped us of soiled clothing. Our mouths and hands were already frantic for each other. Sprays of warm water doused my head as my back met the tile wall. He lowered me to my feet and lathered me with soap, his hands washing away the blood, dirt, and strighoul brain matter from my body. His touch teased and ignited every nerve in me.

He went down on his knees, kissing my thigh. "It's not the sandwich I want to feast on."

I pressed my head back into the tile, moans echoing off them.

Even drained and wounded, he didn't hold anything back. I was quite sure the entire plane—hell, maybe even continents away—heard the sounds of our union.

What we created between us was intense and powerful, and only grew stronger each time we made love.

~~

"Stop fidgeting." Lars placed his hand over mine, pressing down on my bobbing knee.

"I can't help it." I wasn't just nervous; I was terrified. It hadn't really hit me until he mentioned her while we chowed down on the hamburgers and sandwiches in bed. Marguerite's sandwiches won, hands down.

I had set my mind a long time ago that I would never make it back to her. But I was about to see my daughter. Really meet her for the first time.

"I think I'm going to throw up."

"You did eat two hamburgers, a sandwich, fries, and a milkshake."

I glowered at him.

He cupped my face. "She's going to love you."

"Yeah, because I've been such a great mum to her thus far." I turned to look out the window.

"Stop," he said sternly. "It does no good regretting the past. You move forward. Start fresh."

The car stopped in front of the huge English manor, and Lars's door opened instantly.

"Good to have you home, sir." A guard bowed to him, holding the door.

"Thank you." He slid out. It took him two steps to notice I wasn't following. "Fionna." He peered back in the car. I didn't want to move. There was nothing I wanted more than to see my daughter, but fear of rejection or disappointment in her eyes kept me frozen in place. "The strongest woman I know is too scared to face a five-year-old?"

I bit down on my lip.

"She just wants her mother to love her."

"I do love her. So much." I dug my knuckles into my chest.

"Then that is enough," he replied, holding out his hand. "The rest will come in time."

I inhaled, finally nodding. I reached over and grabbed his hand, letting him tug me out of the car.

"Mr. Lars! Mr. Lars!" Marguerite came running out the house, her arms waving excitedly. "You are home. You both are safe!"

He leaned over and kissed her cheek. "Yes, we're home."

Safe? That was debatable.

She jerked her head, darting her wide eyes between our linked hands, a smile taking over her features. "Oh, Mr. Lars, Ms. Fionna!" She rambled on in Spanish so quickly I couldn't pick up a word, but by her joy and the way she pointed at us and grabbed her heart, I knew she understood we were together.

"Shit, breathe, Marguerite." Nik, the panty-dropping Spanish incubus I had seen a few times at the house, stepped into the doorway. But he wasn't what stole the air from my lungs. On his hip, nibbling the last bit of cracker, was my daughter.

My hand went to my mouth, a cry sticking in my throat. She was more beautiful than I remembered from my brief view of her in Lars's basement. The front of her long shiny brown hair was clipped back with barrettes. She wore bright multicolored leggings and a teal "Girls Rock" sweatshirt, her feet in comfy, fuzzy socks. She looked healthy, happy, comfortable, and at home.

Her blue eyes peered curiously at Lars, then at me. I held my breath, feeling her gaze turn critical. Watchful. Nik lowered her slowly to the ground as I tried to swallow, finding my voice.

"Piper."

She stepped behind Nik's leg but did not shun away, her scrutiny drilling into me. I lowered myself onto the steps, even with her.

"Hi, Piper." My voice wobbled. "I don't know if you know who I am—"

"You're my mummy," she said clear and sure, her sweet Irish accent filling my ears like a song.

Tears filled my eyes, burning my lids. "Yes. I'm your mummy."

She looked up at Nik. He rubbed her head and nodded toward me. It was obvious they had bonded over the time we were gone. She took a breath and stepped confidently toward me. Her eyes held so much knowledge and intelligence you could easily forget she was only five.

"I'm so sorry, Piper." My hands itched to wrap her in my arms, but I stayed still, unsure what to do.

"I know, Mummy," she said, reaching up and touching my cheek. I could no longer hold back my tears. "Don't cry."

A sob hiccupped in my throat.

"I knew you'd come back for me." She tapped her head. "I saw it."

Emotion filled me, and I wrapped my arms around her, dragging her into my chest, holding her so tight. "I will never let you go again. I promise." I repeated it over and over, my voice barely able to get all the words out.

Finally, when the tears ebbed, I loosened my grip on her, leaning back enough to see her face. "I love you, Piper. I promise I will make up all those years I wasn't with you." My hands cupped her face.

"It's okay, Mummy. I don't remember when I was a baby."

She meant it to make me feel better, but it only piled on more guilt.

"Nana is making vanilla cake with chocolate chips for dessert. *And with sprinkles.*" She pointed up at Marguerite.

It took everything I had to not shed more tears at Piper calling Marguerite a pet name for grandma. She was so happy here.

I laughed, standing up, wiping my eyes. "My favorite."

"Mine too." She jumped in place. "Come on! It's almost ready." She turned, running back inside, practically knocking Nik over.

"After dinner, squirt." He laughed, following her. Marguerite walked straight to me and gave me a hug, then went in the house too, leaving Lars and me alone.

"You all right?" He came up to me.

"Yes. No. I don't know." I twisted to face him. He drew me to him without a word, knowing I needed a moment to regain myself. He stroked the back of my head, letting me burrow into his chest. Guilt, shame, joy, and love pummeled me like a boxer.

"It will take time, but every day it will get better."

"How can she ever forgive me?"

"I wasn't talking about her. That relationship will build and heal faster than the punishment you are going to put yourself through. Forgive yourself. Otherwise you can't have a true relationship with your daughter." He tipped my head to look at him. "I know what it is like to fight ghosts. You can never win."

I gaped at him. "Where did you come from?" I could hardly believe this was the same man I walked out these doors with a month ago.

"Greece." He smiled, leaning in to kiss me. I wrapped my arms around his neck as he lifted me off my feet, deepening the kiss.

"Mummy? Mr. Darz? Come on!" A little voice called out for us. Piper's face poked out the door, her hand held out for us. "Cake!"

"Darz? Is that me?" Lars put me back on my feet.

"I think so." I smirked. "Come on, Mr. Darz...there's cake."

He grinned, taking her little hand in his, and fresh tears fluttered in my eyes again.

"I can't ever say no to Marguerite's cake." He grinned down at her.

"Me neither." I took her other hand, melting at her touch and at the image of the three of us walking into the house. How open and loving children were. How easily they forgave and moved on to more important things, like cake.

I wished I could so easily forgive myself and forget. I would eventually have to, but it would take a lot more than cake.

~~

I leaned against the doorway watching Piper sleep. Her tiny body curled up around the stuffed animals taking over her bed. Lars had given Marguerite and Nik free rein to redecorate one of the rooms for her. To say they went overboard was an understatement. Eventually I would step in and cut back the toys, a firm believer less was more. She would be loved, but not spoiled to the point where she didn't understand or appreciate what she had.

But looking at her so peaceful and content right then, all I felt was grateful Lars had taken her away from her other family. She was where she belonged. Here, with me.

I didn't know if we would stay here. I wasn't sure if he was ready for Piper and me to live with him. I thought I would long to go back to Ireland, but Olwyn was gone and my sister was here. Lars was here. Seattle was feeling more like home.

I felt his presence instantly, though he made no sound as he approached. Our connection zapped my skin similar to an electrical charge. I could sense him on multiple layers, which was wonderful and disturbing at the same time. I had never needed anyone before. Not like this. He didn't touch me, but the heat of his body compelled mine to step back, longing to be swallowed up by him. I gripped my hands, holding my ground.

"Piper and I will start looking for a place tomorrow," I said low, keeping my gaze on her.

Silence.

"What you've already done for her...I can't thank you enough."

No response.

I gritted my teeth, hating the sense of disappointment and sadness seizing my gut. He wasn't fighting for me to stay. I didn't expect him to, nor did I really want to be "taken care of." I had always done that myself. I would figure it out. Find a job. I was scrappy and determined. Piper and I would be just fine.

I already knew what I wanted to do with my life. The treatment of Druids had always been my cause, but now I wanted to add sub-fae to the list. I would not let Kevin's death be in vain. I would fight for equal rights, work to change the views of society toward those who were "different."

"You agreed you would leave," his voice rumbled behind me.

"What?" I swiveled around, tears stinging my eyes. Lars's hair was wet and slicked back, his face shaven. He was dressed in a pair of posh gray sweatpants, which rode low on his hips, and a tight-fitting black T-shirt. I had never seen him looked so relaxed, but still as though he stepped off the pages of *GQ*.

"You and Piper. I want you safe." His green eyes blazed, his face stone as he moved up to me, clasping my cheek. "I can't protect you as I want. And I will not lie to you and say everything's going to be all right. We both know it is not."

I nipped my lip, looking away.

"Fionna, look at me."

I huffed but obeyed.

"What I want to say is there's no way in hell you're looking for a fucking flat. This should be your home and Piper's home. With me." He nodded toward the sleeping girl. "But we can't." His Adam's apple bobbed. "Neither of us are dreamers. We understand reality and what is coming. Stavros will not quit until I am dead. And that is going to happen sooner than later."

My mouth opened to speak, but his sharp look stopped the denial in my throat. He was right. What-ifs were for romantics and dreamers. We were realists who did what we needed to survive.

"Then come with us." I touched his face, missing the scruff that had grown while we were on the run. "We can figure something out. Find a way to use the other treasures without destroying the world or you. Fight him."

His eyes softened, searching mine. He drew me in closer. "You know I can't." His thumb stroked my cheek. "Kings do not run or hide. I must face him. The Dark law mandates I face my challenger. The stronger, more capable one wins." We both knew it would be Stavros; he already had most of Lars's power. "I've already spoken with Nik and Marguerite. They've agreed to go with you and Piper."

"I am not going to leave you. I just found you. You need me. My magic. Let me stay. I understand we need to get Piper away from here, and Marguerite. But I can fight with you."

"No." He growled. "If things go the way I think they will, I want you far from here. He will not be kind to the people in this house. *Especially* you. You've beaten him twice, and he will be sure you pay dearly for that. I will not let him hurt you…or her. If he even gets an inkling of how powerful Piper already is? No… You have to take her far from here." He tipped his head against mine. "Like I asked you before, I need you to hide the treasures. As a Druid, you can protect them from Stavros. Go to some place in Eastern Europe if you can." He brought up his other hand to my face. "Do this for me. Please."

My jaw clenched, holding back the tide of grief that wanted to flood out. For a brief moment, I had my daughter, a home, and the man I loved all at once. But it existed as a bubble, fragile and popping the moment it was touched.

"Lars," I croaked.

He cut off anything else I was going to say, his lips seeking mine, kissing me slow and deep. His arms curled around my arse, picking me up. He walked us down the hall, laying me back on his bed, and undressed me. While we'd lost ourselves in lust and need every time we had sex, this night was different. For the first time, I felt the difference between lust and love.

We didn't stop until the sun started to rise. It was one of the best nights of my life, and the worst because I knew with each thrust of his hips, with every kiss, he was saying one thing to me.

Goodbye.

Chapter Thirty-Seven

Fionna

I opened my eyes, light sneaking through the blinds and giving the dark room depth. My head turned over to find myself alone, Lars's spot cold.

I propped myself up on my elbows, feeling the soreness and delicious ache from our all-nighter. I replayed everything we did, flushing hot all over again. Some of the things we did I had never done before, but I already wanted to try again. Like now.

Damn, where was he?

I glanced over at the clock, seeing it was almost noon.

"Shite." I scrambled out of bed, my mind on Piper. I grabbed a T-shirt of Lars's out of his closet, the soft cotton amazing against my sensitive skin. I found my leggings from the night before and slipped into those before I moved out.

"Piper?" I peered into her bedroom. The bed was made as though she was never in it, her stuffed animals all arranged perfectly. From downstairs a little girl's voice reached my ears, taking me toward the kitchen.

Dark clouds loomed outside the window, the glass painted with nature's tears, as if it seemed to understand what was coming.

I shook my head, shoving the looming sadness from my head, but it stuck like a claw in my heart. Lars would want me to leave soon, but I wasn't ready to really say goodbye. I still needed to talk to my sister. Shite, she didn't even know about Piper. But most of all Lars and I needed to update her, prepare her for what was coming.

We just needed one more day.

"*Buenas tardes*." Marguerite smiled at me when I entered the room, her eyes glistening with understanding. "Sleep well, Ms. Fionna?"

"Too well." I came up beside Piper.

"You slept in so late, Mummy." She looked up at me and smiled, then went back to her coloring.

"Yeah. I was tired." I kissed the top of Piper's head.

Marguerite made a noise, turning to the stove, her smile growing wider.

"Yeah. Mummy and Daddy were *so* exhausted they kept me up all frickin' night, and my room is on the other side of the house." Nik sauntered into the room, scouring his face as he headed for the fridge, his rumpled hair and outfit signaled he'd just woken up too.

"Nik!" Piper jumped off her stool and ran to him.

He reached down and picked her up. "Hey, squirt." He put her on his hip, rubbing her head.

I tried not to feel the stab of jealousy at the easy way she related to him. I couldn't expect to walk in and have her be comfortable with me. She understood I was her mother, but she still didn't know me.

I knew this, but it still hurt.

Nik grabbed a carton of orange juice and started drinking straight from it.

"*¡Mi hijo!*" Marguerite swiped the back of his head. "Teaching *niña* bad habits."

He grinned at Piper just as wide. I had a feeling it was too late to teach him anything. I loved the instant family she had with Nik and Marguerite. I just wanted to be part of it.

"Piper, we can spend the entire day together and do whatever you want to do." I tugged my hair nervously to one side. What if she didn't want to?

She looked over at me. "Can we watch a movie?"

Nik groaned, letting his head fall back. "Let me guess: *The Secret of Kells*?"

She nodded dramatically. It made me smile that she didn't pick a princess movie, but one about Ireland and magic. Home.

"Sounds perfect."

"With Darz too?" Her brown eyes widened with excitement and hope. "Please!"

"Maybe. I'll have to go find him." I knew we had so much to do. Stavros would be coming soon. I wanted a few hours with my daughter—the three of us—before it was taken away.

"Lunch first." Marguerite pushed past Nik, trying to get into the fridge. "Grilled cheese, *mi niña*?"

"Yesssss!" She wiggled out of Nik's embrace and ran back to her stool.

"I agree!" Nik waved his arms, mimicking her excitement, following her around to another stool. She giggled, her laugh warming my heart, followed by stabs of pain. We were going to have to leave this all behind.

"Have you seen Lars?" I asked.

"I think I saw him head downstairs," Nik responded, picking up a crayon, giving me a look. We both knew what was below.

I had no doubt where he was.

~~

I followed my gut, sensing him and the power of the Druid-made objects. Both pulled on me with a siren's call. I spotted Goran. His expression was icy, but he jerked his head down the hall, telling me what I needed to know.

Nerves began to coil in my gut as my bare feet padded across the cold stone. I wanted to ignore my Druid's intuition as I stepped into the room. It appeared small with different-size compartments lining one wall, resembling a bank vault. Magic swirled in the space, thumping like heartbeats.

Lars was dressed in dark jeans, a black sweater, and boots, not his usual "King" attire, but the one I had grown used to seeing him in.

He stared down, not reacting to my entrance, though I knew he was aware of my presence.

"Lars?" I took a wary step closer. "Lars, what are you doing?"

He didn't even seem to hear me, his focus on an open vault box. My gaze trailed down to see what was in it. The cauldron sat in one, still and lifeless.

Lars's attention was not on the cauldron, however, but on the compartment next to it.

Shite. My heart plummeted like a lump of cement.

A small stone lay in the open container. I knew it was no ordinary beach rock.

The Stone of Fáil.

I had heard plenty of stories about it, and if the magic pulsing off it showed any indication of its power, we were truly screwed.

Out of all the treasures, the Stone of Fáil was rumored to be the worst. It stood, for lack of a better description, the captain of all the others, and it had been searching for centuries to find its companions.

Now it had. *What have we done?*

"Lars?" I reached for his arm, my heart knocking against my ribs. He didn't respond to my touch, his body tight and straight like a plank of wood. Touching him was similar to touching the rails on which a train is steadily coming. Pulsating. Even his aura blurred around him. His hand lifted, moving for the treasure.

"Lars, no!" I flung out my arm and snatched his hand in a bone-crunching grip. The momentum twisted his body slightly toward me. His head jerked up, as if he only just noticed someone else was in the room. His eyes met mine and panic crawled up my throat like a dozen spiders.

Black pits stared back at me, emotionless and lethal.

"Fight it." The lump in my throat bobbed as I swallowed, moving my firm grip to his face. "Don't let it have power over you. You are still a high demon. Don't let it control you. Be stronger."

His lips parted in a snarl, his daggered cuspids displaying their warning.

"You think you scare me?" I moved in closer, yanking his head even with my own, low anger building up in my voice. "Try me. You know I can go toe to toe with you, demon."

Lars didn't move, but a nerve in his cheek twitched.

"You don't want to do this. We can fight what's coming. Together."

"N-o." The word garbled from his lips as if he were struggling to talk. "We can't. It's the only way...otherwise I lose you. My kingdom. I have to fight my uncle. He cannot become King."

"Not this way! You are not leaving me," I growled. Last night my heart was crippled with the idea I would lose him to Stavros. I tried to think of any other option. This wasn't it. I would lose him just the same if he gave into the stone.

My fingers dug into his skin, my muscles shaking trying to hold him in place.

"Do whatever you have to do, but fight it. Do it for me. For the little girl upstairs, who wants nothing more than to cuddle on the sofa and watch a movie with *us*."

His lids finally blinked, a tint of green swelling in around the edges.

As if the stone felt it was losing him, pressure in the room bloomed around us so that my ears popped and my legs bent. I curled over with a cry, tears building up behind my lids.

"I can't fight it anymore. I don't have the strength." Lars choked, pivoting back toward the object, his hand extended.

"No!" I leaped for him, my body crashing into him, but it didn't even bump him off course. "Lars! Don't! Please..." I knew the moment he touched the smooth surface of the rock he was lost to me. Forever. When he had his King power's he could fight the call. Now that he was just a demon...the power was too great.

A terror I had never felt throttled my soul, squeezing out one undeniable, blinding truth. "Lars. I can't lose you." I shook at his arm. "I. *Love*. You."

He jerked to a stop, only his head turning back to me.

"I am so deeply in love with you. I don't know when or how...but I am. Fae, demon, Unseelie, King. It doesn't matter to me. I love *you*. All of you." My hand pressed into my stomach, feeling how true my statement was. "You are needed here. By me. By Piper. The world needs you. Do not let an object or your uncle govern you. *Fight*."

Yellow-green leaked across his irises.

"You aren't getting rid of me. Whatever your uncle brings our way, we can fight him together. Side by side." I inched closer, touching him, hoping to keep him locked on me.

Lars grunted, lifting his fingers to my face, gripping tightly as if I were his anchor. He drew his forehead down to mine. "I was arrogant enough to think I could regulate this kind of power." His voice sounded low and gruff; each syllable strained his vocals. "I was a fool. But I will not let him gain the throne. I must ensure we win this war."

"No." My head brushed against his in denial, my stomach twisting like clothes on the line on a windy day. "Not this way."

His hold constricted, tipping my mouth to his, his lips demanding, filling me with fervor. Desperation, fear, and need deepened our kiss, the magic of our bond glinting off my skin as it took hold of my soul.

He broke away, his mouth a sliver from mine. "It's too late. I'm doing this for my kingdom." His Adam's apple bobbed, his thumbs tracing my mouth. *"For you,* Ms. Cathbad." Without hesitation he whirled around, fingers latching on to the stone.

"No!" I screamed, a blocking chant already bubbling over my lips.

BOOM!

Magic detonated from the stone through the room with waves of energy, crashing into everything blocking its way.

My body flew backward up into the air, my bones cracking as I rammed into the wall. But I felt nothing; the blast had ripped my senses from me, shredding me of emotions. I hit the ground as the lights above flickered, raining down on the room like sparks from fireworks.

Darkness spread throughout me.

~~

My eyes bolted open with a gasp, my lungs contracting as I coughed out the thick layer of dust swirling the room. My head rolled to the side and I groaned. Every bone and muscle ached. My head was fuzzy, unable to hold a thought for long, similar to nailing melting Jell-O to a board.

Understanding started to slip through. I slowly sat up, as bits of the ceiling and walls rolling off of me to the ground.

"Lars?" I hacked, my chest burning. I scanned the room.

Gone.

Shite.

I stumbled trying to rise too fast, then rushed to the wall. I felt no power coming from the compartments.

"Damn," I cried out, wishfully hoping for a different outcome than what I already knew to be true.

Three of the treasures still lay in their place, all as dead and empty as the cauldron. Only one treasure was gone.

And so was the King.

I flipped around, running from the room. *Please, please say it's not too late.* I had to stop him.

I only made it a few steps, my view spotting a twisted massive lump on the ground at the end of the hall.

"No. No. No." Fear lodged in my throat, my knees knocking into the floor with bruising force as I fell next to the body. "Goran?" I grappled for his shoulder. His limp form rolled to face me, his neck hitching in a way that told me it was broken.

I sucked in a gulp, placing my hand on his chest. We may not have liked each other, but I knew how much he loved Lars and would die for him. The stabbing pain in my heart wiggled down into my stomach. Lars would never hurt Goran. Goran was like his brother. They had been together so long that respect and trust ran deep, and nothing would break that.

But Lars was no longer himself.

A severed neck would end a human's life in an instant. Fae were harder to kill, but not impossible. I could sense his energy trying to hang on with mere wisps of life.

Closing my eyes, the chant flowed off my tongue. I shoved the healing spell into his body, but right away I knew it wasn't enough. He was gone. Death had taken him, jumping over into another plane.

A cry splinted from my mouth. I realized what I had to do. Blackness swirled around me, coating my insides and mouth like syrup, the taste disgusting and stale. Similar to death. Ignoring the anxiety in my gut, I chanted the dark spell to bring someone back to life. Black magic was not natural, but bringing a person who is already gone? That went against all laws of nature and fate. If he came back to life, he would never be the same.

I understood this rule. Respected it. But it didn't stop me. Because I couldn't save Lars, I would at least save Lars's friend.

Sweat trickled down my back, my shirt sticking to my skin, but I pressed on.

With a sharp gasp, Goran's eyes flung open, his lungs fluttering, trying to start up again.

"Take it easy. Don't move too fast."

"What happened? Where's my liege?" His head twisted around, his eyebrows wrinkled in confusion.

My mouth opened to try and explain when a girl's cry emanated from upstairs, shooting chills over my skin.

"Piper!" I wailed, already on my feet. I took the next two flights of stairs two at a time until I reached the ground floor of the house, breath locked in my throat with dread. "Piper? Where are you?"

"Ms. Fionna! *¡Aqui! ¡Aqui!*" Marguerite's voice bellowed from the kitchen. My feet hit the wood floor with pounding thuds, terror pumping into my veins.

I turned the corner. Marguerite stood there, Piper in her arms, holding the child to her breast. Nik was nowhere in sight.

"Piper!"

"Mummy." She lifted her head, her arms reaching for me. I swept her up, a relieved sob hiccupping in my throat. She was in my arms. Safe.

"She's all right, Ms. Fionna."

"Are you?"

She nodded as I pulled Piper in tighter to me. Marguerite kept patting me, repeating they were both okay.

I kept hold of her for a long time, needing to feel her in my arms. Now I had her, the thought of ever losing her again was unthinkable. I kissed her head, looking over her shoulder at Marguerite.

"What happened?"

Marguerite's lips pinched together.

"Mr. Lars. Gone."

"Did he say anything? Where he was going?"

Marguerite clicked her tongue. "No." She tapped at her head then her chest. "Mr. Lars is *gone*."

Agony closed my eyes briefly.

I hitched Piper higher onto one hip and moved toward the entry doors. "Shite! Nik!" I held on to Piper, running to the incubus lying on the floor, in front of the open entrance.

"He's okay, Mummy. Darz didn't hurt him."

I still bent down, feeling his pulse. It felt strong against my fingers. Lars must have knocked him out. Frantic hollers from guards outside filtered into the house.

"Where did Darz go?" Piper asked, her voice small.

"I don't know, honey."

"I want Darz."

Despair filled my eyes, hearing the longing in her voice. "Me too, sweetheart. Me too."

Marguerite came up next to me, rubbing Piper's back. Then she squeezed my arm. "He come back," she stated firmly. "He always does...and now he has reasons to." She nodded between Piper and me.

I wanted to believe her. I wanted to believe her so bad it ached. I gritted my teeth, trying to not lose myself to hopelessness.

"He needs you, Ms. Fionna." She still clung to my arm, giving me strength.

I nodded, staring out into stormy afternoon, the clouds making it dark and bleak.

I had no idea what tomorrow would bring. But as I held my daughter, I knew one thing, I would fight with everything I had to get him back.

The world needed the King.

We needed *him*.

"I'm coming for you, demon," I whispered into the air.

My mind flashed. I saw him, surrounded by fog and trees, his black eyes glistening with power. My words traveled over the wind, shooting him in the back. His head jerked over his shoulder. The glow of the house was far in the distance.

"Then come get me, Druid." The stone spoke through him, forming a cruel smirk on his features, but something underneath the facade tugged at my gut. "Your King has fallen. It's my turn now."

My mind snapped back, the image of Lars dissipating.

A slow malicious smile curved my mouth. Lars was still in there; I could feel him.

"But not for long," I promised the stone.

To save the man I loved, there was nowhere I wouldn't go, no line I wouldn't cross. I would destroy the last Treasures of Tuatha Dé Danann once and for all.

I would take back what was mine.

With the fall of a King, a Druid would rise.

Epilogue

Lars

What was left of my humanity hunkered like an animal in a cage. The stone took up residence in my body and most of my mind.

It was power. Alive. Free. Liberated from attachments and emotions. To have nothing holding you back was the ultimate high. I had forgotten how wonderful it felt.

This is only the beginning, King. I have great plans for us, the stone said to me. It moved my body without my input, covering a lot of space quickly. *Getting your pesky uncle out of the way shouldn't be too hard. Even with his growing army of strighoul.*

I didn't need to speak; the stone fed my curiosity.

You will see, Lars, I have been preparing for this for a long time. Players have already been set, waiting for me to lead them.

"And who are these players?" I asked.

Wait and see for yourself.

My legs followed an unseen path for a long time, fatigue never registering. The stone finally took us down a ravine, to a cave. A single torch sat hooked on the wall, flickering with light, as though it waited for me. Us. Clasping it, we followed the tunnel, no longer aware of time. It could have been minutes or hours, but finally the path narrowed, giving way to an arena-sized space inside the earth. Dozens of fire torches flickered along the walls, illuminating the underground with a sinister mood.

My boots jumped onto a boulder. "Come out!" My mouth moved, the stone using my voice. "Your master has arrived."

At first, I heard nothing, but then scuffling echoed through the cave, coming from all directions. Lars, the man, would have been wary, but neither the demon nor the stone felt anything but power and control.

A dozen figures moved in from the shadows, all different shapes and sizes. Their clothes appeared ragged and rank. From a distance they resembled humans, but they made me uneasy.

"What is this?" I asked the stone, my eyes not sure what I was seeing.

The best of human and fae. The new breed of weapons.

What?

One came close enough I could see it had green eyes, brown hair, and a round face. He looked human, but my demon sensed he was not.

"Zeke," the stone greeted him.

"Master." Zeke bowed his head, his attention on his leader, his lips parting.

Deep beneath my skin I jerked in response. Holy fuck. He might look human, but his body, stature, and teeth were pure strighoul. His physique different enough from a human's it made you uncomfortable, spine slightly curving, his skin a shade of gray. He was skinny and tall but muscular. Another one shuffled up to Zeke, also brown haired and green eyed, but it had a tail with a spike on the end. It bowed to me as well. Others had Asian features. One by one more of them surrounded me. Each one was unique and very, very wrong.

Not wrong, Lars. You are not seeing what potential these creatures have. I didn't want Dr. Rapava's creations to go to waste. There is clearly merit in his ideas. I will improve on them, but I need you to help me retrieve something. Something that got away from me.

"What?"

Their mother.

The stone flashed an image in my head, sending a thread of horror through me. *Noooo!*

I don't need your approval, just your body, it said to me. *But before you go, I want to thank you. I could not have done this without you and that Druid. Saving her life was your downfall.*

"What does Fionna have to do with this?"

Everything. She was supposed to die. Her sacrifice and Druid magic would have given my enemy the upper hand.

Dread dripped through the parts of me that could still feel.

Yes. You are beginning to understand. Her fate was to help the cauldron stop me. But you selfishly wouldn't let her do it. Saving your love doomed you all. Your myths about the cauldron as my equal were right, but not in the way the legend made it sound. We were never partners. It was designed to stop me from gaining too much power, to hold me back. So thank you, demon. By destroying that wretched thing, you gave me all the freedom in the world. Nothing to oppose me and stop me from taking all the other treasures' powers once you've brought us together.

This. He waved my arms around. *Is because of you. However, I have no use for you anymore.* The stone pushed my soul, cutting out the last bit of consciousness. Numbness settled in. Locking me away in darkness where nothing could reach me.

"That's better." I adjusted the King's body, getting the feel of it. "Fae think themselves so superior their egos don't let them see the truth. They are so greedy for power. Only the Druids had the wisdom to keep us apart. The demon fell right into my hands, obtaining my fellow treasures so I could drain the others of their power. They are nothing more than junk now."

I rolled my shoulders back, liking how fit and strong this form was. Yes, Lars's physique would work just fine. "I feel amazing. I'd like to keep this one for a while." I turned my attention back up to my men. Because of my connection to their mother, reaching out and twisting their minds to me had been easy enough.

"Now, are you ready to go find your dear mummy and take over the kingdom?"

The creatures yelled, stomping their feet in agreement.

"Let's go get that deceitful bitch, the one who left you to die. She will pay for what she's done."

Zoey Daniels was just the start. She would be for my enjoyment. I will relish taking revenge on her for deceiving me. For getting away.

One King down, one more to go. And the Queen— oh, she would be going down, too—but not in the way she would think. I was going to enjoy this body. Thoroughly.

As the stone, I was like a genie. I had held so much power, but it could only be used if someone touched me, which kept me trapped in a cage for centuries.

Now I was free, and I wasn't going back. I'd burn this world to cinders first.

"Let's go, my pets. We have much to do." I waved them to follow, leading them out to the light, where there would be no more darkness or cages.

Only death, blood, power, and revenge.

The new King has risen.

All hail the King.

Rise from the Embers

Lightness Saga, Book 4

The King has fallen! What will happen to Lars? The world with no King, and a Queen who fae still don't trust? How will they unite and fight against the forces coming to destroy them?

While Stavros moves to take the throne, the fight for Lars begins. But this is no ordinary war. The enemy is the most powerful object in the world.

However, Lars isn't the only one the stone wants. Zoey Daniels is next on its list. And it will do whatever it takes to finally get the girl.

Fae, humans, Druids, pixies, and a certain sprite-monkey will have to come together to try and save the King, along with the world, from destruction.

From ashes, true heroes *Rise from the Embers*.

Don't miss the conclusion, *Rise from the Embers (Lightness Saga #4)* the FINAL installment of the Dark/Light/Collector series, where your favorite characters unite to try and save those they love, and the world from the ultimate opponent.

Not everyone will make it out alive.

Acknowledgements

These might be getting boring, but I feel this way every time I think of my team. I am truly lucky I get to work with the best of the best! A HUGE thanks to:

- Kiki at Next Step PR: I know I can be a pain. Thank you for all your hard work! https://thenextsteppr.org/

- Jordan: You make everything better. And now I have your voice constantly in my head as I write. Thank you. http://jordanrosenfeld.net/

- Hollie "the editor": Don't ever, ever leave me. I will wander the streets in my slippers, mumbling your name. http://www.hollietheeditor.com/

- Dane at Ebook Launch! Thank you for doing your thing and designing such beautiful covers! https://ebooklaunch.com/ebook-cover-design/

- To Judi at http://www.formatting4u.com/: Awesome as always! You always got my back.

- To all the readers who have supported me: My gratitude is for all you do and how much you help indie authors out of the pure love of reading.

- To all the indie/hybrid authors out there who inspire, challenge, support, and push me to be better: I love you!

- And to anyone who has picked up an indie book and given an unknown author a chance. THANK YOU!

About The Author

Stacey Marie Brown is a lover of hot fictional bad boys and sarcastic heroines who kick butt. She also enjoys books, travel, TV shows, hiking, writing, design, and archery. Stacey swears she is part gypsy, being lucky enough to live and travel all over the world.

She grew up in Northern California, where she ran around on her family's farm, raising animals, riding horses, playing flashlight tag, and turning hay bales into cool forts.

When she's not writing she's out hiking, spending time with friends, and traveling. She also volunteers helping animals and is eco-friendly. She feels all animals, people, and the environment should be treated kindly.

To learn more about Stacey or her books, visit her at:

Author website & Newsletter:
www.staceymariebrown.com

Facebook Author page:
www.facebook.com/SMBauthorpage

Pinterest: www.pinterest.com/s.mariebrown

Twitter: @S_MarieBrown

Instagram: www.instagram.com/staceymariebrown/

Twitter: https://twitter.com/S_MarieBrown

Amazon page: www.amazon.com/Stacey-Marie-Brown/e/B00BFWHB9U

Goodreads:
www.goodreads.com/author/show/6938728.Stacey_Marie_Brown

Her Facebook group:
www.facebook.com/groups/1648368945376239/

Bookbub: www.bookbub.com/authors/stacey-marie-brown

CPSIA information can be obtained
at www.ICGtesting.com
Printed in the USA
LVHW080353210322
713971LV00022B/713

9 781977 850782